MUST LOVE

Death

A SISTERS OF THE APOCALYPSE NOVEL

SHELLY CHALMERS

Copyright © 2018 by Shelly Chalmers

All rights reserved. This book or any portion thereof may not be reproduced or used in any manner whatsoever without the express written permission of the publisher except for the use of brief quotations in a book review.

This book is a work of fiction. All names, characters, locations, and incidents are products of the author's imagination. Any resemblance to actual persons living or dead, things, locales, or events is entirely coincidental.

www.scchalmers.com   www.shellychalmers.com

Cover design by Paper & Sage Designs

ISBN 978-1-7750206-6-0

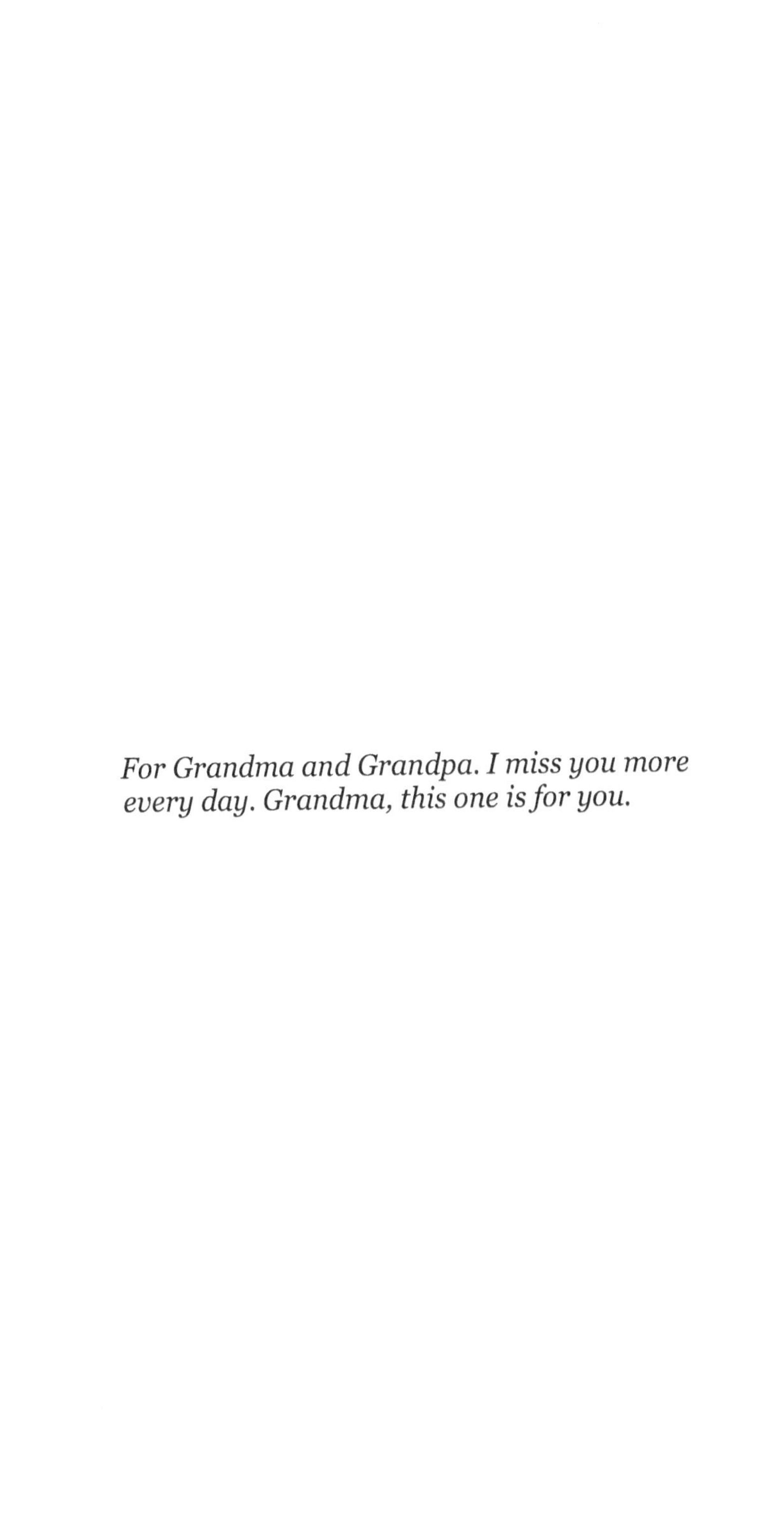

For Grandma and Grandpa. I miss you more every day. Grandma, this one is for you.

ACKNOWLEDGMENTS

This book was challenging on many levels, and I couldn't have done it without a lot of help from others.

Thank you, readers, and those of you who enthusiastically embraced both *Plague* and *Famine*. These books are for you, so it means a lot to me that they've found their audience.

Lana, a shout-out just for you. Thank you for your kind words, enthusiasm, but also your sympathy. You're a big part of why this book was finished in the first place, and I am so grateful. Thank you.

Thank you to Lorne Thomas for your patience answering all my questions about the RCMP and hypothetical situations. Any mistakes are my own, but it really helped bring Mal to life for me.

Thank you as always to my amazing 2014 Dreamweaver sisters. To my wonderful editor, Tera Cuskaden, for helping make this book better. And to Christa Holland with Paper & Sage Design for the gorgeous cover (this one might be my favorite!).

Thank you as always to my critique partner, Shelly Alexander, who fell in love with Mal in book one. Your kind words kept me believing in this story. You're still due a sainthood.

Thank you to my family and friends, who bought and read my first book, and have asked about this book. I couldn't be me without you, and I am touched and honored with your support.

Neelam, thank you for being my best friend, and for always being there for me. You'll always be my first reader, my first fan...and possibly head of marketing. ;) Love you lots!

Mom, thank you for your permission to use Grandma's name, and as always for your patience and love. I know you might not be able to read this one right away. I hope when you do you find that it's worthy of her.

Thank you especially to my husband and my girls, for all your patience and support. I hope someday I can encourage you to follow your dreams as you've allowed me to follow mine.

CHAPTER 1

People sucked.

Both the living and the dead, because both wanted to find a way to hurt her.

Nia Amort stepped into Loki's bar in the center of Beckwell, Alberta, exactly twenty-one minutes late for her meeting. Lou's Place resembled something between a Victorian bordello and a biker bar, with none of the class, all of the weirdness. The deep burgundy walls and scarred round tables typically hosted guests with wings and horns, all variety of paranormal what's-its who made Beckwell their home and sanctuary. Today, only a few tables were occupied.

Her fashionably late entrance should make the point she didn't want to be here, and she wouldn't be pushed around.

Not even by the local demigod himself.

She shoved her hands in the pockets of her black parka, hunched her shoulders, and slinked across the room toward the thick wood bar on the opposite wall. The icy breath of January and the dead of winter still clung to her as the door swung shut and warm air blasted her in the face, ruffling the wild, dark curls around her face. The only good thing about winter was no rain. She shuddered, remembering the last time she'd been caught out in the rain, the clawing fingers grabbing at her, the moans of the dead in her face and reaching into her head.

Damn Loki anyway for insisting on the meeting, one he knew she couldn't refuse. Seriously, was he the freakin' Godfather? As though her life weren't "fun" enough. If "fun" meant still waiting around for the powers of Death to poof into existence. Still waiting for the day she would finally rise as one of the four horsewomen of the apocalypse. Yeah, *those* horsemen, which were more like family clans than just four unlucky losers. It'd been almost four months since her friend Ginny had risen as Famine. And nothin'. No extra powers, just the usual dead people, dead people, and more dead people.

The only good thing about being summoned for today's meeting was being midafternoon Tuesday, the town watering hole was empty. There were only two skinny guys somewhere between teenagers and lifelong loafers who, judging from their pastiness, looked like they'd been kicked out of their moms' basements. Plus, three dead people. The lady in the old-fashioned red dress who kept walking in and out of the same section of wall for no apparent reason didn't worry Nia. The grizzled guy at the end of bar kept drinking his bottomless mug of ale. His unfocused gaze and his pale translucency suggested he might not have known he was dead, but he was fading from this world whether he knew it or not because no one remembered him.

It was the kid—curly blond hair and little boy's sailor suit—whom Nia had to be especially careful to ignore. Because the kid stared at her in a way that made the hairs boogie along the back of her neck.

The skinny dorks froze in their conversation as they

saw her. Pasty dude's mouth fell open until his idiot friend elbowed him. There was a quick, whispered conversation.

Nia looked away and rolled her eyes. Yes, she was really *that* Amort girl. Yes, she'd really discovered her father—or what was left of him. Yes, her nickname used to be "Druggy" in those days when she'd been so desperate to escape the creatures reaching through the veils toward her, creatures Dad invited, she'd do pretty much anything for a few moments of peace, a brief wafer of normal. And, yeah, she'd spent time in an asylum. A couple of them, unhelpful as they'd been. Turned out there wasn't a cure for seeing dead people…and ghosts liked asylums, too.

The kid crossed the bar toward her.

She quickly averted her eyes, her gaze landing on the dorks' table with the beer and glass of water.

Kids were her kryptonite. Didn't have to like them to feel bad for the little buggers. Being short, stuck with whatever parents the Fates dealt them…none of it was their fault. And *dead* kids…ugh. Ghosts came up to her all the time, and sometimes she could ignore them until they left her alone. But when it came to dead kids, it was like she had "sucker" written on her forehead.

Nia grumbled to herself. Five minutes, then she'd make a scene and cut loose. Five minutes.

The skinnier dork gulped, his Adam's apple bobbing and his eyes widening as he straightened in his chair, pushed out his sunken chest.

Ah, shit. He didn't think she was interested or—

The water glass on dork's table trembled.

Nia's gaze zapped straight to it, her breath caught. Water. Always with the freakin' water. Any other fluid was fine, but pure water connected her straight to the Gray, the place between the living and dead and all the nasties trapped there.

A moth burst out of the water, flickering like a faulty

bulb as it shook the damp out of its wings and swooped around the table.

Her heart stuttered. She couldn't look away from the insect.

Both the dorks stared at her and didn't seem to notice it, even as the moth swept in front of both their faces. It hovered in the air, less than a foot from her face, before fluttering toward the big bald man dressed in plaid behind the bar, drying glasses and putting them away.

He'd glanced at Nia when she came in but hadn't looked up since, which was either a good sign…or a bad one. First, because he was the guy who'd summoned her to a meeting she couldn't ignore, considering all she owed him. Second, because while most of the town still looked at him and saw Lou, the fat, bald bartender with a hard-on for plaid, he was also Loki, founder of their weird little paranormal town, general pain in the ass, able to change his appearance at will, and yeah, still a demigod last she'd heard.

He'd also pushed and pulled her friends and most of the citizens of the town however he pleased for whatever game he was playing. It made him not always a villain, but damned close to the line.

The flickering moth appeared and disappeared near Loki before settling on the counter. It froze Nia's step and shortened her breath. A faint buzzing in her head made her wince.

The fact that Loki stopped drying his cup and turned to look at the creature damned near stopped her heart.

The dorks hadn't seen the moth when it'd flown out of the water. Could anyone else it? That moth, whatever it was, had just come out of the Gray into this world.

The demigod raised his gaze to hers, and Nia forced her feet to keep moving.

If that moth was out of the Gray, did that make it her horse?

The world was filled with death, and she was destined to rise as the biggest and baddest of them all. She would be the third horsewoman. Had to be. Of course, until now, powers had been few and far between. Yeah, she was a ghost magnet. Plus, there was the freaky Death voice she could use, and the annoyance of reading people's auras and a hint of their souls whenever she got too close. The whole ending-the-world thing? She and her friends weren't into it. But she wanted the powers. Needed them.

She gulped as Loki quirked a brow at her. She owed him like ten bazillion favors, and it looked like he was about to call in at least one in.

And now of all times that freaky moth showed up.

Damn it.

The moth made an annoyed chirruping sound.

Nia forced her expression into bitch face glory and tried to sidle casually up and take a seat on one of the bar stools. She refused to look at the moth, or the kid ghost, who'd followed her across the room. Of course, stupid stools were made for giraffes, and she had to hop a little to finally get her butt onto it. Finally, she met Loki's gaze.

"Hi, asshole," she said, trying hard not to notice as the moth, still flickering in and out of visibility, took to the air, finally landing directly in front of her.

Loki didn't even twitch. "Petunia." He glanced at the moth. "That yours?"

She'd learned years ago to control the flinch whenever someone used that name. Barely even heard the echo of Dad calling her his precious Petunia…just before he suckered her into something new and awful.

The moth brushed a silken wing against Nia's hand, comfort and warmth flowing through the brief connection. Just in case there'd been any doubt this was a normal moth, its barest touch lit up a vision behind Nia's eyes with the blue and golds of the moth's aura—deep feminine wisdom, temperance and patience, compassion and endurance.

Unfortunately—or maybe fortunately—the stupid kid was now close enough he'd reached out tentatively to touch her knee, his touch like icy tendrils soaking through her and dispelling the moth's aura and whatever the hell that read had been.

Crap, she needed to get out of here.

"What do you want, Loki?"

A small hint of amusement flickered through the demigod's stormy gray-blue eyes. He nodded toward the moth, still between them, pale and flickering like the transmission signal wasn't good and it couldn't quite decide whether it was in this plane or somewhere else.

"That's a death's head hawkmoth. *Archerontia Lachesis*, native to India, Sri Lanka, and the Orient. This one is clearly not of this world. Can you think of any reason it would be here, in the frozen prairies of Canada?"

"You know, I totally figured you for a guy who liked sticking bugs with pins. Kind of like you treat people. Just specimens for your collection and your plans, right?" She leaned closer. "Let's get this very clear, Lou, Loki, whatever the fuck name you want to go by." Until a few months ago, no one had even known Loki *was* Lou. Most people still didn't know that. "I. Don't. Play. Games. Now what do you want so I can go home and get the hell on with the rest of my day?"

If he was irritated by her tone, he didn't show it. He put the last of the glasses he'd been drying on the shelf before leaning back against the counter and crossing his arms over his broad chest. "Despite what you think, I'm worried about you, Nia. All I've ever wanted to do is help you and your friends."

She rolled her eyes. "Oh, for fuck's sake. Cue the violins. Do you think I'm an idiot?"

"Even without the appearance of this moth, we both know you're the next to rise." He continued as though she hadn't spoken. "The world is going to get more dangerous for you, and I'm offering sanctuary."

Her eyes narrowed. She couldn't handle owing him anything else. Hell, at this point she already probably owed him her firstborn, first grandchild, possibly first great-great-grandchild. Plus, all those mortgage payments. Funny how banks got nervous handing out mortgages to broke girls with an online degree and no formal work experience. Loki had helped her out when she'd gotten back two years ago, had been the world's most understanding landlord. They both knew how much she already owed him.

"Not interested."

"Really? I thought you'd enjoy somewhere safe and quiet to relax. A brand-new bathroom, complete with walk-in shower, tiled in staurolite, spirit quartz, selenite crystals, and jet, along with a few other choice gems and minerals to ensure the protection is complete. No spirits will be able to reach you. You sure you're not interested?"

The fuck-you expression had slid off her face somewhere around the mention of "safe," and she struggled to put it back in place and keep her breathing steady. Bathrooms until now were mostly hellholes full of water that'd leave her stuck between this world and the Gray. But what he was offering…

A haven. A bathroom where she could have a shower in peace. She could wash her freaking hands in peace. This was the promise of a room free from spiritual attacks. No ghosts, no death, just the ability to be alone and normal for a few minutes of the day. It might even be a safe place from what hunted her in her sleep.

To be safe. The idea almost made her dizzy.

"Sounds expensive." Her eyes narrowed.

"I'll foot the bill. No strings, no receipts, never a monetary concern for you. Won't even add it to the mortgage."

"What's the catch?" she asked, her voice hoarser than she'd have liked. *Don't be an idiot. This is freakin' Loki. There's a catch. There's always a catch.* But, gods, the idea was captivating. She wanted it. She could already picture it.

"My workman. In your house. Twenty-four seven."

The vision of the perfect haven popped as quickly as an iridescent bubble, and she was already shaking her head. She couldn't have anyone in her house. Especially not all day and night. Especially not now. Keeping everyone out of her house was the only way her life worked.

"How about you buy the stone and I install it? The girls and I—"

"You owe me the last two mortgage payments, so unless you'd like to find somewhere else to live, I call the shots. Besides which, you don't know how to tile, and I'm hardly going to let you experiment with expensive materials or do a shoddy work on a house I might have to repossess."

Damn it, she wanted to get all huffy and storm out, but she really wanted that bathroom now. She'd experimented with crystals and minerals, and they did work. Being a ghost magnet, though, she'd need a whole hell of a lot more than her budget had ever allowed for. If she wanted to eat and all.

"I choose the installer."

"My workman is already selected."

"I get veto."

"You agree sight unseen, or I'll need one of those mortgage payments by the end of the day." He leaned over the counter. "We both know you need this, because you're about to get a whole lot of power, and the League, the gods, and the dead are going to be after you. But you don't like me, and you hate favors. So, this is me helping you, giving you a chance, whether you like it or not."

She ground her teeth. "You're an asshole."

"So you've said. Well, Nia? What will it be? I've got things to do, the rest of my day to get on with," he said, casually tossing her words back at her.

The moth, still flickering in shades of gray, lifted off the counter before landing on Loki's shoulder. A Beatles song flickered into memory— "Here Comes the Sun."

Yeah, right. Loki was not her freakin' sun, and things were not getting brighter. *Shitfuckdamnit.* She sure the hell didn't have money for a mortgage payment. She'd had to give up driving because ghosts popping in and out of the car and appearing in the middle of the road were serious distractions. Which meant bye-bye getting to a job on time, and online work only. Unfortunately, with the attacks during the night, she'd been too exhausted to get many work-for-hire jobs completed, which mostly involved siccing ghosts on slime balls.

How many ghosts would it take to get Loki off her case…

The moth lifted off again, fluttered toward Nia, circled once, then settled back on Loki's left shoulder. Like it wanted her to have something to do with him.

The ghost kid tugged on her hand. "Hey, lady. Lady?"

The grizzled dead guy at the end of the bar looked up at her, and his expression brightened. He turned toward her.

Nia closed her eyes. A haven. Somewhere safe. She wasn't the only one who needed sanctuary. "Just how safe would this room be? I mean…could I bring someone into it?"

"Living or dead?" Loki asked.

She opened her eyes, her lips tight, her heart pounding. How much did he know? He couldn't know everything, could he?

"Does it matter?"

"If you brought them in with you, living wouldn't be

a problem. Dead…well, more your area of expertise, is it not?"

Shit. This could be what she'd been looking for. A way to buy some time until she got her full powers and wasn't just limited to talking with the dead. The moth was probably her horse, which meant soon she'd rise as Death. But until then, what if the bathroom was a sanctuary to hide from the Gray and the monsters? It could buy her time to learn to use her abilities, so finally, she could do more.

She could finally save her daughter.

She stiffly stuck out her hand. "Agreed."

Loki took her hand in his.

She braced herself for what she'd see as his fingers closed around hers. At first, it was like grabbing an electric eel. Power, raw and unadulterated, the bright glare of his immortality.

The moth, still flickering, fluttered off Loki, and landed on their joined hands, as though adding its assent.

The physical touch of her hand against Loki's was starting to give her a headache. Aww, crap. Images flashed through her. Fire, destruction. Her friend Anna's tear-stained face and the sound of screams.

Nia dropped Loki's hand and stepped back, rubbing her sweaty palms on her thighs, trying to erase the images from her mind, trying to ignore the silvery aura surrounding him. Never mind the moth fluttering all over the place, the kid still tugging at her elbow, and the dead guy from the end of the bar was moving toward her.

She had too much shit to worry about already. She did *not* need to know why her vision from Loki, probably his death, had something to do with Anna. She did *not* want to care about his almost silver aura, something she'd never encountered before. She sure as shit did not need the two ghosts coming at her. Another problem with the living: if she was in physical contact for too long, she saw and absorbed more about them than either of them wanted to know.

The moth fluttered up and settled on her shoulder. Though it was flickering and tiny, its touch was like the weight of a calming hand pressing and squeezing her shoulder gently.

The images vanished. Her heart calmed. The grizzled ghost shook his head and settled back down at the bar.

Good.

The dead were attracted to her, partially thanks to the Death clan thing, partially because of Dad and how he'd turned her into a bridge to the Gray. If water was a doorway, she was the hall between this world and the next. It all usually led to Dead People Counseling 101. Dang, she hadn't done much of that lately, either, but it was still a relief when the dead guy returned to his beer.

The child ghost didn't let go of her elbow, but the moth's effect was better than a kick in the head. Nia started to back toward the door of the bar. "Cool. I'm free next week. You can send your guy over then."

"Lady? Lady, can you help me? Do you know who I am? Can I come home with you?" the kid ghost asked, his face beseeching.

She winced. If he didn't know who he was, chances were good he didn't remember he was dead, either. Pretty common with dead kids. Ah, hell. What was one more?

"Sure, kid. Just for the night." She snorted. Like it was ever just for the night. Kids were a problem. Her own the biggest of all. She would rise as Death, and she'd use those powers to protect and save. Because there was no damned way she would let anything happen to her daughter. Not again.

No one knew she even had a daughter. She'd kept the pregnancy, the birth, and the adoption secret. Done everything she'd selfishly told herself at the time would protect the kid. But that hadn't worked, had it?

Instead, she hadn't done the one thing she should have done: protected her own damned daughter in the first place.

"Oh, there's no need to send him over. He's waiting just outside," Loki said, filling peanut bowls. "No, wait. Here he is."

The door to the bar swung open with a slight squeak.

The back of Nia's neck prickled, even with the calming effect of the moth on her shoulder. Her senses were rattled, every one of them suddenly paying close attention to who stepped in behind her, who cast a long shadow eclipsing her own. Her fingertips itched, and her throat tightened.

Loki smiled from behind the bar. "The supplies will arrive at the house later this afternoon. Thank you, Nia. It's always entertaining." He offered her a short bow.

"Hello, Nia," the masculine voice said from behind her. A voice from the past, present, but damn well not the future.

CHAPTER 2

Nia looked good. Damn good. Mal Quilan admired the view from just inside the doorway of Lou's Place, which, since recently, was known to he and his brother as Loki's Lair. One of them at any rate. Wind swept up from outside sending a chill down his neck before the door swung shut behind him, but he didn't care. To hell with anyone else. It was Nia he couldn't take his eyes away from since he hadn't been this close in more than a decade.

She wasn't much taller than she'd been in high school, but there were curves beneath those bulky track pants. Her hair was the same wild mass of black-brown curls he remembered, silken beneath his fingers, caressing her light brown skin and surrounding a small, heart-shaped face that could have been described as elfin—though never to her face, unless you were particularly stupid. When she turned on him, those dark eyes were still irresistible dark-brown pools he could stare into for hours.

All he had to do was talk fast and hope she didn't kill him in the next moment or two.

Her lips thinned, and her eyes narrowed. Her gaze flicked up and down him, just long enough to send a flare of heat licking through him, and he had to wonder whether she liked what she saw.

"Frick. Did Jackasses Anonymous just let out?" she threw at him.

"Yeah, but it's funny, I didn't see you there this week." He kept his tone light and teasing.

She spun away, color staining her high cheekbones as she turned back to the bar. "You have got to be shitting me. Not him. Anyone but him. Hell, *you* can install the tiles," she said to Loki, who stood calmly behind the bar.

Years of practice were the only thing stopping Mal from outwardly flinching. *Not him*. Not that brother. The wrong brother. The "evil" twin, her words implied. He tried to ignore the sting her words caused. It wasn't like it was the first time he'd heard it. But the first time from her. The Jackasses Anonymous thing he could handle. It was just bluster, and Nia's prickly exterior was just show. The loathing in her voice was much worse. Too much like Mom.

He and Loki exchanged a look over Nia's head. A reminder of the deal they'd made a week ago. He owed Loki, and in return for the demigod's help hiding from the Fates, Mal was supposed to install some tiles in Nia's house and play the handyman. In reality he was there for her protection.

When her friend, Ginny, had risen as the incarnation of Famine, it'd made the gods nervous and they'd sent their agents from USELESS to town after Nia and her friends. Despite their name, USELESS agents made the KGB look cuddly in comparison. Plus, there was the League of Assholes, three Fates from town who'd wanted to start an apocalypse and who kept getting stopped by Nia and her friends. And that equaled not their biggest fans. The League also probably wanted to kill him, but that was another story. He might even deserve their fury. Point was, this favor to Loki and keeping Nia safe was his chance to prove he wasn't so different from his twin brother, Daniel, after all. That, for once, he could be the goddamn hero.

If he didn't royally screw it all up. His usual M.O.

"Frick's sakes, are you two flirting with each other or something over my head? Just because you're taller than me doesn't mean I can't see you. Anyone but him, Loki. He's not coming into my house." Nia practically vibrated with fury.

It emanated out from her, tingling against his skin like most people felt the sunlight. It hurried his pulse, heightened his instincts to get on with doing at least one of the three F's that Fomorians like him, practically a lesser form of demon, were good at: fury, fighting, and fucking.

"We had an agreement," Loki said mildly, which in no way calmed Nia down.

Her ass was nicely defined in the black track pants, whether she intended it so or not. Which, as his body hardened, made it clear which one of the F's his Fomorian side voted for.

He took a slow breath to try to calm the base urge. He needed to get Nia on his side, not suggest something dumb enough to get himself dead.

Something she'd probably be good at, being Death and all.

"He was not the deal." She pointed an accusing finger in his direction, still not bothering to dignify him with a name, nor speak directly to him. "If he's not hitting on my best friend, he's trying to end the world. He's a jackass and troublemaker, and I won't have him in my home."

Okay, she did have a point. He had kind of tried to help end the world, or at least helped the League of

Assholes for a little while. He had hit on Nia's friend Piper, but they'd flirted since high school. She and his brother had always belonged together, so the flirting was meaningless. The jackass and troublemaker part… Well, those were his size biker boots. But he was working on those. Starting with taking care of her. He'd tried to save his brother before, and…they'd both ended up dead. They'd come to back to life in the end, so, you know, progress.

"Does this mean you're reneging on our agreement and I can expect a mortgage check this afternoon?" Loki said pleasantly to Nia, hardly a hint of the threat he likely implied. Slippery son of a bitch.

Everything about Loki read "bad guy." Except for the feeling Mal got in his gut. Seven years on the force, and he'd learned his gut was rarely wrong. Even when it came to Loki. The demigod might be playing some bigger game they didn't understand, but his concern for Nia and her friends appeared genuine.

What Mal had dug up this week proved Nia *was* in trouble. She was even more broke than he was and had missed her mortgage payments. At least five USELESS agents were sniffing around town, asking about Nia in particular since she was supposed to be the next horsewoman to rise. Though it was two less than yesterday, after he'd sent them home with a strong warning and some shiny new bruises. Next up were the three Fates, who'd made a habit of going after the four horsewomen. The Fates were keeping a low profile, but their next play would be to come after Nia. His job was to keep them all off her until she could rise as Death, at which point she could probably take care of herself.

"He's a troublemaker and an alcoholic. That's who you trust with all those expensive materials? He'll probably pawn them for the drug money." Nia tried again, still speaking to Loki and ignoring Mal.

"I haven't had a drink in two weeks, I'm not an alcoholic, and I've never done drugs." Even if the escape drugs might have provided had sometimes tempted him on the long, dark nights when all he had were haunting memories and the echo of that scream spiraling through his head. "I'm also not stupid enough to pawn materials belonging to either you or Loki because I like being alive, thanks."

Mal could have sworn he heard Nia's teeth grind and a low growl emanate from her throat. Then there was this weird silvery moth appearing and disappearing, flitting around Nia's head before it landed on her shoulder. At its touch, Nia's shoulders settled a little, and some of the fury ebbed out of her. With her shield gone, there was a gauntness to her features that made him want to pull her into his arms and keep her safe. The shadows in her eyes hadn't been so prominent back in high school.

She'd only let him see the real Nia one rainy afternoon. But like a magician, just when he thought he'd seen behind the curtain, she changed directions by seducing him. Only to toss him as quick as a used condom, like whatever he might have imagined happened between them was only in his head.

Cop's instincts never went away, never mind what he'd been able to uncover about Nia's current situation. The weird, magical moth he filed under "not a threat: possibly useful." While he searched Nia's features for how she fit into all this. Did she know she was in danger? Was she planning something that could make the situation worse?

Nia blew out a breath, enough to scatter the curly black hair hanging in her face. "You're still an asshole," she said to Loki.

The demigod might have responded, but she turned to Mal then, demanding his full attention. Nia gave him another once-over and he resisted straightening for her gaze. Barely. Her hair was curlier and longer than he remembered it, a wild mop of black silk bunching on her shoulders, accentuating high cheekbones, dark eyes, and fine features. Her skin was light brown, a shade or two darker than his. It reminded him of sweet treats and made his Fomorian side wonder if she wanted to taste the salt on his skin as much as he wanted to taste her.

Yeah…that whole plan to resist his baser urges wasn't going so well.

He tried to go over his threat assessment in his head.

But she met his gaze, staring so deeply it was as if she stared into his soul. Hell, she was Death. Maybe she had.

"You really know how to renovate and tile a bathroom? This isn't just some scheme the two of you schmucks cooked up?"

"My uncle owned a construction company, and I worked for them off and on through high school between community service, then with a reno company before I could officially join the RCMP. Yeah, I know what I'm doing."

Renos might have been something he was good at, but when he'd joined the Royal Canadian Mounted Police out of high school, Canada's federal police, for the first time in his life he'd found where he belonged. No one knew his family's story, about his Fomorian genes, that he even had a twin, let alone that his twin was freakin' Saint Daniel.

At least, he'd thought he'd belonged. Until everything had gone FUBAR four years ago and he'd turned in his badge and his weapon.

The moth alighted from Nia's shoulder and fluttered around his face, as though coming in for a closer look. He didn't swat at it since, a) magic moth meant dangerous, and b) with the way it kept flickering like an old black and white movie it was hard to say whether anyone else saw it. Acting like a crazy person swatting at something no one else could see would be one more reason for Nia to get rid of him. One more reason he couldn't prove himself to Loki, the town of Beckwell, and himself.

The moth circled him twice, then finally landed, the slight weight confirming it was on his head. Yeah, because that wasn't creepy at all. A big-ass magical moth on his head. However, he was a grown man, and men did not freak out when a bug got in their hair. At least, not when other people were watching.

Nia's gaze had lifted past his eyes, suggesting she was staring at the moth, which probably meant she could see it, too. She sniffed, a little half-irritated almost-smile on her face. She rolled her eyes.

"Fine. You can come home with me. You work fast, you keep your hands and shit to yourself, and you drive." She shot Loki a quick wave and stalked past Mal out the front door.

Loki crossed his arms and smirked.

Without acknowledging the demigod, Mal had no other choice but to follow Nia outside onto the porch. "Why do I have to drive?"

"Because I don't. Driving with ghosts is way worse than texting and driving. Where's your car?"

He stopped next to Nia and chills that had nothing to do with the weather chased up and down his arms. He took a step back. Cold winter air, but nothing extra. The uneasy sense they weren't alone—not including the magical moth—soaked through him, the Fomorian side more attune to the Other. Whatever. He shouldn't be surprised. This was Nia.

He gestured toward the other end of the parking lot at the old Yamaha motorcycle parked there, more rust than blue. It ran okay...the days it didn't catch on fire first. He'd dug it out of Loki's back shed, and Loki had said he could have it if he could get it to run. It'd run so far, and it was better than walking. He'd been lucky, too, and there'd only been one or two days the roads were too full of snow for the bike, but it was a temporary solution at best.

Nia sighed gustily. "A motorcycle. Figures."

Still, she followed him and plopped on the helmet he handed her. He didn't have a second one for himself, but who was there to arrest him? There was no police force in Beckwell. At least, other than him if his twin brother was to be believed. Daniel didn't understand Mal had left the force because he wasn't good enough. Why would he inflict more pain on unsuspecting innocents?

This job for Loki, keeping an eye on Nia, was because he owed the demigod, not because he was thinking of becoming a cop again. It was just an exception. And it was Nia. Where she'd been after she left high school and before she got back to town two years ago was a bit murky, which made it harder to assess exactly how she fit into the situation. He'd need to feel her out, get a read on her awareness of the threats.

The bike started with a few putts, a small bang, but no flames. When Nia wrapped her thin arms encased in the parka around his waist, he wished the seat were a bit smaller, so she'd have been forced to press closer.

Holding the handlebars, he turned back to look at her, only those dark eyes visible beneath the helmet, the heavy thing making her seem even more petite and vulnerable than usual. The moth fluttered over and landed back on Nia's shoulder.

"Which way?" he said over the sound of the motorcycle.

He'd been back in Beckwell nearly two years. In a town this small, he knew where she lived—everyone pretty much knew where everyone else lived. However, it seemed in his own best interests to pretend he didn't know. They'd both left town around the same time after high school, then both come back to town about the same time, too, two years ago. He'd steered a wide circle around Nia. Even during the stint when he'd pretended to work against her and her friends with the Fates.

"Right at the four-way, down toward Riley Lake. Fourth right, at the driveway with the broken red mailbox. Don't you need tools and things? A truck would seem more practical."

"You have a spare truck I could use? I don't," he said, backing them out of the spot. Even with the added body, Nia was light enough he could hardly feel the difference on the bike. "Just make sure you don't put your feet on the tailpipe. It could burn you. Hold on tight." And not just because he didn't want her to fall off.

He intentionally aimed for the divot, bumping them out of the parking lot. She tightened her grip around him, her hands gathering handfuls of his shirt beneath his leather jacket. His muscles hardened, and his head went back to thinking about the least healthy of the three F's when it came to Nia Amort.

She'd rejected him once and made it damn clear her opinion of him hadn't improved since high school. He paused at the empty four-way, using his arm to signal the right-hand turn, then sped up the bike so Nia held on tight as they flew down the road.

Well, her opinion could be damned. Even if he had to be careful she didn't find out the truth. She be pissed if she knew he'd promised Loki he'd be her in-house bodyguard. It was his job to protect her from threats both living and dead under the ruse of fixing her bathroom. Damned if he'd fail at it.

CHAPTER 3

Nia refused to notice in any way how her hands caressed hard stomach muscle beneath the buttery leather of Mal's jacket and through the soft cotton of his shirt, the rumble of the engine and the road purring between her legs. She sure as shit didn't notice Mal's delicious spicy scent. Nope. Not her. Because he didn't matter, and she'd get rid of him as soon as the first good plan presented itself. Some way *he* could call it off, so she wouldn't owe Loki her ass.

As soon as they pulled into her broad grassy yard, bare trees standing sentry around the perimeter, she barely gave Mal time to stop before she hopped off the bike. She hadn't touched his bare skin, but even the contact they'd had left her with Mal's essence—the shape, color, and feel of his soul.

She rubbed her hands up and down her thighs as though she could rub off the feel of him. Damn if he didn't feel like a harder, stronger version of the boy he'd been. A man with some darkness around the edges, but a deep, yearning, *worthy* glow. The sign of a man who wanted to do better.

The kind of man she needed to stay the hell away from in case the warmth of him and yearning got too attractive. Happy endings might be great for her friends, but not for her. That's part of what made happily ever afters special—not everyone got or deserved one.

Especially not her.

The wind from the ride hadn't blown away either the moth or the ghost kid. The kid had scrambled onto the motorcycle behind her, the moth perched on her shoulder the whole way. Now the kid stood beside her, clutching at her parka and looking around nervously.

The moth fluttered around her head, sound crackling in her ears like radio static that made her wince.

The crackling stopped. Music started. Not playing externally, but more like the faint memory of a song. Urging Nia to reach out.

"I'll be there..."

Nia closed her eyes and rubbed her forehead. Crap. It was like the moth wasn't quite in this world, was still partially in the Gray, which was maybe why it couldn't communicate properly. Hell, it'd resorted to the tricks some ghosts used to communicate with Normals. First, it'd triggered memories of songs. Next, it'd be flickering lights, dream manipulation, scents, and the big guy: electrical manipulation. She sighed. Only her stupid horse would insist on communicating like a ghost instead of in normal words. What next?

The moth settled on her shoulder, the comforting sense of calm soaking through Nia again. Okay, so that was way better than the static.

"Yeah, yeah, I get it," Nia thought to the moth.

The music stopped with the spiritual equivalent of a "humph."

Mal shut off the bike and removed his helmet,

looking too damned sexy as he speared a hand through his dark brown hair, shorter than it'd been in high school. He was all long, hard muscle beneath that hard square jaw darkened by whiskers and those wide shoulders. All covered with gorgeous bronzed skin she knew for a fact continued over every inch of his body, a mark of his Algonquin heritage and not any fondness for the sun.

"You're awfully isolated out here. Security camera? Protection of the magical variety?"

"You made of money? Because I'm not. I have ghosts. Lots of them. Very budget friendly. And what the hell do you care anyway?" Nia spun away and stalked toward the house. What the hell else was going to go wrong today, seriously? Duped by Loki. Harassed by a moth. Stalked by a dead kid. Stuck with Mal.

She had to weave her way through all the ghosts on the front lawn, like demented lawn ornaments only she could see. Her "security system."

The ghost kid shrank against her, his feet so close she practically tripped on him.

She ground her teeth and clenched her hands. Damn if there weren't more spirits littering her lawn than there'd been yesterday. The First Nations warriors, endlessly hunting a herd of ghost elk. The old woman in the nightgown who sometimes showed up in the basement. The headless cowboy on his horse, slowly moseying across the area near the shed. Those were the normal ones. They'd been joined by a family of four, all holding hands. The group of miners, still wearing their mining hats. The mother who cradled her child.

Nia turned away abruptly. Fine. Whatever. Most of them didn't seem aware of her. They were probably some sign she was becoming more powerful—not like any of the horsewomen powers came with a convenient manual. Mostly, though, the spirits were a pain in the ass. They'd wander through her house, wake her at night, crawl into bed with her, sometimes aware enough to ask for help but mostly just drawn to her. Like she was a perverted bug-light for ghosts.

Mal let out a low whistle, and she started, twisting toward him. For a second, she'd thought he saw all the dead people littering her lawn. Nope, he was staring up at the house in all its peeling glory. Her huge old white beast was a square shape, three stories high including the dormers, which popped out of the attic space. Every inch of it hers. Only thanks to Loki.

Two years ago, when she'd coasted back into town on fumes, nowhere to sleep but the back seat of her car, all her worldly goods stuffed in the duffle bag she used as a pillow, she'd been desperate for a miracle. She'd finally accepted there was no psychiatrist or med that could ever cure her affinity for ghosts—or her water allergy. She'd gotten herself a degree, finally felt like she'd put her life back together.

Her gaze slid over the porch, one side of the roof sagging, and she wrapped her arms around herself.

But then she'd taken that fateful trip down the street where her daughter was supposed to have a happy life. Where the kid was supposed to have a life free of a whacko mother, a life that was supposed to make up for everything Nia should have given her.

Heritage, answers, and safety.

Because Nia had abandoned her own daughter. Abandoned her like everyone else in Nia's life had abandoned and failed her. Nia's stomach curdled.

Almost served her right that instead of a happy six-year-old, she'd found a ghost. Another child who didn't remember its name…or death.

They'd rattled around in that beat-up car for almost a year before Nia had brought them back to the only safe place she knew: Beckwell. Out of gas, hope, and cash, she couldn't face her old friends with what she'd done, what she'd become.

Then a miracle appeared on her windshield. An envelope with a key, an address, and a legal contract with a rent-to-own deal from Loki for an old house as hopeless as her. It still needed a lot of work, but then, who didn't? It was hers. A place to keep Asha safe.

At least, it had been.

"Come on then. Loki will just blame me if you freeze to death." She spun away, ramming her hands into the pockets of her parka and hunching her shoulders, stomping up the two steps onto the generous covered porch.

Mal's presence was like a warm shadow, his footsteps and weight making the porch creak as he stepped up beside her. Maybe it was his essence, leaching out toward her. That was the trouble with the living, spreading their aura all over the damned place. Yeah, fine, so Mal wasn't as bad as most since his aura stuck close to him, like the way he kept his thoughts to himself.

The back of her neck tingled, and she chewed her lip. How could she let him inside? Anyone was bad enough. But Mal? He saw too much, always had, even before he'd become a cop. Everyone else had been so surprised, but she hadn't been. He'd never liked bullies and he'd always looked out for the smaller kids on the playground. Had often looked out for her.

Which was exactly the problem. She didn't want anyone seeing anything. She'd kept everyone out of her house for years in case anyone could see ghosts. Her daughter wasn't the only ghost kid inside the house. Nia couldn't risk her daughter or any of the others accidentally finding out they were dead.

Kids could react badly to the news. Like, worse-than-dying-in-the-first-place bad.

And that was only one of the dangers ghost kids faced. There were also things that fed on them, fed on all that unused life potential. Or, like all ghosts, they could fade, a second death for ghosts, when they slowly lost their strength and solidity as they were forgotten by those who'd known them in life.

Her daughter, Asha, was already fading, and something hunted and fed on her. No way was Nia risking the third.

Could she keep Mal out? Could he see ghosts? He was half-Fomorian, so he might have abilities she didn't know about. But she sure the hell didn't have the money to pay Loki the payments she'd missed.

Mal reached around her and lifted the wrinkled paper sign she'd taped up beside the door. Energy buzzed off him as his aura brushed hers, making the hair on her arms rise. She swallowed the gasp at the way his warmth permeated the chill that clung to her, an unexpected burst of summer heat and light spilling through her.

She tried to tamp the warmth down. She couldn't let him close. Death didn't get happy endings. Just the inevitable full stop everyone hated and dreaded. The pain of being left behind.

The sign and its writing, scrawled in black marker, had wrinkled in the wind. It'd been after another long night getting woken up by spirits, all of whom wanted some piece of her. At least the ones in the yard mostly stayed there.

"Attention Dead People, Death can't see you right now. She's in the middle of the apocalypse. Buzz off and bother someone else. If you can read this, I mean you."

It would have been better with more swearing, but some of the kids were old enough to read. Good examples and all that. Speaking of which, where were the rug rats?

Mal chuckled, the sound startling her with all its warm and rumbly-ness, rolling through her body and warming places it had no business going. Like her heart.

"I thought the ghosts were your security system?" he

said.

She sniffed, pulling the cold around her like a cloak, trying to ignore his warmth. She'd been fine without it for years. "Sometimes. Sometimes they're just annoying." She pulled out her key and put it in the lock. Maybe it was the slight sound of metal scraping metal, or maybe they'd been watching for her, but round little faces fluttered the curtain in the living room and near the door, all looking her way.

There they were. The reason she couldn't write out all the swears on her sign. The reason she had to keep fighting.

When she and Asha had arrived at the house, there'd been no ghosts. Those had come after. Dead kids always found her. Around town, knocking on the front door, even in the Gray, they found her, and like the kid from the bar now clinging to her leg, she couldn't ignore them. Maybe it was penance for not accepting responsibility and taking care of her daughter when she'd had the chance—she could have asked for help, could have told someone she knew the truth, could have fought for her daughter then— but now it was up to her to protect these kids. And a damned good reason she shouldn't let anyone inside her house to find out about them.

She paused, her hand on the doorknob. Wait a minute. Maybe this was the answer. Maybe she wouldn't have to convince Mal to back out. Maybe someone else could do it for her. Her lips curled into something like a Grinchy smile.

She flung open the door and stepped through, as though she couldn't feel Mal step in behind her, almost like a physical touch. As though she didn't have to resist the flinch because someone else was in Her Space. Her sanctuary, his essence spreading out and touching hers like fingertips caressing her arms, sparking every nerve.

"Mama, Mama, who's that?" Asha said, running up

to Nia's side, her short, dark curls swaying, dark eyes bright. She sent an elfin grin at the little blond boy now trying to hide behind Nia's back, then a little wave with her still-pudgy fingers.

Nia firmed her resolve and straightened her shoulders. She could let Mal inside, a whole damned parade if she had to if it meant keeping Asha safe. That bathroom could be a way to protect her daughter and buy them some time until she gained her abilities. She'd failed Asha once. She wouldn't fail her again.

Mal stepped over the threshold and blinked. While the house was warmer than outside, there was a noticeable and moving chill in the air. He could swear he'd just heard a little kid's voice from practically beside him, even though he couldn't see anything. It would have been nice to chalk up the voice to imagination and the temperature differences to micro climates or some shit, but he had a bad feeling, the kind that sent the hair on the back of his neck curling upward.

He knew exactly why it was colder inside.

He'd lived in Beckwell more than half his life. His Formorian side had always brought him in close contact with the paranormal undercurrents. Hell, even outside Beckwell there were some experiences science and the mundane could never explain. Still didn't make it comforting, coming right up against it.

The challenging smile Nia threw his way said she saw his discomfort and was more than happy to use it against him. "Don't you want to stay?"

The moth fluttered around her head, toward him, and then away. Still flickering, sometimes visible, sometimes not.

Mal took a steadying breath. Might not like it, probably wasn't going to kill him. "Yeah, sure. Lead the way. Why don't you show me the bathroom I'm going to work on first? We can figure out a rough schedule."

Even though, as per orders, any schedule would be delayed and expanded as needed to make sure Nia had the protection she needed from the League and the gods. Fomorians were one of the few species capable of defeating angels, the gods' soldiers, so if push came to shove, he hit harder. He also had more investigative and undercover experience than anyone in town, plus experience with the twisted Fates to hopefully anticipate their attack. Mostly, he needed to uncover the threats and keep Nia out of trouble until she grew powerful enough to take care of her own protection.

Nia might have an army of ghosts to do her bidding, but so far, that was it. No evidence of a security system that could hold off physical threats. His Fomorian side didn't sense any kind of magical wards, either. Was she cocky or clueless about the danger she was in?

Nia studied his expression a few moments before she shrugged and toed off her shoes. "If you say so."

Mal followed her lead, removing his boots and leaving them by the door beside Nia's worn black ankle boots. Regardless of whether Nia needed help, Loki was giving him the chance to prove himself. To the town, to his brother. To himself. He wasn't going to let a few ghosts change that.

He frowned, catching sight of a rainbow ball in the hall. Were those kids toys in the next room?

Small hands touched his leg, one pressed gently against his back. Then he could have sworn tiny fingers brushed through his.

His throat constricted. His pulse sped, and every instinct—even the Fomorian ones, which were generally too stupid to ever do anything other than fuck or fight—said running would be a damned fine idea right now.

"Aren't you coming?" Nia called.

Somehow, he forced himself to find her with his

gaze. She waited, one foot on the massive staircase with its thick warm oak banisters and spindles leading up to the center floor and dividing the house between the shadowy rooms on the right, and the shadowy rooms on the left.

With his pulse pounding so hard it dimmed his vision, he could have sworn he saw indistinct figures slipping through the space between he and Nia. His training kicked in, and Mal brought his nerves back under control. It was the one thing he'd always been better at than Daniel: controlling and using his Fomorian side. He forced his breath and his heartbeat to slow. He straightened and crossed the short distance to Nia.

Small fingers continued to try to tangle with his. Too small to belong to an adult, even one as petite as Nia. Which meant they were a child. Only a coward would be afraid of a child, even the dead variety. A child who just wanted to hold his hand. A child who needed him.

His throat constricted. He was slammed back into the memory of four years ago. The way the cold damp frosted his breath. The sound of his footsteps in the gravel. The static from his radio before the gunshot had shattered the quiet night. And then the scream. The long, echoing scream as the mother went in to check on her son. The child he'd failed to protect.

His lungs ached as he fought to push the memories down and stop the panic attack. The worse it got, the more Fomorian he'd get. Turning blue and sprouting wings and horns was not going to win him any points with Nia.

He let his hand loosen and his arm hang down. Icy little fingers of a mystery ghost child entangled with his. It was messed up, but that little hand helped box away the memory, helped slow his thundering heartbeat. Helped momentarily cage the Fomorian. There'd be plenty of time to introduce that side of himself later…when it came to keeping Nia safe.

What. The. Hell.

Nia fumed as she led Mal up the staircase to the second floor, the rooms all off a U-shaped hallway that outlined the stairwell. The staircase up to the third floor was pressed against the wall, narrow and intended for servants at some point, even if no servants had ever used it.

The morning after Loki had given her the key, she and Asha had gone to the address, fought through a tangle of weeds glutting the driveway. The beast was much larger than she'd imagined, especially considering the price he'd quoted, but it was obvious the second she stepped on the porch no one had ever loved this house. Neglect hung in the hollow emptiness of the still rooms that didn't echo with family ritual or shimmer with bright memory. No one had ever loved the house, so no one and no entities were attached to it. The lawn ornaments, all the rest of those spirits, those were her fault—ghost magnet issues. But that first day, the house—and Loki—had allowed her to smile for the first time in years.

Mal's warmth billowed against her as he stopped on the stair just below her, his presence scattering the old memories like birds. He was surrounded by all eight kids, plus the ghost parakeet, who perched on his wide shoulder.

She inhaled sharply. Worst of all, Asha held his hand, beaming up at Nia. It damned near made Nia's heart flip.

In an "oh, shit, this is bad, really bad" kind of way, not the romantic kind.

Mal's bronzed skin was a touch grayer than he'd been outside, and there was a noticeable tic he'd developed in his whiskered jaw. Teensy bit satisfying. Yet here he still was. In her house. His essence trying to warm up the place, to feel out hers, to connect.

Nia turned away, frowning and running her hand

along the worn handrail. What did he think of it, her house? Had he noticed the toys she hadn't had a chance to put away? What about the fact even though she kept meaning to pull down the curling rose-print wallpaper in the front hall, she'd never gotten around to it?

No. Wait. She didn't care what he thought. She didn't want him in here. She didn't want anyone in here, and especially not him. Because the one time she'd let him get close, she'd seen he was sexy and sweet and protective, and so damned much more than anyone gave him credit for.

The kind of guy she could fall for, who would break her so much worse when he left.

Because everyone left.

They reached the third-floor attic space, her bedroom. Dormer windows facing in three directions popped out of the room and let in the dim glow of fading sunlight. Looked like snow. Maybe even rain if they were particularly unlucky. It'd trap she and the ghosts in the house, since the water could transport them all back to the Gray, whereas she'd just be stuck in-between, half in the Gray, half here, spirits trying to crawl through her to this side. There was more life energy to feed on here, although the Gray and the ether there called them all back when they needed rest, to join once more with the source of all ether.

Her bed was rumpled, and she kicked a bra underneath it just as Mal stepped into the room. Heat spread from her toes up to her scalp. She'd never had a man in here, never had anyone in here. Mal had been her first, and here he was being her first all over again.

Gah! She wasn't seventeen.

She spun away, stomping toward the bathroom tucked against the east wall, using up one of the four dormers. He was invading her space, spreading his warmth around. His aura brushed hers more here than elsewhere, like fingertips brushing over her skin, all over her body, because this was her personal haven. As much as she'd been able to make it one. The lower floors she hadn't been able to do much about reducing the spirit activity. Limit it, yes. But with the kids, she couldn't completely get rid of it.

Only Asha, still holding Mal's hand, walked across the room toward Nia and the bathroom. The other kids, including the new blond boy, all peeked in from the doorway. The moth fluttered around their heads like a clucking mother hen.

Mal looked like he was working hard at remaining stoic. He straightened with Nia's gaze on him, and raised a dark eyebrow in a sexy, challenging way that made some part of her tremble inside.

She visualized beating those soft feelings down like a plastic gopher down with a plastic mallet.

"This is the shithole you're supposed to transform. Congrats," she said. She flicked on the bathroom light and tried to see it through Mal's eyes.

If the kids hadn't been enough to scare him off, maybe the bathroom would. It did look a bit worse for the wear. Her stuff was scattered over most of the chipboard countertop she'd hacked a circle out of to surround the 1950s chipped pink pedestal sink. She'd propped mostly measured 2x4s beneath it to precariously balance her makeshift countertop. The toilet was likewise pink. For some reason, the bathtub/shower unit was a strange green/yellow shade, kind of like snot, and grimy.

She wasn't up for any housekeeper of the year awards, and although two years ago she could indulge in the occasional spray of water, washing one section of her body at a time, drying between, not recently. Since Piper had risen five months ago, so had spirit activity. The shower was way too much water all at once, left her too vulnerable to their attacks. Water had and always would be a doorway, but most humans had a natural resistance that kept them firmly in world. Thanks to Dad, Nia's resistance was broken. Which meant water partially transported her to the Gray…and anything there could try and take a trip back through her body to this world. Yep, that was her life. So fricking complicated, even taking a shower was dangerous.

Mal scuffed his floor on the lino floor. "This looks like it could be original to the house, around the 1920s maybe?"

She shrugged and crossed her arms. "How long? I say a week, tops."

He snorted. "Demo might take a week." He pointed at the stain on the ceiling that also traversed down one wall. "That dealt with?"

"Nothing drips down it if that's what you mean." She'd made damned sure. Water was enough of a problem without having it drip on her in a highly unpleasant surprise.

"Mmm." He poked around the room a bit more, even undid the sole plugin over the toilet, poked at something around the window trim. He rubbed his chin with his free hand, one hand still clutched in Asha's. "A week for the demo at least. The construction of the steam shower will take the longest. We've got to entirely seal the stall properly, so you don't get moisture problems in the rest of the bathroom and house. Plus, we'll need to make room to accommodate the steam generator. You sure you want one?"

"It's only steam, no actual water?"

He gave her a strange look. Like she was the only one in the universe who didn't know how fancy things like steam showers worked.

Her face was going to start to steam soon.

Fortunately, he answered before calling her out on her cluelessness. "It's a separate unit that creates steam, which many people find relaxing. Water can condense on the ceiling, and there will still be a separate showerhead in the stall. But the steam unit itself is just steam, yeah."

Steam wasn't wet enough to count as actual water. Sure, if her water allergy grew, eventually it could be a problem. Hell, breathing moisture in the air could be a problem. But the moth had arrived. She was on the way to becoming Death, right?

Holy hell, she'd get to luxuriate in a freaking steam shower? It was like heaven was moving into her ensuite.

"Yes, I want one. Fast as you can do it." She steeled herself. "Okay. Let me have it. How long am I stuck with you?" More like, how long did he think he was staying?

He looked around some more. "Three weeks maybe?"

Her gaze found his fingers, still twined with Asha's. Funny he hadn't let go. Did he even know she was there?

Cold stabbed through Nia. He wasn't wholly human. She'd assumed he couldn't see the spirits, but what if he could?

Oh, gods. What if he or anyone else found out about Asha, and who she really was? Bad enough Asha was getting weaker every day, and something was hunting her in the Gray. Nia couldn't risk her daughter finding out she was dead. Three weeks was not happening. She wanted him gone tomorrow.

CHAPTER 4

Forty-five minutes later, sitting in Nia's blue and white kitchen that walked a fine line between vintage charm and old and battered, Mal wondered how much longer he'd be able to handle this. Sure, Beckwell hosted residents with wings, horns, and all variety of mythological and paranormal family descendants you could find on the internet. Heck, a good cross-section of paranormal weirdness was just a typical Friday night at Loki's bar.

But the inexplicable cold spots, the sounds of children's voices coming out of thin air, and the faint shadowy hints of something moving just out of the corner of his eye had him strung out and on edge. The child who'd held his hand continued to pat his fingers now and then, whether to further freak him out or in comfort it was hard to say. It was mostly accomplishing the former. His Fomorian side wanted to fight, but it was impossible to fight a shadow, counter cold air. Besides, ghost or not, he was certain it was a kid. Even with his childhood he knew adults were supposed to protect kids, not the other way around.

He ground his teeth and watched Nia at the counter, pulling four frozen pizzas out of the fridge and tossing them on the counter.

This was all part of the gig though, right? He'd be useless as a bodyguard if he wasn't at the house. Nia, soon to rise as the personification of Death and notoriously connected to and inundated with the dead. All through school she'd talked to people no one else could see, been one of the four girls from the horseman clans everyone gave wide berth.

But she'd still freaked out when water touched her. She'd still needed his help then, and whether she knew it or not, she did now, too. It wasn't a question of if she'd be attacked by one of the groups after her, more like when. The physical attacks, those he was ready for.

The touching. The voices. He hadn't thought they'd be so damned unsettling. Hell, he'd rather be getting grilled by the defense while he went to trial for one of the cases he'd worked, or reamed out by one of the upper officers for a mistake.

Someone—or something—touched him on the back through the spindles of the kitchen chair, and he couldn't help it. He jumped to his feet. The kitchen chair skidded backward.

There was a muffled sound of children's giggles.

Nia looked up from the counter, a frozen pizza in her hand, paused in the act of putting it on a battered pizza tin. A dark eyebrow curved upward in challenge, and her lips twitched. "Everything okay?"

Oh, so now she was going to laugh at him with her ghosts, was she? Both masculine and Formorian sides bristled at the thought. He sidled closer to her, since the heat crackling between them seemed to be about the only thing that could keep him warm in this house. "Having some fun, are you?"

Her eyes widened and she clutched at the pizza box, crumpling it between her fingers. She licked her lips, and her breath shortened. "I'm making dinner. About as fun as the typical root canal."

He should have felt bad he was making her nervous. He almost did. Almost. But then, there was proof he really was more Fomorian than human, considering he was supposed to be here to protect her. Her nervousness didn't stop him. Instead, he was inundated with thoughts about the girl she'd been, his stupid crush.

Memories of the one day she hadn't turned him down. In the old maintenance shed, the scent of grass clippings warm around them, and Nia's spicy-sweet scent. The image of her staring up him, naked beneath him, finally looking at him. It'd almost seemed like she saw the real him no one else did.

He stepped closer, until less than a foot separated them. Not close enough to be creepy, but not far enough away she could ignore him like she'd always seemed able to do. He'd never been able to ignore her. Not the way her hair was like this wild mass of curls and black silk his fingers itched to touch. Or the hints of something vulnerable in her dark gaze he'd always longed to ask about, wanted to find some way to protect her from.

Not that she'd tell him. Then or now. She looked up, her eyes darkening, she didn't look like the girl—no, the woman everyone was always afraid of, whispered about just beyond her hearing. There was a gauntness to her face he hated seeing, the tired shadows around her eyes.

She looked vulnerable. Like someone who needed his help.

The thought should have made him back off. Didn't.

Evil twin, remember?

He made a show of looking over the pizzas. "That's a lot of pizza for just one person, isn't it?" His voice was rough and raspy, and he was getting hungrier for something much more dangerous than pizza. Obviously, it couldn't all be for her, and he wasn't dumb enough to think Nia was somehow planning to cook for him.

Unless there was arsenic involved.

She shrugged, crossing and then uncrossing her arms over her chest. Then turned to look at something on the other side of the kitchen. Her features hardened, and when she turned back, any trace of vulnerability was carefully disguised. She tossed her head and gave him a look full of sass and vinegar.

"You have a problem with women eating?" She pushed him, hard, forcing him back a few steps, and flung open the oven door and tossed her pizza in. "I get hungry, and cold pizza rocks." She straightened, and her gaze narrowed. "You're not getting any, if that's what you thought."

The dual meaning of "getting any" perked up his Fomorian side, which never had been particularly bright. He had enough brain cells to know it was time to back off. His job was to protect her. Not antagonize, not seduce, and sure the fuck not to get involved.

Still, he couldn't seem to resist teasing her.

Maybe it wasn't just his Fomorian side asking for a beating.

"Oh, I get plenty, don't worry," he said. He shifted slightly closer, until his enhanced senses could pick up the hitch in her breath, the way her pulse sped, and the soft perfumed scent of Nia, something kind of spicy, kind of sharp. He remembered her scent from high school, all those days he'd studied the fine lines and the delicate skin at the nape of her neck from behind her in at least half their classes. No, it wasn't perfume or anything. It was Nia. A strong urge to taste her skin slipped through him, to see if that spicy-sharpness sparked on his tongue.

Her dark gaze flashed to his. Color blossomed over her cheekbones. "What do you think you're doing?" she said, though her voice was raspier than usual. She turned to face him, and she raised her chin in challenge.

There. Right there was the Nia he remembered, that spark of rebellion, that hint of fight in her he'd always admired but which had seemed absent since they'd both come back to town. Not entirely gone, though. It was the spark that had always drawn him. Or, rather, the other side hidden beneath.

The other side he'd glimpsed, for a moment or two, that day of the high school dance, when the kids had pulled the fire alarm.

Yeah, well, that was ancient history. Or at least, it should have been.

He raised his hands and stepped back, putting the kitchen island between them. "Nothing. Just…testing. Figuring out where we stand. You know, break the ice." The bullshit rolled off his tongue with ease. "I'm here to do a job, nothing more." He paused. He'd practically jumped at the chance to protect Nia, proof there was no growing out of stupidity. Trouble was, all those old thoughts about her rattled around in his head, better left to a lonely teenager with raging hormones. "For an old friend."

Nia snorted, putting the last of her pizzas in the oven before she slammed the oven and turned, crossing her arms. "You better mean Loki. Because whatever we are, we're not old friends. Now, are you just going to stand there looking pretty, or are you going to help them unload all the crap you'll need for the reno? I don't want anyone else in my house."

He blinked mentally a second. She thought he was pretty. Oh, shit. He really was a teenager in a man's body. Then he frowned. "Wait, what? Help who?"

Someone banged on the door, and Nia spun away. She jerked her thumb over her shoulder. "Them."

"Delivery for Malcolm Quilan," a man shouted from

outside.

The moment, whatever it had been, was lost. Nia had turned away, and Mal was left answering the doors for deliverymen with their truck of supplies for the bathroom. And the other supplies he'd added to the order: security cameras, a few weapons, things he'd need to keep her safe if anyone came after her. As he hauled in supplies for the bathroom reno, storing some of the others out on the porch, it was clear he had to rethink his strategy. Seemed clear time hadn't made Nia's heart grow fonder. Which was good. He needed to focus on getting the reno done, and more importantly, keeping Nia safe without her realizing he was doing it.

&

Two hours later, Nia tossed the empty pizza tin from the part of the pizza she'd eaten in the sink, glancing up at the rapidly darkening sky outside. The other three empty pizza tins sat stacked on the cupboard, just waiting for the incinerator to finish its job. Pizzas went in, ghost pizzas came out. That is, the equivalent of the pizzas' spirit after the physical portion was incinerated. Turned out it was true what some cultures believed: everything had a spirit.

Her kids didn't know they were dead, which meant they thought they still needed to eat. Just like they needed the normal-ish life she tried to give them. Half were under five, which meant they didn't expect to go to school. A few of the older ones knew they were dead and helped look after the littles. Helped to explain why they lived a simple life, most of it spent at the house doing crafts, playing games. Field trips to the library, sometimes going for walks cross-country. She should give them more, but what else could she do for them without making anyone, particularly her friends, suspicious?

The sky was pale gray. It was cold it enough it should be snow, but she always worried it could be rain. Just the thought of it, or worse, getting trapped out in it, made her stomach churn. More freakin' problems. Like Mal. Showing up, seeing too much, reminding her of a past she'd sure as shit rather forget.

After he'd finished unloading all the supplies, even though she'd been tempted to share some pizza with him, he'd said he needed to get his things and visit his aunt at the Senior Center. More like he probably needed a break from her, her ghosts, and her house.

Nia snorted, gripping the cold edge of the steel sink. A break from her life. Wouldn't that be nice. Maybe this bathroom reno thing would be worth it in the end. A place where she could escape, if even for just a few minutes. That monster from the Gray had started hunting Asha a few months ago while Asha slept, which meant even nights were spent fighting for her daughter's survival. Then last month, Asha had started to look paler, more transparent. At first Nia had blamed it on the monster from the Gray, but it was more than that.

Asha was fading.

Whoever had known her as a living child was either forgetting her or was dead themselves. The fact that Nia knew her as a ghost, loved her, wasn't enough. Fading took time, differed from ghost-to-ghost, but unless Nia did something about it, one way or the other, she'd lose Asha all over again.

The moth, still translucent and flickering, fluttered into view and landed on Nia's shoulder. Calm soaked through the moth's gentle touch, like a mother's hug. No, better. A grandmother's hug. The subtle, slightly flowery-smoky scent of jasmine tea wafted through the air.

"Thanks, bug," she muttered and finished wrapping up the rest of her pizza before storing it in the fridge. "Should have known from your taste in music you were an old lady type."

As though affronted, the moth took to the air, fluttered

a few feet, and vanished, taking the comfort with it. The soft scent of jasmine tea remained.

Nia snorted. Touchy and temperamental insect. Definitely an apocalypse horse.

"Maaammmaaa, we're hungry!" Asha said, running into the room, followed by a stampeding mini army of ghost children.

Nia rolled her eyes, pushing back the ache in her chest. "You're always hungry, you." She leaned forward and tickled Asha, who erupted into giggles, then tickled each of the other six children.

It should have been because they were growing kids. It should have been because they'd hit another growth spurt. It shouldn't have been because hunger, like most of their body's physical responses, were residual memory of a living child's autonomic responses. If there was a heaven or an afterlife, what the hell kind of place was it that wouldn't accept and invite these children in, even if they didn't know they were dead?

She didn't tickle, but ruffled the blond hair of the eighth child, the little blond boy from the bar who seemed to have joined the household, for now at least. Eight kids and the assorted pets and other spirit critters she'd lost track of some time ago. Plus, the odd random and confused ones who wandered the halls, like the lady in the entryway. The kids, though, those were on her. Those she'd fight for.

She straightened and massaged her aching neck. "Set the table. Food should be ready." Hopefully it meant she could get back in before even a drop of rain hit her.

Amid the clatter of dishes as the kids started to set the table, Nia scooped up the three empty pizza tins and headed out through the mudroom and back door just off the kitchen. The storm door was already unlocked and open, from when she'd gone out an hour or so earlier, and the old screen door was loose and squeaky enough she could back against it to walk through.

The kids knew enough to stay inside where they belonged. Where it was safe. Hell, maybe it wasn't even safe for them there anymore, not with the kind of attention she was attracting.

Her friends were worried about the gods and their USELESS agents coming after them. The stupid old Fates, aka the League of Assholes, and their plots. Nope. Nia had to be more worried about the growing number of dead in and around her home and what else they attracted. Kind of like leaving food out attracted animals.

The cracked cement patio was cold beneath her stocking feet as she wound her way through all the dead people littering the space toward the incinerator, like a literal version of the walking dead, but less smelly. Many of those were new, too. Some of them watched the incinerator hungrily.

Some of them watched her hungrily. She sent the latter a proper fuck-off glare.

The moth reappeared, hovering over her and doing circles around her. It flew at a couple of spirits who edged closer, sending them backward, startled.

Huh. Was it trying to protect her?

"Thought you were pissed at me," Nia said, shoving her hands into the welders' gloves she'd left on the tilting metal patio table. She opened the doors on the small gray incinerator. The squat, kind of gray, mailbox-looking thing that stood not much taller than her had cooled, but still put off enough heat the gloves made it safer.

Another song, this time a little fainter and only enough to get the main words, started, leading into Stevie Wonder's "Don't You Worry 'bout a Thing" before it stopped. The moth kept circling, keeping the spirits at a distance.

Despite herself, and glancing again at the gathering clouds, Nia chuckled. "Thought you were into older stuff than that, you old *bouri* you," she said, using the word her grandmother, or *bibiji*, had said was a really insulting way of saying "old woman." Insulting enough that Bibiji had pinched Nia's ear hard before the explanation.

The moth chirped in annoyance, the scent of jasmine tea singed, but it kept diving at the ghosts.

Nia's ear began to ache, as though at just the memory of Bibiji's grip. She rubbed at it impatiently, hands shaking. She'd just been talking to the moth, not her East Indian grandmother. The one who might have been around in ghost form to take care of Nia when she was little, but ready to ditch and run the second Nia's mother had died.

Mom had promised she'd be back the day she walked out on Dad. Bibiji had promised she'd always be there for Nia. Both had lied.

Nia's eyes narrowed on the insect. "Yeah, well, you ever figure out how to talk and you just let me know what your real name is then, huh?" To heck with being intimidated by a bug.

She leaned over and peered inside the incinerator. The fire burned below the grated shelves where she placed the food, and the shelves held the ghost pizzas—the physical remains of the pizza turned to ash. She collected and stacked the three ghost pizzas on her pizza tins. The incinerator door squeaked as she closed it, and she balanced the tins on her arm.

One of the pizzas she set down on the battered and tilted metal patio table near the edge of the cracked concrete. A few of the ghosts nodded at her in thanks, while some of the others descended like locusts.

The other two pizzas she carried inside, returning through the kitchen door. She waited for the moth, then latched it. The kids all scurried to the table, chairs sliding back and into place as they took their places.

"Good job setting the table tonight, guys," she said, a

mismatched set of plates set at every spot.

An extra set had been set out for Mal.

Ignoring his plate, she set the pizzas down on the table.

The kids all joyously dug in, filled with chatter but quieting as they filled themselves. Almost like they were still alive. The new little boy jostled with another of the boys, an older boy who was maybe ten and probably the oldest of the group. Or, at least, the one who'd lived the longest.

Nia sat to Asha's left and tried to smile at her daughter. Her pale, increasingly translucent daughter.

Asha grinned back, her dark eyes sparkling as she chomped a piece of pizza, cheese strings sticking to her chin. She giggled, the sound young, the baby fat never having had a chance to fade from her face.

In April, she should have been celebrating her tenth birthday.

But that would never happen because Nia had given Asha away without ever trying to find a way to provide a better life for her. She could have gone to Loki, asked him for help. She'd been eighteen, not eight, not helpless. If she hadn't been weak and cowardly, hadn't abandoned Asha, maybe her daughter would still be alive.

Nia couldn't be weak anymore. She'd damn well protect them from anything that came their way, whether that meant Mal, her friends, or the darker beings that preyed on spiritual energy. It was why she needed to rise as Death.

The moth fluttered back and settled quietly on Nia's shoulder. Quiet strength soaked through the contact. The assurance that Nia wouldn't be alone anymore.

"Yeah, well, we'll see. Long as you stick around, I guess," she communicated back. Because no one stuck around long enough to depend on. By the time Nia met Piper, Ginny, and Anna, she'd learned the only one she could really depend on was herself.

The lights above the table flickered, and the scent of jasmine tea increased with the weight of the moth's touch, pressing into her, like it wanted her to remember it was there.

Whatever. For now.

For now, she'd take all the moth had to offer, especially when it came to keeping other spirits away. Spirits who could clue the kids into the truth. The young rarely understood the concept of death, and often the trauma of their passing created a memory blank that could just conceal their demise or, as in Asha's case, completely hide all memory of who they'd been.

Finding out the truth unexpectedly didn't usually go over well. A few could accept it, but others, especially children with high potential soul energy, those could turn bad. Some of them might turn to poltergeist activity in a misguided attempt to interact with other kids.

Far worse was their other potential future.

Bibiji had told Nia about them when she was three, the first time she'd accidentally fallen into the Gray. Bibiji had other names for them, the nightmare creatures who haunted the Gray and fed on other souls. She'd thought they were the spirits of murderers and demons.

She'd been wrong.

Nia had known that the first time one had attacked her two months ago. That creature who haunted her dreams and hunted her daughter. In that brief touch, she'd connected with what it had been. A child, destroyed by the knowledge of all that had been stolen from it, turned into a mindless hunting beast. A monster. A killer.

Soul devourer.

She wouldn't let that happen to her kids. Which meant she had to protect them from every threat. Including Mal.

CHAPTER 5

Mal stepped into the bright open atrium of the Beckwell Senior Center trying to shake the chill out of his bones—one part ghost-related, one part his damned leather jacket wasn't warm enough and motorcycle season was months past its prime. His fingers were half frozen around the package of cookies he'd stopped at the store to pick up for Aunt Junie to check in on her and see what she knew about Nia.

He'd lucked out and at the stop in the store he'd run into Louise Dole, one of the Fates who'd been after Nia. The collision was both literal and intentional when he'd crashed his cart into hers and started small talk with the middle-aged woman just long enough to make it clear where he was staying, that he and Nia were good friends, and they didn't like visitors. The woman had nodded stiffly, acknowledging he'd made his point.

Damned irritating knowing who the Fates were, that they were one step off from criminals but he wasn't a cop any more. Even if they committed a crime, he couldn't do anything about it. Still, his step lightened the way it always did on a visit to Aunt Junie, even one where he was going to ask questions and might not like the answers. A visit with Aunt Junie was always a welcome distraction. To Daniel she'd always been "Aunt June," but Mal's nickname dated back to childhood when he'd wanted to call her Mommy, but at Mom's freak-out had settled for his own version—Junie. Hell, unlike his own mother, at least Aunt Junie had seen something good in him. And besides being the family historian, she'd also been about the only damned person other than Daniel who cared whether Mal ate or starved.

Two purple-haired grannies flapped their wings, cackling as they circled the high atrium ceiling, up near the apex of the dome and the glass panels. The moment Mal stepped through the door, they started to bicker. Two old men, one in pajamas, another in slacks and suspenders over an undershirt, both using walkers, started to curse each other in different languages.

Mal walked quickly past them. Hopefully the fight and the violence would pass as he did. It was like his shadow, something he carried with him whether he liked it or not. With sometimes deadly effect.

Damn, but the staff were efficient here. Any hint of burn marks from past battles was scrubbed away. These were Beckwell seniors, old wizards and sorcerers among them, who tended to make weapons out of their mobility devices. Most of them looked fairly human, if one ignored the odd tail, horns, or green skin.

In many ways, the Senior Center was at the heart of Beckwell. Like the rest of the town, it housed dangerous outsiders the rest of the paranormal world didn't really know how to handle. Or want to handle.

A few pajama-clad men shuffling past on their walkers scowled at him, then turned and scowled at each other. One of them lifted his walker and shook it threateningly.

Another pair of purple-haired old ladies—these ones without wings —whispered about him, or at least, tried to whisper. Sounded like their hearing aids weren't cutting it.

"There's that Quilan boy. The younger one, not the doctor."

"Malcolm Quilan. Troublemaker." The second lady tsked, playing with her pearls and shaking her head. "His poor aunt. Just the shame of that one." Pretty sure she shot him the evil eye.

He made a point to smile and wink at her.

At which point she turned and jabbed the woman next to her with an elbow.

Mal hurried past before it became a brawl. Not like what she'd said was anything different than he'd heard all his life. Hell, they'd been generous compared to most of what was said about him. The "other" Quilan. The mess-up. The one who'd tried to run away, joined the RCMP, and screwed that up too, not that anyone was surprised. If it didn't mean so much to Aunt Junie that he visited, he would have avoided the Senior Center for her sake, even if it would be like cutting off his right arm.

The whole center was circular shaped, the atrium near the front, the café in the center, and the nurses station just to the left of the atrium to spot anyone who'd circled once too many times and might need some help back to their room. Mal swung left, past the glass-walled home of the medical center, located in the Senior Center but open to the town. The chairs in the waiting room were mostly empty, and his twin, Daniel, perused a patient file. They had the same height, same muscular physique, same bronzed skin and dark hair.

That's where the similarities ended.

Mal couldn't resist tapping on the glass and giving a jaunty wave.

Daniel looked up. His eyes narrowed and suspicion filtered through their connection.

Mal just shook his head but hurried out of view. He didn't have time for a Daniel lecture today. Daniel had been born maybe a minute earlier but took the whole older brother thing much too seriously. In an annoying, kind-of-nice-but-Mal-would-never-admit-it kind of way.

It also meant Daniel had had to shoulder the responsibility of being the town good guy for too long alone. He was right. It was time Mal stepped up. Which he was trying to do. Despite the ghosts and the cold and Nia probably hating him. Then again, it hadn't been all anger that sparked heat between them.

He'd entered a corridor with doors on the right and paused in front of a mauve door with the label "June Benoit," his hand raised to knock.

Yeah, well, great. His focus needed to be on protecting Nia and keeping the reno-job cover up to snuff, not seducing her. Hopefully Aunt Junie could give him some tips and intel to figure out Nia, so he'd have some idea where she stood if or when threats came calling. She might not know it, probably wouldn't like it, but he had Nia's back. He knocked brusquely.

There went his stupid Fomorian side. Thinking of that interesting but terrible idea when it came to Nia, her back, and the F word.

The door opened, and Aunt Junie clapped her hands in delight. "Malcolm! Sweetie, what a surprise. Is your brother coming, too?" She peered into the hall around Mal, then touched his cheek, her eyes narrowing as she studied his face. "You're not trying to kill each other again, are you? Come in, come in," she said, stringing all the questions together faster than he could answer.

Aunt Junie was only in her fifties, but somehow seemed to have skipped middle age and gone straight for the granny phase, or at least, that's what he'd always figured. Daniel thought she might have a mental illness, possibly even early onset dementia. Dad had always said she was just slow. Mal considered the woman in front of him, her long black braids more silver today than last month it seemed, her neon pink jogging suit with its yellow smiley face across her chest, her smile as kind and as loving as it'd always been. Even at the worst times in his life, she'd told him everything would be okay, and because it was her, he'd wanted to believe. Yeah, fine. Maybe she wasn't as sharp at the everyday practical things most people considered important, but the things that really *were* important? Like family and taking care of her loved ones, especially her two nephews? In those areas she ought to have a couple of PhDs.

He held out the cookies in one hand and gave her a one-handed hug with the other. "Aunt Junie. You're looking lovely as always. Is that a new sweatshirt? I like the smiley face." He stepped into the room, and she closed the door behind them.

She took the cookies and shooed him toward the rose-colored loveseat and chair beside the wall-height window overlooking the field and a small copse of poplar trees, barren of all their leaves, their branches silver with frost.

"It is!" she cooed, setting about getting tea for the two of them, her usual ritual. "Daniel's Piper helped me pick it out. We ordered it on the internets. Did you know they have clothes now?"

His lips twitched, but he refused to smile too broadly and possibly embarrass her.

"I did. It looks good. Piper has been here to see you then?"

He'd barely seen his brother and his new sister-in-law-to-be since the big bachelorette party at the bar, where Piper had gained the powers of Pestilence…and after he might have kidnapped her in a misguided attempt to save his brother. Yeah…probably not too surprising he hadn't seen much of them. He glanced out the window as the wind whipped among the trees, shaking the tall grass sticking out of the snow beneath an angry sky. Moisture spit onto the glass. Damn. Looked like an even colder ride back to Nia's tonight.

"Yes, Daniel and Piper had me over to their house for dinner last night. You should come next time, Malcolm," Aunt Junie said, coming back with the teapot in one hand and a plate of cookies in the other.

Mal jumped up to go retrieve the teacups before she could ask, and they both settled onto the loveseat. She'd never ask for help, but it was the least he could do for the woman he owed so much. The woman who'd loved him even when his own mother couldn't, when his father only tolerated him because it looked like Mal had inherited more of the Fomorian genes than his brother had. Which mostly meant he was better at getting in fights and causing trouble.

"It would be just like old times, the whole family together again," Aunt Junie said, smiling and pouring them both tea.

Mal's smile dimmed. Yeah, just like old times. Golden-boy Daniel, making a home with his perfect fiancée. His aunt, the sweetest lady in town. And him. The evil twin, who last time he'd spent any significant time with either Daniel or Piper had tried to kidnap one and had almost gotten the other killed. Well, it'd be as fucked up as old times, so there was that. Maybe he could even get shit-faced in memory of Mom and Dad's notorious benders.

He took the tea Aunt Junie offered, as well as one of the cookies. Her favorite, a double-chocolate variety he had the store special order in just for her.

"You're doing okay here? There's nothing else I could get you? Anything you need?" No, he didn't make as much as, say, a doctor did, and money was tight these days. But Loki had promised payment for the job, which meant Mal could probably borrow against it if necessary.

"Of course, I don't need anything else. You and Daniel spoil me." She patted his knee. "Now, why don't you tell me why you're here, and we can get to it." She sipped her tea around a small smile.

Mal chuckled, shaking his head and looking down a second. "I'm that obvious, am I?" He leaned back in the loveseat and stretched out his long legs. As much as he could in the small space anyway. "What do you know about ghosts, Aunt Junie?"

Her eyes lit up and she set down her tea, turning towards him. "Do you mean ghosts or spirits?"

"There's a difference?"

She swatted him on the knee and shook her head before straightening and folding her hands in her lap. "Our people, the *Omàmiwinini,* believe all things, living and otherwise, are inhabited by the presence of Kitchie Manitou, or the Great Spirit. Therefore, spirits surround us all the time, both good and bad, lesser and greater. When we die, we return to the spirit world where we began, and the cycle of life is complete."

"Um, I don't think that's what I mean."

"Ghosts are spirits of the dead who are trapped here. Is that what you meant?"

"At this point, I'm not sure."

Aunt Junie took a sip of tea. "Well, we're all supposed to return to the spirit realm and our Creator. But, just like in life, there are always the ornery ones, those who lose their way. I saw my first spirit before I could speak, and I've continued to see them all my life. Don't tell Daniel; he'll worry." She shrugged. "Some spirits just want to cause trouble and pain. Like the soul devourers, the wendigo."

Huh. Aunt Junie saw spirits. Although, considering

the town and how pretty much all of them had paranormal ability, made sense. Mal munched a cookie, waving it to articulate his words. "That's like a werewolf, right?"

"No, it's like a wendigo. In spirit form, they can possess humans and turn them into cannibals. I knew one shaman who believed the wendigo legend was never about the physical, but that wendigo devoured souls, in this realm and others. He's the one who called them soul devourers." She shrugged again and blinked, looking up at him. "Now, I'm sorry, it's me who's confused. Why do you want to know about ghosts? Are you being haunted? Perhaps we could get my friend Mr. Death to stop by. I don't think anyone's doing that poorly, so he's unlikely to be by tonight otherwise, but he might know more about your trouble."

"No, that's okay." To distract his aunt, Mal offered her another cookie.

Aunt Junie's friend Mr. Death was real despite Daniel's belief that he was one of Aunt Junie's delusions and a symptom of dementia. They'd met him, and as a favor to Aunt Junie, he'd reluctantly saved Mal's sorry ass. Which made the Death guy strong, paranormal, and something of a mystery. Nia was supposed to be Death, right? Which made Mr. Death what? A reaper? A pseudonym?

A troubling mystery that didn't need to be solved this second, that's what.

Aunt Junie dunked her cookie and munched with a small, blissful smile for a few moments. "I don't think you should kidnap Piper again. She's almost family now, and that's quite rude," she said, waving her cookie to punctuate her sentence before she dunked it again and popped the rest in her mouth. "I worry about you, Malcolm. Kidnapper isn't a very good profession for a grown man. And I certainly don't want you and your brother fulfilling the silly curse that stole my brothers."

"Silly curse." Yeah, sure, great name for the thing that had meant all the twins in their family line ended up killing each other. Nah, he and Daniel probably wouldn't do that.

At least…not a second time.

"I have a job. Not kidnapping—which no, isn't a job, but an indictable offense, and not one I intend on repeating. I have a real job. Well, a temporary one." Better not to mention the protecting part. Aunt Junie would worry. "I'm helping a friend renovate her bathroom, and I think she might be haunted."

"Renovations? You aren't working for your uncle again, are you? When are you going back to the RCMP? You're a police officer, Malcolm. Did you forget?"

Forget the training, the camaraderie, the meaning he'd found in his life before his past had come back to haunt him? Then, just when he didn't think things could get any worse, a month after the shooting, Mom and Dad had died in a car accident. Yeah, he could only dream of forgetting some of those nightmares.

"I left the force four years ago, Aunt Junie, remember?" he said gently.

"Well, it hardly means you can't go back tomorrow. They'd be lucky to have you. I could call them if you like. Your friend is haunted? Oh, you mean Petunia Amort, that nice Death girl, don't you?" Aunt Junie tsked while Mal struggled to catch up. "That poor child. What her father did to her? It's little wonder she has ghost trouble."

"How could you—"

His aunt waved off the question. "Marguerite snuck out to get Jell-O for tonight's shots at the store, and you, Petunia, and Mr. Lou were hardly quiet in your discussion right next door at the bar."

As ever, his aunt proved she wasn't slow, but at least three steps ahead of all the rest of them. He just shook his head. "What did her father do?"

Aunt Junie scowled, cupping her tea. "Nasty fellow. Necromancer, he fancied himself. As though he had any right or the knowledge of the shamans to go messing around with things he shouldn't. They say he used his daughter to tear a hole into the spirit world, and eventually some of those spirits—some of the nasty ones, mind—came and tore him apart for it."

Mal set his tea down, any pretense of drinking it gone. "He what?"

Aunt Junie shrugged, lifting her tea again. "Suppose he got what was coming to him. A shame for the girl, finding him and all. Then all that mess with the asylums and the baby."

Time froze for a moment or two as Mal tried to make sense of her words before it rushed back toward him and slammed him hard into reality. "Nia has a *baby*?" He'd heard rumors about the asylums, but never a kid.

Aunt Junie's eyes widened, and she brought a hand to her lips. "Oh dear. I wonder if that was something Mr. Death and I talked about? I forget sometimes where I hear things, and that poor girl doesn't need more gossip about her. You won't say anything, will you?"

"Of course not." At least, he sure the hell wouldn't spread any gossip. But it was clear he and Nia needed to chat. If she had a child no one knew about, what other secrets was she hiding? And with the threats facing her, just how much more trouble could she get both of them into?

CHAPTER 6

Nia rolled her neck and blinked gritty, tired eyes, her laptop balanced on her lap where she sat cross-legged on her bed. She was maybe an hour into a job siccing ghosts on a perv, but even though she'd found him with no trouble, it was always good to make sure it was the right perv.

The kids were tucked into bed with their stories but wouldn't go to sleep and be off to the Gray for an hour or so. Which gave her some time to make some money. Plus, *not* think about where Mal was and why he hadn't come back as darkness gathered and snow spit against the windows. He'd said he was going to visit his aunt and pick up some of his things. Gah! Not that she cared. Better he didn't come back. Better he didn't find out about Asha…or Asha any more about him.

She tucked her hair behind her ears and tried to focus on the laptop screen again. Not on the way Mal's eyes crinkled when he smiled. Or his comforting warmth. Nope. Totally focused on this latest email, someone who needed help getting rid of a stalker-ish ex.

It wasn't too hard. She had some ghosts who weren't ready to move on, even after some ghost therapy, and the friendly ones helped her out sometimes. She liked to refer to them as her ghost army, even though they rarely acted in concert, and obeyed her about as well as an army of cats. But when she needed inside information, like the address of the family who'd adopted her daughter, they could sneak in places she couldn't, could travel halfway around the world to investigate if it really was JohnF@jerkhead.net sending his neighbor sleazy dick pics.

The revenge racket was a lucrative business…when she was diligent about it. After a good haunting and a clear message to back off, even pervs backed down. The inquiries came in via Nia's website, then seeing as ghosts traveled easily through electrical connections, she'd send the ghosts back through the IP address of the email and do some snooping around before giving pervs a good scare—and getting paid for it. Nia got cash, the ghosts got other deals. Sometimes messages to loved ones, sometimes ghost food, sometimes other small favors they wanted. She wasn't rolling in money, but it could pay the bills.

Note to self: Attack more pervs. Make more money, owe Loki less.

She'd just opened her messages requesting more help and offering a paying job—yay!—when a new message appeared in her email.

Her neck tightened when she recognized the name, and her fingers froze, perched above the keys. Deirdre Boniface. Aka Beckwell School's principal, mean old Boney-face, plus one of the Fates who'd formed the League of Assholes, and who wanted Nia and her friends to start the apocalypse. They'd threatened Piper, first to rise and Pestilence clan, to get her to start a worldwide plague. When that hadn't worked, they'd gone after Ginny, manipulating her dead brother to steal her powers and, yep, end the world. They were obsessed. And stupid if they thought after Piper and Ginny had turned them down—the more agreeable of The Four—that either Nia or Anna, the War horsewoman, would ever agree to their insane terms.

Looked like it was Nia's turn.

She licked her lips and opened the email.

Dear Ms. Amort,

We would like to offer you a trade. Help us usher in a better age for humanity by ending the repugnant state all are forced to live in now, and we'll help you save your daughter. She doesn't have much time.

Sincerely,

Deirdre Boniface.

Icy cold slid through Nia's veins. They knew about Asha? Was it a bluff? Her fingers trembled above the keyboard, and her chest squeezed.

The moth fluttered across the room and landed on the corner of the laptop screen. The screen flickered, and the word processing program opened. "Where is boy man?" it wrote. "He helps."

Damn. Looked like the moth'd figured out the trick with electricity, too.

"I don't have time for this, bug. Can you read? Do you not see the message on the screen?"

Another window opened. "I read. They are Fates. Know past, present, future. Trap."

"No shit it's a trap." Yet some of the tension went out of Nia's shoulders. Sure, okay. They knew the past, present, and future, so maybe that was how they knew about Asha. And that she was fading. Did that also mean they could know how much time Asha had left? "But they cut the thread of living creatures, not ghosts, right?"

"Trap." The moth stretched its wings. "Yes. Thread of living. You living. Get him. Need help. Trap. Danger." The words danced across the screen.

"Yes, but what if they know something? Maybe something happened to the people who adopted Asha. Or is happening, if Asha is only starting to fade. Maybe they're in a coma. Maybe…"

The word "trap" began to repeat and print itself across the page.

Nia rubbed her forehead. "Frick. You're probably right." She typed a quick, eloquent reply.

F you. Not interested.

Hit send.

Almost immediately two more emails popped into her inbox, suggesting not only was the wireless connection up to speed tonight…but the Fates were online and watching.

The first email was from Louise Dole, the middle Fate.

You might not like visitors or reality—" Whoa, where'd that come from? *"—but the Apocalypse is inevitable. Wouldn't you rather choose when it happens? She's just a child. Help us, protect her.*

The second was from Daphne Spinner, youngest of three, and most batshit.

We're the Fates, bitch. We know how this plays out. We know WE win, you lose. The kid is as good as gone. You should have accepted our offer.

Nia's jaw ground. Definitely batshit.

Another email binged. This one Deirdre Boniface again.

Nia closed her eyes a second, then hit open.

Please forgive Daphne. She's under a great deal of stress. We are sincere in our offer. You could save her. We know the identity and location of the individual who could keep your daughter strong. Rise, help convince your friends to join us, and we'll ensure that individual lives a long, healthy life and remembers your daughter many years to come.

Sincerely,

D. Boniface

What the hell. Was it drive Nia nuts day or something? First Loki and the moth. Then Mal. Now the freakin' League of Assholes.

Another window popped up. "Trap. Danger," appeared across the screen while the moth flattened itself on the glowing laptop screen. "Get man."

"We don't need him. And I know they're full of crap. They seriously think I'd convince my friends to help end the world? Even if I could, why would I? Definitely wouldn't guarantee a long existence for anyone." Nia said, closing the program again. She didn't need Mal. Or his warmth. Or the way he looked at her, all that sexiness rolled up in one man.

She sent a reply all message to all three of the Fates. *Not interested.*

The Fates knew Asha was in danger. Which only confirmed what Nia already suspected: Asha was fading because whoever remembered the child she'd been was either dying or dead, or otherwise incapable of remembering. Even if Nia did listen to the Fates' terms, it would be one hoop after another to jump through. Asha would be no safer.

Unless Nia found a way to keep her safe from all the threats ghost children faced.

Three more emails binged in Nia's inbox.

The program window popped open again. The words

were in caps now. "NEED HELP. MAN CAN HELP. DAUGHTER. YOU. ME."

"Okay, this is getting annoying. He's not here. What do I need him for? I've got you, got the ghosts, must mean I'm rising as Death, then I'll be powerful enough to stop anything. We're good." Nia pressed the power button on the laptop.

The moth rose into the air just before it closed in the laptop screen, settling on the bedside lamp.

Nia put the laptop on the floor beside her, tucking it slightly under the bed.

Her phone, plugged in on the nightside table, buzzed. A new message from an unknown sender. "Protect you. Daughter in danger. YOU in danger. Betiya."

A chill scuttled down Nia's neck, and she squeezed handfuls of her quilt. "Don't call me that. You're not Bibiji."

Betiya. Only her grandmother had called her that. Just the word conjured Bibiji's smiling face, the way she'd lean in with a big smile and press her hands to Nia's face. The way she'd stay with Nia all night long to keep the other ghosts away, to guide Nia home if she accidentally fell into the Gray. The way she'd always smelled of cinnamon gum. She was Nia's guide in the Gray, and her protector.

Until Mom walked out when Nia was five, and Bibiji left with her.

Everyone else seemed willing to visit her in their afterlife. Except the people who'd mattered the most.

"You might be an old woman, but you're not my grandmother," Nia whispered.

The moth chirped in annoyance. Another message. "Spirit wisdom. Name Esther."

Esther. An old name. Biblical. One letter off from "ether."

Her phone started to ring.

Nia flinched, and she twisted to glare at it, expecting another moth text. Instead, Anna's photo popped up, the one where Anna hadn't wanted a picture taken and was trying to cover her face; only her hand, middle finger, and a hint of brown hair was visible.

Nia picked up the phone and answered the call. "Anna?"

She and Anna, the heir to the War horseman clan, had never been exactly close. Usually they ended up arguing, because it was way too much fun to poke the War horsewoman, especially because not many other people would. That was something they both understood: what it was like to be feared in a town of weirdos, where for some reason, they were ranked higher. Or lower, depending on your perspective. Their friends Piper and Ginny, the Pestilence and Famine horsewomen respectively, had never quite gotten it the same way. Guess people weren't quite as afraid of getting sick or starving as they were of Death and War. Go figure.

Static crackled on the other end "Nia? What do you want?" Anna sounded more wary than pissed off. There was the sound of pages turning in the background, like Anna was still reading despite having answered the phone.

"You called me."

"No, you called me. What do you want, Nia?" On top of being the heir to War, Anna was also the town librarian and overly keen on research. She knew more about the horsemen clans than anyone else did, and it had proved helpful. Sometimes equally irritating, when she thought that made her their leader.

If a moth could look smug, Esther sure the hell did. Nia glanced at it where it perched on the lamp, wings slowly opening and closing, revealing a skull-like pattern on its abdomen. She wasn't taking orders from an insect...but maybe suggestions were okay. Talking to

Anna wasn't the worst idea; Anna had a connection to Loki that could be useful.

"How well do you know Loki?" Nia couldn't resist adding, "Like, how's the fucktationship going?"

Anna's growl rumbled over the phone. "He brought me to town when I was a kid, and he was technically my guardian. That's the beginning and end of the story. Why do you have to be so crude?"

"It's a gift. So, no chance you could blow him and, I don't know, ask him to let me out of this deal where Mal lives in my house and renovates my bathroom?" It was a challenge to keep the words light when so much was riding on getting rid of Mal and keeping her kids safe.

"Mal, as in Mal Quilan, Daniel's brother? And you made a deal with Loki? Nia, what were you thinking?"

"I'm sorry, did you have a spare house laying around?" There was a snap to her voice. Crap. No, not fair. She'd been too ashamed to tell her friends anything about where she'd been or how desperate she was when she'd come back two years ago. Plus, pissing Anna off was not going to help.

Nia took a calming breath. "He holds my mortgage, and when he called me in for a meeting, I had to go. He says he's doing the favor for me, but you know how it is. There's always a catch with Loki."

Anna snorted. "There's probably a scheme, too." Her voice turned more serious. "Are you in trouble? Has Mal threatened or hurt you in any way?"

Anna's darkening tone tempted Nia only for about half a second, because it was cruel, even to Mal, to turn Anna loose on him. Anna might be a librarian, but she sure the hell wasn't mild-mannered.

Nia sighed. "No. Loki wants Mal staying with me like an unwanted squatter until he's done this renovation job. Claims it's a favor to me. I just...I don't like him being here." The last words were hard to admit. She'd do anything for her friends…but she had to protect herself, too. If you let people get to close, it was a sure recipe for getting hurt.

"What are the terms?" Thank gods, Anna went all business-like instead of sympathetic.

"He stays here until the bathroom renovation is done." All that warmth, his deep blue gaze and broad shoulders. "If I back out, I owe him a lot of money."

"You don't have the money?"

Nia's voice dropped, her face heated, and she picked at a loose thread on the duvet. "No."

Fortunately, Anna didn't seem to notice. "It's definitely about more than just a reno, and I can't see that Loki would need the money. Do you think he's working for the League again?" Yet another way Loki had tried to manipulate she and her friends.

"Those losers? No, I think he's done with them." She'd tell her friends about the emails from the League later. When she didn't have to explain who Asha was. Loki claimed he wanted to help her, but was that really what he was doing? "He saw my moth today, though. I mean, you know, my horse. At least, I'm pretty sure that's what it is."

Esther. The moth had become Esther.

"Which means you're rising as Death." The way Anna said it might as well have been a life sentence. "But…" Anna hesitated. "Do you think Loki could be trying to help? I mean, obviously there's a scheme in it somewhere, but he did give us sanctuary when the USELESS agents came after Ginny and us."

"Why would he help?"

The War horsewoman growled to herself. "I don't know. It just…never mind. Dumb idea. I'll look into it, see what I can find." The line went dead.

Nia pulled back to look at the screen. Nope, it hadn't been her cell. Anna had hung up on her. Nia rolled her eyes and plugged her phone in again.

It binged almost immediately with a message, and Esther fluttered down to land on top of it. *"You need help. Friends help. Man help. I help. All help."*

Nia swung her legs out of bed and padded toward the doorway. "What if you can't? I mean, what if this is just a Death thing I'm supposed to handle on my own? I'll need the girls to help me bring back Asha, but until then, I can't risk letting them in the house. They might not be able to see ghosts, but what if they accidentally let slip that the kids aren't alive? And stop using my phone unless you plan on paying the bill." She didn't turn back to see if there was another message, or if the moth followed her.

Instead, she headed down the stairs to check on the kids. Not at all to see if Mal was downstairs somewhere.

Nope. It was still quiet, no lights on, no sense of his essence.

Had to give Esther some credit. Asking Anna for help was genius...even if right now, other than Anna's connection with Loki, Nia didn't really know what help she could ask for. She'd eventually have to get them all involved once she rose as Death and was strong enough to bring Asha back.

She turned the knob to the kids' bedroom slowly, in case she woke them.

Of course, most of them were in their beds, and almost none of them were asleep.

"Another story," Asha murmured.

Nia kissed each one gently on the forehead, lingering longer beside Asha, brushing the dark hair back from her daughter's forehead and semi-translucent skin. "You had your story at bedtime. It's time to rest now. But it's okay. I'll be there. You won't be alone."

As the children fell asleep, they disappeared, one by one. Just as they didn't need food, technically they didn't need sleep, though they did need to recharge their energy.

Which for them, as for most spirits, meant journeying into the Gray, the place between life and death. Of course, they just thought it was a dream.

Not a dangerous parallel world where some things, awful things like the soul devourers, were trapped and waiting. Hungry.

Returning to her own room, Nia shut the door, then checked her windows were shut tight, the taps were turned off, not a trace or droplet of water escaped anywhere. She placed a heavy crystal over the toilet lid, to keep that water contained. No doorway to the Gray here, thanks. Then checked the four corners of her room that the other protective rocks and crystals were in place. No chance of water getting on her and potentially making her physical form even more vulnerable in the Gray. Because like the ghosts, when she went to sleep, the Gray and its ether drew her, too.

Finally, she was able to settle down in bed and, reluctantly, flick out the lamp. She closed her eyes and prepared for battle.

&

It was after ten thirty, black and icy by the time Mal rolled into Nia's yard, keeping it slow so the bike tires wouldn't slide out from beneath him. Plus, he hadn't paid close enough attention when he'd driven into the yard the first time to know if there were stumps or potholes in the driveway. The equipment he'd set up at Nia's showed zero movement outside, which meant neither the Fates nor the USELESS agents had made a move. The gods would be trickier—part of why Loki thought Mal should be in-house with Nia twenty-four seven.

At least knowing Nia was safe for now, he'd tried to wait out the sleet with Aunt Junie, watching the hockey game. But when it'd only gotten worse, he'd given in to the fact he'd be headed back through the sticky wet snow back to Nia's, where the welcome was sure to be as warm as the weather.

He parked the bike against the house, somewhat sheltered by the porch roof. His icy fingers slipped and fumbled with the clasp to untie his duffle bag from the back. Frozen rivulets of sleet dripped down his neck by the time he made it onto the covered porch. Sure enough, there were no lights on, and the door was locked. He dug his cell out of his jacket and dialed Nia's number, the one Loki had given him. Twice, and no answer. Crud. He reached in his pocket, found the cold shape of the key. The demigod had said in case she locked him out, but did this count? It sure the hell wasn't a way to start this relationship, him basically breaking into her house.

The faint wail that carried on the wind found his ears, more sensitive than a regular human's, and froze him in place. It echoed that other scream, from four years ago, that terrible night. For a second, he wasn't sure if it was in his head again, or real. His Fomorian side sent adrenaline racing through him, tightened and increased his muscle-mass. Another cry, slightly louder this time, and he knew it was coming from the house.

He jammed the key in, barely pulling it out before charging inside.

The cries were louder inside, but still muffled. He pounded up the stairs. Not on the second floor, but above him. Nia's room.

The door stuck near the top of the stairs, and he had to shove his shoulder into it. He burst into the room. It was dark and shadowy. He fumbled for a light switch, couldn't find it, and instead used his cell as a flashlight.

"Nia? Nia, it's Mal."

Wind and sleet blew in through one of the windows where a section of tree had crashed through, broken branches littering the floor, the wind howling through the broken glass. Mixed rain and snow splattered onto the bed and Nia.

She thrashed and moaned on the bed.

He approached slowly, the hair on the back of his neck rising.

"Nia!" he called again, louder this time to be heard over the wind and rain. He crouched beside the bed. Wet splattered him as it did her, soaking her bed and plastering her hair to her head. "Nia, wake up. It's just a dream."

She flinched as though struck, and a bright red mark appeared along the side of her neck.

He grasped her shoulder and shook, gently but firmly. "Wake up. Come on, Nia. Wake up, baby."

She continued to moan and thrash as though he wasn't even there.

He shook her again, a little less gently this time. Fomorian gray-blue tinted his arms and fingers as the fight response raged through his body.

Still no response. Icy water continued to splatter over them, so that wouldn't work. But whatever the hell she was trapped in, it seemed clear it was more than just a bad dream. He shook her again, lifting her against him. No response as she flopped against him, wet, cold, and boneless. He checked for a pulse. Rapid and panicked. Her eyes moved rapidly behind her eyelids.

The moth, silvery in the darkness, appeared out of nowhere and fluttered close to her, landing gently on her face. Fluttering near her lips. The memory of a song, that one from the kid's mermaid show about kissing the girl echoed through his head, even though he hadn't seen it since elementary school maybe? If ever. The longer he ignored it, the louder the song became.

Well, shit. Nothing else was working, and if it worked for Prince Charming, he'd worry about Nia's reaction when she woke up. Because it was the waking part that was important.

The moth vanished to wherever it'd been.

"This would not be my first choice, sweetheart, but I

need you to wake up. Wake up and slap me if you want, but you damn well wake up." He held her gently in his arms and lowered his lips to hers.

Hers were icy beneath his.

His chest tightened and he grimaced at the wrongness of kissing her while she slept. But her moth seemed to believe it was the only way to wake her up.

He pressed tiny kiss after kiss against her lips, whispering a prayer to whoever was listening that she'd come to. It didn't seem like it was working. He'd have to—

Her lips began to move beneath his. She grabbed his shoulder and pulled herself closer. Deepened the kiss.

His Fomorian and human sides heated with pleasure.

Her eyes popped open, and she shoved away from him. She panted, her eyes wide, face all shadows in the darkness. "What the fuck?"

Rain-snow mix splattered over them again, as it had continued to do since he'd come into the room.

She jumped back, scurrying toward the door to her room and flicked on the light. She shoved a hand through her damp curls, started shaking as her hand came away wet. Racing into the bathroom, she grabbed a towel and started scrubbing at her hair. Then finding her clothes wet, started to strip them off.

Mal was frozen in place. Partially because a gorgeous woman was stripping in front of him. And because this was familiar. That day in high school, near the end of the year, when he'd finally found the courage to speak to Nia. He'd barely said four words when someone had set off the gym sprinklers and they'd all run outside to find it pouring rain. Only, Nia had reacted as though the water practically burned her. How was he supposed to protect her from this threat?

She needs you, moron.

He dashed forward, grabbing what looked like a

hoodie or robe off a chair, and wrapping it around her.

She stilled, his arms around her. Her dark eyes, wide and dilated, met his gaze. She'd been stripped of her usual black armor of heavy hoodies and clothes to hide her body, her wild mane tamed and dripping around her shoulders. All she had was the single sweater around her, gaping at the neck and revealing silken light brown flesh. The universe paused. They were back in that shed, and Nia Amort, the coolest girl he'd ever seen, was looking at him, talking to him.

He swallowed. For a second, staring down into her deep brown eyes, tear tracks drying on her cheekbones, all his past screw-ups melted away until he became someone worthy of her, worthy of keeping her safe forever. Maybe he should have tried harder back then. Maybe he shouldn't have let her push him away like everyone else.

Oh, yeah, like she'd respond well to that. Him trying to smother her. Mal Quilan, evil twin and smothering asshole. Nope. No time for that now.

"Go downstairs. Get dry," he said brusquely, forcing himself to let her go. "I'll go find some wood and close up this window, keep things dry up here."

She stared at him a moment longer, the water leaving her hair in heavy, limp curls down her neck. It only accentuated the angry gouge on one side, deep enough in some places that bright ruby droplets formed.

"Clean up your neck. You'll need a bandage for that."

She seemed to shake herself out of whatever held her then, as she started, blinked, then turned for the stairs. "Yes. Of course. That's a good idea."

He followed her close behind on the stairs because she still seemed unsteady. Only when she turned and glared at him did it feel like he could leave her for a second to go repair the window and dry things up.

Still, he paused her, a hand gentle on her elbow.

"What happened back there just now?" He watched her expression for the truth, any shifting that might indicate a lie.

She swallowed, opened her mouth, then closed it again. She studied him a moment longer. "I…I was trapped. The water makes it worse. It always has."

"Makes what worse?"

Her smile was a harsh twisting of her lips. "Everything. Everything that makes me who and what I am." Then she turned, tugging away and heading into one of the second-floor bedrooms. She closed the door firmly behind her.

He finally dared to breathe and added keeping Nia dry to the list of things he needed to do to protect her. Question was, how the hell did he protect her from something that could attack her in her dreams?

CHAPTER 7

Nia perched on the edge of the bed, stroking Asha's hair with trembling fingers, another arm around the other kids. They all clustered together on Asha's bed in silence while her daughter whimpered. The moth settled on Nia's shoulder, but even the sense of comfort was hollow. The sound of hammering and wood shifting wafted down the stairs from Nia's room as Mal repaired the broken window.

The water had triggered something, and she'd been trapped in the Gray, unable to wake up. A broken window because a tree fell through. What were the chances? Had a ghost made it happen? Was there some other reason for it?

Had she pissed off the Fates with her email to them?

Nia tried not to look at the angry red welt forming around Asha's wrist, even though the scratch on her neck seemed to throb in response to it. That had been too close tonight. Asha's whimpers grew.

Nia gave up with the stroking and just pulled Asha's

small body against hers.

"It's okay. I'm here," she lied.

Because it wasn't okay. It should have been, but it wasn't fucking okay. It would never be fucking okay, not unless she found a way to save Asha forever. Unless she found some way to bring Asha back to life.

Maybe she'd be able to help the other kids, too, someday. But they weren't fading like Asha. They weren't being hunted by the soul devourer.

They weren't her daughter. She hadn't abandoned them when it was her damned job in this life to protect her child, protect her in a way Nia never had been protected. Which made her as bad as Mom and Bibiji.

She'd been there tonight. She was supposed to be rising as fucking all-powerful Death and she hadn't been able to fight the soul devourer, hadn't been able to stop it. If it hadn't been for Mal, if he hadn't come in when he did, found some way to pull her out, she wouldn't have been able to pull Asha out with her. Then what would have happened? How long would the pain have lasted? How long would the thing have been able to feed on them? Asha wouldn't have survived. Hell, Nia probably wouldn't have, either.

The hammering stopped. More footsteps upstairs, the sound of furniture shifting. Mal was probably stripping the bed, drying things up like he'd said.

"Mama, you're squishing me," Asha finally said.

Nia let her go immediately, looking down to find all the kids watching her. "I'm sorry. I didn't mean—"

This time it was Asha who reached up a hand and stroked Nia's cheek. Then gently traced the deep scratch mark on Nia's neck. "It's okay, Mama. Just bad dream, right?"

Nia gave Asha another squeeze and blinked back the sting in her eyes, unable to repeat the lie she'd told the kids before. That the Gray and the things in it were just part of a bad dream, because better that than they realized the truth and became one of the nightmares who lived there. Spirits needed to connect to the Gray and the ether there to refuel. It should have been safe.

At least, that's what she'd thought. Before the Gray and the soul devourer had become a bad dream that could kill them both if given the chance. Asha was too young to realize bad dreams shouldn't leave physical marks like those on both of their bodies. She was still in danger. And the soul devourer was getting more persistent.

When it had first appeared, maybe a year ago, it had found she and Asha only occasionally, maybe every few months or longer. Now, though, it seemed to be waiting for them. Hunted them on a nightly basis.

"It's okay, Mama," Asha said, still trying to comfort Nia.

"It will be okay. We'll figure this out." She focused on Asha as she said it, because it was Asha the soul devourer wanted most. The others might be safe. Asha had been to the Gray to recharge. She was safe for the rest of the night. "I have to go check on our houseguest and see if he needs help with anything. I'll get breakfast in a few hours."

If the sleet had turned to snow and she could get out to the incinerator. There might still be some spirit cereal left in the cupboard, but the residual spiritual energy of things faded faster than the spirits of the living, so if the kids hadn't eaten it, hard to say if there was anything left.

She gave Asha one more hug and climbed to her feet before she exchanged another look with a couple of the older kids, who knew what the Gray was. What they were. "You'll take care of them, right?"

The boy and girl, both dead probably early last century, or even from the nineteenth, nodded solemnly. They didn't speak much, so she didn't even know their names. Sometimes the dead couldn't remember those, either. They'd showed up at the house around when she'd moved in two years ago, and they seemed to like helping take care of the other kids. Sometimes they even helped with her online investigations. Their intentions and essences emanated good, just lonely. They were welcome here.

Esther settled once more on her shoulder as she closed the kids' bedroom door. She could feel its weariness, but still there was the sense of comfort it gave with the touch, that grandmotherly touch. It'd been there in the Gray, too, and for the first time she hadn't been alone in the fight for survival through the night. In the Gray, Esther's wingspan was nearly a foot, and she'd wove and dove at the shadowy darkness of the soul devourer, giving Nia time to collect the kids and run, then vanishing for a moment only to reappear. But it hadn't been enough. Even with the help of her horse, it wasn't enough.

"Thank you. For back there."

The faintest whisper scratched through Nia's mind. *"Trapped. Man help. Kiss."*

"Wait a second…you had something to do with Mal kissing me?"

"Need help. Kiss. You happy."

Nia opened her mouth to ream out the moth when it spoke again.

"Our Asha. Our fight." It was accompanied again by the scent of jasmine tea and the warmth of an embrace.

The anger sagged out of Nia's shoulders. It'd been trying to help her. And…maybe they did need help. Tonight, when the soul devourer let the other kids go and only went after Asha, it made it clear that the attacks were targeted. But why only Asha?

"It's going to be a nasty battle, Esther. I'm going to need your help keeping Asha and the kids safe."

The hammering and other noise had stopped, and Mal's footsteps were on the stairs. The warmth he brought with him flooded through her. He'd been there, he'd pulled she and Asha out of the Gray. Real life hero stuff. Now he was doing all the cleaning up for her, duties she'd usually have to do herself. She winced, closing her eyes. He'd been around for less than a day, and already she owed him.

He was going to have questions, some of which she might even have to answer.

"Maybe you could go keep an eye on the kids while Mal and I talk?"

Another soft wave of comfort from Esther, but it wasn't enough to dispel the dread.

Talk. Such a simple word that usually meant just opening yourself up to pain. Crap. Sharing anything about herself ranked right up there with obstetrical exams and doing her taxes. If she let anyone close, it just made it easier for them to hurt her. She couldn't afford any weakness, not with a nightly battle for Asha, and the even bigger one to save her still ahead. She needed to focus on becoming Death for Asha, not doing the crazy relationship dance that might as well have been juggling with knives.

Ugh. She made a face and blew out a breath, then cocked her head toward the moth. What she needed was an easier way to get Mal's help without letting him invade her life any more than he already had.

☙

Mal took the last few stairs slowly, his arms full of Nia's wet blankets and sheets. Nia was waiting down at the bottom for him. A different Nia than he'd seen thus far. She'd pulled on a pair of sweats beneath the hoodie, and had her hands stuffed deep in the hoodie pockets, her shoulders hunched. She bit her lip, tracking his approach, watching him from beneath her lashes.

Uh huh. Considering her house and the nightmare he'd somehow pulled her out of, what was bad enough it even made *her* nervous?

Though the hoodie, zipped right to the top, didn't show anything all that interesting, it did show the angry red slash on the side of her slim brown neck. A droplet of blood had slid down her skin and made him scowl. Some job he was doing protecting her so far. He'd only been on the job for a day, and it'd already gone to shit. He could monitor the Fates, watch for the gods, do all the threat assessments he'd wanted. He'd planned for physical attacks, anticipated ghosts, but didn't have a plan to protect her from nightmares. Yeah, his Fomorian blood made him more sensitive to the unseen paranormal world, but not enough to follow her into her dreams. Not without help from Aunt Junie's Mr. Death.

"You were supposed to bandage that," he said, coming down the last few steps. It brought them almost face-to-face, other than the armful of wet linens in his arms. They were scented of her, that spicy-sharp Nia scent, and her damp hair made the scent even stronger. The urge to press his face into her hair and pull her closer grabbed him. He squeezed the wet sheets tighter. Stupid Fomorian side.

"Do you have a dryer? I propped up the mattress, so hopefully it will dry by tomorrow night, but you'd better find somewhere else to sleep tonight."

She studied him a moment longer, brow wrinkling as though she'd expected him to ask something else. "I'm not tired." She turned and headed for the main staircase. "Come on, dryer is in the basement. Want me to throw in your clothes?"

Oh, yeah, because Nia suddenly turning into little Suzie Homemaker wasn't suspicious at all.

"If you don't mind. Or I can just hang them to dry."

She wouldn't quite meet his eyes, already nodding as they reached the cellar door. "Sure. Whatever. Great. Living room's that way."

She pointed so quickly he missed the exact direction, then practically ran down the stairs before he could ask for clarification.

His scalp prickled, cop sense saying something was off. He moved in the general direction of Nia's wave, turning on lights when he bumped into the length of a sofa. More kids toys in here. For the mystery child his aunt had told him about?

He peeled off his wet jacket and hung it near the front door with his boots. His shirt beneath was equally soaked. He unbuttoned the long sleeve shirt he wore on top, leaving only the white undershirt, and had just hung up the other shirt to dry when he turned and found Nia watching him from the doorway.

Her gaze licked over him in a heated caress, taking in where the snug white shirt clung to his chest. He didn't need to ask if she liked what she saw. The way she licked her lips and boldly continued to assess him made that clear.

Yep, the Fomorian side took note, too. There went its favorite F word shooting heat straight to his shaft.

Nia sidled up to him, and he watched her with narrowing eyes.

"You know," she said, her voice raspy. "I figure there's two ways we deal with this whole stuck-with-each-other thing." She slowly let her gaze move up his body until she met his eyes. "First is talking, questions, boring stuff." She rolled her eyes, walking her fingers up his chest and making his muscles jump. "Of course, we could just skip all that and be fuck buddies instead. Help each other out, that sort of thing."

He frowned and shut down the Fomorian instinct so he could filter through the situation. She'd met him at the bottom of the stairs looking nervous as shit, but a quick jaunt to the laundry room and suddenly she was ready to get intimate?

She'd done this before. That day at the school dance, ten years ago. When the sprinklers went off in the gymnasium, and she'd run outside with him into the pouring rain. She'd been so afraid. They'd taken shelter in the maintenance shelter, and after she'd made them both strip down, leaving them shivering in each other's arms, she'd started to explain that water hurt her. But when he'd tried to ask a question, tried to understand, she'd shut down, suggested they make out instead. He'd been too infatuated and too much of a horny teenager to see it didn't add up.

He wasn't so stupid now, and he'd waited ten years for an answer.

She was playing the same damned game. Trying to distract him and avoid explaining what she'd started to tell him upstairs. The truth about why water hurt her.

"I think the polite term is 'friends with benefits,'" he said, catching her fingers and taking them off his chest. Instead, he brought her hand to his lips and pressed a soft kiss into her palm.

Her eyes widened, all pretense of sex kitten slipping away. Her fingers trembled in his.

"While I still think you are insanely hot, I don't do the 'friends with benefits' thing.'" At least, not since two minutes ago. Not when this was Nia he was talking about. He touched her chin, tipping her gaze up to meet his. "You don't have to do this. If or when we sleep together, it will be because it's what we both want. The sex, and all the rest that goes with it. But for now, what's going on? We need to talk about why water hurts you, what your father did to you. And about your child."

CHAPTER 8

Ohshitdamnfuckshit. Nia jerked her hand free of Mal's and wrapped her arms around herself as though somehow, they'd kept her safe, keep her secrets locked inside. Panic raged through her like an escaped bull. She staggered farther into the living room, shutting off all the lights except the table lamp. She told herself it was so the light didn't wake the kids, but it was because she wanted to hide from him. He saw through her too easily already. What would he think when he knew the truth?

Mal's heavier step followed her into the room, and the springs of the flowered thrift-store sofa wheezed as he sank onto them. He said nothing, just watched her, that cobalt gaze steady, muscles bunching and flexing beneath that tight white shirt while he patiently waited for her to fall into a conversation trap.

She scooped a blanket off the floor and started folding it, but her hands were shaking too bad and she made a mess of it.

"Right in with the easy stuff, huh?" she said, trying for

a sarcastic tone, but it came off as high and warbly.

Couldn't he just have been a typical guy? Couldn't she just have distracted him with sex? The idea had occurred to her when she'd walked into the living room and found him practically stripping, all that mouth-watering yumminess, muscles flexing and bronzed skin. Sex with Mal would be fun as hell, no matter the terms. She used her black, oversized clothes to avoid attention of the unwanted variety, the kind of unwelcome attention from the living and dead that'd been a reality most of her life. But Mal…Mal'd always been different. She'd never been afraid to touch him, or afraid of his touch.

"Nia, sit down," he said, his voice warm and calm. "I want to help."

Turned away from him, she clenched the blanket in her hands and squeezed her eyes shut a second. She needed his help. Crap, crap, crap. How come that meant giving him answers, too? Blowing out a breath, she opened her eyes, forced herself to turn and look at him.

He seemed to take up most of her couch, muscled forearms resting on his knees, leaning forward and focused on her, entirely on her.

Her stomach roiled. She'd faced headless ghosts, ones so mangled they hardly looked human anymore. Each night she fought a monster that was like a dragon, a shark, and a tiger had a mean-ass baby. She was fully prepared to take on the full powers of Death and fight like hell for Asha.

But facing Mal and answering his questions? That was scary as shit.

She tossed the crumpled blanket aside and forced herself to meet his gaze. "What do you know?" she said, her voice raspy.

His gaze was steady, like he'd played this kind of game before. Hell, he'd been a cop. Of course, he had.

"I know water hurts you somehow, like it did back in

high school." He paused a second. "My aunt says your father was in to necromancy, and he used you to create a doorway of some kind to the other side."

Okay, nothing too hard yet. She forced herself to breathe, even took a seat on the battered little plaid footstool that didn't match anything. She nodded. "Not the other side, the Gray, the place between life and death. The other side, heaven, whatever the fuck you call it, that's somewhere else," she corrected, mostly because mouthing off meant a distraction from what he'd probably ask about next: Asha. What did she tell him?

There was so much she couldn't tell him.

"Okay…" he said slowly. "I think I've been there. All kind of misty and post-apocalyptic-like?"

She blinked. "Yeah." What the fuck? Regular mortals weren't supposed to be able to survive the Gray.

Then again…Mal wasn't a Normal.

And he didn't elaborate.

"So, your father used you to create a doorway to the Gray. What does that have to do with water? You said earlier water makes everything 'worse'? What does that mean?"

"Creating a doorway" sounded so much better than "tearing a hole through the worlds and shoving his little daughter through it, turning her into the bridge." She shifted, crossed her arms more tightly, but the memory of that day slid over her like a cold reptile. She'd been maybe Asha's age, three or four at the time. That bastard had promised her a treat if she just helped him with "his work" for a minute.

Standing fully clothed in the plastic wading pool, the water, at first warm, grew colder and colder around her legs as Dad continued to chant. Cold water soaked through her overalls and up through her T-shirt. She'd started to shiver, teeth chattering while the water grew ever icier. The air thickened and darkness closed in around the little pool, like looking at the world through a sheer curtain. At first, only shadows moved on the other side of the curtain, shifting and filing the basement. Dad continued to shout and chant, drowning out Nia's whimpers, unable to hear the growing whispers and rustles. The icy water froze Nia in place.

And then the creatures started to reach through the curtains. Long, fleshless limbs, terrible claws, reaching toward her, tearing at her, trying to pull her apart. She'd screamed for his help, slipped and fallen, water filling her mouth as those hands reached for her. But all he wanted were descriptions of what she saw. Descriptions while she choked and sputtered on icy water, pinned down by their bodies, half in this world, half in theirs.

An imagined swarm of wasps circled in Nia's stomach at the memory, and she rubbed at the cut on the side of her neck. *Shitshitshit.* She didn't want to tell him, tell anyone this, but she needed his help. Looked like his price was answers.

"Water is a conduit to ether, the substance that makes up everything. And the source of all ether is the Gray. Ghosts are also made of ether, which means they need to reconnect with the source—or the Gray—every so often, like we need sleep. When water touches me, it means I can't...well...I can't avoid them, you know? I'm like a bridge, between this world and the Gray. And all the things that live there. They want to get here, to the living."

All those spirits and nasty things trapped in the Gray were more than willing to claw, bite, even possess her if it meant reaching the warm energy of the living. Any time she connected with water, it pulled part of her into the Gray, which had been extremely dangerous before she'd learned to protect herself, to center her aura and essence and keep other spirits out. She'd been a teenager before she'd figured out how to keep that out, how to defend herself from possession and them feeding off her spiritual energy. Too bad no one else was alive at that point or had cared enough about her to stick around and teach her what they knew.

Too bad before she'd learned to protect herself, being possessed by the spirits hadn't been the worst thing they'd done to her. Possessing her, they'd made her do terrible things. Sometimes, they'd just done terrible things to her themselves. Gave her a reason to feel her body was just a physical vessel and somehow distanced from her spirit. Just something to be used. Like they'd used it.

Asha would know everything Nia knew, would always have the answers, would learn how to protect herself if Nia could save her. Because Nia would never abandon her daughter again, and when she rose as Death, nothing alive or dead better try to threaten Asha.

Mal's gaze, more gray than blue for the moment, met hers steadily, like he knew there was a lot she wasn't telling him—no shit—but wouldn't pursue it for now. There was sympathy there, but at least not pity. Probably only because he didn't know the whole of it.

"And your child. How do they fit into all of this?" he asked.

The fact that Mal was asking about Asha made Nia jump up, start picking up a few toys that were laying over on the floor and toss them into their baskets against the wall. How had he heard about Asha? She'd been so careful, even her friends didn't know.

"Aren't you supposed to go chronologically? The gossip usually includes the asylum trip, right?"

"Was there an asylum trip?"

"Yep. A couple of them. There was that little jaunt when I was in second grade. It was because of the experiments. Dad got me out of that one. Then the others, well, those ones I chose. I mean, watching your father torn apart by ghosts? That's got to mess a person up, right? Like I needed any help. Signed my rights away lickety-split. No more having to take care of myself, kind of hoped they could convince me all the ghost stuff was bullshit but I guess that didn't happen."

The worst was that she hadn't been as upset as she should have been when Dad died, when she'd found the mushy, gory pieces that didn't even look like they'd ever made up a human, let alone her father. "His precious Petunia" he'd always called her. Yeah, more like precious lab rat. Every time she heard that name it reminded her of him, of what he'd done to her. Of the cold that stole into her heart, froze her reactions and emotions when she'd found him, or the pieces that used to be him. She'd had herself voluntarily committed because there had to be something wrong with someone like that, someone who looked at that horror show and found some relief in the fact he was gone, never mind the terrible death he must have suffered.

"What happened to your baby, Nia?" Mal's voice was quiet, patient, and steady.

She started fluffing pillows. "You know, it's pretty hard to get locked up in an asylum. I mean, unless you're a danger to others and all. I didn't know where to get a gun to go waving it around, so I tried some delinquency and such in the city. Helped get my case up the ranks at any rate."

"Your baby, Nia."

Nia slumped down onto the bean-bag chair across the room, the one that had lost most of its filling and left her practically sitting on the floor. Guess that's what came of getting everything secondhand.

"I didn't know I was pregnant when I institutionalized myself. Probably wouldn't have made a difference. I would have made a shitty mother."

At least, that's what she'd told herself when she'd told the doctors she wanted to give the baby up. They'd said there were other options. They'd offered to help her find those other options, to connect with family even. She hadn't wanted to. Made up every reason she needed to abandon her daughter, to become the person she'd promised herself she'd never be after Mom died and Bibiji left.

"I gave her up for adoption."

"Where was the father?"

She looked up at Mal, searched his expression for the judgment she was certain had to be there. Damn, he was good. She couldn't find a trace of it.

"Not around," she said vaguely.

"Do you have any idea where she is now?"

Nia's smile was hollow. "Haven't you figured it out yet? She's upstairs, in the second bedroom with the rest of the kids. The rest of the ghosts. I didn't keep her safe, I abandoned her, and she ended up dead."

There was a moment when the only sound was the howl of the angry wind outside, and the sleet spitting against the windows.

Mal was silent, not even a sharp inhale. There was just this small twitch in his brow. His gaze was still calm, still steady.

Well, she'd gotten this far.

"Which is why I need your help." She leaned forward, twisting her fingers between her knees, unable to meet Mal's gaze as she spoke. "Something is hunting her in the Gray." Her fingers grazed the scratch on her neck that still throbbed, as it deserved to. "A soul devourer. It feeds on our spiritual energy, which hurts like hell. For the living, we replenish our energy all the time. For the dead, it's a finite amount. Especially when they're no longer remembered by someone who knew them in life, and they begin to fade. If something like what happened tonight happens again, and we're trapped there, that monster will kill Asha and she will cease to exist." Her throat squeezed, and she paused a second before she could breathe, let alone speak. "I need your help. To keep her safe in the Gray and here." She forced herself to raise her gaze. "Until I can find a way to bring her back to life and save her permanently."

℥℥

Mal didn't know what he'd been expecting. Maybe some story about a boyfriend gone bad, or maybe the father had custody of Nia's daughter. But he hadn't expected this. Only all his training—surviving under Mom and her constant attacks, then interrogation and police training—had kept his reaction under wraps. He was reeling and wanted time to process, to form a proper plan of attack. A glance down at his hands showed a tint of blue creeping through his veins. But if he retreated now, he might never get the truth from Nia.

"You think…you can bring your daughter back to life?" he said slowly.

Nia nodded, the movement so small it was a good thing he was completely focused on her to see it. "I think so, yeah. When I gain my full powers. When Ginny rose, she had this friend who was shot. The four of us, we brought him back."

"Yeah, but that's when he was just shot. Maybe that was more healing him? Your daughter—"

"Asha. Her name is Asha. And I know it's different. I'm not an idiot. She doesn't have a body." She got up and started to pace, her arms still around herself.

"So, you can make her a body? And aren't there risks to bringing someone back from beyond? I mean, there are legends and entire film franchises based on it."

"Some of it, like with necromancy, can be dangerous. But so long as her spirit doesn't have anything dangerous associated with it and she's in this world, not the Gray, it's just another spirit, and everything has a spirit." She continued to pace, her shoulders hunched. "The body will be the tricky part. But I'll figure it out."

He ached to wrap his arms around her, to somehow make this all okay. Geezus, the kind of pain she had to have survived. She'd checked herself into a mental institution? How bad did things get to want to do that?

"You have a plan I take it?"

She stopped to scowl at him. "I just told you the plan. Gain the powers of Death. Bring her back." She waved her hands in a vague motion. "I don't know exactly how it will work, or how it works for me. But Piper and Ginny? They didn't just get the powers of Pestilence and Famine. They got what Anna calls 'companion abilities,' too. Like, the opposite of their abilities. Piper can heal people as well as make them sick. Ginny can kill plants, but also make them grow."

"You think you can reverse death," he said slowly. Holy shit. He'd seen some strange things here in Beckwell, even contributed to some happening, so it was possible. Maybe. He smoothed a hand over his face, as though that would somehow make all this make more sense, and his fingers dragged against stubble. "So…she's all for this I take it? There must be some risk involved, bringing someone back to life."

Nia paused again, tucking a few curls that were regaining their springiness behind an ear. She looked so freakin'…elfin, it was a bit hard to think of her as Death. Besides her attitude, of course.

"Yeah, well, that's the thing. She doesn't exactly remember dying. Or who she was before."

"I'm sorry, what?"

"Sometimes when people die, especially the young, they don't understand that they died." Her voice dropped, and her gaze shot to his. "You can't tell Asha. Don't even use the words 'ghost' or 'dead' around them. A lot of the kids don't know. If they find out, well, the shock could turn them into soul devourers."

Kids turning into monsters. That painted a scary-ass

picture. "How many kids are we talking?"

She turned away, rubbing her arms up and down. "Maybe I shouldn't have told you. I mean, what are you supposed to do about any of this? You can't even see them. Which means you probably can't see the Other. Which means this is all ridiculous. You know what? Forget I said—"

He stood, catching her gently in his arms, and waited until she looked up at him. "I'm not some Normal you're talking to. My Fomorian bloodlines let me see things others can't, and even if I can't see your ghosts, I can feel them. I'll find a way to help you." Those words held so much more weight than when he'd promised the same thing to Loki. Because he was saying them to Nia this time, and he meant every syllable.

Because it wasn't just her in danger. It was her daughter, too. He thought of the little fingers that had twined with his. Maybe that had been Asha. Maybe by helping Asha and Nia, it was a small start to repay the debt he owed that other child, the one he couldn't save.

"I've been to the Gray before, so it probably means I can do it again, right?"

"Sure. When you're dead," she said dryly. "You're less useful dead. I'm certain. Like, seventy percent certain."

He ignored that last part. "Point is, Nia, you're not alone. Not anymore."

She looked up at him, her gaze raw and vulnerable.

"I know," she said, her voice barely a whisper. "That's the part that worries me."

CHAPTER 9

Nia woke, lying in the warm, safe circle of Mal's arms as the sun burned through the curtainless windows and the kids ran in shrieking circles around and around the sofa.

A thin man with short, curled ram horns sticking out of his curly, brown hair, and a round, seeping hole in his forehead stood next to the sofa. Next to him was a pretty woman with blonde hair, probably in her thirties, one seeping hole in her throat, a larger one in her chest soaking through her pink dress. She had her arm wrapped around the little boy in front of her, his curly, brown hair and tiny ram horns like the man's. Plus the same seeping forehead wound and gaping chest wound.

Aw hell. Poor kid. Nia winced and blinked up at them.

"She's coming. To kill you like she killed us," the woman whispered, the words driving straight into Nia's brain.

There was a flash of impossibly bright light, and all three of them vanished.

Nia grimaced and rubbed her eyes. Yep, they were really gone. What the hell. Couldn't she have gone a tad less cryptic? She who? Was it whoever had shot them? Nia didn't even recognize them, not like she knew everyone in town.

She smothered a yawn. Too early for cryptic dead people. There was a crick in her neck, and stretching, she peeked at Mal through one eye. He frowned in his sleep, his knees all bent up to fit on the sofa and uncomfortable, not surprising seeing as somehow or other they'd spent the night together on the ancient lumpy furniture. *Fuuuccckk!* Let's see…there'd been the horrible no good talk where she'd told him so much she might as well have been drunk. Even though it'd been the middle of the night, she sure the hell wasn't going to sleep, which seemed to mean Mal wasn't going to sleep. So, they'd put in some DVD. Hell if she could even remember what it was. Because somehow or other, she had fallen asleep on Mal like some ditsy teenager.

Nia paused, the shrieking of the kids and the cryptic dead family message suddenly dull compared to the roar in her head.

She'd fallen asleep on Mal…and she hadn't ended up in the Gray. There was hardly a night or time when she fell asleep that she didn't end up there. The soul devourer hadn't been able to get her. She cut Mal a sideways glance—kind of cute and innocent asleep. Mal, who didn't seem to hear the kids, and who could somehow block out the ghosts and her connection to the Gray.

"We're hungry! We're hungry!" Asha said, leading the chant and getting the rest of the kids involved.

Leaving Mal sleeping, Nia stumbled into the kitchen on the hunt for caffeine. There was still stale, cold coffee in the coffee pot from yesterday. Done and done. Sipping directly from the pot, she searched for food for the kids. No spirit cereal.

Shit. A thin sheet of ice and snow covered the patio. Was it cold enough that all the puddles were frozen to the bottom? There was a particularly large one directly in front of the incinerator. She didn't need to find thin ice and slip into water and the Gray this morning.

"What do you need done out there? I'll get it," Mal said, all solicitous and helpful-like as he strode into the kitchen. He stretched, pulling his shirt tight against his hard, sculpted chest, lifting the bottom and showing a narrow band of sculpted abs.

She dragged her gaze away from the show and put on her bitch face. She didn't need distractions. "I asked for your help, but this changes nothing you know. We're still not friends. I don't think I even like you." Okay, that last part sounded lame even to her.

His lips twitched, and he leaned in close. "We slept together, sweetheart. I think you more than like me."

Warmth spread through her, like it was leaching from his aura into the iciness of hers. A trap, just waiting to catch her unawares and hurt. "Jacka—"

He stopped her words with a finger on her lips that sent heat streaking through her, of the angry and turned-on varieties, which shouldn't have worked in collusion against her. "Language. The kids, remember?" He plucked the cereal from her fingers, raised a dark brow at the sugary crap.

She rolled her eyes and stamped down any hint of heat. "The incinerator is out on the patio. You light it from the bottom, leave the cereal inside on the shelf. I'll go get it in about an hour."

"Is an hour a long time?" Asha whined.

Nia grabbed some fruit spirits off the counter that hadn't made it to the incinerator but had died a natural, kind of smelly death. Somehow or other, their spirit hadn't ended up smelly. Two apples and an orange. "Divide this up to hold off starvation. Sorry, guys, food is going to be a little late this morning."

Because somehow or other she'd, a) told Mal actual real stuff that mattered, and b) she'd fallen asleep on the sofa with him? *Seriously?* What was *wrong* with her?

She made it up the stairs to get changed, choosing a turtleneck to hide the deep gouges on her neck and the gauze she put over them. They didn't look much better in the morning light than they had when fresh. She finished off her beauty routine by dragging a brush through the frizzy mess of her hair, brushing her teeth, and grabbing her phone. Then back down the stairs. And all without falling and killing herself despite a lack of caffeine.

The faint weight of extra auras brushed hers as she reached the foot of the stairs and the main floor a second or two before there was a knock on the door. Her eyes narrowed. A glance toward the kitchen showed Mal was still outside, probably fiddling with the incinerator. More stuff for the bathroom reno. Oh, yeah, was he going to do that anyway? With everything else that'd happened last night, it'd kind of slipped her mind.

Esther landed lightly and comfortingly on Nia's shoulder as she started for the door. She peeked through the curtains on the side first, which was probably kind of dumb and obvious, seeing as the curtains were lacey and motheaten, and the window part made it obvious she was looking. She straightened. Her three friends were standing outside. On her front porch. Oh, hell. The town was too small to hide where she'd lived, but she'd made a million excuses why they couldn't come over. Last one had been a mouse infestation.

She contemplated creeping away from the door without opening it.

"Nia, open the door." Anna's voice was cross.

"Yeah, it's cold out here," Piper said, her shape the other short-ish and skinny one dancing around outside.

"I brought muffins." Ginny, ever the one to offer a

little sugar with her words. Her muffins really were irresistible—enough that she'd started a flourishing local business. Though no one was quite certain if, with her powers of Famine, eating too many of her muffins could be dangerous.

"What kind?" Nia asked through the door.

"Dark chocolate with coffee bean buttercream." Ginny was way too cheerful for this early.

"Why does it matter what type?" Anna grumbled.

"Because we need her to open the door is why," Ginny shot back.

Damn. Her favorite. Nia could practically taste all that rich dark chocolate, just the right side of not-too-sweet with a delicious hit of coffee. Her mouth watered. Nia unlocked the door and swung it open.

Tall, brunette Anna with the old lady clothes was War clan. Blonde pretty Piper was Pestilence, looking like a short model. The tall, curvy redhead was Ginny, Famine clan. Nia would die for them, but she also held back a certain amount of truth out of self-protection. Not like they could complain. Piper had run off for almost a decade with hardly a word to any of them. Ginny had concealed her powers and a dead mostly evil twin brother. Who the hell knew what skeletons Anna had hidden.

Still, Nia crossed her arms and leaned in the doorway, blocking their way and trying to squelch the lump of guilt deep down inside. "What are you doing here?"

Anna held up her phone and frowned. "You texted. Said you needed us all here, ASAP. What, first you call me, now you text me and can't remember?"

Nia's eyes narrowed. "I texted? When?" She stood on tiptoe and peered around them. The large black ice cream truck without serving windows that was Ginny's horse flashed a headlight at her, whereas the snot green Porta Potty truck that was Piper's horse was more dignified and remained looking like an actual truck. Anna must have caught a ride with one of the two.

Ginny was already scanning through her texts. "Twice, actually. Once just past midnight—"

Uh huh. About the time she'd put on the movie with Mal.

"—and the second time this morning, about two hours ago." The redhead looked up and flushed. "Sorry, I didn't see the first one."

"Yeah, yeah, because you and hubby were probably banging," Nia said, being deliberately crude to make Ginny's face flame more. Ginny had married another Famine descendant back in October and they were completely ooey-gooey in love. The crudeness did not, however, make any of them budge from their spot on her porch.

"Well? Are you going to let us in?" Anna, ever blunt as she gestured toward the door.

"I didn't call you last night, and I didn't text." She pointed at the unrepentant moth on her shoulder. "Not sure if you can see her—"

Piper leaned back, making a face. "Big ugly butterfly? Yeah, I see her. What does a butterfly have to do with death? I mean, toad was with plagues I guess." Her horse had started out as a toad.

"She's a moth, and butterflies and moths are sometimes thought to carry the souls of the dead. Yes, Anna, I read a book…or maybe I found it online. Whatever. This one's Esther. Pretty sure she's the one who contacted you." Nia found her phone in her pocket, and sure enough, a new message binged.

"You nerd their helping," it read. Or rather, Esther said. The moth chirruped with annoyance. The phone binged. *"You need their help."*

"I'm letting the boy-toy stick around. Isn't that enough?" she communicated back, since somehow

Esther seemed to understand her better than she could understand Esther.

The phone binged again. *"It is not."*

Another bing. *"You need them."*

Another. *"You need your fries."* The moth flew up with the scent of burned tea leaves, then settled back on Nia's shoulder. *"You need your friends. And new phone."*

"I'm not giving you texting lessons. I can't afford a new phone," Nia communicated back.

"I'm sorry," Anna growled, not sounding the least bit sorry. "Are we interrupting your texting time?"

"It's not—look, okay?" she held her phone out to the War horsewoman. "It's how she's communicating with me. Well, one of the ways. There's also the buzzing, and the songs, and the touching— You know what, never mind."

Anna frowned down at the messages, one brown eyebrow arching. "Fascinating." She looked back at Piper and Ginny. "Neither of your horses ever used modern communication devices, did they?"

"Mostly showtunes and gutter humor," Ginny said dryly. She held up the muffins again. "Don't we at least get to come in?" She peered around and over Nia's head. "This is an amazing house, Nia! I can't believe you never invited us here."

"No kidding. You totally would have had room for me to stay when I first got back to town, you liar," Piper said, partially smiling as she said it. Probably because instead she'd stayed with her ex, Mal's twin brother, which had worked out for them, too. Not only were she and Daniel engaged, they were expecting their first child.

Happily ever afters all over the place. Their group was obviously over its quota.

"I…haven't cleaned," Nia lied lamely. Like she ever cleaned.

"Piper? Is that you?" Mal's voice coming up from

behind her.

Piper squeezed her way past Nia. "Mal? What are you doing here?"

"Nia, what haven't you been telling us?" Ginny said, all excited whisper and big eyes.

"Loki pulled one of his tricks and saddled Nia with Mal for a while. At least until I figure out how to dissolve it." The look Anna shot Mal was borderline hostile. At least someone got it. Then she had to go and ruin the good feeling when she leaned down, as though to give Nia a hug.

Nia scuttled backward.

Which opened the door for her friends to waltz right in.

Anna's lips turned up, as though that'd been the plan all along.

Nia scowled at all of them as they removed their jackets and shoes. "No using the g-h-o-s-t word or the d-e-a-d word, got it?" They probably couldn't see the kids. She flicked the moth off her shoulder, which lifted off with a shimmer of light and possibly annoyance.

Piper had grabbed onto Mal and they were doing that annoying flirty thing they always did. Piper was dedicated to Daniel, so it meant nothing. Still, it made Nia's teeth grind and produced the rather strong urge to put her fist into Piper's pretty face. Anna had marched right in, commenting on the molding and something about the history of the house. Anna speak for time-for-Nia-to-ignore-her. Which left Ginny, carefully folding her pretty princess-cut red coat revealing a stunning vintage black and white polka dot blouse with bright blue slacks.

She grinned at Nia and held up the basket. "It's okay. I still have the muffins. And I know what it's like, everyone just walking all over you. I'm surprised you let Anna do that."

Me, too, Nia thought but chose not to say. Why had

she? Maybe because her friends had shown up out of the blue at her house? All because they thought she'd asked for help. She could feel them, their essences spreading out over her house like bright splashes of color. It wasn't super horrible. Maybe because of that part where they were supposed to be immune to each other's abilities, but their essences didn't aggravate her as much as most other people did.

She gestured toward the kitchen. "May as well head after them all before Anna reorganizes the whole damned house without me."

"She means well, you know. That bossiness is her way of taking care of us," Ginny said, keeping step with Nia.

Nia scrubbed a hand through her hair, the curls heavy. "I know. Still annoying as fuck, but I know."

"There were also a few burned muffins I brought, like you said to—I mean, your, er, moth said? In the text. There was mention of burned food?" This time Ginny held up a separate 4L yellow ice cream pail with the lid still labeled as ice cream.

She stopped dead and turned to Ginny. "How burned?"

Ginny's pale face flushed deep crimson. "Well I started a batch earlier this morning, but then James and I, uh…"

"Unless he's changing colors or whatever, I don't want to know about your sex life." Nia's face heated as hot as Ginny's looked. "But, like, really, really burned?"

Her friend nodded miserably. "I don't know why you'd want them. I should have just tossed them."

As though it knew she was thinking of it, the moth fluttered back into view, back from wherever it occasionally disappeared to.

"Okay, Esther. You get a point for that. The kids are going to be excited," Nia acknowledged.

Ginny barely blinked when Nia talked to the moth. She got it. Her horse had started as a grasshopper. She did, however, frown at the latter part. "Kids?"

"Er…never mind."

The phone binged again with a new text from, surprise, surprise, the moth. *"See? I'm good at texting. Phone is problem. I told you, betiya."*

Nia tensed again at the nickname. What kind of game did the moth think it was playing? Esther wasn't her grandmother. Hadn't they cleared that up?

Nia fake smiled as her friends talked around her and hurried toward the kitchen, lowering the volume on her phone. The moth had made its point, but she didn't need any more messages right now. She had to focus on the girls and what she'd tell them. She'd already told Mal about Asha. She didn't know if she was ready to tell the rest of them yet. In fact, she was so distracted picking and choosing her truth in the kitchen with her friends, she didn't even notice the next three messages that arrived.

CHAPTER 10

Being such close witness to the four horsewomen of the apocalypse was both a fascinating and terrifying experience. Mal kept a safe distance, pretending to be monitoring the incinerator outside and sipping his coffee while leaning against the counter. Outside he'd been able to do a quick walk of the yard to make sure no one was lurking before jogging back inside. Having the other horsewomen around wasn't a bad thing. They could help protect Nia, too. The double bonus was that his abilities didn't seem to affect them—otherwise they'd probably be bickering more than they naturally seemed to.

The women all took seats along Nia's long ranch-style table with its mismatched chairs. Back in high school, it'd been Daniel who'd been part of their group after he and Piper hooked up, not Mal. He'd always been more of a loner, both by chance and inclination. More likely they didn't care he was there, but it was nice to think he might have been welcome now.

Ginny was relatively quiet, so much prettier than he

remembered her, like she'd blossomed since marriage. She served muffins and brewed fresh tea and coffee in what appeared to be her way of controlling her part in the situation and avoiding conflict, though she piped up when something caught her attention.

Piper, as she'd been in high school, was more than happy being the center of attention, though she had to fight for it here among Nia and Anna.

Few people had ever really intimidated him, not with the rough way Dad and his uncles and cousins had been, all big guys like himself. But there was something about the way Anna could look at you that made a guy just kind of…shrivel. Like, nope, that fight was just way out of his league.

Which led to Nia, smallest of The Four and caustic in her remarks, there was an ease about her he hadn't seen otherwise. Yeah, some people were just as uncomfortable around her as they were Anna, but only because they didn't see the softness to Nia. Seriously, look at her house: she'd filled it with dead children who had no other homes. He'd heard what sounded like animals, too, so maybe there were even abandoned ghost pets. Who knew. Tough as she tried to play it, she'd brought them here. She kept everyone out of this house to keep them safe. He had a hunch it was to keep her safe, too.

All while fighting scary-ass unimaginable things in that Gray place. Alone. She needed help, and he wanted to be the one to give it to her.

Gods help make sure he didn't screw this up. Because it would be Nia and her daughter at stake if he did.

He'd just held his coffee cup out for refill from a smiling Ginny, convinced he'd have to stop eating the muffins or they'd have to roll him out of here, when his phone went crazy, buzzing and ringing at full volume.

Mal dug it out of his pocket as Nia climbed to her

feet, a small frown creasing her forehead. She turned toward the front door, like she was attuned to something invisible to all of them.

He answered the call on autopilot, more interested in watching Nia. Her friends were watching her like he was, but he was faster to start after her. The moth flew in crazy circles in front of her, enough that Nia gently swatted at it as she moved forward.

"Whatever you do, don't kill her!" Loki shouted from the other side of the phone into Mal's ear, so loudly it was like he was standing and shouting in the same room. "I'm on my way. Don't kill her. Do you hear me?"

"Don't kill—"

The line went dead.

Who? He wasn't eager to kill anyone, but good to know exactly who Loki meant. Nia? One of her friends?

Nia's hand was on the front doorknob before he'd even reached the foyer, before he had a chance to check the cameras or stop her.

The hair rose on the back of his neck, his gut telling him he should stop her, that this was bad. His shoulders bunched, his Fomorian side ready for a fight.

Someone banged on the door, making it rattle in its frame.

"Let me in, let me in, little piggies," a woman sing-songed from outside. "Or I will blow this house sky high from out here." The stranger cackled manically.

Crazy and threatening. Bad combination. Mal's senses and every muscle in his body went on high alert. The words of his first training officer went through his head: a cop's biggest weapon was his voice. He needed to evaluate and de-escalate the situation, something he'd often struggled with thanks to his Fomorian side, which preferred to knock heads and ask questions later. Maybe this stranger at the door was whom Loki meant, whoever "she" was. Her voice niggled a memory, and when it came to batshit crazy, the ladies that checked that box were the three Fates.

At one point, he'd tried to work with them when they'd promised him a way to save Daniel, but when he'd switched sides, it'd put him squarely in their crosshairs. He'd warned them yesterday to stay away but looked like they hadn't gotten the message.

"Whatever you're selling, we don't need any," Nia shouted back through the door. She took a small step backward, the tiniest hint of tremble in her words. "If it's crazy—because you clearly have lots of that—we're full up. Sorry."

Two palms slammed against the door window, the face pressed close but still a pinkish silhouette. "So that's a yes to blowing your house up? I mean, I have enough shit here to blow up like half the town. Not that that's saying much."

The temperature in the room dropped a few more degrees until he could see his breath.

Nia took a step back toward the door. "I told you yesterday in the email, I wasn't interested in your offer."

What offer? From the Fates?

No damned way he wanted that psycho in here, but he couldn't assess if the threat was real without seeing her and the alleged explosive. "Anna, dial 911. Nia, let me deal with this."

Nia didn't even glance his direction. "This bitch is threatening my home. My kids." A dark silvery-black mask, somewhere between shadow and substance seemed to collect over her eyes. Her focus was entirely on the stranger outside. "I'm sorry. Just to clarify: you're coming to *my* house and threatening *me*?" The tremble had gone from her voice.

Ah, crap.

"Nia, wait—"

He didn't have time to lunge for her before Nia

yanked open the door, leaving the unwanted visitor falling forward into the hall.

The woman straightened quickly, a curly-haired brunette who might have been pretty if it wasn't for all the explosives strapped to her curvy figure. The wrap job she'd done was sloppy, but they sure looked like sticks of dynamite, maybe stolen from a nearby mining operation. Damn straight she could probably take out most of the town, and maybe half of next decade. The glittering mania in her expression was even more volatile.

"Why, Petunia, how good of you to let me in. You should have been politer when you answered our emails yesterday. 'Cause that offer has gone bye-bye," she cooed, waving bye like a little kid.

What the fuck offer? He hadn't known he needed to question Nia's email. Mal ground his jaw and focused on the threat, blue sliding up his forearms. Daphne Spinner. She was a relative newcomer in town, but Loki had pegged her as trouble. Unfortunately, a few months too late.

Nia crossed her arms and gave the woman a razor-thin smile. The darkness over her eyes still hadn't settled into something definite, and a longer shadow seemed to grow around Nia, like a cloak of smoke that elongated and stretched her figure until she looked bigger.

"I let you in. Is this the part where you explain why you're here threatening my home and friends, bitch?"

He didn't look but could feel the presence of the other three women near his back. Two of them full horsewomen of the apocalypse, the other War, who could create conflict just by opening her mouth—which was not what they needed right now.

Nope, upgrade the assessment to "oh, shit."

The woman might be certifiable. If or when she recognized him, chances were good she'd turn that rage on him. Even so, he had to find some common ground and get her to surrender if possible.

He drew in a breath and forced a small smile onto his lips.

"Daphne, sweetheart, is that you?" He strolled toward the front door like a clueless schmuck. Hopefully she didn't notice the blue-gray Fomorian tint.

He let his gaze linger on her as though he wasn't calculating just how fast he could take her down, and if it would make any difference with all that shit stuck to her body. Dynamite was more stable than some explosives, but not exactly the kind of thing you wanted to smash around. "You're looking good," he said. He walked right up to Nia and draped an arm loosely around her shoulders. It meant she was close enough he could throw her away from danger when or if that got necessary.

Her narrow shoulders twitched beneath his touch, already tight with tension. "Mal…" she growled through clenched teeth. "I'm handling this."

"Handle? What's to handle? You know Daphne, right? I mean, you must. Don't all the gorgeous women in town know each other? Sounds like you guys have been emailing each other anyway." Oh, gods. His mouth was running away with him like a two-year-old on Halloween. Blame it on the Fomorian side, which pumped up the adrenaline and was primed for a fight. "Daphne, darlin', why don't you take off that vest. You come in, we all have some wine and some of Ginny's spectacular muffins. You have tried one, haven't you? And—"

"She ignored our offer. She thinks she's better than us. It's her fault I'm here. You think I won't really do this?" Daphne cried, clutching what appeared to be a trigger.

His shoulders swelled, his heartbeat slowing, ready for battle, and he held up a hand. "You don't want to do this, Daphne. Let's talk about this. The muffins really are good."

A new arrival, Louise Dole, the middle Fate he'd spoken to in the store yesterday, stepped into the doorway behind Daphne. Louise was in her late fifties, white, wearing a blue tracksuit and a headscarf around her head. Tears tracked down her pale face.

Daphne turned.

Louise lifted her hand, revealing a gun.

Daphne smiled and opened her arms wide, as though welcoming the bullet. "Hello, Louise."

Mal grabbed Nia and twisted her to the ground, covering her with his body.

The gunshot tore through the air, a loud crack.

Daphne crumpled in toward the impact and then to the floor.

The middle Fate, Daphne, continued to fire, emptying the revolver into the younger woman, her expression blank except for those tears.

Seeing as the dynamite didn't explode, looked like the threat had been a bluff after all. With Nia down on the ground, Mal's muscles coiled to spring and take down the shooter. She didn't seem interested in anyone but Daphne, but that could change.

Before he could jump, the third and eldest of the Fates raced up the porch steps and into the house. Tall, slim, and silver-haired, Deirdre Boniface grabbed Louise, wrapping her arms around her. Mrs. Boniface's eyes widened. "Oh, Louise. What have you done?" She reached for the gun.

The shooter, Louise, collapsed to her knees. She didn't fight to regain the weapon. Her voice was a flat whisper. "She killed them. She killed them all. My Randy. His wife." Her voice cracked and her hands spasmed, pain etching her face. "Johnny. Even my sweet Johnny-seed."

Nia, who was trying to shove him off with no success, had turned to vicious pokes. He rolled off her, lifting her to her feet mostly so he could keep himself between her and the other women.

From the corner of his eye, he could see blood beginning to pool over Nia's wood floors beneath the body. He was more concerned with that weapon, and however many bullets it might still hold.

"Mrs. Boniface. The weapon," he said, edging toward her with his hand out.

The silver-haired woman lifted her hand as though surprised to find a gun there. She looked up at him through eyes gone blank and weary and held the weapon out to him with no protest, then glanced at Nia. "You should have accepted our offer. Now? No one will survive." Her gaze slid back to Daphne.

Mal checked and emptied the weapon and went over to Daphne, kneeling beside the body. Damn it all. Her supposed dynamite was a convincing fake. He checked for a pulse. Nothing.

Loki roared into the yard in his slick car, jumped out, and raced up the stairs, his big belly jiggling beneath the plaid shirt.

The demigod took in the scene with one look and turned a searing glare on Mal. "I told you not to kill her."

"You didn't even give me a name." Mal climbed to his feet. Hell, he was beating himself up enough as it was. "You couldn't have told me more?"

"He didn't know more. Not soon enough," Mrs. Boniface, the eldest of the Fates said, strength returning to her voice though she still looked...defeated. She turned again on Nia, took a step toward her.

Mal intercepted, placing himself between Nia and the older woman.

Mrs. Boniface stopped, speaking to Nia as though he wasn't there. "It was a good offer. If you'd helped us, at least some of them could have survived. Now..." She gestured toward Daphne, now little more than a twisted mass of flesh in a growing blood pool. Mrs. Boniface sniffed, the sound desolate. "Well, you are Death I suppose. What do you care for life?"

Loki stomped over to the body, checked her pulse for himself. Shook his head and looked away, his jaw twitching.

"I'm sorry. This is not my fault. Your offer was bullshit, but I didn't make anyone strap a bomb to their chest or pick up a gun. But now there's a dead woman bleeding all over my front hall," Nia snapped.

"She's only mostly dead. And you're more concerned about your hall than you are her murder," the dry male voice said before a body materialized in the air around it. When it did, there was a medium-height, dapper little man with a neatly trimmed brown mustache, natty gray suit with waistcoat. And a fiery glare directed at Nia.

∞

Nia met the little interloper's glare with an icy one of her own. She couldn't bring herself to look at the woman whose soul hadn't quite broken away from the earthly form, the body still twitching. The ghosts had tried to warn her this morning. But she'd understood the message too late.

Esther settled on Nia's shoulder, sending strength and cool calm through the touch.

Okay, fine, so the guy in the waistcoat was taller than she was, but he was short for a man.

She was pissed. Mal and her friends flanked her, proving they seemed to be able to see the Death twerp, too.

Enough people had invaded her house for a decade, let alone the day, plus there was a dead one now, and that was going to cause all sorts of fuckery. Seriously, there wasn't a good way to clear dead-person out of your house if they didn't want to go, especially being her.

"Who the fuck are you? Why are you in my house?"

The guy gave her a thin, cold smile. "One of the

people who actually does any work when it comes to death." He glanced around her house with a sneer. "Not all of us can just wander the halls aimlessly and eat bonbons." He plucked at his pinstriped trousers before he knelt to examine the body, dismissing her.

If it was possible for steam to come out of her ears, it should have been. "You little ass—"

Mal caught her elbow gently. "Nia, this is Mr. Death. Aunt Junie's…friend."

She shook off Mal's warmth, the reality that he'd probably have thrown himself in front of her or something if Louise hadn't shown up and shot Daphne first.

The reality that this might have happened because she'd told them to eff off in the email last night instead of just ignoring the Fates' offer.

This was *her* house. She did the protecting around here. Oh, crap. The kids were all watching, their eyes huge, from the entrance to the living room.

"Look, buddy, the only death around here is me. Though, if you're here to take the dead woman off my hands, great."

"No, not great," Loki said, kneeling on the opposite side of the body from the twerp. "You can't take her."

A twerp *and* Loki the asshole *and* the League of Assholes, all in her house, all on the same day? So not frickin' fair.

Twerp, aka supposed "Mr. Death"—what was with that? It made him sound like her husband or something. Gross—flicked a thumb back over his shoulder in Mal's direction. "Of course, I can. Ask him, or more correctly, his aunt. I work this sector. These souls are mine."

"Then look again. You can't have this one," Loki said, a dark edge of urgency in his voice. "You don't want this one."

Mr. Death held a hand out over the body, froze, then slowly pulled back. He and Loki exchanged a dark look.

Despite herself, Nia edged closer, careful to avoid the blood pool. A look, sure, but what about words? Why didn't he want Daphne?

Unfortunately, Loki turned on her instead, then landed on each of her friends. "You have to bring her back. Now."

"Bring her back? Look, maybe you didn't get the memo, but I'm not Death yet. Not fully," Nia said.

Mr. Death made a dismissive snort. "Oh, we've all had that memo, sweetheart."

It would be really convenient if the ability to incinerate someone on the spot with a glare was one of her powers, even though that was probably more likely to be an Anna War clan thing. Still, Nia gave it a good shot.

Mr. Death sniffed, adjusting the spectacles on his nose.

"Wait, we could resurrect her maybe. Right?" Ginny said, the redhead coming forward with the scent of muffins and the warmth of sunshine and hugs and all sorts of things nice. "We brought Maddox back." She met Nia's gaze, then glanced back at Piper and Anna, who were also venturing closer. "The four of us."

"Do it," Loki demanded.

"Yeah, but he was only mostly dead. And—"

The corpse trembled.

Like something had shaken it from the inside.

The floorboards beneath rattled.

Yeah…that wasn't good…

"Do it now! Hurry," Loki urged, jumping back out of the way.

Mr. Death did the same, looking a tad concerned himself.

The body and the floor trembled again. Harder this time.

Asha and some of the younger children whimpered.

Nia's head whipped up. She wanted to comfort them.

She wanted to tell them it would be okay, that this wasn't as scary as it seemed. Seeing as it probably *was* as scary as it seemed, it was a waste of breath. Hell, selfishly, she wanted to feel Asha's cold little arms around her to feel like at least one tiny part of this world was still okay. But what right did she have to do that? Not unless she found a way to make her home safe again.

Nia wiped damp palms down her thighs, stepped over and knelt beside the body. Okay, right, just bring the mostly dead person back to life. The last time she and her friends had done this, the man hadn't been so far gone.

Then again, she expected to be able to bring Asha back to life. Maybe if she thought of this as practice.

Her three friends, Ginny beside her, Anna and Piper on the other side, each laid a hand gently on the corpse even as it shuddered again, almost throwing their grip off.

"Piper, heal the wounds," Ginny said, referring to Piper's companion ability to pestilence: the ability to heal. "Anna, fight back mortality. I'm hunger for life." Anna even as not-officially-War could fight back anything, whereas Ginny could create directed, insatiable hunger for anything she wanted, including life.

But it'd be Nia's job to force back to Death, to keep the spirit tethered to the physical body.

The corpse shook, harder still this time, flinging dark hair over Daphne's face.

Nia closed her eyes, reached out her hands to find the soft, torn edges of the spirit. The dying and the recently deceased had an edge that separated their soul from their physical form, like a flapping ragged sheet in the wind, ether that wanted to rip away and fly off to the spirit world, the Gray, or whatever great beyond awaited them. She could sense the green freshness of Ginny's abilities next to her, that rich vibrancy for life calling to the spirit, willing it to live. The raging fire of Anna's fight demanded the spirit fight back, never go quietly into death. The oozing thickness of Piper's healing and pestilence, somewhere between a salve and phlegm, tried to mend the wounds, restart the heart.

But none of it would matter if Nia couldn't stop the spirit from escaping. Once it was freed from the body, hell if she knew how to catch it.

"Nia, you've got the heavy lifting on this one. You were right," Ginny said, and it was like her voice came from far away. "She's further gone than Maddox was. Can we do this? Can we save her?"

If they could save her together, could they save Asha?

The next tremor was almost enough to throw them all off the body, but the others had done their jobs, and now it was up to Nia. She saw the edges of the soul flapping and almost free. There was something beneath, something other than the physical form that was a hell of a lot scarier and more disturbing than a soul devourer as it tried to claw its way free. Its aura was pitch black, shoving and tearing at the remains of the soul. Nia caught the edge of the ether spirit, her hands and arms tensing as though she physically held it and pulled it down tight like a tarp.

Chills chased up and down her body, damp clung to her skin, even as sweat trickled down her neck, but she had to keep focusing on holding that frayed edge of the soul and tucking it back into place. She could have been flailing in the watery wading pool, trapped and terrified as spirits attacked her, only this time she was in charge of the spirit and more scared of whatever the hell was hiding inside the body. Tucking and joining it back with the physical form even as whatever the hell it was tried to jab and claw its way through. The soul was too strong for it, stretching and jumping like a rubber balloon. Until Nia got all the edges tied down tight. Except…it was like sewing. How did she connect it fully? She'd never done this. Not this part. Not when the soul was already almost gone.

If she couldn't do this, how did she think she could save Asha? In that situation, there wasn't even a body. A soul, tethered to nothing.

Whatever this thing was, if it got out, what would it do to her kids? To her friends?

"MR. DEATH, A LITTLE HELP OVER HERE," she said, accidentally using the Death voice that made most people pee themselves a little.

With her eyes still closed, the vision behind her eyelids part of this world, part of the Gray, she sensed more than saw Mr. Death's aura, like a lighter smoky-white version of her own, the same dove color as his suit, settle next to her. He almost looked like he belonged in the Gray, which might mean without an affinity for death, people like her friends wouldn't be able to see him any more than they could see ghosts.

"You don't know how to do anything, do you?" he sniped, but still helped her get to work. Helped her with the tucking and…stitching, if that was the right word, to connect the soul and physical form more tightly. Trapping that other thing more firmly inside.

The frayed-ether edges of Daphne's spirit were attached to the physical body, and Nia's fingertips were icy with the contact.

She knew it was done when the woman, Daphne, took a fresh breath, and the colors of her aura flickered back to life. All sludgy browns and blacks, which never meant anything good. But the flickering aura meant alive.

Nia fell back on her butt. She'd done it. She'd saved Daphne. Brought her back from the freakin' dead.

Which meant maybe, somehow, there was a chance she really could save Asha. She could bring her back. No more Gray. No more monsters out to eat her. Just that detail of creating a body for Asha.

"Help me get Daphne out of here." Loki's voice, bossing someone else other than her around, thank gods. Maybe Mr. Death.

Nia opened her eyes, her head bobbing lightly around where her neck should have been. The whole world kind of swayed like a drunken pirate. Her three friends were watching her. The two leftover Fates watched her in kind of a nervous looking way, like they'd never really looked at her before. Loki, Mr. Death, and the body—along with any hint there'd been a murder here—were gone. Asha and the others, they were watching, too, along with a whole lot of dead people who seemed to have wandered inside. Damn it. Didn't they read the sign?

Warmth spread through the gentle grip on her arms, the roughened fingertips that smoothed along her cheek and turned to face him. Gee, Mal's eyes really were blue. Like, really, *blue*. His mouth opened, and words were probably coming out of it.

"Nia? Nia, can you hear me?" Oh, there were the words.

I can hear you. You think bringing back the dead makes me deaf? At least, that's what she meant to say, but her tongue didn't cooperate. Her eyes, no matter how wide she tried to make them focus were making Mal go all fuzzy and indistinct.

Well, poop.

Everything went black.

CHAPTER 11

Mal had barely reached Nia's side when a black sedan roared into the yard, still visible through the open door. The car jerked to a stop beside Loki's sleek luxury car parked out front, Mrs. Boniface's classic silver convertible, and Louise Dole's blue Honda Civic. Two dark-suited USELESS agents he recognized from the bar—one a muscle-bound blond, the other dark skinned and slim, both in dark agency suits—jumped out of the car and pounded into Nia's front foyer, smashing the door into the opposite wall. Glass shattered.

If his muscles hadn't already been tight, the Fomorian genes riding him, that would have done it.

"Everyone freeze!" the blond guy shouted. "Petunia Amort, Death clan, you are officially under arrest by order of the United Supernatural Exalted Deities for committing an act against nature. You will be taken and tried before a court of said gods for your crimes."

Frigid air blew in through the open door. Anna and Piper started shouting at the agents.

Since the choice was go after the asswipes for breaking Nia's door and probably get himself in trouble, or let the women deal with it, he let them deal with it as Nia went limp in his arms. The only thing that mattered was sliding two fingers against her soft brown skin and holding his breath. When a faint rhythm thumped against his fingertips, it wrung the air from his lungs.

He hadn't failed yet.

Iciness surrounded him, and little hands brushed his arms, surrounding Nia. More than one child. And one of them her daughter. Geezus, what could the poor little thing be feeling? Did she even understand half of what had happened? There'd been the bomb threat, a homicide, then Nia and her friends had brought someone back from the dead. Oh, then the agents in matching dark suits showed up out of nowhere. Hell, if the kid understood more than half, that was possibly more than him at this point.

"It's okay. I've got her. She's going to be okay," he murmured softly for them, shifting Nia so he could slide his arm beneath her legs and climb to his feet. Her slight form weighed a hell of a lot less than it should. It would have been better if the pizzas she'd cooked last night had all been for her. At least it would mean she'd been eating.

"Hey! Where do you think you're going with her? I said freeze. You're under arrest," the big USELESS agent with the slicked back blond hair shouted, wearing a suit he'd probably paid too much for, small white horns just above his eyebrows.

"No, you said *she's* under arrest. If you plan on taking her right now, you'll be going through me." Mal never broke stride as he cradled her against him and headed for the living room and the lumpy flowered sofa where she'd slept against him all night. The icy shadow of the ghost children followed him across the room, and tiny fingers rested against his where he supported Nia's legs.

"What the hell do you mean crimes against nature? What are you doing, stalking us?" Anna demanded, rounding on the agents.

"I thought I made it quite clear you weren't wanted here," Ginny said, the house trembling slightly with her anger. She might even have done that thing where her eyes kind of glowed green. Famine abilities were about the earth.

Mal gently lowered Nia onto the sofa, coming down onto his knees on the floor so he could fluff the pillow beneath her head. Right now, he didn't give a shit if Ginny started an earthquake, so long as it didn't hurt Nia.

"You are impeding a crime scene. Step back and stand down," the USELESS agent said. Same guy as before, whereas the second guy hadn't said anything yet.

"If there's been a crime, shouldn't there be evidence? We're all witnesses. Nothing happened here," Piper snapped back at the agents. Hopefully she didn't go and disease all of them. Nia might be immune, but he wasn't. Plus, better Piper stopped talking before she got them all in more trouble. Witnesses, yeah, and potentially at as much fault as Nia for bringing back Daphne.

"Wake up the Amort girl. She's under arrest," the big, blond agent demanded again, looking jittery with his hand on that weapon of his, a combination of a wand and a gun.

"We sent agents like you away before. You think we're scared of you?" Ginny said, getting in the agent's face.

For fuck's sake, soon all of them would be under arrest. Mal ground his jaw, his free hand clenched at his side and Fomorian gray-blue.

There was a worn-looking blue fleece blanket near the end of the sofa, and Mal pulled that over Nia.

She didn't respond.

"All of you shut up. I need to check her heart rate," he shouted at the lot of them, again placing his fingers against Nia's throat. She still had a pulse, a solid, steady one, too. Breathing was even. He sat back on his heels. Guess bringing someone back from the dead took a lot out of a person.

The vague shape of a figure wavered in front of Mal, brushed against his arm and brought his complete focus back to Nia and the sofa. The sofa cushion dipped and indented beside Nia, just a tiny little indent for a tiny little body. His insides ached. Too tiny. How old would she have been?

A cold breeze brushed his face, and a largish feathered shape, maybe a foot high, settled on the back of the sofa above Nia. Ghostly talons dug into the cushions. Large shining eyes blinked and regarded him before the owl turned toward the foyer then back to him, shaking out its large wings. Occasionally, its silhouette flickered, the way the moth had. This was the same creature. Nia's "horse."

Nia had just taken a step closer to becoming one of the four horsewomen with the full powers of Death. Piper and Ginny had gone through the same thing, their horses morphing shape as their powers grew.

The owl turned again toward the foyer and the increasingly raised voices. Then looked pointedly back at him.

He nodded and rose to his feet, rolling his broad shoulders. "I'm going," he grumbled. "You guys take care of her, got it? I'll go…make sure no one else dies."

He'd rather have stayed at Nia's side, but things were escalating in the foyer. Someone had to deal with the situation.

Anna had progressed to poking a finger repeatedly into the suited chest of the blond USELESS agent, while Ginny had the other guy, the quiet one, tensed and frozen in place. Mrs. Boniface and Louise Dole were limping toward the door.

Mrs. Boniface glanced back at him for a second, a spark of defiance lighting her steely gaze, daring him to try and stop her.

It wouldn't be that hard. From what he heard, USELESS was almost as interested in the League and the Fates as they were in Nia and her friends. But…there was no telling how Mrs. Boniface would play it, and there was a good chance she'd be willing to throw Nia under whatever moving vehicle was closest.

He gave her the tiniest of nods, and she and Louise slipped out the door. The Fomorian snarled for blood inside, and the closer to the foyer he got, the more agitated the conversation grew. Hell, the fact that Anna was talking and he was in the room wasn't great, both likely to escalate violence.

His Fomorian side wanted to smile, eager for blood.

"We will not let you take our friend, gods or not," Anna snarled dangerously, in a flurry of enraged poking. "You two-bit brainless excuse for flesh."

Shouty-guy narrowed his eyes on her but didn't seem otherwise affected, especially considering this was the War horsewoman, whose voice alone usually incited violence.

Mal cocked his head, considering the big blond. Ah, there it was. A quick look at the other agent revealed the same. They were wearing magical hearing protection, the edges of which he could see as a dim shadow around their heads thanks only to his Fomorian side. Maybe it explained the shouting, and why the other guy was so quiet. If they weren't supposed to be affected by the voices and commands of the horsewomen, maybe it made it difficult to hear anything.

Still, red color had risen to stain the blond's face, and his fingers twitched, close to drawing his weapon.

Interesting he hadn't done so already.

"Anna, back off. They'll arrest you on some trumped-up interference charge," Mal said quietly, his gaze meeting the blond agent's. They exchanged a hard, measuring glance, weighing the outcomes of coming to blows, similar size, high likelihood of unexpected paranormal abilities. Although maybe the other USELESS agents had told these two about Mal. And his fists.

He let his lips curl up in a slow, feral smile.

Good. Let them remember that Fomorians almost always came out on top when it came to a fight. Especially because they weren't afraid to fight dirty.

"Oh, so you're suddenly going to prove yourself useful and get rid of them?" Anna snapped, the words pulling at his Fomorian side that already wanted to hit something.

He tamped the urge down carefully, never breaking eye contact with the agent. "You and the others, go see to Nia. I'll handle this." Maybe there was a chance, however miniscule, this could all end here. If he convinced the agents they were wrong, that they lacked any evidence, maybe they wouldn't try dragging Nia back to face charges before the gods.

"What, like good little girls you mean?" Anna snarled.

"No. Like three responsible, intelligent beings who realize getting in a fight with agents of the gods would be stupid right now," he said quietly. Something he should probably remember himself. His clothes strained around his increased muscle bulk, and as he flexed his fingers, he caught sight of his skin, gone completely blue-gray. Next would be the horns and wings, but if he went that far, the agents better run.

"Go Mal, sounding all Daniel-like," Piper said, taking one of Anna's arms. "Come on, Anna. Let Mal handle this. He's on our side."

In his peripheral, he could see Anna struggle to calm down enough before she let Piper tug her toward the living room.

Ginny cast a troubled look back at him, like maybe she'd figured out as he had that this time, there was no simple "getting out of this." After she'd risen, it had been confirmation to the gods that The Four really would rise…and potentially challenge their supremacy when it came to power. Even if the four women weren't interested in taking over, the gods never saw it that way. They considered every rise of power a threat, because in their small, power-hungry, backstabbing little world, it was.

Mal crossed his blue arms over his straining chest, making it clear he wasn't holding a weapon, wasn't even close to reaching for one.

"What about introductions first? I'm Malcolm Quilan. Fomorian and the local law enforcement."

Strictly speaking, not true, though he had been *invited* to become the town peace officer. He resisted adding the invitation to just give him a reason to throw down. The blue skin probably implied that.

The blond waved a hand near his one ear, whatever shield he'd been using removed enough that he could hear, before he mirrored Mal's movements. Good. Hands away from the weapon that was something between a wand and a gun—which meant a strike from it would hurt plenty. "I'm Agent Bertram. That's Agent Simons."

"I'd say it's nice to meet you, but I'd be lying. What are you doing here?" he asked, keeping his tone neutral.

Bertram answered again. Either Simons didn't speak, or this was part of their good cop/bad cop routine. "We've been monitoring the situation from outside the yard. When several targets all coalesced, it seemed wise to have a presence nearby."

Which probably meant the agents his fists had

already met were still in town, or there were other agents in town, or at least close enough to be called in for backup. Hell, it was possible they were on their way now, had been monitoring all along, might even be outside. Just the idea made his neck tighter.

The possibility of keeping Nia away from the gods and here in Beckwell was evaporating like a puddle in the hot sun.

The USELESS agents would want to drag Nia off to their monkey court where the crimes, whether real or imagined, almost always resulted in a death sentence. Didn't matter that the others had been involved. Piper and Ginny were too high risk, Anna was too volatile to expose in an open court, which left Nia, not quite Death, probably less threatening because of her size. The gods liked to make an example now and then, of what came if anyone even dared crossing them, and looked like Nia was next on their list, even if he'd bet she didn't give a shit about them, their court, or their games. The defendant never had a chance because it was rigged from the beginning. Any kind of defense was highly discouraged, seeing as anyone who stuck their neck out for one of the gods' targets was guaranteed the same sentence. The justice system for Normals had its issues, but at least he could live with it. The idea of having to be a puppet to the gods' corruption, though, was a good part of why he refused to be town peace officer, where he might be expected to turn someone over to their circuit court. I.e. turn them over for execution.

Damned if he'd let that happen to Nia.

He scanned through everything he remembered of that time Dad had taken him to see a High Court trial. Poor old Uncle Lem. Mal had been too young to remember the details.

"What evidence do you have?" he demanded.

Dad hadn't taken him there to see justice. It'd been a

lesson. Do what you like, break the laws, just don't get caught, because this was the consequence for their kind. Yes, usually there were local circuit judges that would come through, which included a slim chance one of them had a sliver of compassion and might drop the case. Because if the case went directly in front of the gods, you were as good as fit for a noose.

Bertram gestured to the other agent. The other guy, Simons, likewise removed the hearing protection from one ear. Then drew a small device out of his pocket. About the size of a smart phone, it had some other enhancements, with a kind of spicy scent to it his Fomorian nose picked up as magic.

"We were monitoring life signs," Simons said, speaking up for the first time, playing back what looked like a recording of bright lights moving around inside the house.

Two were brighter than the other three. Guessing Piper and Ginny with their abilities? From placement and movement through the scene, he could pick out Nia. She was brighter than his little spot was, but not glowing as brightly as her friends.

"First there were five life signs before the arrival of the sixth. Two more arrived, but life signs dropped to seven." The agent continued.

Five of them in the house before Daphne arrived, then crazy Daphne made six. Before Louise, number seven, shot the hell out of Daphne. Yeah, so they were aware there might have been a murder. Of course, *that* wasn't their concern. They didn't care about life, especially not the lives of mortals. They only cared about power, and even the mere chance that when Nia and her friends rose, they could be more powerful than the gods.

Mal watched the bright colored figures collect in the main foyer. That was a hell of a lot of witnesses. Then an extremely bright light arrived, almost eclipsing the light of the others. Loki.

"Eight with the arrival of Subject Serpent," Simons continued. Some justice having Loki described as a "subject."

Four of the figures—that had to be Nia and her friends—clustered together. Bringing back Daphne. This time, one of the figures started to glow, more and more brightly, almost as brightly as Loki. Ah, hell. Maybe it was what Nia looked like bringing someone back to life.

"Then, we're back up to nine," Agent Simons said. He shut off the screen and returned to looking stoic.

"Circumstantial at best," Mal said, keeping his tone neutral. *Shit, shit, shit.* It was better evidence than most of the gods' cases had. Evidence that would make it easy for the gods to play the case out exactly as they wanted: Nia as the power-hungry villainess who would be taught a permanent lesson in case anyone else was thinking of looking for a little power.

Agent Bertram smirked. "That's today's evidence. Coupled with evidence collected about the other two supposed 'horsewomen' and their activities, we have more than enough to suggest a conspiracy."

"You're going to go with crimes against nature, huh? Since when is it illegal to bring someone back to life?"

"Since two months ago," the guy said, his smirk widening.

"That's bullshit."

"So is that little bitch thinking she can do whatever she feels like."

"I thought we were keeping things civil," Mal said, a low growl in his voice. He took a threatening step toward Bertram. The charges were trumped up, the law changed just to entrap Nia. The gods must have figured out that like her friends, Nia would probably rise to have both the abilities of Death as well as companion abilities—life. Or… His insides froze.

Or they knew about Asha and Nia's desperate battle to save her. Hell, they might even have set whatever it was that attacked Asha and Nia in the Gray after them.

He fisted his hands at his side, the Fomorian side raging up inside him, roaring and demanding he put this guy down. His hands ached, he clenched them so hard against the urge to punch the jackass.

"Now, see, I was pretty sure a crime against nature was, like, having sex with a corpse or something, and that's been illegal for a long time," Nia said, her voice raspier than usual as she stepped up beside him.

Dammit, she still looked too pale, and she wavered a bit where she stood.

"Nia, go sit down," he said quietly. Preferably farther away from him when he announced his intentions and the vague hint of a plan to save her. It wasn't much, but it was pretty much certain to piss her off when she figured out the ramifications.

She didn't take her gaze off the two agents. "Yeah, but if I'm being charged with having sex with a corpse, I'd at least like a chance to defend myself. I mean, if I'm guilty, shouldn't I at least have gotten to have some of the fun, too? Not the corpse part. That doesn't sound fun at all, but the sin. You know what I mean," she said, gesturing toward the agents.

The blond asshole smirked again. "I believe we have evidence of your sins on all levels, Ms. Amort," he said, looking her up and down in a way that made Mal's skin crawl and the Fomorian part of him growl low in his throat. "You are a crime against nature, by your very existence, by the way you think you're somehow above the two most basic laws in our world: life and death. You're not. No one is. By the end, you will know that, too."

Mal'd had enough with the smirking and now threatening Nia. This time, he couldn't talk himself into behaving responsibly. He took a small step forward and decked the bastard.

CHAPTER 12

It was almost sweet, Mal punching the other guy on her behalf. If it hadn't been so incredibly moronic and irritating as fuck. Did he think she needed protection, that she couldn't have punched the jerk on her own if she wanted to? What was the blond douche's name? Agent Bertram.

Mal and Agent Bertram rolled on the floor, equally matched. Their fists made sickening thuds as they made contact. They collided with the edge of the door with a bang.

It was like that kid's book with the mouse and the cookie, only with men and the way they had to one-up each other. Mostly it meant she hadn't got to hit Agent Buttwipe. People called her a bitch all the time, which, frankly, was not a word she especially minded when it meant she didn't take shit from other people and spoke her own mind. Yep, she could be a bitch. And proud of it.

She wrapped her arms around herself and glared at the men, the other agent beside her doing the same. Agent

Simons. She put that name down in memory of the guy who wasn't as bad as his partner.

A bitch probably wouldn't be as scared spitless as she was that the gods had come after her and planned to arrest her. Mal punching the guy probably didn't make things better, but how could it get much worse? From what the agents had said to Mal, even if she got away from these guys, there'd be others. She couldn't leave. There'd be no one to look after her kids. Who would fight the soul devourer in the Gray? Just when it had seemed like maybe she could figure this out, like maybe she and Asha had a chance, now this. Could Asha come with her, wherever the agents took her? Where would it be? What would it be like? From what Ginny's husband and Loki had said, Nia didn't stand much of a chance of surviving the gods' so-called justice. A tremor slid through her, along with panic creeping its way up her throat like vomit. Her breath started coming faster.

Then she caught sight of Anna, Ginny, and Piper in the doorway to the dining room. Clustered in front of them stood her kids. Asha in the front, her eyes huge and round. Witnessing violence she shouldn't have to see.

Dammit, dammit, dammit. Nia squeezed her hands tight, put on her best bitch face, then put two fingers in her mouth and whistled. Once Mal and Agent Bertram paused and turned to her, she scowled at them. "Yo, dumbasses. Knock it off!"

Agent Bertram looked like he wanted to give Mal a jab in the back when Mal's back was turned, but Mal cleared away warily, never completely turning his back until he reached Nia's side.

"Damn, Mal, why'd you have to go and do that? Agent Dickhead and I were just getting to know each other," she said, pretending to speak to Mal even as she eyed the two agents warily, both of whom waved their hands near their ears a second before they came and stood back in front of her. A hint of a bubble surrounded their heads, so probably some kind of protection. A jockstrap probably would have been smarter.

Agent Dickhead, aka Agent Bertram, glowered at her. He was unfortunately close enough she could feel the nastiness of his arrogant dark brown aura brushing hers, catch the echoes of violence in his past and the way he gloried in it, gloried in making people miserable with his own power.

The other guy, Agent Simons, was quieter, maybe smarter, and while his purple aura was likewise touched with violence, this job meant something more to him than just kicking asses and causing pain. Damn. The dummy thought he was making a difference, could make the world a better place.

"You're playing for the wrong team, dude," Nia said quietly to the Agent Simons.

The tiniest flicker of movement between his eyebrows was his only reaction.

"Whatever. So. What's the deal? I get, like, a couple of days to clear up my affairs or something, right? You stay here while I'm in custody before a court date or something?" Her mind quickly raced, sorting through plans. Maybe she could convince Loki to take care of the custody thing. Maybe he could also strongarm Mr. Death, and that guy could help her, and she'd only need a day or two and she could save Asha then to hell with the gods. They could do what they liked. Yeah, so maybe she wouldn't be with Asha, but maybe Loki could see Asha was taken care of. Watch over her friends.

And Mal…

Her mind shied away from the idea. Her daughter with Mal. The way he'd probably teach her to fight her own battles, even if he might punch out jerks who called her a bitch.

"You're under arrest now, and you will accompany

us immediately to Braelyn for trial," the quiet agent said.

Nia gulped. *Braelyn*. Bibiji had taught her about that. The world of the gods. Pretty and everything, but crappy place to go unless you were a god. No one went there because they wanted to.

"Playtime's over," Agent Dickhead-Bertram couldn't seem able to resist saying.

Nia's mouth was dry and sticky, making it hard to work up the spit to swallow, let alone mouth off. The owl swooped over and settled on her shoulder, and if the agents saw it, they gave no indication. That feeling of calm swept over her, but not nearly enough to wash away all the panic.

"I have to go to Braelyn?" she said stupidly since the idea hadn't occurred to her. That was only for serious crimes, wasn't it? Mom and Dad hadn't been born in Beckwell, so some of the finer details about paranormal justice and laws she'd never heard. Or never paid attention to. Stupid naps in history class. Okay, so she knew Braelyn was the parallel world of the gods. A whole other world away from Asha and home. "I-isn't there like some local judge we see first?" There had to still be a way she could protect Asha. But she was too weak right now to try anything. How would she make a body? Was she strong enough to bring Asha back?

Dickhead's smile was wide and smarmy. "Not this time. Not this case. This goes straight to the high court."

"Oh, I'm sure it does. Anything for the gods to play their games," Anna said, stalking closer.

"Anna, chill." Nia grabbed her friend before Anna did something stupid, like do some punching of her own. Anna needed to stay here. To look out for the others.

Anna turned her back on the agents, pitching her voice low. "Nia, you don't understand. They'll take you away, use you to make an example. To try and punish us all. Maybe if I went with you—"

"Oh, sweetheart, tell me you're stepping up as defense council. You'd get to stay with your friend. Right up to and with her at the end," Agent Dickhead-Bertram said with a smirk.

Nia's heart sped. *Up to and with her to the end.* The way he said it held permanent menace. In Braelyn, a whole other world they didn't understand, they'd be alone and powerless. Subject to the whims of spiteful gods.

"Don't. Anna, *don't*," she whispered. Please, no. It would be bad enough not seeing Asha again. Not being here for her. She couldn't allow anything to happen to her friends. She'd need all of them to somehow save Asha. If she could.

Worse, challenge sparked in Anna's eyes. "If I do—"

"If you do, they have both of us, then where are we at? It's what they want, don't you see that?"

Mal cleared his throat. "Besides which, position is already filled. I'll stand as the defense."

"No. Don't do this," Nia said, spinning instead to Mal. Her fear turned her words to fury. He looked perfectly calm about the whole thing. Calm about following her to the gods and then letting them do whatever the hell they wanted. "Mal. Stop it. Take it back."

He just shook his head.

She spun toward the agents. "I don't want him. I have no defense." She stuck out her hands. "Come on. Get on with the arresting then. Just me. Got that? Just. Me."

But Agent Dickhead-Bertram was looking at Mal. "I heard him. Agent Simons, did you hear him?"

The other agent nodded. "I did. Defense of Petunia Amort registered as one Malcolm Quilan." He glanced at his wristwatch. "We should be going. The transport loop will be arriving in five."

He and his partner took a concerted step toward Mal

and Nia.

"No!" Nia rounded back on Mal. "Mal, you moron, what are you thinking?" She grabbed his chest and shoved him back a few feet, probably, infuriatingly, because he let her. "Who's going to take care of my kids?" she whispered. "Who the hell said I wanted your defense anyway? I don't want you. I don't even like you."

Finally, he looked down at her. Reached a hand up and stroked it down her cheek, the simple touch sending shivers and warmth shooting through her and straight to the erogenous zone, which should have been the erroneous zone. "Then I guess it shouldn't matter too much what happens to me, should it?"

Her mouth opened but there were no words. Because it would matter to her if anything happened to him. If, like Asha, someone else died because of her stupidity, died because of this curse of her blood that promised power but never gave her enough to protect anyone she cared about. Stupid Mal, she didn't care about him, of course, she didn't. She barely knew him. He'd invaded her life since yesterday and she hadn't been able to get rid of him and he reminded her of the warmth of the sun, and the hope there'd still been when she was young. The hope that this wasn't all there was.

That just maybe, sometimes the happily ever afters got shared a lot more equally around the world, even to some of those who didn't really deserve them.

Agent Dickhead-Bertram clamped a hand on her shoulder, turning her around and holding out a glowing chain thing.

The owl screeched and dove toward him. He knocked it effortlessly out of the air.

Esther fell in a pile of feathers, flickering out and vanishing.

Crap. *"Esther, you okay?"* No response. Not that the owl talked anyway. Besides, she had other things she needed to deal with. Nia turned to her friends, fighting the panic that threatened to swamp her, the moisture that pricked her eyes.

"You tell Mr. Death he owes me." How, she had no idea, but it was worth a try. She had no other choice. "He needs to look after my kids. No one can use the d-e-a-d or g-h-o-s-t words, got that?" Nia called to her friends, seeing no choice but to let the agents secure her hands with the glowy thing. Let them take her to Braelyn. It gave her time to recover her strength, time to develop a plan.

"If Mr. Death gives you any guff, tell my aunt. You also need to let Lou know what's happened," Mal said, using one of Loki's pseudonyms as he spoke to Anna and her friends. He glanced at Nia as he too let them secure his hands. "Tell him I'm doing what I promised. That I'll keep my word." His eyes were only on her as he spoke, as though swearing an oath. "I'll keep her safe."

A chill shivered through her at the weight of his words, as if they echoed through this world and all the others.

"What the—" Just when she was about to ask what the hell he meant by that, Agent Dickhead-Bertram pulled out another device, pressed it, and blue light danced before her eyes. Then, for the second time that hour, the world went black.

CHAPTER 13

Ugh. Who left all the curtains open? Nia squinted against the bright light burning through her eyelids, raising a hand to shield her eyes. Pain exploded in her head like fireworks, her shoulder blades digging into cold, unrelenting stone beneath her. Reality and memory flashed through her, and she popped open her eyes, pushing upright against the cold floor.

She was in a dazzling semicircular, bright room. She staggered to her feet, her bare toes icy against the polished stone floor. Guess no one had bothered finding her shoes when they'd arrested her. No telling how long she'd been left on the floor there, but it was even worse for her back than her shabby sofa was. A small sink and toilet of the same stone were built into the opposite wall. A faint outline indicated what might be a door, though it was as smooth as the wall with no latch or knob.

Her gaze was drawn toward the source of all the brightness: a tall, narrow window, starting about four feet off the ground and rising to the vaulted ceiling. Also stone.

Trying to focus on the architecture and go look out the window was about the only thing quieting the screaming voice inside that wanted to know how she'd gotten here, where "here" was exactly, and what would happen next. Where was Mal? She didn't want him to face the same fate as her, yet there'd been something comforting in knowing she wouldn't be here alone.

That she wouldn't die alone.

She approached the window, having to raise her hand to her eyes against the dazzling light until they started to adjust. The bottom of the window was about chest height, the window a narrow slit barely wide enough for her arm. Though peering down, it was a dizzying drop down to greenery below.

Activity bustled around her building. Stunning creatures too beautiful and perfect to be human rode around on flying carpets. Others drove flying chariots drawn by winged beasts, all in a cacophony of noise and chaos, rush hour traffic in the air and on the ground. Around her were other structures, some of them almost modern in their design, others like this one more castle-like, although all seemed to be made of the same pale, creamy stone, whether the modern skyscraper off to the right, or the Greek temple over on the hill. Servants swept out balconies. Lovers embraced. On a towering balcony to the right an orange guy in a business suit talked on what looked like a cellphone. The sky was a bright pink, warming to yellow at the apex, above which might have been the sun, but wasn't visible from here.

Even with the drop, Nia studied the wall, completely smooth, no chance of a handhold. Just a nasty fall.

"Esther says: 'don't you even contempwate it, betiya,'" Asha's sweet little voice said from behind Nia, trying to imitate the stern sound of an adult.

Nia spun, her heart pounding. Oh, no. Oh, no, no, no.

She wasn't supposed to be here. She was supposed to be back in Beckwell. Asha was dressed in her usual bright pink sweatpants and white T-shirt with the kitten, her hair wild around her head in dark curls. Perched on her shoulder was a large gray owl. Nia ignored the damned owl. Knees weak, when she reached Asha, she dropped down, dragging her daughter's cool body into her arms.

"Sweetheart, what are you doing here?" *How? This shouldn't have been possible. Oh, gods, this wasn't fair.*

"Surprise, Mama! We came, too," Asha said proudly, pulling back and patting Nia's cheek. She frowned. "You sad, Mama?" Her shoulders slumped. "I do something bad?"

Nia's insides melted and cracked all at once. She gave Asha another squeeze. "No, sweetie. You didn't do anything wrong." She turned a glower on the owl. "Though I've got a few choice words for you." She gave a tight smile. "Of course, most of them aren't for Asha's ears. What are you two doing here?"

Asha cocked her head, and though Nia heard only a bare crackle and whisper, like the hint of words, Asha turned back to Nia. "She says, of course, she's here. Someone has to look after silly girl." Her daughter turned and frowned at the owl. "I'm not silly." More conversation, evidently, because then Asha beamed. "Oh. Not me." She turned to Nia. "*You* silly girl."

"Fine. You want to look after me? Get her out of here. Take her home," she said, still speaking to the bird.

The owl blinked at her, its eyelids lowering in an annoyed, half-mast fashion.

"She says no, Mama," Asha filled in.

Yeah, that much Nia had kind of picked up. "Sweetie, Mommy and the bird need to have a little chat. A grown-up one, okay? Can you maybe stand over there while we talk? That's a girl." Barely waiting for Asha to nod, Nia grabbed the owl by the feet. It flapped its wings wildly, almost lifting her from the floor, but she was too pissed to care, and hauled it toward the window, farther from Asha. The scent of singed jasmine tea bloomed.

"Mama, she says you won't understand," Asha called from the other side of the room.

"That's okay, sweetie." Nia narrowed her eyes on the bird. "She's the one who needs to understand." She lowered her voice to a growling whisper. "You need to take Asha and get her back to Beckwell."

"She…your…safety," were the words that came through, that almost-whisper in Nia's head again. The owl flapped its wings again, then let them droop. *"Can't. I…stay,"* it said, then flickered wildly, almost disappearing, as though the effort had cost it a lot of energy.

Nia rolled her shoulders. "Look, I know you probably mean well, trying to protect me and all. But I need *her* safe."

The owl shook its head. *"Not safe…here…stay."* A bit of the chorus for "Stand by Me" rolled through Nia's head. The owl almost vanished from sight, though Nia could still feel the slight form of it in her hands, the tickle of feathers against her skin.

She let it go, and a rush of air accompanied it as it circled and swooped, back over toward Asha, then back toward Nia.

Asha looked up from where she was playing with her shoes and walking them across the floor with her hands. "She says she stay, Mama. Take care of us."

The owl settled on the floor between them, bowed its head again.

Nia sighed. "Crap. Okay, fine." She went over to the part of the wall that looked like it might be an outline of a door, but there wasn't even enough space in the outline for her to fit a fingernail. The window might be the only way out, if she could fit through. Plus figured out how to fly. Well, at least she could keep an eye on Asha. At night. Great. Fighting the gods during the day, and the soul devourer during the night. Was it possible to save Asha before one of them got Nia first?

ℜ

"He's coming to!" a female voice said above Mal. Ginny maybe, from the muffin-sweet scent of her.

Someone slapped his cheek, none too gently.

"Anna, that isn't helpful," was the dry reply. Loki's voice, from the sound of it.

Little hands touched his face more gently. One of them pulled at his nose. Another poked his eyelid. He twitched away but didn't move too quickly in case he bumped into one of the kids.

"Okay, I just got off the phone with Daniel. He's on his way." Piper this time, her voice getting louder as she got closer.

Mal forced his eyes open. Kids. Nia's ghost kids. This was Nia's house. Daphne had attacked, then she'd been shot. Then the USELESS agents had come. He tried to scramble upright. Dizziness attacked, and he collapsed back onto the sofa. "Nia?" he asked weakly.

He was in Nia's living room on the same lumpy sofa where they'd spent the night. Loki sat on the opposite chair texting, his brow furrowed. Ginny chewed on her lip, then started handing out coffee and muffins, like she'd done before everything had gone to shit. Mal tried to sit up again more slowly and the world came into less blurred focus.

"Daniel said symptoms of a concussion could include dizziness and vomiting," Piper said, coming over and kneeling in front of him.

Anna paced around the room, arms crossed across her chest casting him glowers. "See? I didn't hurt him. His head is probably too hard and full of rocks to cause any damage."

"It's such a wonder people ever call you hard to get along with," Loki said mildly, without looking up from his phone.

Piper leaned down and offered a tentative smile. "How are you doing? Your brother's on the way. He said not to get up too fast and to take it slow just now. You might have a concussion. I don't really sense anything, but my read on you might not be as good as it'd be on a full human."

"Is anyone going to tell me where Nia is?" He'd taken responsibility, even knowing it was probably entering a losing battle with one arm behind his back: he'd signed up to be Nia's defense. So…where was she, and why wasn't he with her?

The little hands patted his arms, making goose bumps slide over his skin.

"They took her," Loki said, his voice tight. A muscle twitched in his jaw, and it took Mal a second to realize Loki wasn't wearing his Lou disguise, but looked like a younger man, similar size and build as Mal, the oversized plaid shirt loose all but across the shoulders. The demigod swore softly beneath his breath at whatever he read on his phone, then flipped it over in his lap before he speared Mal with a look. "I understand you volunteered as Nia's counsel?"

"Yes. Before I could volunteer and give Nia a better option," Anna said bitterly, wrapping her arms around herself. "He probably doesn't even know what Braelyn is, let alone how to behave there."

"You said it was the same as here. A parallel world, right? Is it more dangerous for Nia there?" Ginny asked, rounding on Anna, coffee pot forgotten.

"Wait. There's how many worlds? Like infinite possibilities?" Piper asked, joining the party.

"It isn't infinite worlds. Or it might be, but the only ones we're concerned with are the three parallel ones that guide our universe and its inhabitants." Anna scowled again. "Doesn't anyone remember history class? Big sandwich of parallel worlds. Braelyn, the gods' world and what humans sometimes think of as heaven on top." She was using hand gestures. "Us, the mortal world in the middle. Daimoleigh, the demon realm in the bottom, which some religions have posited as hell."

Speaking of hell, he couldn't handle hand gestures and all this sitting around right now. He needed to know where Nia was. Mal tried shaking his head, and the world wobbled. Yeah, bad idea.

One of the kids placed a cold hand on the back of his neck.

The cool soaked through his tense muscles, easing some of the ache in his head. Touch creepy since it was a dead kid, but it seemed meant in kindness. He cradled his head in his hand to hold it still and tried not to groan.

"I couldn't let you volunteer, Anna. You didn't know what you're getting into. Because yeah, I do know what Braelyn is. I've been there. Besides, it would have been what they wanted. The two of you, vulnerable to them."

Instead, it was Nia, alone and vulnerable, gods knew where. Was she all right? Had they hurt her? His stomach churned at the idea. He should have been there with her, there to fight for her. Shit, maybe she even thought he'd reneged on his offer.

"What can you possibly offer her I can't? Besides muscle and the ability to get everyone into trouble?" Anna snapped.

"He was just trying to help," Ginny, ever the peacemaker, tried to volunteer.

"Yeah, but what does he know about defending Nia?" Piper said. "No offense, Mal. I mean, I like you and everything. But this is Nia. And the gods. The flipping gods!"

"He was right to volunteer," Loki said, rising and

walking over to a window to look out. "Anna and Nia haven't risen yet. It was the opportunity the gods wanted—especially with Anna's tendency to jump into a fight without fully considering the consequences."

"With my tendency to—" Anna's face had taken on a peculiar shade of crimson, and she bit off her words and pressed her lips closed for a second, breathing through her nose. Didn't seem to be calming her down much. "He can't possibly have done the amount of research on the gods that I have."

Ignoring Anna, Mal turned to Loki. "This is usual procedure? I volunteered, they took note of it. I should be with her." Where he could be at least halfway less useless then he was here. All sides of him—Fomorian and human—itched to fight instead of this sitting around. Well, not his head. That part still wanted to lie down. Or implode. Kind of a toss-up.

"What a great choice to defend our friend from almost certain death. He doesn't even know usual procedure for high court sentences," Anna said, pretending to mutter it beneath her breath, but her volume high enough it was clear she wanted the others to know.

"The dizziness should pass soon," Loki said mildly. "General stun spell, and they may have upped the strength knowing your heritage." He turned and strode back into the main part of the room. "Nothing about this is 'usual.' The gods are after blood. They think they've found a loophole, a way to stop Nia and hurt all the rest of you through her. Technically Mal's not needed until the trial, which could be as soon as the end of the week, or as long as a year away if we don't find a way to set our terms." He stopped near Anna's turned back and reached a hand out to her shoulder.

She visibly stiffened.

"I know you're worried about her. We all are. Taking your fear out on Malcolm won't help. Go after me if you must, but he needs to be prepared."

She jerked away from him, spinning back, teeth bared. "Blame you? Oh, I do. It's your fault, you and your games, that she's in this position in the first place." She jabbed a hand in Mal's direction but didn't take her glare off Loki. "This was all part of some game, wasn't it? Trap her with him? What was the result you wanted? Accelerate her rising like you did Piper's, when you used the League to pull our strings?"

Good question. He stayed still, just in case the other two remembered they weren't alone in the room. Ginny and Piper were likewise watching, wide-eyed.

Loki dropped his gaze to the floor, and he massaged the back of his neck. "I've been concerned about Daphne's stability for some time, though I didn't think she'd take such drastic action. She has a destruction goddess inside of her, who will be released on the world if Daphne dies. But only if she's killed in a destructive act of fury—rather symptomatic of the goddess's own danger." He rubbed a hand over his face, his voice dropping. "Daphne murdered Louise Dole's entire family, including son, daughter-in-law, and grandson this morning."

There were gasps from the girls.

Mal wanted to puke. Shit. He didn't know the Doles well, but they were young. Another child, stolen too soon.

Loki continued quietly. "That was the first part of her plan, the second being the attack on Nia. I suspect she felt with Nia's association with death, her end would be certain. I have Daphne safely imprisoned in my home, where I can ensure she lives a long, peaceful life and that the goddess stays inside of her."

Silence fell in the room as they considered the waste of life because of yet another plan for power and destruction. Mal winced the most, thinking of the grandson. Another kid who'd never had a fair shot.

Finally, since he had to act if he was going to prevent more death, he cleared his throat. "So, you'll bring in the others?"

Loki shrugged. "Louise Dole has been hospitalized over at the Senior Center, and I suspect without her family she won't fight the cancer any longer."

"It's already bad," Piper said. "I don't think she had long anyway."

"What about Boniface?"

Loki looked considering. "Deirdre Boniface blames herself for the death of Louise's family. It was her decision to recruit Daphne as the third Fate, and it was her suggestion to install the goddess within Daphne as a final measure, though I doubt she expected or wanted to use it. Deirdre is not above making sacrifices for her vision, but she would never knowingly harm a child. Daphne, on the other hand, remains a very dangerous threat, even confined. Whether she was mad to begin with, or the goddess has driven her so, she wants to die a violent death, which means should she seize the opportunity, she will commit more horrific acts."

"You knew all this when you were working with them, and yet you just let them get on with it?" Mal demanded, not feeling exactly sympathetic for any of the three Fates.

Anna crossed her arms and glowered at Loki. Piper and Ginny mirrored their friend.

The demigod leaned back in the chair, sliding his hands along the chair arms. "Yes, well, better I monitored them, wasn't it? The deed with the goddess had already been done once I caught wind of the League's intentions." His gaze flickered toward Anna, then back toward Mal. "Besides which, at the time, they were a convenient distraction from my own plans. I thought at the time— arrogantly—that I could control the situation."

"Play us all for idiots," Anna said bitterly. "Just

pawns in your chess game."

Loki leaned forward, shaking his head. "No, never pawns. Never disposable. I've done all I can to protect you. All of you." He gestured toward Piper. "I tried to tell you how much potential power you had, hoping the four of you would be able to stop the League some time ago."

Mal blew out a breath. "That's where I come in, too, isn't it? You were concerned someone would go after Nia next, so you got me to look after her."

The demigod nodded. "That, and the issue with the gods. I suspected they would come after her next. After all of you ladies, following what happened after Genevieve's marriage." He gestured toward Ginny, referring to where two other USELESS agents had gone after her and she'd sent them home with their tails between their legs.

"Yes, fine, she was in danger," Anna said, putting her hands on hips. "But why him of all people?"

"Yeah, don't worry that I'm sitting right here," Mal muttered. No one else, especially Mom, had ever minded, telling him and whoever would listen how little he was worth. Shouldn't be surprised at anything different now.

"Anna, my brother may be many things, but he is definitely capable," Daniel said, pausing to consider the damaged front door as he strode into the house. Then he headed straight for Mal, doctor bag in hand.

Mal tried to swat Daniel away, but he and his twin were both of the same muscular stature and stubbornness level. Eventually he settled for unhelpfully glaring while Daniel listened to his heart, felt up his head, and flashed a light in his eyes.

"Your wife already examined me. Anna's right. My head's too hard for there to be much damage," he grumbled.

Daniel continued to study Mal's eyes. "A hard head, definitely, but we're not invincible." Finally, he lowered the flashlight and packed away his doctor kit even as Piper joined him on the sofa. They clasped hands in a seemingly coordinated fashion, what with the way they didn't even have to look to reach out and find each other. "What's this about Nia?"

Mal looked up from where he'd been staring at his brother and Piper's joined hands. The closeness of it, all it implied. "The gods have her. I volunteered as counsel because I gave my word to Loki to protect her." He paused. "I gave Nia my word, too." Was her daughter still here, frightened and confused because she didn't understand what had happened? He hadn't seen any sign of the moth-turned-owl, and it probably would have gone with Nia. Just how strong was it? It barely seemed able to communicate with Nia, let alone defend her from any threat.

"Counsel? Defending her from the gods?" Daniel dropped his voice to a whisper. "Mal, I'm glad you're trying to help, but do you think you're prepared for that responsibility?"

"What happened to confidence in my abilities?" Mal half-joked.

"As a police officer and here in Beckwell, there's no one I'd trust more. But this is courtroom procedure and the gods. Are you sure you know enough?" Daniel asked.

Anna threw her hands in the air. "Finally. Someone who sees reason."

"Yes, but no one would fight as hard as Mal. I mean, it's not like he could come back here and face us if anything happened to Nia," Ginny said.

A chill slid through Mal. They thought he'd come back if Nia was found guilty. He rubbed his head, which had started pounding all over again. Shit. Dad might have taken Mal to Braelyn and the high court, might have shown him the gods' distorted view of justice, but Dad would never have taken Daniel there. Here in Beckwell,

Daniel was a doctor. What did he know about the legal system? He hadn't thought that if this all went to shit, just like four years ago, Daniel would be the one to have to clean it up. Less than a month after the shooting, Mom and Dad had been killed in that accident, and Mal'd been too messed up to help. Daniel had done everything.

Now he had to tell his brother he might be the last Quilan standing.

Daniel leaned over him, trying to examine him all over again. "Are the symptoms worsening?" He held up a finger. "How many fingers do you see?"

Mal shoved Daniel away. "Leave off. I'm fine." Except for the fact he had to tell his brother and the girls what signing up as defense meant. "Look, I don't know how long I have, so I'll just spit it out." Fast, like a Band-Aid.

Or a bullet. He winced.

Everyone was looking at him. Even Loki, with a look that might have been sympathetic.

"I'm the best choice for Nia's defense, because I know the most about the legal system—yes, Anna, even more than you—and I'll fight like hell to make sure she isn't dragged through some monkey court."

He forced himself to look at his brother as he said the words, even though through the connection they'd shared since birth, he'd feel Daniel's reaction, since it would probably be a strong one.

"And because, if things come to the worse, better me than anyone else. Because in the gods' high court, the defendant's counsel suffers the same sentence." Which meant come what may, at least Nia wouldn't have to go through everything alone again.

Ginny made a small sound, touching her throat.

Piper's eyes widened. "Oh, Mal…"

Anna's lips thinned but she looked otherwise unmoved. With her research, she'd probably known that, and it said something about her that she'd volunteered herself for Nia anyway.

A punch of shock and a hit of fear jolted through the connection Mal and Daniel shared the second Daniel realized what volunteering as Nia's Defender meant.

Daniel dropped his gaze to his feet, sucking in a breath.

Mal clenched his jaw. Worse, though, was the accompanying pang of pity, like maybe he'd also put together why Mal would volunteer in the first place.

Daniel met Mal's gaze. "Which means, if it's a death sentence for her, it's the same for you," he said slowly, as though confirming the truth for himself.

Mal rubbed his eyes, gritty and aching. "Yeah." He couldn't quite bring himself to look at Daniel, and shoved his brother's emotion down. He had enough of his own to deal with without adding any. "If I don't come back, you'll soften the blow for Aunt Junie?"

Daniel nodded stiffly, staring down at his feet for a second. He looked up, clearing his throat. "Of course. But you're not going to just let anything happen, got that? If necessary, you fight and take as many down with you as you can."

Mal raised a brow. "Damn. You really are Fomorian now, aren't you? Six months ago, you might have asked I be careful not to hurt anyone."

"No. Not then, not now. You're my brother and I want you safe, one way or the other."

The two exchanged a weighted look full of all the memories they shared, both the shitty and the good ones. Mal turned away first, massaging the aching muscles in the back of his neck.

Maybe there was some good in the fact that he and Daniel seemed to finally have come to some peace with each other. That didn't change the fact that Nia was in trouble, and he'd volunteered to defend her when he'd only been to a high court trial once and was a much better cop than he was a lawyer. Maybe it would have been better if Anna had defended Nia rather than him, who knew more about the paranormal legal system mostly by skirting arrest for most of his youth, and sometimes in modern years. Still, better than she was alone, no matter the outcome.

He straightened, dividing his gaze between Anna and Loki. "So, now that we've cleared that up, let's move on, shall we? We all know the game will be fixed. The gods can call it a trial and justice, but it's all just a show. Which means we need a backup plan. How do we get Nia out of there alive?"

"Unfortunately, a lot of that will be up to you once we get you there," Loki said. "Alas, I've never been a favorite in Braelyn, so I don't know enough of the layout or the routines." He lifted his phone and offered a wry look. "Anyone I do know who's more familiar, including my family, is rather reluctant to part with that information."

"Outside communication?" Mal asked.

"Defendants are permitted little additional freedoms," Anna said, then tried to act nonchalant when everyone looked at her. She grumbled beneath her breath before she started again, perching on the sofa arm near Piper. "Besides counsel, she'll be allowed limited outside contact. Like phone calls here, but for the gods it will mean in-person visits from additional advisors." She nodded her head toward Loki. "He's probably your best bet."

"Perhaps 'unpopular' is putting it too mildly. If I go to Braelyn, under any circumstance, I'm just as likely to be incarcerated as Nia," Loki said with a small grimace. "My presence and association will do Nia no favors. Anna, you would probably be the best contact. You can help Mal with your knowledge of what's to come, as well as act as a go-between for all of us back here."

Ann gave Loki a somewhat inscrutable look. "I can do that."

"Priority is getting her out of there permanently, no matter the verdict," Mal emphasized, sharing a look with each of the others, ending with his brother. "Whatever it takes."

Maybe some of his desperation and fear leached through their connection to Daniel. Maybe Daniel just got it because of the situation, but whatever the case, his brother gave Mal a minuscule nod. Approval and support, a total I-have-your-back moment between the brothers that said Daniel would be there if needed. Whether for Mal, or for Nia.

"Another interesting fact. When the agents were showing me their so-called evidence against Nia, their sensors didn't pick up the death guy, or 'Mr. Death' as Aunt Junie calls him." He glanced at Loki. "Think he could be persuaded to help us?"

Loki crossed his arms over a broad chest and leaned back against the wall. "Anyone can be persuaded given the right trigger points. Whether he'll be persuaded to be helpful is a different question. I can talk to him if you like." For perhaps the first time, there was something in his demeanor that hinted at the warrior he was reputed to have been, something lethal.

Mal stored that information away, too. "Thank you, but—" he turned to Piper, "—do you think you could bake some of your cookies and talk to Aunt Junie? I think she might be able to talk him into it." He cleared his throat. "She, uh, was fairly helpful when it came to convincing him to help me with Daniel's situation." Mr. Death was the only reason the two brothers were still alive. They probably owed the guy a lot more than he did them, but if there was a chance to get any extra help for Nia, he'd take it.

Piper blinked. "Um, maybe if Ginny helps me. Sure. I can do that." She stood. "Should we get started now?"

"In a minute, absolutely. I just…" He couldn't help thinking about Nia, far away and worried about her kids back home. Her simple request to get them some help. "Who's up for volunteering to take care of some kids who need your help?"

CHAPTER 14

Everyone stared at Mal like he'd grown a second head for a moment after his question about the kids. Scratch that. Everyone but Loki.

"Yeah, I'm all for helping kids and stuff," Piper said, raising a protective hand to her still-flat belly. "But shouldn't we save Nia first?"

"Is this about that weird thing Nia said, asking Mr. Death to take care of her kids?" Ginny added.

Anna just looked suspicious. It was becoming a common expression for the War horsewoman.

It was an odd moment, all of them looking to him like he was in charge, like he had any idea what the hell he was doing. Yes, he'd had that before, back on the force, but not with these people. Not with anyone who knew his history. It was a bit like he was pretending to be one of the good guys and someone would call him out at any moment, laughing.

They all waited for him to speak, no one cracking a smile.

"Be careful, Malcolm. Nia does like her secrets," Loki said, confirming yep, he definitely knew more than he'd said or let on.

Mal blew out a breath. No, he didn't want to reveal Nia's secrets, since if she hadn't told her friends before, she probably had her reasons. What had just been a crush when he was a kid, something he was sure he'd grown out of, didn't seem to have vanished where Nia was concerned. Instead, it seemed to keep growing. The desire for her physically, yes, but more than that. He wanted to know her, to make her life better. To be part of her life.

When they'd been about to get dragged off, she'd wanted someone to take care of her kids. If it were his daughter, he'd want someone looking after her, too. Even if that meant someone had to share his secrets, things he'd much rather no one knew about, either.

"If Nia knows things are handled here at home, she can focus on escaping and getting home herself." If they came up with a plan to get her home. Without having to become one of her ghosts first. "Nia has children living here with her. Children who could use your help and protection until she gets back."

"Children? Like d—" Anna started.

"Not that word thanks. Nothing related to d-e-a-t-h." Mal cut her off. At her frown, he struggled to explain without explaining, seeing as there were still little hands touching him. "Some of them are…unclear exactly where they fit in the spectrum of things," he said, widening his eyes and speaking slowly to try and emphasize his meaning. "According to Nia, it's best they stay that way. I guess there can be trouble if they find out certain…realities. Like anything other than that they're healthy, living children."

Anna crossed her arms with a frown. "Fine. But shouldn't our focus be on Nia? Surely they'll be fine."

When Ginny and Piper started to nod, Mal winced.

Crap. He was losing them, and he knew this was important to Nia.

He paused to take a breath and contemplated his next words carefully. Finding out Nia had a child had thrown him, too. Hell, he'd even done the quick math wondering if there was any possibility it was his, but they'd only been together that once. Even he wasn't that unlucky. Plus she'd implied the father didn't want to be involved. She'd kept this quiet for a reason. He hated sharing her secrets. *Crap, Nia, I hope you can forgive me for this.*

"One of whom is her daughter," he finally added quietly.

Everyone in the room had known Nia at least as long if not longer and better than he had. She hadn't told any of them about her daughter. Certainly not from the startled expressions on their faces.

Anna was the first to recover. "What can we do to help?" she asked, and the others just nodded and determined.

His lips tried to move toward a smile, and warmth bloomed inside that this was the first thing any of them had wanted to know: how they could help. No attempt to dig deeper into Nia's secrets, no judgment, no hypocrisy. These were good people.

The children's song "One of these things is not like the other" started through his head, smothering the warmth. He hunkered down to start the explanation. "First thing: the kids need to eat. Out back is this incinerator…"

An hour later, Mal stalked through the house. Restless energy haunted him and demanded he do something when instead he was forced to just wait. He needed to know how Nia was doing. More importantly, how he could break her out.

Ginny and Piper had returned from the store and were busy in the kitchen, preparing the most delectable version of Piper's cookies for Aunt Junie that had ever been made, adding in a little of Ginny's special ability that made everything she cooked irresistible. Loki was on the phone in an intense conversation with someone in a language Mal couldn't even identify, but from the sounds of it and the frustrated look on the demigod's face, getting nowhere fast. Anna was at the kitchen table surrounded by books, going through them and scribbling notes for him to take with him—the first of her demands for reasonable treatment of a defendant, something the gods were reluctant to offer.

His pacing took him through the foyer and into the living room. The cold chill surrounding him said that the kids still followed him, some of them at any rate. Was Nia's daughter among them? While he should have been prepared, all he could keep thinking about was that night when he'd thought he'd been prepared. A routine call, they said. A night that shouldn't have ended like it did. Maybe wouldn't have if he hadn't been there, if whatever bad luck that stalked him hadn't maybe affected the outcome.

Hadn't resulted in the bullet ricocheting and ending that kid's life.

What if in the same way he was dooming Nia? What if he wasn't the one who should be going with her? Too late to back out now—and he damn well did want to be at her side. But did he know enough about the law— paranormal and otherwise?

"Stop pacing, or pace somewhere else," Anna said, without looking up from the long kitchen table.

"Oh. Sorry," he turned and headed for the foyer.

"You truly care about her, don't you?" the War horsewoman said, her voice soft, almost like she was half asking herself the question.

He paused and turned. "I promised I'd keep her and her daughter safe. That's what I'm good at, right? Muscle and a hard head, to paraphrase your words."

She winced slightly and glanced back at Piper and Ginny, who, of course, had stopped their conversation and were staring at him.

Talk about feeling like a kid caught with his hand in the cookie jar.

"She doesn't even like me," he said, as way of explanation.

Telling them there was nothing for them to see would have been the easier explanation. Hell, maybe it was the way they seemed to welcome him on to "team good guy" that made him hesitate in letting the lie slip easily past his lips.

Because Nia might say she didn't like him, hell, maybe it was even true, but he'd be lying if he said there was nothing between them. More than the teenage crush. More than a memory. Maybe just a part of the longing to do better, be better than he was possibly capable of. For her.

Yeah, little wonder he didn't say any of that.

"Huh. You totally still have the hots for her, don't you?" Piper said, crossing her arms across her chest and inadvertently getting flour all over her shirt.

Ginny swept her off almost absently, not a speck of flour on the more experienced baker. "Yes, but that was years ago. They were just kids."

"I dunno. Worked out okay for Daniel and me," Piper said, referring to the fact she and Daniel had fallen in love in high school, and, despite a decade-long breakup, had never gotten over each other.

"No. It's nothing like that," he started to say.

"How do both of you know what he felt in school and I didn't?" Anna demanded of the other two.

They both gave her an identical look. Ginny put it into words. "Sweetie, you know we love you…but you're not the most observant. Especially when it comes to…interpersonal stuff."

Yeah, that was putting it mildly. Even though, damn it, his face burned. Must be because the oven was on. "I'll just, uh, go pack some stuff," he said, clueless what he'd pack.

"If you really care about her, don't be afraid your Fomorian side will scare her off. If she's the right woman for you, nothing will," Piper said with a grin before she turned away to finish tidying up the kitchen.

Yep. Definitely the oven making his face hot…and him feel like a kid. He stalked away, stopped midway through the foyer by Ginny's hand on his arm. She glanced back at the others, Piper who was happily washing dishes, and Anna who had returned to flipping pages and scribbling notes.

"Look, I don't know everything Nia has been through, I don't even know whether I should say anything I just…I know it hasn't been easy. She deserves some happy in her life, you know?" Ginny said, keeping her voice low.

He nodded, waiting for her to say the rest he sensed she was thinking.

She didn't make him wait long, meeting his gaze directly. "You take care of her for us, won't you? If you two have the chance for happy, don't be scared to take it because you think someone else deserves it more, okay? Because they don't. You two deserve whatever you can get."

Maybe he was allergic to flour, because now his throat was all clogged up, too. He nodded since he couldn't quite speak.

"But if you hurt her or cause her more pain, I'll make you never want to eat food again and only long for a death you'll never find," she said, with the sweetest smile.

"I'll give you a really nasty STD," Piper called from the kitchen over the sound of clanging dishes.

"I'll just rip out your spine," Anna said, never looking up from her book.

Ginny patted him on the arm. "Go on. Get packed. Make sure you grab some things for Nia, too. We know you'll do the right thing, Mal. I hope you do, too." She headed back to the kitchen, a bounce in her step.

He just shook his head as he headed upstairs to collect some clothes for Nia, even though a small smile hovered over his lips. Must have been the death threats.

CHAPTER 15

The gods on their flying carpets and with their chariots and magical animals in Braelyn's pink sky had started coming to peer in her window as though Nia was a circus freak. Her only defense was to slump down low against the wall directly below the window, making herself difficult so see. She was glad she'd never gotten around to taking Asha to a zoo and had a great deal of sympathy for the animals hiding in whatever shelter they had available to them.

She had no defense, nothing to cover the window. All she could do was feel the cold stone soak through her clothes, Asha's little body curled against her side as they listened to the strange, indecipherable voices of those who'd come to gawk at her. When it rained, she lost even the solace of hiding beside the window as water splashed through, the faces of the dead reflected in the puddle as they tried to reach through to her. The sun never set in Braelyn, so it was hard to tell how much time had passed. Food arrived every few hours through a small opening in the bottom of the door outline, the flap vanishing without even a seam to show where it'd been.

Sometimes they slept. That made her think days had passed, not just hours. Time moved differently here. Too much time to think about how everyone seemed to have forgotten about her—other than the gawkers. All the people she cared about. Would it have been different if she'd let them know her more, if she'd shared her secrets? Most likely it would have just hurt more when they didn't come. Like it had hurt after Mom had died, and she and her grandmother hadn't even come back to see Nia again, not even for one last farewell.

Letting people matter just made it hurt more when they made it clear you'd never mattered as much to them.

Nia's eyes drifted shut.

When she opened them, she and Asha were back in the stark, parched world of the Gray. It was colder here than in the part of the Gray she normally visited, and the landscape looked different. The shattered ruins of temples surrounded them, the soil beneath them dry and cracked.

"Where are we, Mama? Monster here?" Asha said, clutching Nia's hand and staying close.

"It's just the Gray. No, it isn't here. We're okay." She could feel the soul devourer, like a distant hunger, the angry dark brown and pulsing black puss of its aura hunting them. Perhaps because they weren't even in the same realm, it hadn't found them yet. Not that there couldn't be other threats lurking.

"Yes, but you're hardly safe," the distinguished woman's voice said from beside her, and a large gray owl settled on the crumbling remains of a pillar. Her owl. Esther. "You can understand me clearly now, I hope?"

Nia stared at the owl, the subtle glow surrounding it. The owl had never spoken aloud before…but then, this was the Gray, where it seemed to come from.

"Huh. Yep." She shrugged. "I just thought your

English sucked."

The owl ruffled its feathers and its eyes narrowed. "My English is perfectly good. As is my Persian, Hindi, Italian, Urdu, and Greek, to name a few. It's you who can't seem to understand properly, betiya."

"Enough with the nickname, okay? I'm hardly your granddaughter. You should be my age, maybe even younger." At least the sound of Esther's voice wasn't the same as Bibiji's, but she sounded like an old lady.

A tiny part of her had started to wonder if somehow, Bibiji had come back as her horse. But no, her grandmother was long gone. It was naïve to think she'd ever come back. At least she'd taught Nia a good lesson: don't let yourself get too close, because the people you care about the most are also the ones most likely to break your heart.

"She was a good woman. But human. She made mistakes as we all do," Esther said softly. "I call you betiya because of our connection. And your foolish insistence on behaving like a child."

"Stay out of my head," Nia growled. The owl might not be speaking telepathically, but seemed to slip into Nia's thoughts too easily. She climbed up onto a fallen column to see if she could see farther, but it was just endless gray, most of it indistinct unless it was up close. Still, a plan began to emerge. "If we're in the Gray, the same Gray, that means you can take Asha through and take her home."

"It would be possible," Esther said slowly.

"Then take her home."

"It would be possible, were I willing to leave you here alone. But that wouldn't minimize the risk for either you or Asha. The Pishacha will eventually track you down. Your energy is too strong, too enticing for it to ignore. And Asha…it appears to like her best of all."

"Hold on. The Pistachio?" Nia said, deliberately

mangling the name.

The owl's eyes narrowed to slits. "You do try the patience, betiya. I understand why you do so. Yet it will not always keep you safe, will not protect your heart from the hurt you fear. The Pishacha—the flesh-eating demon spirits of your grandmother's home. You know them as soul devourers." The owl's head did a three-sixty, like it was listening to something, then turned back to Nia. "We have little time. You must open to the young man. He's coming for you. And for Asha."

"Mal?" Asha piped up, a big grin spreading over her face.

"If you even think of suggesting it's time I marry and settle down—"

"Don't be foolish. I don't have to say it. When you're with him, you think it for me. Let him help you. It's the only way you'll both survive. Because soon you will battle the soul devourer and these so-called gods." Esther paused. "I will do what I can, but it's difficult when you can't understand me. I will have to devise something more efficient than the child. Because you are right. Asha should not be involved in this. We must find a way to remove her from the situation."

"Wow. We agree on something. I was kind of wondering if it was possible. You know, my friend Ginny says her horse cracks dirty jokes all the time and can be entertaining. Don't suppose you might consider that."

The owl closed its eyes and turned its head.

"He comes," she said. "Wake. Now."

Nia woke with a gasp back in the brightness of Braelyn just as the door to the cell opened for the first time since she'd been there. She scrambled to her feet, her knees weak, her heart practically choking her. Was this it? Was it time for court? For execution?

Mal stepped through the opening, his broad shoulders taking up most of the width, dark hair ruffled, his whiskered jaw hard.

She gulped, and heat spread through her, the first heat blossoming inside her since she'd arrived in this place. She couldn't decide whether she was glad to see him, pissed, a bit of both. How long had it been since she'd seen him? He barely knew her. It'd only been a few days together at her house, and yet…he'd come. He'd come for her, when no one else had.

"What are you doing here?" She forced the words through her tight throat.

His gaze ran over her greedily, returning to her face to search her expression. "You've been treated all right? They haven't hurt you?"

"Uh, yeah, I'm fine." Her insides were all mixed up, relief that she wasn't alone anymore, that he hadn't ditched her like everyone else, and fear being here put him in danger. "I didn't think you were coming. Any of you. Not after this long."

Mal's expression darkened, and he leaned closer until she could see the way his dark lashes brushed coppery skin beneath those amazeballs-blue eyes. He dropped his voice. "How long do you think you've been here?"

He'd abandoned her, they all had, just like she'd known they would, and now he wanted to play games?

"Oh, that's rich. I don't know. A week, at least. You mean you've missed me so little?"

He was already shaking his head. "Nia, they only took you from the house this morning. I've been doing everything I can to get here. You were taken this morning from Beckwell."

Time had seemed to move more slowly here…but she had that all wrong? A heavy freezing sludge hit the bottom of her stomach and her skin tingled as her vision blurred for a second.

"What? No. Y-you're wrong."

"Let's argue later, huh?" he said, his voice rough. He lifted what looked like a little medallion on a soft piece of leather and placed it over her head, settling it around her shoulders, his fingertips brushing her neck and setting off sparks.

"It's like a translator. You'll be able to understand what everyone is saying, no matter the language."

She noted the same medallion around his neck, too. He hadn't abandoned her. He'd come the same day…even if it didn't feel that way to her. Her heart expanded, her head grew buoyant, and…oh no. Her eyes started to sting. She blinked rapidly. That was so not happening.

"You shouldn't be here, you big dummy." Her throat thickened. If for Mal this was the same day she'd been taken, it meant two days after she'd met him in Loki's bar, agreed to Loki's scheme, he'd volunteered to be her defense.

He'd put his life in danger, all for her.

"Well, it'd be pretty hard to keep you safe from back home," he said. As though it didn't matter, this huge sacrifice he'd made for her.

Asha crept up behind her, giving Nia's fingers a squeeze.

A silvery, translucent moth fluttered around Nia's head before landing lightly on her shoulder, the warm scent of jasmine tea surrounding her, but the comfort didn't feel the same. Not even the fact that the owl had turned back into a moth made a difference.

"Is she okay?" Anna's voice called from outside in the hall, and she popped her head around the corner, her dark braid swinging.

Nia's knees softened to jelly, and her eyes stung. Anna had come, too?

Anna's expression darkened just before her head disappeared. "We'll need to speak with your supervisor. Now," she growled to someone else in the hall.

Lips compressed to a thin line, Mal wrapped an arm around her, drawing her against his side. His warmth soaked through her like spring sunshine, trying to thaw all the frozen places, trying to crack and melt away the fear, the certainty she'd had that they'd all just abandoned her, that no one was coming, and it was just her, just like it'd been for so damned long.

It was too much, too fast. She tried to jerk away.

He kept her pulled gently but firmly against him, leading her toward the door.

Out in the hall stood a red-faced Anna, her hands on her hips. In her sights stood a skinny little guy dressed in white suit with curling goat horns protruding from his shaggy brown hair and a terrified expression on his pale face.

The little snot's gaze dodged from side to side, as though looking for an escape.

"S-supervisor?" he squeaked. His eyes widened as he caught sight of Mal and Nia stepping out of the cell. He held up a shaking hand. "You, um, she's s-supposed to stay in there. P-please," he whimpered, stumbling back a step down the endless white stone hall, away from the War horsewoman and Mal.

Mal towered over the pipsqueak, grabbed him by the collar, and shoved him against the wall. Blue-gray color climbed Mal's muscular forearm. "I knew your justice system was fucked, but it's far worse than I thought if you lock up defendants before they've even been convicted." His voice was barely more than a guttural growl, his golden-brown skin taking on a faint silvery-blue hue.

Nia could only blink. She'd never seen Mal so pissed. Anna, well, it was a dumb move getting into a fight with the War horsewoman on a good day. Here they both were. Fighting for her. Her mouth wasn't hanging open was it? Maybe this was some weird hallucination.

"Section 4.56, Addendum 12 of the Olympus

convention of 1912, clearly states all defendants are no longer to be situated in any less than humane and hospitable conditions," Anna said, her expression no less intractable, her voice echoing down the long hall. She turned to Nia and offered a brief hint of a smile. "I am *so* glad to see you." Her gaze zapped back to the pipsqueak with horns, her expression hardening. "I am appalled by the conditions we found you in. Hospitable conditions were clearly defined as providing bed linens and basic comforts." Anna's lip curled, and for a second, red flames danced in her steel blue eyes. "Care to explain why we've found different?"

"She's, uh, a p-prisoner?" the snot said, his voice cracking like the pathetic teenager he was.

"She has been accused of a crime, not convicted," Anna said.

"Which means you're not allowed to treat her as a prisoner, you little shit," Mal ground out, shoving the little guard away from him.

It was like watching a messed-up reality show. Mal and Anna were seriously pissed. On her behalf. They were here in Braelyn, and they hadn't abandoned her. Oh, frick, no, no, no. Moisture pricked her eyes, and she blinked rapidly, turning a second to suck in a breath and pretend to be glancing back into the room when really, she just needed a second.

They'd come for *her*. A strange lightness suffused her along with Mal's warmth.

"I, uh, I need my supervisor," the little snot said. He ran off, his keys jangling while her door hung open.

"Damn. You guys are good." Nia tried to keep her tone light. Hopefully it was just her who heard the slight catch in her throat. She looked up at Mal and might have swayed.

Holy crapadoodle. The blue of Mal's eyes had deepened to the blue of a bright midnight sky. He seemed bigger, more muscular than ever, a living superhero of shadow and starlight, the perfect hero for her.

She blinked. *Nu-uh. Bad Nia.* She must have been locked up longer than she thought, because that was just crazy thinking. Mal was no superhero, and he sure as shit wasn't "hers" in any way other than possibly the sentences "my problem" and "my past."

"I'm sorry I didn't get here sooner, but they're not getting rid of me now," he said, the deep timbre of his voice rumbling over her, sending warmth spiraling through her and pooling in her core.

"You okay? Have they fed you at least? Given you anything?" Anna said, touching Nia's arms and breaking the spell Mal seemed to be weaving.

Phew. Good. Didn't need none of that.

Wanted, maybe. Needed, nope.

Nia blinked. "Um, food, yeah. Like protein shake kind of stuff. They haven't mistreated me, exactly."

Anna's eyes widened. "You're in a cell, with no curtains when the daylight never ends, no bed, no basic shelter. I'd definitely call that mistreatment." She grabbed Nia for a hard, fast hug, whispering fast in her ear. "Mal's going to be here with you, but I swear to you, I'm not going to let these assholes win or hurt you. We are going to make them pay for this."

"No. Anna, don't—" she began.

The War horsewoman cut her off with a quick hand movement a second before Nia heard jangling keys signaling the return of skinny snot and, presumably, someone with half a brain cell more than the kid.

She was forced to content herself with a glare at her friend. *I meant don't make promises you can't keep. Don't you get dragged into this, too.* First Mal, now Anna. What was it, an epidemic? Her throat tightened. She couldn't let someone else hurt because of her.

A woman whose hair and skin were as white and

colorless as her long robes rounded the corner toward them, her expression carefully neutral. When she was close enough, her pointed ears and amber eyes did not make her appearance any less unsettling. Though outwardly calm, her predominantly red aura, indicating a proud person, was muddied with brown uncertainty and negative blacks. The colors only calmed when she saw that Nia was still among them.

"My humblest apologies. There must have been some kind of…clerical error that resulted in Ms. Amort being in this tower," she said, her voice melodic.

"I trust there won't be any more similar *errors* during her stay," Anna said, her hard tone making it clear what her opinion of the lie was, and at the same time sounding as though Nia was just visiting here.

"Please, let me show you all to her actual quarters," the woman said, her aura spiking briefly with black hatred at Anna's words. She dismissed the skinny snot with a small flick of her hand, like shooing a dog, before she held out her arm in indication to follow. They followed her through the white stone halls.

"To make sure we have it correct for the court, how many days was she wrongly incarcerated in one of your prison cells before she was even tried? An exact number, please," Anna said, biting off every word.

Another flash of black hatred and brown uncertainty in the white-robe lady's red aura, and her hand trembled as she raised a hand, pointing down the hall. Either it was Anna's war abilities getting to her, or Anna's questions. The woman tried to force a smile. "Surely—"

"How many days?" Mal repeated, his voice hard.

White-robe lady swallowed, looked down a second and licked her lips, then back up. "Merely one day's worth in the mortal realm," she said quietly.

"How long was that here?" Mal's tone was smooth, with an undercurrent of violence.

The woman's aura shadowed with brown shame. Her amber gaze flicked up to meet Nia's for a brief second before flitting away. "One week and three days," she finally whispered.

Mal swore, the blue climbing up his neck now.

White-robe lady flinched, and she spun, speeding up her step as they neared a second hall that finally straightened and had large oval windows with views of the bustling city and pink skies outside. "My apologies."

"We're going to need better," Anna snapped. "We expect reparation."

The woman stopped, back still turned. "Reparation?"

"It means an apology you actually mean," Anna defined, sweet as a knife blade, crossing her arms over her chest and raising a brow in challenge.

Damn. With lines like that, she didn't leave Nia any room to edge in anything good.

The woman slowly turned. "You have something in mind?"

"Full release."

The woman was already shaking her head. "Impossible."

"Then luxury quarters, for the duration of her and her Defender's stay, with all added amenities any guest in such a suite would expect."

"That's completely—"

"Inadequate after what she's already suffered? Yes. We'll make do."

More black hatred and dark brown criticism and shame marred the woman's aura in an awesome way. Damn, Anna could be badass when she wanted to.

"If you will allow me a moment, I'll see what I can arrange," she said, turning her back, then lifting a small device out of a pocket and speaking softly and quickly into it.

"If I by some strange miracle survive this, you and I

have to travel together. You'll always get us all the best rooms for the cheapest price." Nia gave Anna a bump against her arm and a wink.

Anna turned back, her look bleak. "You are getting out of here."

"One way or the other," Mal murmured darkly.

Nia struggled to swallow. Yeah, that's what she was afraid of.

<h1 style="text-align:center">CHAPTER 16</h1>

Thanks to Anna's help, in under an hour, he and Nia had been shown to a room that looked like something out of a Charlton Heston sword and sandals flick, the kind that used to sometimes come on one of the only three TV channels they'd had at home when he was a kid. No cable in the country, and their neighbors were too far away to steal their satellite. All white marble, pillars, floaty fabric and a single large bed on a raised dais. There was even a separate dressing room and bathroom suite Nia and Anna poked their heads in while he watched from near the doorway. Partially to give the two friends some privacy, partially to make sure no one was coming in after them. Yeah, sure, the room was nice and all, but it was still a pretty jail cell, and it'd be a fight to get Nia out alive. One door, windows were too high to climb out.

She still looked too pale, even her attempt at the usual Nia sarcasm coming off as forced.

One week and three days of that cold, sterile cell. She claimed they'd fed her, something that technically counted as food, but there'd been no sign of even anything soft to lay on, not a sniff of privacy. Alone and convinced he and her friends had abandoned her.

Small fingers squeezed his, and he gave a gentle squeeze back. She hadn't spoken, but he was almost certain it was Nia's daughter, Asha.

When Nia had pulled away from him not long after her white-robed jailer had investigated getting a better room, small, cold fingers had gripped his hand. Which made his heart compress.

Not all alone, then. He thought he'd spotted the moth briefly. But a child didn't belong in a place like that. Not under any circumstance.

It was his fault Nia had been in the situation in the first place. If he'd answered his phone, if he'd gotten Loki's messages—one of which he'd only listened to later and which had clearly said Daphne was coming and he needed to get everyone out of the house before she got there—maybe the gods wouldn't have had the excuse they were looking for to arrest Nia. Maybe she and Asha would still be home in Beckwell, safe and where they belonged.

Maybe if Loki had found someone better to watch out for her, she wouldn't be in here and in more danger than she'd been when he'd first walked into her life.

"You look like you're thinking deep thoughts," Anna said, approaching with Nia at her side. "I hope some of them include what you're going to say tomorrow at the preliminary court appearance." She grimaced, glancing at Nia. "I'll try, but I don't think they'll let me come back here soon, and besides, now we know time moves differently here than back home. By the time I got back, it might already be over."

Which meant it was up to him. His shoulders tightened, and his stomach twisted. His position with the RCMP meant he was more familiar with the Canadian legal system than he was with the paranormal one.

"It's unlikely to make much difference anyway. They're just going through the motions. The chance of dismissing the case is probably a negative number value. I had an uncle go through the process. It should have been dismissed at this level, but never was."

Nia's brow furrowed, and she paled. "Did he get off?"

Crud. Bad example. They'd strung old Lem up. A few times. "Um, totally different situation."

"Don't lie to her," Anna said. She took Nia's hands. "Once it gets this far, there has only been once case I've found in the entire history since the creation of the USED organization where someone has been found innocent."

Huh. He'd never heard of even one.

Nia blinked. "One. In what, like fifty years?"

"Five hundred, but that's not the point," Anna said. "The point is there *was* one. From what I can gather, since information is scarce, it looks like the case created enough conflict and doubt within the supernatural community, and among the gods themselves. An execution would have resulted in potential war. That, and the accused was very powerful in his own right."

That did sound promising. "I'm hearing a lot of similarities to your case," Mal agreed.

"Exactly," Anna agreed.

Nia looked less convinced.

There was a knock on the door. "Transportation is ready for Hadrianna Fray."

The War horsewoman frowned at the closed door, biting her lip. "I have to go. According to Loki, there's at least a chance they'll let me come back if I try to be agreeable. I don't like it, or having to trust him, but it's all we have." She gave Nia a warm hug, enveloping the smaller woman in her embrace. "Try not to say anything stupid and piss them off any more than they already are, okay? Just let Mal do the talking. Try to look innocent.

No tears. Better not to show weakness. Maybe strong but calm?" She pulled back, assessing her friend.

"What about pissed off and strong?"

"So long as you don't speak, sure." Anna ducked in for another quicker hug. "Just stay alive, okay? We're all working on this, we're on all your side, and Loki is gathering other allies."

Finally, the two friends parted.

Another knock on the door.

"One minute, Ms. Fray," the voice said, sounding like the white-robed prison official.

Anna turned to him. "Don't do anything stupid. Don't make it worse." She hesitated, then pulled a small black book out of a pocket and pressed it into his hand, placing another finger over her lips.

"Keep it secret," she mouthed.

He nodded, slipping it into his pocket.

The door opened. Outside the opposite wall and on either side of the door were guards who looked like they'd gotten their job by checking "yes" on the "highly intimidating," "extra muscle and horns," and "good with murdering on command" application boxes. Most of them had concealed their wings, but there was no doubt they were angels. Quite possibly the most dangerous paranormal creatures out there, and more than capable of taking on a Fomorian.

The white-robed official from before was trying to look serene, but there was a tightness around her lips.

"Ms. Fray, we do not have all day."

Anna leaned in to give Mal a hug, quite possibly the first time he'd even been this close to the War horsewoman who he'd never thought as being especially huggy in all the years he'd known her.

"Tell her the backup plan in the bathroom. I've used a spell Loki gave me to secure the area from any kind of eavesdropping," she whispered into his ear. "We're working on the next part of the plan and hopefully you should hear from him before you hear from me." She pulled back. "Take care of her, Quilan. We're counting on you."

Damn, what a terrifying idea: everyone counting on him, the evil twin, to somehow be the hero and keep Nia safe. Great job he'd done of it so far.

Still, no sense making Nia or Asha more nervous, so he kept his face carefully blank, his tone even. "Got it, boss lady. No parting threats?"

That earned him a brief flicker of a smile. "I think we've clarified our intentions." She nodded to him, gave Nia a brief wave, then followed the white-robed female out the door.

It closed behind Anna and the official, leaving he, Nia, and Asha alone.

Leaving him responsible in this dangerous new world.

Damn.

&

The room, which was easily the size of her living room and kitchen combined, seemed to get smaller the second the door closed and she was alone with Mal. Okay, not completely alone. Asha was there, and Esther, who fluttered off her shoulder as soon as the door closed, the flap of wings growing as it doubled in size, assuming the owl form once more.

Nia looked at Mal, who didn't look quite as huge and muscly as he had when he'd been pissed.

"Daniel turns all bronze and muscly in his Fomorian form, yet you turn into Steroid Smurf? Seems kind of unfair."

"Not sure if it's quite Smurf blue, but since when is life fair." He cast a significant look down in Asha's direction, even though he couldn't see her.

No, life hadn't been fair in that situation. The child

clung to his hand and stared up at him with something that looked suspiciously like hero-worship.

Damn. Better than a crush probably—the small grace of Asha being so young. Better it was her daughter looking at him than her, even if in the bottom corner of her heart she might be the teensiest bit tempted. He'd never been hard on the eyes, and even back in high school she'd snuck the occasional peek at him. Who wasn't the tiniest bit curious about the town bad boy?

"I would have thought—maybe even hoped—she'd have stayed back home. How has she been holding up?" he asked.

He wasn't even touching her, and warmth spiraled through Nia that he'd ask, that from the concern furrowing his brow and, in his voice, he gave a shit.

"She's still paler than I'd like her to be." Every sign that Asha continued to fade, though she couldn't say that with Asha listening. "And she says sometimes she's bored, but I guess when you can make up a game playing with your shoes, nothing is that bad."

He took a step toward her, and her pulse jumped. "How are you? Really?"

The heat increased, bouncing through her like a ball in a pinball machine. The symptoms got even worse as she met his deep blue gaze. "I…"

Was she seriously thinking of telling him how frightened, alone, and desperate she'd felt? Aka her recent life as a chief zoo exhibit in an alien world? That, worst of all, she'd wondered if anyone at home even missed her, even cared she was gone. Yeah, she could be a crummy friend, and there was a possibility she even had a small attitude problem. Even when she'd been too young to have done anything wrong, there seemed to be something about her that meant people either wanted to use her or lose her.

"Nia?" Mal said, touching her cheek with his

fingertips, the touch softer than the brush of the moth's wings. "Sweetheart, please. Tell me what I can do to help you."

Crud. There went that irritating sting of her eyes. Must be invisible dust everywhere. She tucked her hair behind her ears and turned away, stalking across the room toward the floor-to-ceiling windows, broken by graceful arching pillars.

"I'm cool. Don't worry about me." She glanced up. "I thought robe-lady said there was some way to close the windows?"

She'd barely spoken the word, before the bright clear openings seemed to solidify, pitching the room into black.

"Huh. Lights?"

Glowing orbs, growing in brightness, appeared all over the ceiling, giving the room a warmth and clear light almost the same as when the windows were open.

There was a delighted childish giggle from Asha, who dragged on Mal's arm as she jumped excitedly up and down.

Mal, meanwhile, visibly stiffened, his eyes searching out the light orbs like they might attack him.

She couldn't resist the pull of him and sidled closer. "Is the big bad Fomorian scared of a little magic?" Could he be any cuter? Somehow, this revelation made him all the sexier.

He'd come back. For her. After all she'd done to him. All she owed him.

He turned the glare on her, his jaw tight. "Magic doesn't scare me."

"Oh, sure it doesn't," she said, crossing her arms and raising a challenging brow. Even if she did have to crane her neck back a bit to see him.

A smile pulled at his lips. "It doesn't scare me. I just don't trust it."

She had to step closer, had to reach out and touch

him, tapping him on the, yum, very muscular chest. Muscle jumped beneath her touch. Everything he risked coming here flooded over her. A genuine hero stood in front of her, wanted to fight for her. She let it crowd out the fear that haunted her days and nights for so long, the certainty she was alone, had to be alone.

Her libido came back from the dead, cold place it'd been hiding for a few years now. Back like a freaking phoenix, and twice as hot. Dear gods, *life* seared through her, filled her lungs, pumped her heart in a way it hadn't for a long damned time. And lust, like any woman might feel for the sexy-as-hell man in front of her who was unlike anyone else. He hadn't ditched her. He'd come back. Hell, he was ready to risk his whole damned life for her. Which she should probably feel guilty about too and would. Later.

"You're a magical being. And you're scared of magic," she said, for once not minding the sex-kitten rasp her voice had been described as before.

"Not scared. Suspicious," he said, his voice husky as his gaze flickered over her.

"Esther, can you take Asha somewhere? Somewhere you're both safe but so the adults can have a bit of…adult conversation." She flattened her hands against his chest, the heat beneath her fingertips scorching. So different from everything her life had been for so long, a barrier against the terror that had gripped her since she'd arrived in Braelyn.

"She says yes, Mama," Asha says. "I stay?"

"Not right now, love," Nia said. "Maybe you and Esther can work on that code you were going to develop? The one to make it easier to talk to her?"

"Okay, Mommy." Asha happily went off with the owl into the dressing room.

Nia stepped closer, just short of pressing herself against Mal. She slid her hands up his hard chest, reaching for his shoulders. She lifted on tiptoe, which still wasn't enough to reach his lips, not without his cooperation. "Now, where shall we start?"

His hands came around her waist, living licks of flame wherever they touched. He leaned down slightly, bringing their lips almost together. "You mean our discussion."

"Yeah, sure, let's call it that," she said, twining upward. His breath brushed her lips, and she could almost reach him, almost initiate a kiss.

"I have never met another woman like you all my life, and I never will," he said, sliding one hand up and tucking her hair behind her ear, smoothing rough fingertips over her cheekbones. "I have never stopped wanting you."

"What are you waiting for?" Since she couldn't reach his lips, she'd start with small kisses pressed along the side of his neck. Pulling herself closer to him, she found the hard length of him as proof he was serious about the wanting part.

"We talked about what sex would be like between us."

"Fast, hard, and fuck-tastic?" She took a small nip at his neck.

He groaned. Then straightened to his full height, too damned high to reach properly. Well, except for one part that was sure to get his attention and clarify her intentions.

As though anticipating her plan, he took a step back. "I told you. When it happens, it will be because we both want it. Because it will mean more. Not because you're scared and you need a distraction."

She crossed her arms over breasts that ached for his touch. "Yeah, well, don't expect this offer comes around every day, dummy."

His smile was rueful, and he pushed a hand back through his dark hair. "I don't expect it does. Yeah, I probably am a dummy." They both glanced down at the erection tenting his jeans. He sighed, looking up at her. "But we do need some actual adult conversation—the non-sex kind." He waved her toward the bathroom.

She raised an eyebrow. "Seriously? If you shove me into the bathtub—"

"Just follow me already, will you?" He held out his hand. "Come on, Nia. Trust me."

She hesitated a second, looking up into those midnight blue eyes of his. That was the strangest thing. She already did trust him. It was just everything else and the universe that might be the problem. She reached out and placed her fingers in his. "Yeah, well, just so we're clear, sexy-times would have been much more fun."

Mal chuckled. "Probably. But good guys don't just get sex and fun."

"Says you." Ugh, maybe it was just as well. Because somehow or other, she had a feeling they'd passed the point when sex could be meaningless between them. If that point had ever existed.

CHAPTER 17

With Nia's hand in his, it was tempting to pull her closer to him, continue what they'd began out in the room. Mal released her, letting her precede him into the substantial bathroom that was half walk-in tub, surrounded by pillars on either side. Better to avoid temptation, because he'd meant what he'd said. If they were together again, he didn't want it to just be because he was convenient or because he made a good runner-up for whatever or whomever she'd prefer.

He scowled a second at his reflection in the mirror. Same lean features that were too hard with experience to ever be mistaken for his brother, or a kind man.

When it came to Nia, he wanted her to see him. Which also meant she deserved the whole truth. He rubbed a hand over his face, turning away from the reflection.

Yeah, she was right. He watched as she trailed her fingers along the dry edge of the massive tub, imagined those fingers on him instead. Yep, he was a dummy. But a well-intentioned one.

"Are you going to talk or are we here for the ambiance?" she said wryly, turning and hopping to jump up onto the side of the empty tub, swinging her feet once she'd found her perch. She cocked her head. "Or is this because of that nasty perfume stuff Anna sprayed in here?"

He considered sitting next to her. His body leaped at the idea. He opted to lean against the opposite counter. "She said she somehow secured the room so it's safe for us to talk in here. From what Loki says, it's likely the gods will be listening and looking for any vulnerability, any way they can guarantee their success with the case. If they're not going to play fair, there's no reason we should. While Anna and I plan to give this case our all, we're not accepting a defeat. A backup plan is in the works to get you out of here, should things go bad."

She snorted, cocking her head and sending the dark, silky curls shifting and lifting against one another. "You mean when, don't you? That's all fine and good, but we need to plan for if that all fails." She swallowed and seemed to force herself on. "For if I don't come home."

"Nia…" he said, trying to sound scary when mostly the word should have been scared. Shit, he didn't want to think about that possibility, why did she? In fact, he'd created at least three dozen additional backup plans to back up the backup plans.

She just shook her head. "I need to know what will happen. Who will look after what. Who will take care of the kids? Some of them are— You're sure Asha can't hear us, either?"

"Anna just said the room was secure or hinted at it. If Asha isn't in here, then no, she shouldn't be able to hear us. Look, there's something you should understand first—"

Nia waved a hand, cutting him off. "Some of the

older kids know what they are, and they'll look out for the little ones, but they can't go around getting food. Some of the spirits outside can make a nuisance of themselves. They'll go after the kids even, all that bright vitality of their souls, the soul potential unused. Never mind the danger if they find out they're dead and react badly. Who's going to look after them?"

"Piper and Daniel are on it." He couldn't resist the small smile, remembering Daniel's expression the first time one of the kids touched him. Mal hadn't been the only Fomorian who'd wanted to run. "Piper says it's practice for when their own are born. They can't see the food like you to get it out of the incinerator, but Daniel's going to run defense for one of the older kids, and they'll bring it inside for everyone else. Look, Nia, there's something else you should know—"

"So, they're like…living in my house?" She cut him off, again, and crossed her arms over her chest. She tried to say it casually, but the way she crossed and uncrossed her arms, and the bounce of her knee gave her away.

Nia seemed more bothered at the idea Piper and Daniel could be staying at her house than she did at the fact the gods might find her guilty and try to execute her by the end of the week. He didn't have a house, never had, and maybe he wouldn't like it, people staying at his place while he wasn't there either. Still…

"Maybe. I don't know. They're helping out, right?" he said gently. "Nia, could you just let me talk—"

"Pfft, I know they're helping," she said, tucking back the hair behind her ear for the second or third time, her knee still bouncing. "So how—"

"You should know that I was hired by Loki to protect you back in Beckwell, not just reno your bathroom," he said, cutting her off this time.

She froze, her mouth still open a second.

He took the opportunity to push on, hating the

tension crawling inside him. He forced himself to watch her expression when it would have been easier to look away. "Which has nothing to do with why I'm here now, or why I want to help you." He cleared his throat. "Or why I volunteered to become your Defender. But you need to understand what that position means."

Her face had lost all color. "That you're with me when we lose, and they execute me." Color raced up to stain her cheekbones. "I knew it!" She jumped off the edge of the tub and poked a hard finger into his chest. "You were colluding with Loki. Protecting me? What the hell do I need protection from?"

Mal looked down at her finger, poking him hard in the chest, and back at her. He lifted an eyebrow and crossed his arms. "I dunno…what about the gods who were following you and looking for any reason to drag you here? The League and batshit insane Daphne?" He dropped his voice in case there was any chance they could be overheard. "What about the part where water can hurt you, huh? Shit, Nia. You needed help, you still need help, and sometimes you have to accept some."

Her eyes narrowed, and her lips thinned. "How much did Loki pay you to come here, huh? What's the retainer as Defender?"

"I volunteered."

"Oh. Sure. Likely story. Get paid, go home whatever the outcome, and you're—"

"If you lose, we both lose. You die…" His throat thickened, forcing him to stop, soften his tone as Nia's eyes began to widen. "You die, I die with you."

She just stared at him mutely, her lips moving, brow furrowed. "But that means…" She shook her head, kept shaking it, her eyes growing shiny with tears. "Mal. Please. Tell me this is one shitty-ass joke."

He reached forward and slid his hands down her arms. "No joke. I still meant what I said before. I'm here for you, and I have no regrets."

She pulled out of his reach and turned her back to him.

Mal let his gaze find the floor to give her some privacy. "Look, I didn't want to interrupt you. I know you need to make plans. We both do. But you also deserved the truth. The whole truth." She knew now, so at least there weren't secrets between them. Not on his side. Now they could get to the business of fighting as a team.

"How do we get Asha out of here?" she whispered. "I thought you—" She shook her head, as though she'd somehow thought he could take Asha back to Beckwell. She cleared her throat. "I think Loki could see the moth, which means there's a chance some of the other gods might be able to see Asha. I don't want her getting caught up in any of this."

The gods would be looking for any weakness, anything they could use against her. Which included her vulnerability to water and Asha. Hell, from what Loki had suggested, they'd use anything and anyone they could to get the verdict they wanted. Even if the trial was fixed, there was the outside paranormal community to consider. Not all of them would be on the gods' side, even if they weren't exactly on Nia's, either.

"Can she just go home? Stay under cover?"

Nia turned back to face him and scrubbed her hands through her hair, shaking out the curls. "No. She shouldn't have come with me in the first place, and it's not like she can just walk there anyway. Not through the Gray."

"Because that thing is hunting her." The edge of the deep gouge was still visible just below the high collar of her turtleneck.

She covered it with her hand, avoiding his eyes. "Maybe Loki can come get her?"

"I doubt it. From what he said, his coming here could cause you more problems." Besides which, they were already depending more on the demigod than was altogether comfortable. Loki said he wanted to help, Mal's gut said it was true, but this was still Loki, troublemaker extraordinaire.

"Crap." She hopped down from the tub, wrapping her arms around her and starting to pace. "I know you guys probably think you can save me or something, but it's her who matters, okay?" She closed her eyes, pressing her hands against them a second. "If I'd just had time, if I'd somehow been able to save her before we left, at least I'd know she'd get on without me."

"By save her…you mean bringing her back to life? Like you did with Daphne?"

Nia made a face. "Yeah, but it's more complicated. Daphne I kind of reattached to her physical form. Asha doesn't have one. Hell if I know how to make one. If I had the full powers of Death, I dunno, maybe I could just grab one out of the ether or something." She slumped down against the massive tub again. "Other than when I found her, she's barely left the house."

Despite the fact they should be discussing tactics for tomorrow, in what little time they might have left if Mr. Death didn't come through, he wanted to know as much about the woman she'd kept hidden from everyone for so long.

"How did you find her?" he asked quietly.

She sniffed, a mirthless kind of sound, staring down at the tiled floor. "By that point I'd been in and out of the sanitarium, and I'd figured out there was nothing they could do for me. Finished a bookkeeping degree there, though, finally started to get my life back on track. I just…I wondered about her, you know? Even though I'd given her up. Even though I had no damned right to know anything about her."

"She was still your daughter," he said quietly. He ached for her. Geezus, that must have been hard. He couldn't imagine how much so. Yet at the same time, growing up with a mother who'd always hated him, had suggested she should have aborted when she'd found out she carried twins, he'd often wondered what life would have been like if she'd at least given them up. If maybe he and Daniel could have grown up somewhere else, with someone else.

Nia met his gaze and held it briefly. Nodded, before her stare broke away. "I had a ghost break into the records for me." Another snort. "So much for getting my life on track, but whatever. I convinced myself I needed to see her, just from a distance, and I'd see how much better she was without me." Her voice dropped, barely a whisper. "I drove down that street, where she should have been happy, growing, getting in trouble. I found her all right. This lonely little ghost who didn't remember what'd happened to her. Who didn't know she was dead, didn't even know her name."

"Shit."

"Yeah. No kidding." Nia smoothed back her hair again, gathering it into one hand and pulling it to the side where she finger-braided it. "I just…knew she was mine. Looked it up later, and I was right."

"Looked up, what? What happened to her?"

Another nod. "Someone driving too fast down the residential street. A little kid chasing her ball, too little to know better."

Bile burned his throat and roiled his stomach. His chest ached, and he rubbed the spot as though that'd make any difference. "You brought her home."

"I called her Asha." The shadow of a smile. "The name I would have called her. If I hadn't given her up for what was supposed to be a better life." She paused, taking in and releasing a deep breath. "For a while, things weren't bad. I mean, I couldn't tell her the truth, not with the chance of what could happen to her, let her be destroyed all over again. I've tried to give her as normal a life as I can, under the circumstances. Until that thing in the Gray started hunting her. The soul devourer. I don't know how to stop it. I don't know how to make up for what I cost her."

"Nia, it wasn't your fault." Not the way it was his fault that other child had died.

"Maybe not directly, but my decisions caused the end result. Different decisions, different outcome."

"Maybe, but you don't know that."

She glared at him. "You're saying she was destined to be a child who died too young?"

"That's not what—"

She cut him off with a flick of her hand. "I don't buy it. Fate isn't real. Just like this BS with me becoming Death. The Fates didn't make Piper gain her powers, nor Ginny. My friends learned to use their powers, they made themselves powerful. I just need to, I dunno, get stronger, gain the rest of my abilities. Then, when I'm Death, I can save her."

If she were a more powerful figure, she'd be more likely to get off at the trial, like the case Anna had mentioned.

"Let's do it, then," he said, pushing off from the counter and holding out his arms. "Let's get you to rise as Death, be more powerful, get the hell out of here."

Nia turned and gave him a sideways look, a hint of a smile pulling at her lips. "Don't suppose you have a spare 'How to be Death in Five Easy Steps' manual just laying around or anything, huh?"

"No, but Anna might." Remembering the book the War horsewoman had slipped him, he dug it out of his pocket. The thing was only about four inches high, a tiny bound black book. Inside was crammed with Anna's scrawling notes. All the text appropriate in scale for Barbie, a lot less so for a real person. He brought the book almost to his nose. "Well, hell. There's even an index," he muttered.

He held his breath, a flutter of the tiniest variety flickering inside him. The text might be small, but the meaning was mighty. Hell, she'd helped build his whole case right here, a good one, with full precedent examples, suggested witnesses and protocol.

Knowing Asha's story, he was more determined than ever to get both her and Nia out of this situation, help them return to their normal life, and hopefully, in Asha's case, something better. This little book might help them do that.

He looked up to find Nia watching him, her dark gaze shining. Maybe if he could save her and her daughter, maybe there was some tiny chance he wouldn't have to be runner-up or the consolation prize. Maybe for Nia at least, he could be the one she really wanted.

CHAPTER 18

Mal stared at her with a warm intensity that melted some of the ice that solidified within her the day she'd found Asha. The complete failing desolation had almost wiped out any hint of hope in her. Then she'd spent so long hiding Asha and so much of herself from everyone else, even her closest friends, terrified they'd reject her and her, frankly, kind of crazy plan. She wanted to bring back Asha, who some people might already think was beyond saving. Hell, even as a ghost, Asha was in trouble as she faded into a second death.

Yet here was Mal, ready to help her seize her powers and take on the gods. Volunteering his whole damned life on the small chance, a) she could choose to gain her powers and figure out how to do so, and b) somehow, they could make it out of this alive, considering how fixed the game was. Her pulse sped, heart hammering, warmth flooding her as she looked at him, almost as though seeing him for the first time. This amazeballs gorgeous guy, dark hair just the right amount scruffy, built like a warrior-god, and all his sweet ferocity in those beautiful blue eyes. Focused on her, waiting on her and wanting something longer, more meaningful with her before he said they'd sleep together.

He looked up from the book, those dazzling cobalt eyes snaring her gaze. "Anna gave this to me, and since she did so in secret, I'm guessing she wasn't supposed to. Lucky for us. Most of this has to do with her notes on procedure and suggestions for how to handle the court appearances, what she thinks might be in store. But…" He paused, flipping to the section, then holding it out to her. "This part is about the Death horseman."

Electricity tingled in the brief brush of their fingertips, and her body heated even more than when they'd been out in the bedroom and she'd suggested sexy times. The tremble that went through her almost made her drop the damned book. Through most of school, he'd been there, on the periphery of their group in high school after Piper and Daniel got together, always the sexy bad boy all the girls talked about but most were too scared to approach. Until that one day *he'd* approached *her*. She'd learned even then he was much more than just the bad boy. So much potentially harder on her heart. He was dependable, kind, gentle, trustworthy, all the things she'd searched for all her life and never found. Which was why she'd pushed him away. Hard, fast, and mean.

What would have happened if she hadn't?

"Nia? You okay? Aren't you going to look at the book?" he said, giving her a look that said he thought maybe she'd spent long enough in a cell to have lost her mind.

"Fine. I'm fine. Why wouldn't I be fine?" Heat crept up her face, and she dropped her gaze to the tiny book blindly. Maybe he was right. Maybe she had lost it, thinking such stupid thoughts when she should be thinking how to gain her powers.

Speaking of which… She tried to read Anna's scrawl. Brought it closer to her face. "Damn. Did she use a magnifying glass or something?" Still, once she got used to the size, she could mostly follow it along. It was like Anna had created a miniature version of her Bigass Book of Scary—a book with everything she knew about the four horsemen of the apocalypse that weighed about as much as a VW Bug.

Aww, hell. There went that warm and squidgy feeling in her, making her feel all loved and appreciated inside when what she'd really like to do was start flailing around like the Grinch as his heart grew too big. Unfortunately, the book didn't include much more information than she'd already read.

Death was usually the fourth rider on a pale or corpse-like horse. *Huh, maybe that explained the gray moth and owl.* Could see and speak to ghosts, as well as attracting them. *Duh. Since she was born.* Association with wild beasts. *Was that why the soul devourer was after she and Asha?* Abilities could include walking the Gray, soul reading, and necrokinesis. *Yep, just in case she wanted to kill anything with a touch, yuck.* Association with water and ether… Nia's breath caught.

She looked up, caught Mal staring at her, and her face heated more. Ignoring that, she showed him the spot in the book, as though he could read the miniscule writing from that far away.

"Look at this. 'Can lift the veil, blurring the division between life and death.' Something about zombies… No, that's not it… Here! 'Resurrection is believed to be one of Death's abilities, in truth a companion ability. Can take back death.'" She frowned. "What, like, give them a refund? That's a stupid way to put it." She flipped through the pages, but there was no description for how she was supposed to take back death or assume her abilities. "Frick."

She handed it back to Mal and started pacing. "Maybe I can't do it without the others, like we did with Daphne and with Maddox when we brought them back. Maybe it's not really one of my abilities and the book is full of shit. Either way, it doesn't provide anything better. I mean, I've been seeing and talking to ghosts all my life. What else am I supposed to do to advance my powers? To become Death? Because I am seriously not in to zombies or going around killing people."

"Good to know," Mal said. He stopped her pacing with gentle hands on her shoulders, turning her to face him and gently massaging some of the tension out of her muscles. "What it means is that there's probably no going anywhere tonight." A deep breath. "We're going to have to at least attend the prelim trial tomorrow."

Her throat squeezed, in direct contradiction to her desire to close her eyes and moan at how his hands turned her to molten lust. Made her want to beg him to just keep touching her. Usually she hated being touched and accidentally reading the person's soul. That and a history of grabby ghosts and the times she'd traded first-base touches with boys at school for drugs and an escape from reality. But with Mal, on top of his genuine, sexy-as-fuck desire to do the right thing, be the goddamned hero clouded her mind, filled her with him. Plus, ooohh, he knew how to give a massage.

"But that's all it will be, right? Just some talking at us, vague threats of all the horrible things about to befall us?" Her voice had gone raspy and she found it hard to keep her eyes open.

"Yeah. Sure," he said, his voice deeper and rougher. Possibly because she might not have been able to bite back the last moan. "You should probably get cleaned up, get some rest," he said, starting to pull away.

She caught his hand and pulled him closer to her. Her eyelids were heavy, and her body hummed with life and warmth. So damned alive and pumping. She spent so much time with dead people, she'd almost forgotten she wasn't one of them. To want, to need another person's touch. There'd been a couple of guys in the past, just enough to satisfy a momentary craving but nothing more. Even then she'd had to tolerate their touch and keep it fast before she saw too much, their souls stripped bare in front of her.

None of them compared to Mal. She met his gaze, those dark cobalt eyes grown darker with desire. "I could…use some help," she said, stepping back into the circle of his body.

"Nia." A hint of begging in his tone. Probably that nonsense about wanting to wait, about their being together meaning more.

What more was it going to mean?

"We might not have after tomorrow," she said, lifting his hand and pressing small kisses to his knuckles. She placed it back around her neck and reached for the bottom hem of her shirt. "Besides, you know what water is like for me. You were able to pull me out back home. I need you."

He swallowed hard, his Adam's apple bobbing. "You sure about this?" His voice had gone husky with want that matched the bulge in his jeans.

She smirked. "Hell no. I only meant you help me get a little cleaned up. Then maybe a little dirty, too."

He lifted his hand and helped her pull the turtleneck over her head. He smoothed her hair back over her bare shoulders, the curls tickling her skin even as his rough fingertips set off a path of sparks where he touched. Her not-spectacular chest was covered by a magenta bra and not the sexiest thing she owned, but the way he looked at her, it was like she'd been transformed into a lingerie model.

Those deep blue eyes, gone almost black, met hers.

"What do you want me to do?"

A heady thrill of lust and heat shot through her. All that man, all that muscle, at her command.

"We can both use a washcloth, little soap, as little water as possible. I don't want to risk getting pulled into the Gray. You can help me reach a few spots."

Honestly, she hadn't been able to resist a few sponge baths in the other cell, which fortunately meant she wasn't nearly as gross as she could be. She did want to feel clean, and more than that, she wanted his hands on her.

His nostrils flared, and he headed for the sink and the pile of white fluffy towels.

"Oh, you better take off your shirt. We wouldn't want you to get splashed," she added. Obviously, some daring, sexually powerful woman had possessed her, but that was cool. She'd happily reap the benefits.

Mal's lips twitched with an almost-smile in the reflection in the mirror before he slowly turned, leaning a hip against the counter. "Better not risk it." He unbuttoned the top two buttons of the black polo shirt, then lifted it over his head, muscles rippling, revealing a sculpted chest and coppery flesh. "This meet with approval?"

"You better undo your jeans. Just in case they get wet."

He quirked a dark brow and didn't break her gaze as he reached down and flicked open the top button of the dark denim. Then slowly unzipped the fly.

She broke the stare first, because she couldn't resist looking at him, was hungry for him in a way she'd never experienced before. Maybe it was the desperation of the situation, maybe it was the fact that he'd come here, put his life at risk for her when he barely knew her, not the whole truth.

Not the things that might have changed his mind.

She pushed those thoughts aside to revel in the hint of dark blue fabric over his swollen shaft she could see through the fly. He pushed the jeans a little lower with the underwear, until the top of the shaft was almost visible. Then stopped.

She frowned, letting her gaze slowly wander back to his gaze. "That's it?"

He wet the washcloths, squeezed them out, not looking at what he was doing. His eyes were only on her. "How are we going to get you clean wearing all those clothes?"

Her muscles tensed. Getting naked with someone was just another way to be weak in front of them. Showing off her body attracted attention she didn't want to bother with, didn't need. The kind of attention sleazy attendants at the asylum took advantage of when she'd been sedated, and hell, that'd just been the hospital gown. She hadn't let anyone see her wholly naked for years now.

Not since ten years ago, when someone had pulled the fire alarm and set the school fire sprinklers off. She'd been soaked and with the bridge to the Gray open, spirits had clawed their way over and through her.

Mal had been there to help her. He'd found her shelter, he'd helped her get dry. He'd been her haven.

"We could stop," he said, turning and facing her, completely open. Yeah, his underwear was tented, but she had no doubt he'd button up and go about his business if she said the word.

Or if she hesitated any longer. She tried to shake it off and shoved her pants down. Kept her panties on. No sense going crazy, and she wasn't feeling quite that brave. She stepped out of her pants under Mal's heated gaze. His appraisal trailed up her body as potent as a touch, sending a lick of fire through her, searing her skin as he stepped closer.

She squeezed her hands into fists and watched his approach. This didn't mean anything. This was sex, it'd be great sex, but it was just sex. With Mal. Surprisingly sweet Mal who was coming to mean so much more than he was supposed to. Who risked his life coming here. "Have I told you recently that you shouldn't be here?"

He stopped when his toes touched hers, and the fly of his jeans brushed her belly button. He slid the washcloth over her skin, around her neck and down her arms. Then cocked his head, those eyes almost black with desire. "Where the hell else would I be?"

Her throat was too thick with emotion to speak, so she told him how grateful she was, how much he meant to her the only way she could. She grabbed the washcloths, tossed them over her shoulder, and on tiptoe, pressed her body and her lips to his with all the passion, all the regret, all that could have been and never would be in her kiss.

Mal hesitated a heartbeat before his arms came around her, and he returned the kiss, deepening it, tasting her and heating her down through her toes and up again with a wash of glorious desire.

The kiss quickly progressed and heated until he lifted her, wrapping her legs around his waist and pulling her against his impressive erection. She moaned, dizzy with the feel of him, the urgency of him, the heat of his kisses and the feel of Mal. His aura wrapped around her, the fear he wasn't good enough, the guilt for past mistakes, the desire to be so much better, the desire to better *for her*, all of it so familiar, so achingly real. She lost herself to the sensation, to his heated touches. Her palms found his chest, playing with the hardness of muscle there and then raking his back with her nails to bring him closer, to keep him with her.

Still kissing her, then placing hot, open-mouthed kisses down the length of her neck, he set her on the cool marble of the countertop while he pulled down the straps of her bra. First one, then the other, kissing and placing light bites along her arms. She tried to reach for him, to reach her hand into his fly and caress him, but he shifted out of the way with a rough chuckle and grasped her hands in one hand, pinning her to the mirror behind her. Her back arched, her body eager for his touch.

Her legs still around his waist, she hooked her feet into his jeans and shoved them down, lifting her body to cup his length, rub against herself.

He groaned and laughed at the same time before their kisses grew even more frenzied. "I wanted to make this better," he said, his mouth against her neck, his hand sliding down between them and inside her panties.

She could barely speak as he found her with one smooth touch. White light flashed behind her eyes with the intensity of her pleasure. "We can…perfect it…later. Inside me. Now," she demanded. She shoved down her panties as far as she could with her hands, opening herself and pressing against his length.

"Protection—" he tried to say.

She grasped him in her hand and guided him to her opening. Then surged against him, taking his whole length inside her. She might have said something like she didn't give a rat's ass, she was clean, and because of complications during Asha's birth, there was a high likelihood pregnancy was impossible for her anyway. But that was way too complicated, and instead she let her body adjust to his long, hard length inside her. Damn, he was bigger than she remembered. She pulled back, prepared to rock against him again.

Mal gripped her hips, stilling the movement with a hiss of breath from between his teeth, his forehead pressed to hers. He pulled back until she could see his gaze, the deep blue of his eyes, the slight glint that hinted at his inhuman side.

"You're going to kill me, you know that? Give me a second. I'm going to make this last, but I can't—"

She squeezed him with her inner muscles, milking him as much as she could.

He groaned again, choking on a ragged chuckle. "Well, there are worse ways to go." Then his lips caught hers, and this time he surged into her.

She gasped as he went even deeper than he had before, striking just the right spot that made her see at least triple.

They lost themselves to the surging rhythm and the pleasure of their joining. It was beyond anything she'd ever experienced. The very air seemed to thicken between them, heighten the pleasure and tighten her core into a hard knot of want and desire until it drowned out everything else. She was blind to the world, only feeling. Mal against her, Mal with her, inside her. Just as she splintered with a guttural cry, she went deeper, saw further into him. The image of a little boy, shattered and crying with discarded crushed flower petals around him, alone in a darkened room. Then he pushed her over the edge. A guttural cry tore from his throat, and Nia screamed his name, collapsing limp and damp against his chest.

Ten years later, or maybe ten minutes if one insisted on reality and stuff, she finally built up the strength to lift her head to slide a hand up the massive bulk of his bicep, caress a hand…over his warm blue-gray jaw. Her gaze followed farther upward, to the large curling horns on his forehead. His full Fomorian form. Her breath shortened as she took in the dimmed light, the faint fog in the air. The cold, clammy damp of the air, like wet sheets hanging over them.

Oh, gods, they were in the Gray.

CHAPTER 19

The way Nia stiffened around him was Mal's first hint that something was wrong.

The flap of his wings as he stretched and resettled himself was the second. His eyes popped open, the post-sex bliss evaporating even though he was still cocooned in the warmth of Nia's body and, frankly, could have found a second wind. If not for the wings. And the fact that wherever the hell they were, they weren't in the bathroom where they had been.

He looked down at his arms, still wrapped around Nia's body. Yep, they were that gray-blue ash color. Which was, well, slightly disturbing considering the circumstances.

But it was Nia who caught his attention, dark eyes wide, little upturned nose and pointed chin. She was like a creature of shadow and light. Her skin shimmered with internal light, a black mask shadowing her eyes and a black dusky cloak of smoke billowing out around her reminiscent of the cloud of her curly, black hair. If she wasn't stunning enough, he could feel her. Not just her body, her. The woman who struggled to remain strong, to give more shit than she took but inside trembled and ached so badly to do better, to be better, who was eaten with regret and fear. The love, the warmth that radiated from her, all she had to give stole his breath.

Holy shit. Had he…was he…could he see her actual soul?

Nia licked her lips, holding on to both of his shoulders so he couldn't turn away.

As if he'd had any intention of looking away from all that beauty. Normal Nia was gorgeous, cute, and sexy all balled up in one. Here…she was regal, otherworldly and ethereal.

She was Death.

"I don't want to panic you or anything, but, um…" She licked her lips and swallowed. "I'm pretty sure we're in the Gray." Her eyes widened, and her fingers dug into his shoulders. "Oh, dear gods. You're— I've killed you! We must have fallen into the bathtub or something. There must have been too much water and I pulled you into the Gray." Her breath came in pants. "Anna told us we shouldn't just have sex. Not after what happened to Daniel and James. But this…" Tears pricked her eyes, and she held him tighter. "I've killed you." Her words were a bare whisper.

"Um, you sure about that? We've had sex before and didn't end up here."

"But I wasn't rising as Death, was I? Able to go through the veils like Anna's book says. Mal, this…" She lifted her head, looking around at the foggy ruined landscape they were in, like castle ruins surrounded by an indistinct and misty desert. She met his eyes again, moisture making hers shine even more. "This is the Gray. A-and mortals only come here when they've died. Before they move on to whatever it is that comes next."

He glanced around. There wasn't much to see. The Gray was an accurate term, since everything was kind of that indistinct color, or shades thereof. If it wasn't for the heavy mist/fog rolling around their feet and obscuring the view, maybe they could see more.

He turned back to Nia and shrugged. "I might only be mostly dead. I've been that and been here before, remember? What's the big deal? You're Death. Fix it."

Her eyes narrowed, and she smacked him on the shoulder. "Be serious. You could be dead." Her voice turned to a grumble. "If I have to fix it with that attitude, I'll make sure there'll be nothing accidental about your death."

Well, at least death threats must mean she wasn't as scared. Then, because she didn't seem particularly upset about his appearance, he lifted a hand and cupped her jaw, turning her to him again. "At least it means you can still visit me. After what we experienced, what I feel when I'm with you, it makes it worth it."

Ah, hell, now his mouth had gone and run off without permission. Though nothing he said was a lie. He didn't just mean the sex. It was everything. It was the way Nia tempted and teased him in every world. It was the way being with her made him see more, and that even before he'd had a brief glimpse of her soul—if that's what that had been—he'd already started to see that woman. Saw her, and cared about her. Would become a better man for her.

She swallowed, her expression softening. "You're a dumbass, you know that?"

"You don't even care that I look like this, do you? You aren't scared? Considering."

They both looked down at their still-joined bodies, then back up into each other's eyes.

"It doesn't make a difference to you?" He held his breath. Damn. Maybe he wasn't prepared for her answer.

She cupped his jaw and leaned closer. "I see *you*, Mal. That's all I've seen. Here we can't hide who we are. The soul is laid bare, its true essence. But that's what I can always see, especially if I touch someone. Horns, skin color, it doesn't matter. I see you, beneath whatever skin you wear." She paused, glancing down a second and biting her lip a second before she met his gaze again, her voice rough. "I'd never forgive myself if something happened to you because of me. Don't you get that?"

He had no words. Hell, he had to grit his jaw and just focus on the stunning beauty in his arms instead of the weight of her words. When Mom had looked at him, she'd always seen either the Fomorian side she hated, or the evil twin destined to kill her precious Daniel, which she'd hated even more. Dad had only ever liked the Fomorian traits he recognized.

Nia didn't seem to give a shit about either. It might mean she was deluded, and maybe seeing beyond all that wasn't a big deal to her, but it was to him. He was overwhelmed with desire and something deeper, something more meaningful he didn't want to dissect right now. He leaned forward, intent on a kiss. And more.

She gave his shoulder a light swat.

He jerked away. How had he misread her so badly? Hadn't she said the horns and skin didn't matter?

She growled at him. "Not here." She leaned in close. "It's not you, it's this place. It's dangerous." She cast a significant look down at his erection, then met his gaze. "All our focus needs to be on surviving and getting out of here. Nothing else."

He searched her expression a moment for some hint that wasn't all she meant. No, she seemed convinced.

"Come on, get off me. We need to be ready," she said, tension already tightening her body.

Reluctantly, he pulled out and away from her, trying to focus his brain on what they needed to think about.

Which it wasn't especially keen to do. Even better, they were supposed to be prepared for a fight, and not only did he not have a weapon, he was naked.

A chilling howl, unlike any animal he'd ever heard, carried on the mist. It wasn't far and froze away any remaining ardor.

Nia turned toward the sound.

"The soul devourer," she whispered, some of the shimmer around her dimming.

"Sounds like a good time to leave," he said, trying to keep his tone light. He held out his arms. "Snap us back to where we were."

She paused a moment, then slowly turned, her expression tight. "You don't get it, do you? I've been to the Gray before, every time I go to sleep. But we're not asleep. Our bodies aren't back in that room. *We* are here. Our actual, very-killable bodies." She wrapped her arms around herself, the black smokiness floating around her like a cloak, hiding most of her body. "I don't know how to get back."

His shoulders tensed. Ah. That made things…a whole lot worse. Still, his training helped him force back any kind of panic. "Okay then. Are there exits?"

She shook her head miserably. "Not that I know of."

He tried to remember the one and only other time he'd been in the Gray. When he'd followed Daniel down after a fight and Mal had almost died to save his brother. He hadn't gotten there on his own, either. Aunt Junie's Mr. Death had helped. "Mr. Death. Let's call him. He can get us out of here."

There was another howl, and they both stared at the direction it'd come from. Getting closer.

Nia just shook her head. "Unless you happen to have his cell number…or any other known way to communicate with him. I didn't know he existed until he showed up at the house for Daphne, all pissy and entitled."

"Damn. What about your horse?"

This got her to turn to him. "Maybe. I don't really know how to call her, either."

"What do you mean you don't know how to call her? I thought you were trying to gain your abilities."

She stuck her hands on her hips. "I'm sorry. I've been a bit distracted. What with the being arrested, imprisoned, dragged to a different world."

He rubbed his forehead, found the stupid horns were in the way from doing it properly. "Okay, so maybe if you focus on her? Say her name?"

Nia closed her eyes. Seemed to be doing what he said.

Another howl, along with a snarl.

Nia's eyes snapped open.

Mal searched for it in the fog. Even his Fomorian side shivered. He tightened his muscles and prepared for battle as the creature's howl sent chills dancing along his spine. It was close. Really close. Then again, he looked at Nia, and yeah, she did seem to shimmer and glow. Literally putting off a glow.

Ah, hell. A glow that probably made her stand out in this place.

"We need to find weapons," he said, hunting through the fog on the ground. He picked up a sizeable rock. Discarded it for a bigger one, weighing it in his hand. Of course, to hurt something with a rock, either he had to throw it accurately…or better, he had to be in close enough to smash the rock into his enemy. Which meant close enough to get torn to shreds in the meantime.

Nia found a stick and swung it like she was up to bat. And probably about to be struck out. Damn.

"Let's see what we can find for shelter." He tried to joke. "Any spare clothes hanging around would be handy, too."

"Ending up here because we had sex seems really unfair. I mean, Daniel only changed color. You did that and then some," she said, searching the ground for a different stick. "Of course, with those wings you'd really rock some leather pants.

She'd barely said the word when the chill around his ass disappeared. He was wearing leather pants.

"Uh, Nia…" She didn't even seem aware she'd done anything, still searching for the stick. What if that was the key, her not knowing? "Wouldn't some great defensive shelter be good, too?"

"Ha! Yeah, something with really thick walls to keep out that sonofa—"

The ground trembled beneath their feet before thick rock walls shot out of the ground, surrounding them in an open towering tube of stone that blotted out the little light from the sky. Only Nia's glow illuminated the maybe fifteen-foot diameter of the interior tower with them in it.

Nia turned to him. Took in the leather pants. Took in the tower. A brief second later she was clothed, too, head to toe in a black catsuit.

"What. The. Hell," she murmured.

The howl came again, this time from just outside the walls. There was a massive boom, as whatever the hell it was threw itself against the walls. The tower shuddered but held. Only…if that thing could make it shake, there was a chance it could make the tower fall, too.

Another boom, and then claws skittered against the outside of the wall. Oh, hell. "It's scaling the walls," Mal said. "Looking for a way in."

They both looked up.

A dark shape appeared at the top. It howled, and maybe that was a smile, because there sure were a lot of glittering teeth. It was thing fit for nightmares. Part black tiger, part dragon, scales and teeth, long claws, rows of eyes glinting in the dim light ringing its head. It lunged down at them with another blood-chilling roar.

Nia raised her stick.

Mal clutched his rock.

The world dissolved around them and both she and Mal landed on a carpeted floor, hard.

Mal's gaze traced upward from the polished patent leather shoes, up the gray pinstriped double-breasted suit, to the thin moustache and spectacles.

Mr. Death raised a brow. "Honestly. It's a wonder you two have survived this long."

Mal made it to his feet before her, and Nia accepted his hand up, mostly because it gave her a second to ensure the clothes she'd created still existed. She still wore the black leather catsuit and knee-high biker boots. Why she'd chosen the catsuit, hard to say. Maybe it was to look something like Mal, who still had his leather pants. Though his flesh retained some of the blue-gray hue, he'd lost the massive leathery wings and horns.

She took in the office where they stood, full of cubicles, people gathering paperwork, clicking away on their computers, all normal office-type stuff, and taking no notice of them at all. Her mind still raced at what had happened. How they'd been transported to the Gray, she'd made stuff by thinking it, and then they'd almost been eaten. What the hell was going on, and what did it all mean?

Finally, she crossed her arms over her chest and gave the slim man a look. Mal towered over him, and he looked like a preppy jerk from a century ago or so, judging from the clothes. Plus, the pocket watch.

"Okay, so I know your answer is probably going to be that I should already know, but how did we get here, and why did you save us back there?"

Mr. Death didn't look impressed, tucking his fingers into his vest. "Would you rather I put you back in the

Gray?”

"No, no we wouldn't." Mal put an arm between the two of them. "Could you two play nice? We could help each other, I think."

Both she and Mr. Death glared at him until Mal gave up and raised his hands in surrender. He took a few steps back. "Fine. Kill each other. Do the job for the gods." He was still grumbling as he turned away, massaging the back of his neck.

Nia did some grumbling of her own. "Thanks for saving us and all."

Mr. Death inclined his head slightly. "Not really for you, but because I like his aunt and I like the idea of Loki owing me some favors."

She looked around the office some more for clues. There was a sign near the front that marked the days without a workplace incident—eighty-two, it would seem. Even cat posters in a few of the cubicles. Yet, there was something about the people working them.

Then she got it. Their auras weren't right. Considering the number of people in the room, they didn't spread all over and cling to her like the normally did.

"All these people are dead," she murmured.

"Oh, point to you. You do know something," Mr. Death cracked.

She turned back to him, cocking her head. "Dude, please. You made it clear back at my place when Daphne died that I don't know anything about the Death business and you do. But I have no idea what your beef is with me, or what any of this is." She waved a hand to encompass the room, then finally him. "Or what it has to do with me. Although if you'd like to help with more than resurrecting psychopaths—which I'm on trial for, by the way, that'd be cool."

He narrowed his eyes. "You did the actual resurrecting. I just didn't severe the connection. Indeed, we have plenty of attorneys and assistance. Were you actually Death."

She rubbed her eyes, then scratched her chin with her middle finger and sent a dark look in his direction. "You're not going to help us, are you?"

He mimicked her expression, crossing his arms over his chest. "Give you a back door exit out of Braelyn? No. It wouldn't make any difference anyway. First, because the gods would just send the angels after you, and there's nowhere you could outrun them. Second, because—"

"I'm not Death. Yeah, I got that," Nia said, exhaustion suddenly weighing heavily on her. She held a hand over her eyes a moment, before finally looking at the slim man again. "Look, I'm sorry for whatever it is you think I did to you, what I owe you. All I want is to help my daughter and my friends. After that, well, so be it I guess."

He studied her for a time. Long enough even Mal turned and joined in staring at her.

She fought not to squirm. Damn, she really shouldn't have gone with the catsuit. First, it left her feeling far more exposed than she usually was in her every day, oversized wardrobe. Second, it rode up in some uncomfortable places, only made worse by the scrutiny the two men placed her under. She tried to look bored with the whole situation.

"You...don't want to rise as Death?" Mr. Death finally asked, saying the words slowly as though trying to understand them.

"All the power, being a big shot or whatever? No, I don't really care about that. Even Spiderman knew great power just means more damned work. I'm sick of twenty-four seven ghosts. But I would take on whatever responsibility necessary just to have the knowledge and ability to save my daughter. The power of resurrection is supposed to be one of my abilities. If getting that means I gain all the rest, too, fine."

This was followed by another painfully long study of her, even if it probably only lasted a second or two. Then he dropped his arms and spun on his heel. "Come on. This way. There's something I want you to see."

She and Mal exchanged a glance. This place seemed a lot less scary than the Gray, even if all the office workers were dead. They fell into step following Mr. Death through the maze of cubicles. Mal fell back somewhat. To watch her back, and possibly her butt definitely. She glanced back. Yep, he was doing both. Still looking so damned sexy it made her shiver, even with the blue skin. He was bigger, more powerful than ever, made more evident since he was shirtless. His shoulders rolled with every step, and he kept watch, a warrior. Yet he caught her look and gave her a wink, and she knew he'd probably do whatever she asked of him. He'd been fine with the idea she might have killed him. Told her the only place he belonged was at her side.

She couldn't let anything happen to him. Her stomach clenched at how much it would hurt when he left her. It didn't matter what they promised. Everyone always left her. When Mal found out the truth, he'd leave, too.

Mr. Death stopped in front of doublewide wood doors, turned the knob to open them, and gestured Mal and Nia inside.

Nia stepped in first, her boots sinking into plush carpeting. Lights came on with their entry, revealing a sparse if luxurious office with a massive black wood desk near one side, subtle carved skulls forming a border along the top. Black club chairs were clustered near an immense fireplace that flared to life when she looked at it. Curtains rose on three vast windows, which spanned the width of the room. Three windows. Three different views.

"Three windows to overlook the three realms where Death holds power." Mr. Death pointed at the one on the far left, with the pink sky, some soaring marble-sculptures. "Braelyn, home of the gods." He pointed to the window in the middle, one with a bright blue sky and soaring birds. "Your world, or the human mortal world." Finally, he pointed to the one on the far right, which featured a burning red sky and land below that looked like fire and brimstone. "Daimoleigh, the demon world that also contains a corner humans call Hell."

She checked out the three windows again. Stepped closer. The surface of the windows wasn't glass, but water. Really cool…but not her problem right now. She turned back to Mr. Death, crossing her arms over her chest. "Whose office are we in? Am I about to meet your boss?"

Mr. Death chuckled. "Hardly. No one has occupied this office for more than a thousand years. Not formally, anyway." He pointed out the window on the opposite side of the room, the one overlooking the cubicles. "Everyone out there does the real work, along with the reapers. We make sure people live their lives and die at their appointed time and according to plan."

"You mean fate?"

"I mean plan. We get word of what's expected about a day in advance, enough time to hand out the assignments, although there are occasionally some unexpected ones we get called in on."

Her head was trying to make sense of all this. "Which makes you…Death?"

"No, I'm a reaper. I do the business of death." He turned, tucking his hands in a pocket and walking over to look out the middle window over the human realm. "Most of us reapers were alive once. This is the human world branch. Since mortality is more common here, we're also the head branch, though there are offices in both Braelyn and Daimoleigh." He turned back, crossing his arms over his chest and leaning against the windowsill, crossing his ankles. "I'm assigned a sector, including Beckwell. We do all the work, reaping and assigning the souls, while you—or, pardon me, some nebulous figurehead called 'Death'—" here he used air quotes, "—gets all the credit."

Mal snorted. "I can see why you might be pissed." He padded across the carpet, sitting on the arm of one of the chairs.

"Thank you. You are unusual for a Fomorian." He snorted. "I suppose it's little surprise she—" he nodded in Nia's direction, "—recruited you."

"Hey, you two." Nia said, looking from one man to the other. "I didn't do anything wrong. I was born into the Death clan. I'm supposed to be a horsewoman, not any of this." She waved her hands to indicate the room and the three windows, which, frankly, kind of freaked her out. Realms and worlds, what the hell? Anna so did not have any of this in the Bigass Book of Scary. "I didn't recruit Mal. He—" Made her heart pound. Was willing to sacrifice everything for her. Made her wonder at the possibility of happy endings. "—just keeps hanging around."

"*He* is Fomorian, one of the few other species capable of walking the Gray without being dead. I've heard stories that Death used to employ Fomorian bodyguards for when he traversed the Gray."

Mal perked up, clearly interested and surprised by the news he could walk the Gray.

Nia kept her expression dark. See, that would have been useful information to have had earlier. She wouldn't have been terrified she'd accidentally killed Mal. Talk about killing the post-coital glow.

"So…Mal pulled us into the Gray? That's how we ended up there?"

Mr. Death raised a slim dark eyebrow above his spectacles. "Of course not. That's your ability, not his. I suspect you clumsily fell through the veils in a moment when your guard was down."

"People can't just fall through the veils between the worlds," she scoffed, squeezing her arms across her chest.

"Not ordinary mortals, who have a natural internal barrier that keeps them in their world. But, the veils are thinner in Braelyn owing to the traffic going through all the time from there into the mortal realm. And…" he paused, his dark gaze curious behind his spectacles, "you're broken."

Nia opened her mouth to swear at him, closed it.

"Hey, there's no need for that," Mal said, swaggering closer to Mr. Death, his skin growing bluer.

"No. It's fine. He's right," she said quietly and wrapped her trembling arms around herself more tightly. *Broken*. Not like she hadn't known it, hadn't thought it. If people had a natural resistance, maybe that's what Dad had broken with the necromancy books down in the basement.

Mr. Death studied her a moment before he cleared his throat and continued. "Death was never like the other horsemen. He joined the others out of duty, but death existed before and after his rise. He lasted long after the others, rejoining his normal routine. Then, maybe because we have it all handled, another Death never came around. The reapers had everything handled. We work from the machinery the original Death set up. We neither need nor want our absentee CEO."

"That's hardly my fault," Nia sputtered.

Mr. Death gave her a hard look. "Your clan didn't even bother to remember us or the rest of your duties. Hell, few members of your family ever get called up for reaper duty. You're untouchable, like rich children with no responsibility."

"Dude, you've told me more about the Death clan that Dad ever did, so back off, okay?"

She considered the desk, which looked like it'd been

made for some guy more Mal's Fomorian size. All the black, masculine furniture. Of all the ghosts multiplying out on her lawn and that had come after her, ever since Dad and his experiment. All the spirits in the Gray who'd tried to use her as a doorway, had even stolen her body and used it against her to try and access her ability. All the things she'd suffered because she'd been born Death clan, while this little twerp and undoubtedly the others in the office resented her and her clan. She was already responsible for her daughter, her horse, Mal, her friends. As Death, suddenly she'd be responsible for all these people too, these reapers and random office workers? What did that even mean, anyway? Being CEO of Death Corp?

Asha's face came to mind. Her little face and sparkling brown eyes. The feel of her skinny arms around Nia, the touch of her small cold fingers.

"Whoever rises, they'll have the power of resurrection?"

Mr. Death gave a small nod. "Yes. They'll be strongest in the Gray, where Death can create anything, and walk the byways of the Gray. But there's always a threat from the restless and dangerous beings who survive there, the lost and broken souls."

"Walk the Gray?" Her brain struggled to put it all together. So, wait…they'd ended up in what was the same Gray even from Braelyn. The soul devourer, the thing that chased her, it had sensed and followed her. "You mean, like you?"

Mr. Death's smile was slim. "No, not like me. Death is always at greater risk in the Gray, in any realm for that matter, because of the power they wield. Power other beings will always crave. Rogue demons, things far worse than the mad creature you just faced."

"Plus, you glow. Which really makes you stand out back there," Mal pointed out.

"I do not glow," she denied.

"Oh, you do." He nodded at the other man. "She does, doesn't she?"

"She does," Mr. Death agreed. Stupid, typical males taking the same side against her.

Nia satisfied herself with a glare, walking closer to the windows and taking in all three views through their watery panes. Death could view and walk all the realms. "The Gray connects them, doesn't it? The Gray is made of ether, and ether is between and in all things. That makes the Gray not just the place between the living and the dead, it's the place between the realms."

"Perhaps you're smarter than you look," Mr. Death said wryly from beside her.

She turned to him. "You better watch out. I might be your boss someday."

His smile was small, but for the first time since she'd met him, it had lost its hostile edge. "Only if you survive the gods and their machinations first. The office has been empty for a long time. It is likely to remain so."

"If it wasn't empty, if you did get a new boss, they'd have the whole force of this…Death Corp behind them?"

Mr. Death looked somewhat considering. "They might. If they could survive and prove themselves worthy."

Nia pushed back her shoulders and straightened to her full height, then stepped closer to Mr. Death. "Then listen up. Prep the legal team, start that paperwork. Because you're about to get a new boss, and I'm going to be kind of busy resurrecting the dead, so I'll need you to help out with the gods." She turned to Mal. "If you don't object, I think we'd better get back to Braelyn. We've got a prelim trial tomorrow."

CHAPTER 20

The next morning, Nia hadn't magically assumed Death's powers overnight. Which meant they really were stuck headed to the trial until she had a second to start practicing the new abilities she'd learned about and then kick some ass. Her stomach rolled as a group of angels, led by the white-robed chick Anna had ticked off, marched Nia and Mal through a winding maze of marble corridors to the courtroom for the preliminary trial. All the marble walls looked the same, and none of the soaring views of the city outside were familiar enough yet to orient herself. If she did make a run for it, she counted her chances of finding her way back to the room and Asha as damned slim.

Nia tried to smother a small yawn, tired with the little sleep she'd gotten after getting back from the Gray and Mr. Death's world, aka Death Corp. She wasn't the only one tired. Asha was as well, since it was too dangerous to allow her into the Gray to recharge last night. They'd have to let her back to the Gray soon, though, or Asha would become even weaker.

Fade even more.

Nia gulped, fully awake. By some miracle the dressing room was full of beautiful clothes, evidently for the gods to wear to fancy dress parties or something. Whatever the reason, it gave her daughter something to play with and hopefully occupy her until either Esther could check in on her, or Mal and Nia returned.

If Asha discovered the truth about her death, would she become one of those soul devourers? Would she become another mindless beast out to hunt Nia?

Her gaze sought out Mal, marching down the hall beside her. He had to be tired, too. He'd been up most of the night after they'd gotten back reviewing Anna's little book. "Building their case," he'd said. Which evidently didn't include much sleeping time.

She cringed as her stomach twinged. It had been turning somersaults all morning, leaving her unable to eat anything off the beautiful breakfast tray this morning. She'd only washed quickly, the reflection of the soul devourer pacing and snarling in the water in the sink. Pulling the plug as fast as possible, she'd changed out of the catsuit into a black tank top and simple black slacks she'd found in the bag Mal had brought.

They were usually clothes she'd layer under a whole bunch of other ones, but today it didn't matter as much if anyone else looked at her. She didn't have to hide from unwelcome touching, anyone else pointing out just how petite she was for the woman destined to become Death. All she cared about was if Mal looked at her.

She slid him another sideways glance. Damn him, anyway. Looking so stoic and cool, his strong jaw hard, eyes straight ahead. He'd made a simple toy for Asha out of one of the scarves from the closet, though no one had asked him to. It was just a little rag doll made with knots and drawn-on eyes, but it meant a kind of playmate for the child. The action had only further cemented him as a hero in her daughter's eyes.

Trouble was, it wasn't only Asha looking at him that way.

As though he'd sensed her gaze, he turned to look at her. Gave her a wink and a quick gone-too-soon grin.

She flicked her gaze away from him, her face burning. Again. Ugh. She kept blushing like a teenager. What was wrong with her?

Esther landed lightly on her shoulder, sending a cool wave of calm over Nia. Not enough to cool her face or get her brain back on track and not thinking about Mal, but no sense asking for miracles.

"Good...man," Esther managed inside Nia's head, the sound still a broken radio signal.

She stole another peek at him. Yeah, he was. Better than practically anyone gave him credit for. Including she suspected, himself.

Last night, their foray into the Gray had been unexpected—could she just have "fallen" through the veils and taken Mal with her? But it had given her so much more information than she'd expected. All the potential she'd learned about from Mr. Death, even if it meant her friends' plan to get her away wouldn't work.

Then there was the fact that she and Mal had slept together. Even without the ending-up-in-the-Gray part, it'd been world shattering. She could tell him it'd just been sex, but deep inside, she knew it'd been more. There'd been the same connection that they'd had when they were younger. For a moment, there'd even been the hope of something deeper, something more.

She scowled. She was racking up way too many debts she owed him. Too many to possibly repay. She needed to think of Asha, of gaining her Death abilities. No matter if last night had made her dream happy endings might be real, eventually Mal would leave. Just when she started to trust someone, care about them, like Bibiji, they'd leave. And if Mal found out the truth, he'd have reason to hate her, too. The worst part was that this time, opening herself up to someone else might not hurt only her. It could get Mal hurt. It could get him killed. The gods were frightened of her potential power, and they'd use that fear as justification to destroy her and anyone unlucky enough to be close to her.

Mal stalked down the hall after the white-robed prison guard, Nia at his side, half a dozen angel guards giving him the stink eye. Hell, rumors had questioned for years if a Fomorian was strong enough to take on an angel: similar weight, similar skills, similar nasty nature. Yeah, his skin was faintly blue, his muscles were Fomorian-big, and his mood was shitty after spending most of the night studying Anna's notes in that headache-inducing tiny writing and making more of his own in preparation for this morning. Adrenaline and instinct had his muscles prepped and itching for the fight he anticipated in court.

Nia looked too pale this morning.

His fingers dug into his palms as he and the angel next to him locked gazes. Between those winged jackasses and the god, she was scared enough that he hadn't been able to get her to smile when he'd winked.

She hadn't even sworn at him.

Could mean she was petrified.

Looking away from the angel, he continued reconnaissance of their path to the courtroom, in case they had to retrace it in a run. But either there were parts of the towering marble city outside identical to other parts, or they'd taken a circuitous and repetitive route specifically to throw them off and make it difficult to situate themselves.

He ground his teeth. Damn.

Asha had squeezed his hand again this morning.

They couldn't leave her behind. He was getting used to the kid, which was maybe why he could sometimes see a vague shape of her, like a partial shadow moving around the room. Did she look like Nia? Or did she look like the nameless father?

That just brought up the urge to punch the angels *and* the unknown father.

They approached two towering carved wood doors depicting a tree of life, along with writing in at least two different languages, neither of them being ones he recognized or could read.

He rolled his shoulders and focused on courtroom procedure instead of punching. Anna's notes fit with his experience, and his gut that said the gods would do whatever they could to speed through this preliminary in hopes of skipping to their favorite part: the execution.

The massive doors swung open, and a cacophony of voices and languages swam out toward them, many of them muddled as his translation charm struggled to keep up with the input.

Nia froze. Her face lost all color, and she looked like she'd either puke, pass out, or maybe both.

Ignoring the angels trying to shove him forward, he stopped dead beside her, took a deep breath until he could hold back some of the blue tint to his skin, then gently touched her chin until her gaze met his.

"Screw them. They're terrified of you. They should be. Remember that."

She stared at him a moment or two, but color crept up her cheekbones.

Electricity zinged back and forth between the two of them, reminding him of the heat of her body, her breathless cries when she'd come. They'd damn well make it through the day, because he had plans for a repeat performance.

Humor sparked in her eyes, despite her gray

complexion. "This you being a cheerleader?"

He raised a brow. Energy flowed through him, prepped him for the opening statement…and for the reward tonight when they got back to the room.

"I even have pompoms." He leaned in closer, his gaze finding her lips, then moving back to her eyes. His voice rasped, "If you're good, I'll show them to you."

More color tinted her face, and her pupils dilated. Her voice was equally husky. "I'd like that."

The urge to throw her over his shoulder and find somewhere private poured through him.

One of the angels gave Mal a poke with his ceremonial spear.

Mal grabbed the handle, jerked it out of the angel's hands, and threw it to the ground.

Swords slid free of scabbards.

He didn't look away from Nia, from her dark eyes, while he took in a breath and held it a second until the Fomorian quieted down enough for court. At least she wasn't noticing the rowdy crowd, or the angels who wanted to kill him.

"They'll want a reaction as they search for evidence of how you've broken their laws. Don't let them get to you. They won't hurt you today." Though they hadn't held back from intimidation tactics with the first jail cell. "We've got a few friends who've made sure of it. Screw them, right?"

"Ms. Amort, Mr. Quilan, if you please," the stiff-necked lady in the white robe said, color staining her cheekbones as she came up beside the angels and their drawn swords. Bastards couldn't hurt Mal yet, not until the trial had at least begun.

Nia started to turn toward the pissed-off angels, who she hadn't seemed to notice yet.

No sense freaking her out more. He quickly wrapped an arm around her, turning her and steering her through the doors, his hand in the small of her back. Even as his neck itched at the thought the armed angels were now behind him.

They moved into a soaring room with a blue sky, complete with birds and wind. Angels lined the front and back walls of the courtroom, not holding their swords at ready, but full of their usual menace. Dad used to tell Mal and Daniel only a stupid man turned his back on an angel. The pompous asses didn't care about honor, only their duty, and they were just as likely to stab someone in the back.

The room was also inhabited by a hell of a lot of people who filled the courtroom. The voices grew louder as he and Nia stepped in, more aggressive—that was probably his Fomorian side whipping them up.

He focused on the courtroom, set up like others he'd been in—minus the living sky—as well as the first and second balcony above. Plenty of witnesses, thanks to his brother, Anna, Loki, Ginny, Piper, and whoever else might have helped. They'd force the gods to play by the rules.

No seats were free, other than the humble scarred table and two chairs in front of the divider, which was a far cry from the marble slab table with chunky legs the prosecution enjoyed. All six of them. The gods' prosecution team included two beautiful women, one a green-skinned female with slicked-back Medusa hair, a gold guy who looked as if he were made of metal, the probably-a-guy with the black sphinx head, and, finally, Agent Bertram, who'd arrested Nia.

The courtroom quieted until it was almost easy to believe they were the only ones there.

Mal pulled out Nia's chair, the legs scraping the floor loudly. They sat only after everyone else did.

A small guy in white robes flew out on undersized wings from the other side of the room and blew on a horn.

Everyone climbed to their feet, including Nia and Mal.

It wasn't a single judge, but ten of them, representing each of the ten major mythologies experiencing the greatest current popularity. From Anna's research, USED operated a lot like the human UN…only with even more in-fighting and the occasional incineration. There was the guy in full wings with a halo. Another with blue skin and multiple arms. Two in togas. A Viking–looking dude. A male with a green-scaled snake head, yellow eyes, and a flicking forked tongue. A sphinx. An angel made of both snow and fire. A woman-sized Chinese dragon. And a guy who could have been Ganesh, with the elephant's head and multiple arms.

While some were quite human-like in appearance, others were more monstrous. Anna had warned him to expect that, too. These gods were more like middle management within their pantheons. The only similarity between all of them were the pure white robes…and the dark expressions on their faces, like someone had peed in their Goddios. No one liked cereal with yellow milk. A few glanced at the full seats, obviously discomfited.

Good. His lips almost curled upward. If he had his way, they'd continue to get a hell of a lot less comfortable. Anna figured the prelim would be an attempt to rattle he and Nia. Paint them as guilty from the start. People had been trying to make him feel guilty all his life, so what was new?

The harp played again, and one of the gods, the guy who looked like he was part snake, complete with green scaled skin, yellow eyes, and a forked tongue, leaned over the dais, as though he could barely see Mal and Nia from way up there.

"I am Judge Thesku, Head Judge in this trial. Defender Malcolm Quilan, you are marked in the court report as choosing to stand for the defendant, Petunia Amort, Death clan. We will first determine the validity of the case."

Mal rose to his feet. "In that case, your honor—" to hell with saying *your godship*, "—we move for dismissal on grounds of improper venue. This case should have proceeded through a circuit judge before ever proceeding this far, especially in a case of mortality and with a defendant with no prior criminal record. Furthermore, a case involving mortality seems inappropriate and out of your jurisdiction, when all in the court are otherwise immortal."

Judge Thesku quirked his head, forked tongue flicking a second. There was a brief discussion among the gods before Judge Thesku spoke. "Request denied. Defender Quilan, we find your causes for dismissal without merit. Yes, a defendant with no prior offenses and no direct threat against the realm would indeed usually have proceeded to circuit courts. However—" the snake looked too pleased with himself, and Mal's stomach tightened, "—such cannot be the case when the circuit judge is otherwise indisposed."

Mal didn't so much as blink. Call him suspicious, but he had a feeling something very bad had happened to the circuit judge. Not that the case ever would have been likely to have gone that route—this was about the gods' fear of the four horsewomen and hatred of anyone with even a pretense of power. Dismissal had been a long shot, but Anna had advised starting with it, and he agreed.

"Furthermore," Judge Thesku continued, "we are more than versed in the subject matter of mortality and the natural order, as we have in large part helped create the natural order. As such, we are more than capable of judging the defendant guilty." There was the slightest of heavy pauses. "If it should prove necessary."

Yeah, like that hadn't sounded like a thinly veiled threat. "Then you are undoubtedly aware Ms. Amort has committed no crimes other than the alleged resurrection of on Daphne Spinner. At the time, there is no clear evidence Ms. Spinner was fully dead, merely dying."

"Objection," came from the prosecution's side. The overeager blond brute, Agent Bertram, from the arrest. "Ms. Spinner had been shot multiple times. She was clearly deceased."

Mal turned to address the punk directly. "Is that your professional medical opinion? She was dying, not dead. Therefore, we suggest there was no crime, no breaking of the natural order."

The harp played again, which evidently meant "everyone shut up and listen to the judges."

The protests continued a while before the sound of steel scraping in scabbards seemed to quiet folks down.

Judge Thesku leaned forward again. "The specificity of Ms. Spinner's life status is of little note. Ms. Amort had the intent to resurrect."

Mal held up a hand and opened his mouth to interject.

Ol' Snake-y held up a green finger, and Mal's voice vanished. He turned his gold eyes on Nia, his forked tongue flicking again. "We have carefully examined the history of the defendant. From her early years, when she was a pawn between her parents. The trauma her father inflicted on her when he made her a bridge into the Gray left her damaged and broken, susceptible to weakness."

Nia twisted her hands together until her knuckles were white against the table.

Mal glared at the judge, heat whipping through him. Bastards probably knew about the water, too, since they seemed to know all of Nia's other secrets and were gleefully parading them out in court. He pounded a fist against the table.

Judge Thesku sighed, but Mal's voice returned to him.

"It isn't Ms. Amort's character on trial, nor is this a

trial, merely a preliminary," Mal snapped. "The evidence needs to be provided that Ms. Amort would have broken the laws of nature should Ms. Spinner have actually been dead."

The snake god stared at Mal for a moment or two, hints of what might have been a small smile turning up his lips. "Then let us turn to you, Malcolm Quilan, for the character of a Defender is indeed of import in determining the validity of the case. A history of petty crime before, ludicrously, joining a human police force. Where it is notable you failed, your failure resulting in the death of a child."

Mal squeezed his hands into fists at his side, forced himself to keep breathing, to not show any sign he'd just been sucker-punched in the gut. Anna hadn't warned him how much they might come after him besides the Fomorian thing and general history. Then again, she didn't know about the child. Nia's gaze burned him. Hell, could feel the gazes of everyone in the whole damned courtroom. He wanted to shout that, yeah, he damned well knew it was his fault and the guilt ate at him every day of his life. None of which would help Nia's case.

He took a calming breath. "Let the record show the child's name was Paul Loyer. He was five."

Murmurs rose in the courtroom and even some among the judges. The harp sounded, but no one seemed to notice it.

Nia leaned closer, "Mal, what are you doing? You're not helping," she whispered frantically.

Finally, someone found a gavel—more useful than the harp—and the sound brought the courtroom back under some semblance of control.

"You admit to responsibility in the death of this child?" Judge Thesku said, his gold gaze hungry for entrapment.

"I have never denied I feel responsible for his death,

but I was not the one who fired the weapon," Mal answered carefully. He'd been there. The Fomorian side had stirred up what should have been a small incident. "I would ask the court what this history has on the current case, especially at this stage?"

"All will become clear," was the reply. "Have you anything else to say in favor of the defendant?"

"I maintain no crime was committed, and therefore the case should be dismissed."

Unease roiled in Mal's belly when Judge Thesku flicked his tongue again and smiled before he turned to the prosecution. "As the Defender has nothing more he wishes to add, I turn it over to you, Procurator fiscal."

It was Agent Bertram who stood and nodded to one of the angels near the door. Two angels pushed in what for all appearance looked like a large gilded cage on wheels.

Curled up, clutching her knees in the middle of it, was Asha.

Blood pounded in his ears, his vision clouded momentarily with red.

The toddler was visible, from the top of her curly-haired little head, to her pink toes and pink kitten shirt. She saw her mother, climbed to her feet, and tried to reach her hand through the cage. There was a flash, and the child was flung back from the bars.

Nia made a small cry.

Her horse transformed from a moth to an owl and swooped toward the child. It turned back into a moth to fit between the bars but encountered a barrier. There was a brief flash, and the moth was gone.

Nia started to hyperventilate.

He opened his mouth to object.

Judge Thesku raised a hand and stole Mal's voice again.

Since grabbing one of the angel's swords, fighting

them off, and prying open the cage probably wouldn't end well, he forced himself to just grab Nia's hand and squeeze as gently as he could, when he'd rather have them around that snake's throat. How had they gotten Asha? How had they even known about her?

"We present the defendant's daughter, a spirit kept prisoner by her mother, the defendant," one of the prosecution said. It sounded like one of the women.

Mal didn't turn to look, couldn't look away from the tiny, whimpering child, who'd curled in the bottom of the cage again. Facing her mother, facing her one chance at salvation.

"We posit that given the opportunity, the defendant would use her abilities to distort the laws of nature again on the spirit's behalf. A dangerous and illegal activity."

She's just a child you assholes, he wanted to roar. Then get to work with a sword.

Maybe good he couldn't speak.

"The spirit was given away callously by her mother, the defendant, with no further regard for her welfare, also suggesting a marked lack of empathy." The prosecutor, indeed a woman in a sharp suit, marched in high heels across the marble floor, curling her lip as she glanced in at Asha as though she didn't even see a child. She waved a hand toward Nia. "We would suggest this pattern of behavior is the result of parental interference when she herself was young and believe this makes the defendant a high-risk offender in this situation."

Mal closed his eyes a second and ground his jaw. Because Nia had a fucking conscience and wanted to help her daughter, save anyone, she was on trial.

Nia was almost limp against him, crying, and there was nothing he could do.

"Furthermore, we would add for the court record further evidence of the nature of the Defender. Who abandoned the defendant and his unborn child. With his record of disreputable activities and Fomorian nature, it seems likely he could pose a significant danger to the mortal public and should be dealt with accordingly."

Mal stopped breathing. The woman rattled on with something more, more shit about his sins. His brain had frozen on the part about the unborn child.

Nia's unborn child.

Asha.

He was Asha's father.

Blood roared in his ears, the thud of his heart overwhelming all other sound.

Nia had stiffened at his side. She slowly looked up at him.

Nia. Who had never told him she was pregnant. Never told him there'd been a child. Never told him the child who held his hand, the child he was trying to save was also *his* child.

He dropped her hand because he was afraid of squeezing too hard. Too afraid he was losing complete control. Blue-gray swept over his features no matter how hard he tried for control, no matter all the lessons drilled into him.

Asha was his daughter.

Red crept into his narrow focus of vision that didn't see much more than the sweet child, his child in a cage and the skinny bitch who stepped between him and his little girl.

His hands shook, and he could feel the pain of horns trying to burst from his forehead. Never mind the trouble wings could pose.

An edgy, twitchy feeling filled him.

Nia had lied to him. She'd hidden his daughter from him. And if he was supposed to defend her.

Or they'd all die.

Oh helldamnshitfuck. Nia struggled to catch her

breath, and couldn't take her eyes off Asha. Her periphery caught Mal beside her, hands clenched, eyes closed. His skin had turned Fomorian blue-gray, and he was so disgusted with her he couldn't even bear to hold her hand. Asha was up in a fucking cage in the middle of the room. Esther had been vaporized into moth-dust. It was all Nia's fault. Because she hadn't told Mal the truth about Asha. Because she hadn't told anyone the truth.

If she'd told her friends that day in the house, before Daphne came, maybe they could have resurrected Asha then. Maybe none of this would have happened. They were right. She'd break every damned law there was if it meant saving Asha. Now she'd be found guilty and all of them punished for a law she'd never even broken.

She should have told Mal. She'd been terrified of his reaction. At first because what if he'd wanted a relationship? He could have said all the right words but eventually he'd have left her, broken and alone. Everyone always did if she didn't leave first or didn't keep her distance. After…what if Asha would love him more? Mal hadn't abandoned Asha. All he'd done was protect her. All the horrible things that had happened to Asha weren't Mal's fault.

There was a rising din of murmurs and discontent in the room, though she could still hear Asha's whimpers. Every one tore a strip off Nia's heart. Hell, what chance did she have of becoming Death? Maybe she didn't deserve the Death ability and responsibility. She shouldn't oversee Death Corp when she couldn't take care of Asha or Mal. She might have doomed them. There was no one else to ask for help. No one else she could involve.

"Give them a fair trial!" someone shouted from near the back, and the echo of such started to grow.

The voice penetrated her frozen shell of horror. A familiar voice. She had to turn, and sure enough, it looked like one of Beckwell's former mayors, Old Henry everyone called him. Except he looked kind of gold in color, dressed in flowing robes that wouldn't have blended in back at home. Wait, wasn't that the school janitor over there? Over there was Ginny's skinny dad, Mr. Lack, near the far wall. The more she looked, the more Beckwellians she could pick out. Somehow, people from home were not only here, they were here to support her. Her, the one they'd often been scared to let their kids play with because she was Death clan. The one who they'd always kept wide berth around. Yet when she needed them the most, here they were.

Here even though she hadn't asked them to be.

Oh, hell. She was going to have a Grinch moment soon, the way her heart seemed to swell. She blinked rapidly. Just call her green and melting. The tiniest glimmer of hope refused to die, even if it was stupid and impossible.

Maybe she could explain to Mal. Maybe...maybe he'd understand.

The volume rose until the gavel had to pound a few times. Doors opened, and angels marched in through the aisles, all of them holding their golden sword in front of them. That got people to settle down and quiet quickly.

The only judge who'd spoken, the snake guy, Judge Thesku, looked her over with one creepy tongue flick. "In light of recent evidence, the court has an offer for the defendant. Should the defendant plead guilty and no-contest to all charges, the spirit—" he waved a scale-y hand at Asha, "—will be returned home unharmed." There was the briefest pause. "The soul devourer will be halted."

Soul devourer. They could halt the soul devourer that hunted them? It meant Asha could recharge in the Gray safely. Maybe this was the answer. It didn't matter what happened to her, right? She should take the deal, for Asha's sake. She'd—

"The answer is no," Mal said, his voice booming and loud.

She jerked on his arm until he looked at her. "That isn't your decision to make," she growled.

"She's my daughter, too," he said, all the softness, all the kindness she'd grown used to seeing in his face gone. Then he turned back to the judge raising his voice to be heard. "The child will be released immediately. She's guilty of no crime."

"The spirit will be returned to the defendant's quarters but will be recalled when court is next in session. We find enough evidence to proceed with trial." Judge Thesku didn't give Mal a chance to object. He grabbed the gavel and pounded it hard. "This court is recessed." His lips turned up in a menacing smile as his yellow gaze fell on Mal and Nia. "We look forward to the trial tomorrow."

CHAPTER 21

Mal forced himself to wait until they were back in their room to confront Nia. The angels had left, Esther had reappeared, and Asha had been settled in the dressing room under Esther's watchful eye.

Why the fuck hadn't Nia told him about Asha?

She closed the door on the dressing room quietly, looking up through her lashes at him, small, petite, elfin little face. She'd lied to him through omission.

He jabbed a finger, indicating the bathroom for its magical soundproofing or whatever the hell Anna had done to it, and stalked ahead of her. He waited for her to precede him before he forced himself to close the door gently behind her. His belly knotted. The classical Greek columns and huge spa bath was all hard surfaces and marble, too hard on his knuckles and his strong urge to smash something.

Nia blew out a loud breath, lifting her heavy curls off her neck and shaking them out before she perched on the edge of the massive bath spa and glared at him first.

"Should we do rock, paper, scissors for who gets to go first? I'm getting a turn to demand what the hell right you think you had turning down that offer without even asking me first. Or, do you want to start giving me hell for not telling you about Asha?"

He growled low in his throat and leaned against the sink countertop, crossing his arms over his chest. "You're going to give me shit about turning down a bullshit offer? They were never going to let Asha go. Did you even consider that if they know about the soul devourer, there's a damned good chance they were the ones who sent it after you?"

She pressed her lips into a hard line for a moment or two. "You don't know that."

"You know otherwise? Look at the timing." He started checking them off on his fingers. "Rumors start about Piper, you get more powerful, and that thing starts coming after you. You think that's coincidence?"

She scowled down at her feet, rubbing the back of her neck. Her hair slid down and shielded her face, her shoulders hunched. "I...I just thought it was because of me. It's not the first." Her voice grew so quiet, he could barely hear her. "I thought that's why it was after Asha. Because of me."

Despite his anger, he softened his tone. "Nia, not everything is your fault."

She'd gone through all that shit alone, then blamed herself.

Of course, if she'd told him the truth, she wouldn't have been alone.

Nonetheless, he tried to coax a smile from her. "I mean, I know you're a badass and you're going to be in charge of the very state of death and all, but still. Not everything."

She peeked up at him through a curtain of hair before she pushed it back. "This isn't funny."

Dual urges to shout at her until she explained herself, or pull her into his arms and keep her safe warred with each other. He pushed off from the counter, came across the room and took a seat on the wide bath edge beside her, clasping his hands so he didn't touch her. His body perked up just being close to her, the warmth of her thigh brushing his, remembering his promise to show her his pompoms.

Yeah, well, that wasn't happening now.

"Fine. Everything's your fault. But if that thing was attracted to you, why'd it come after Asha? Why not the other kids? They didn't seem to be as at much risk."

"They're not. I just…I thought maybe because of the Death thing…maybe she'd inherited part of it or something."

Yeah, well, could be her part Fomorian side, too. His jaw tightened. "You thought it had to be your fault in some way."

Her narrow shoulders lifted in a shrug, and she avoided his gaze. "I…should have told you about her. I don't know if I could have back when I found out. We were together just once. I mean, talk about rotten luck, right?" Her smile was humorless and tinted with regret. She shrugged. "Then…then there was the thing with Dad."

His belly knotted. "The thing with Dad" being the horrible death her father had suffered. Descriptions of just how bad it'd been had whipped through town like wildfire. At the center of it, Nia. Who'd walked in to find what was left of her father's body.

But she'd chosen to do it alone. Hadn't wanted to have him around. Shit, she'd pushed him away as hard as she could. What could he have done differently?

Nia shrugged off what had to have been one of the worst moments of her life and continued. "I waited out the month until I left town. I didn't know I was pregnant until

I had to do a bunch of tests to commit myself. But…I could have told you about her since you found out she existed in the first place."

He snorted, clasping his hands loosely between his knees and, like her, looking down at the tiled floor. "No shit."

Weight settled over him like a heavy fog, squeezing his lungs. All this while he'd been up to useless shit, getting in trouble while she'd faced it all alone. Pregnant, orphaned, that garbage her father had pulled driving her insane. He should have been there. He should have been with her.

He *could* have been there if she'd told him. His Fomorian side said this was *his* woman and *his* child, damn worth battling for, worth dying for.

The more rational side of him said he maybe he hadn't deserved to know when he was a teenager, and she was protecting herself now.

The Fomorian snarled bullshit. She'd lied to him through omission, he'd lost something he didn't know he'd had, and she could have told him.

"Why didn't you? Tell me the truth the night you told me about Asha." His voice dropped, throat thick. "Didn't you trust me?"

Her gaze flashed up to his, then just as quickly away, color staining her cheekbones. "You'd been gone a long time."

He stared down at the tiles and clenched his jaw until it hurt. His fingers dug into his thighs, his lungs wringing out all the air, cutting off all ability to speak.

She might see him, but she didn't trust him. Not with Asha.

His Fomorian side bellowed and howled for blood.

Mal sucked in one breath. Two, until the spots didn't still do the hula in front of his eyes.

"Mal?" Nia whispered and touched his arm.

He flinched. "Just…give me a second," he ground out. His shoulders could have been turned to granite, and the breathing wasn't doing fuck all to shut up the side that wanted to rage. The side that wouldn't understand they needed to move forward, there was no back.

"I'm sorry. I'm so damned sorry," Nia said. Her voice fractured, and he looked up to meet her watery gaze.

She slammed her fingers over her lips, and shook her head, tears sliding down her face. "I-I screwed up. Big time. But I was just trying to protect her."

"When you were seventeen is one thing. But now? How was not telling me protecting her when I promised to help you bring her back?" he demanded, his voice harsh, growling.

She scrubbed the tears out of her eyes, hopped off the edge of the bathtub and got in his face. "I'm sorry. I am. But you're going to sit there and tell me you've never messed up? That you're fricking perfect?"

Her accusation punched him in the gut. "I'm not."

Nia crossed her arms over her chest, swiping at a getaway tear. "Gee, really convincing."

"A little boy died because of me."

The words slipped out without him quite meaning to, words to describe something he'd avoided talking about, couldn't stop thinking about that had haunted his nightmares for four long years. Now that they'd escaped, they refused to be caged to the clinical description in the reports he'd filed before he left the force.

Nia's brow furrowed, and she slowly returned to his side, perching on the edge of the empty walk-in tub.

The damp of that night, the way the red and blue lights from his patrol car had whirled in the dark fields dragging him back to the chill of four years ago, tightening his chest, chilling his fingers. "You know, if you do rise as Death, the first thing you should abolish is kids dying young. It's bullshit."

"I don't think I can."

He snorted. "Yeah, well, someone should. They don't deserve that pain. *He* didn't deserve it. Five years old. Three months from his sixth birthday when he was going to get that bike he'd been asking for." It was hard to swallow past the thickness in his throat.

"What happened?" Nia asked quietly.

The night was so black and clear, even the moon barely cast any light. It was only his headlights, picking out that group of teen thugs in their T-shirts and low-slung pants, pushing each other, messing around.

"Four years ago, I get dispatched out on this routine call to one of the reserves near the city. Two rival gangs, just stupid kids like I'd been. Backup was on the way, but I was there first, my shiny new corporal badge puffing up my head to think I could—or should—handle it on my own. See, I'd convinced myself the Fomorian side made me stronger. That I was in control of it, and not the other way around."

He sucked in a breath tinted with that night's foggy air, the scent of fresh cut hay. Those kids had come at him, and the Fomorian saw a fight. Got out of the cruiser. Said he was deescalating the situation, but the other side of him was itching for a fight.

"If it'd been someone else, maybe they could have deescalated it without incident. Maybe they would have called for backup, hell, scared the kids off just by showing up in the cruiser instead of making one of those rival gangs bolder, circling the cruiser. Maybe someone else wouldn't have missed that rifle that kid shot when I got in his face. He fired it to scare me. By the time I got him and half his friends down, weapon secured…" His voice faltered. "That's when the screaming started."

The fog that'd hung over the moon seemed to clear with the first piercing scream that shattered the night. It'd echoed and rung in his ears, sent a deep shiver tunneling down his spine.

His mouth was almost too dry to speak. "It was the mother in a nearby house. She'd gone in to check on her five-year-old son." He swallowed past the tightness closing his throat. "Paramedics said after it was quick. Maybe he didn't even feel anything."

Nia lifted her hands to his face, cupping his jaw, her thumb stroking over whiskers. "The young usually don't remember," she said softly. "If it happened quickly, he probably didn't feel anything."

He'd shouted at the kids to stay put, torn between dealing with them and investigating the screams. Backup came around the corner, and they were barely out of the car before he'd torn up the steps of the little house. Burst through the door, the blue glow of the TV in the living room. Down the narrow dark hall and into the back room, the only room with the bright light. And the mother kneeling on the bed cradling that tiny, limp body, blood all over her arms, the metallic hint of it in the air. The echoing pain of her screams.

"I've wondered so many times, if it hadn't been me that night—"

"Oh, Mal. You didn't fire the gun."

"But bad things follow me. You've seen what the Fomorian side does, the way it can get a crowd raging, almost as fast as Anna. Hell, I cause an 'incident' at the Senior Center practically every time I visit, just by walking through. The violence, the rage of the Fomorian side seems to bring it out in other people."

"You don't bring it out in me."

He snorted and gave her a sidelong look. "That's just your charming personality then?"

She punched him lightly in the arm before she wrapped her arms around his biceps and leaned against him. "I should have told you about her. You're right."

Heat flared inside as the Fomorian again howled.

Demanded to know how he could trust her when she'd kept something that big from him.

Yet, here she was, right after he'd confessed something that should make her hate him—hell, something that'd made him hate himself—and she seemed to accept him. Something inside shifted. His shoulders and muscles swelled, like he'd gone Fomorian without turning blue. To hell with the gods. To hell with all the reasons everyone had always said a Fomorian had to be one thing or another.

The ache inside wasn't ready to forgive her quite yet, but Nia would never find anyone who'd fight as hard for her. He was Fomorian: it was their raison d'etre. And pissed or not, protecting Nia was his meaning.

He caught her mouth in his and pressed an open-mouthed kiss to her lips. Tasted the salt of her tears on her lips, her fear, her regret, the sharp tart-sweet taste of her on his tongue. He wrapped his hand around the back of her head and angled his mouth to deepen the kiss. She might not believe him if he told her now, but he wanted to show her. How he'd protect her, body and soul, from this universe to the next. His hand slid around from her back to her front, cupping her breast. Heat flared, whipped around and between them.

She made a small mewling sound in her throat as his thumb found her nipple, massaging it to a hard peak. A tasty treat. He pressed kisses to the corner of her lips, working his way down her neck, toward his target, and leaving one hand to slip beneath her hem and unhook her bra while his other hand slid between her knees.

"Um, so, uh, this is nice and all," she said, voice high and breathy. "But…weren't we talking?"

"We need to have sex," he said, gently pinching and pulling her nipple while his hand found the apex of her thighs.

She chuckled, the sound turning to a moan as he

lifted her shirt and pulled her breast into his mouth. "Need…is, ah…ooh…a strong…word."

He broke away from her glistening nipple to meet her gaze, massaging the back of her neck. "The gods are going to cream us if given half a chance. It won't matter how good I am at defending you. They're never going to allow a not-guilty verdict. We go with Plan C." His fingers, meanwhile, rubbed slowly back and forth along the seam of her black pants, and her legs fell open to allow him better access.

She frowned, grabbed his hand a second, a heated flush staining her cheekbones as she forced her gaze to his. She licked her lips, narrowing her eyes as though struggling to focus. "Um, what?"

"Plan C. You rise as Death and kick all their asses." His free hand found her breast again.

She grabbed that one, too, blinking, her gaze unfocused, her voice raspy. "How does sex play into that?"

"Aunt Junie's Mr. Death seemed to think you were strongest in the Gray. Which means you need to fall through the veils again and take me with you. It will also make it harder for the gods to track what you're up to. We go there, you work on your abilities, you rise as Death."

"Okay. That part I get. But the sex?"

"Know a better—or more fun—way to get to the Gray?"

Her brows lifted. "Good point." She released his hands, probably so she could cup the bulge of his cock, not that he was complaining. "Let's get on with it then," she said, smiling against his lips.

ॐ

Good Parenting 101 probably said moms weren't supposed to leave their kid in the closet while running off to have sex and enter the Gray. Probably rules on rising as Death while being a full-time mom, too. Stupid rules.

But court would resume tomorrow, and Mal was right. This was their best method of getting to the Gray, especially when she couldn't think of any other way to get Mal there. Without the killing him part.

They'd barely come down from another earth-shattering climax—it'd been two for her this time since Mal was an overachiever—and she opened her eyes to find they'd arrived in the desolate, near-colorless landscape of the Gray. They'd taken care not to remove all their clothing this time, and Mal was recovering as she was, doing up buttons, zippers, and hooks. On the watch for the soul devourer.

They'd ended up in the same place as last time. There was the tower she'd built last time, resembling something out of the Stone Age, but whatever. It'd kind of worked.

A blood-freezing howl tore through the air.

"Want to magic me up a weapon of some kind? And fast, please?" Mal said, his wings flicking out and tensing as he did, those big leathery shapes kind of fascinating. He was so much larger here. Her mind wandered over what else might be larger, too.

Another bloodcurdling scream put her lust on pause.

"I thought you didn't trust magic," she teased, mostly to try not to think of the beast with too many eyes and teeth coming after them any second now. She closed her eyes, letting the feel of the ether soak into her, like sinking into a cold bathtub of water. Then she imagined the shape of the thing she wanted, the form solidifying like ice in her hand, first the handle, growing in weight as it gained the head, only it all happened almost faster than she could think of it. She opened her eyes and handed Mal the battle-ax that had materialized in her hand.

Mal took it, frowning at it, then her. "I'm sorry…what is this?"

"You weren't specific. It kind of goes with the wings and horns, don't you think?"

"I want a weapon, not a fashion accessory," he said, his voice flat.

A snarl came from nearby. Too close for comfort. She whipped around, searching for it in the shifting shadows, her palms damp, a sour taste in her mouth.

"Then what do you want? What do I know about weapons?"

The soul devourer screamed again, closer still, somewhere in the surrounding fog. She could sense it watching them. Stalking them.

Mal took a defensive position, the five-foot handle of the battle-ax clutched in his hands. "Make me a Benelli M4 Super 90 semi-automatic shotgun. That'll take down this bastard," he said, still moving on the balls of his feet, studying the thick fog.

"What?" She touched his shoulder and closed her eyes. Saw the weapon he'd envisioned in his head, and it appeared in her hand, heavy and icy cold. Huh. A big gun. Why didn't he just say a big gun?

There was movement, a flick of a dark tail, a flash of shining teeth about eight feet to their left.

"Here!" she said quickly, shoving the weapon into his hands.

This time it was Mal's teeth that glinted in a grin as he handed her the battle-ax, caressing the gun as he slid things into place, slotted other things upward with assurance. Just in time, too.

The soul devourer launched itself at Nia.

Mal stepped between them and the gun rained out thunder and lightning as it poured bullets into the monster.

This time the thing's scream was pained, and it disappeared again back into the fog.

Mal touched her hand. "More shells. Lots of them. A bandolier of them."

She picked up the vision of what he needed from his head, and almost as soon as they appeared in her hand he'd taken them, a strap of some kind that held them across his chest, other shotgun shells jammed into his pockets. He'd been serious about the "lots" part. There had to be almost a hundred shells altogether.

The soul devourer leaped at Nia again.

Mal pounded the thing with shells and it retreated, from the sounds of its cries, even farther away than it had the first time.

"Well? What are you waiting for?" He reloaded the weapon, still keeping watch and circling. "Start practicing your abilities. Get all powerful. I'll keep the soul devourer off us."

"I think it needs a different name. Like, Fluffy maybe. Something a lot less scary."

Fluffy roared and raced out of the fog without warning.

Mal spun and shot off what seemed like a million shots.

Fluffy raced off again.

"Nia, get to work," Mal growled, back to defense mode.

Yeah, great…but what did she try to do? She licked her lips. "It's not exactly easy to focus with that thing and all the noise your gun makes."

"I'll try to shoot it more quietly next time," he said dryly, his gaze piercing the shadows and fog surrounding them. "Get. To. Work."

Her hands dampened and her heart pounded. Yeah, okay. Pretend like she had any idea what she was doing. Pretend she wasn't starting to feel those warm and mushy feelings every time Mal looked her way, and already wondered just how much it would hurt when he left. Because he would. If she managed to somehow get them all out of Braelyn alive. She'd have to learn how to live like she had before. Alone. Hiding. It would be harder, going back after today had given her a tiny glimpse into a warm world of not alone, of partnership.

Of what life could be with Mal. If she let herself fully trust him and earned back his trust.

"Nia," Mal rumbled. Another scream, more booming shots.

She snapped her eyes closed, sank into the icy damp of the Gray, and pictured a castle. A big, stone, scary one. No, not a castle, a keep. With a drawbridge and a moat and a flag on top where she and Mal were standing looking out over—

"Holy shit!" Mal shouted, fighting for balance.

The world rumbled beneath their feet. Stone shot up out of the ground, lifting them as the keep she'd imagined assembled itself beneath them. Last to pop up was the flag flapping in nonexistent wind.

Fluffy screamed and snarled from far below them.

"Like to dream big, huh?" Mal said, taking a hesitant first step, then walked around examining the keep that was easily about twenty square feet, and probably more than double in height.

It wouldn't be easy for Fluffy to get them all the way up here. Or maybe at all. If she could create buildings, could she get rid of that thing, too? The soul devourer was an enraged soul, and if she was Death, that put her in charge of all the dead souls, enraged or otherwise. Didn't it?

Nia couldn't help it. She grinned at Mal. She'd done it. She'd done it. She'd built this. With her *mind*.

A small smile tugged at his lips. He hung his gun over his shoulder. "How about dreaming a door or something so we can get down into the keep and off this thing?"

Her face warmed, and she turned. Sure enough, no door. All she had to do was picture a kind of room on top, with a door that led to the stairs… They all started to appear as she thought of them. "There, smartass. How's—

"

"Nia!" The gray owl swooped through the sky, screeching and expanding, growing to the size of a flying horse. Esther. "Nia, it's after Asha."

CHAPTER 22

Mal hadn't needed any special powers to hear Nia's horse speak, clear as day, and tell him Nia's daughter was in danger while he was up here on the castle roof cracking jokes. He raced toward the door Nia had just built.

The Fomorian side claimed that little girl, said it was their daughter in danger.

The human part wasn't quite ready for all that meant. But was good with letting the frustration and confusion all build into the anger he hadn't quite forgotten yet and use it to fuel his strength.

"There's no time! Jump. I'll catch you," the owl said, even as it began to grow in size.

The soul devourer screeched again.

More chilling was the high, terrified scream of the little girl that followed, raising the hair on his neck, tightening his muscles.

Nia never hesitated. She raced toward the edge of the high keep and leaped.

He raced after her. He had wings, didn't know how to use them. He rarely went Fomorian enough that his wings popped, let alone gave him time to learn how to use them. He jumped, too.

They fell maybe five feet before they landed on the soft, warm, feathery bed that was the owl. Unfortunately, they'd hit hard and fast. And they were rolling.

The owl swept them toward the ground. "Can't…maintain…size," it gasped, shrinking back down to normal.

He was almost on the ground when he fell. He landed on his feet, Fomorian reflexes kicking in. Full-warrior mode, he tore toward the sound of the little girl's second scream.

At least if she could still scream, there was still time.

He ran faster than he knew he could run, more strength pulsing through him than he'd ever experienced. His heart pounded in time with every step, but he didn't get winded, only dug his feet in and picked up speed a little more. The anger of what he'd missed out on, of another child in danger, fueled him. He saw the glint of the battle-ax on the ground, swooped down to grab it, never breaking stride.

He had his eyes, vision sharper than ever, on the shadowy beast in front of him. Those unblinking dozens of eyes, rows of glistening razor teeth.

His gaze flicked to the small child cowering in a pink shirt and sweat pants, curly, black hair and big, dark eyes.

He forced himself to push harder, the scene in front of him playing out like a slow-motion car crash.

She tried to run but wasn't fast enough. She tripped, seemed almost dizzy, her movements clumsy. The beast mirrored her, always a few feet away, circling her.

His lip curled with realization. The monster was playing with her. It crept ever closer, increasing the scent of her terror. When it inhaled, bright light seemed to dance through the air from the child to it.

His heartbeat pounded in his ears. Geezus, it wasn't even touching her, and it was stealing something from her.

Devouring her.

Another inhale.

Asha wavered and fell to her knees.

The thing lowered its head like a wolf about to go in for the kill.

Nope. Not on his watch.

His muscles tightened, and his resolve solidified. Mal leaped, his wings flared behind him, lifting him higher, in sync with his intentions. He raised the battle-ax above his head. Brought it down to hit squarely in the center of the creature.

Maybe he made some sound. Maybe it sensed the movement behind him. It twisted and jerked aside. His ax drove deep down into hard-packed soil. He dropped it, reaching for the gun and firing at the monster. Placed himself between the monster and the child.

The beast snarled and snapped at him, staying farther back, farther from harm. Still circling Asha.

Nia ducked in past him, diving for Asha. She cradled their daughter in her arms.

The soul devourer snarled again then made the bloodcurdling howl, all those eyes narrowing in on mother and daughter.

Mal mirrored the monster, kept himself between that snarling maw and them. He fired at the monster again. No, not monster. Gave the bastard more power than it deserved. Nia called it Fluffy, like some overgrown pet. Fluffy was learning. It seemed to have some idea of the weapon's range and stayed clear. Sticky, purple blood oozed from its undulating shoulder blades, but it wouldn't back down.

Worse was the sound of answering howls in the distance. The soul devourer raised its head and called out a reply. Once. Twice. Then sprang again, trying to get over Mal's head.

He fired, backing closer to Nia and Asha, shielding them with his body.

The beast screeched and fell off to the side. It made a yipping, snarling sound.

At least two distinct replies yowled back from off in the surrounding mist. They were getting closer.

"We need an exit strategy. Now," he said tersely.

"On my back. We'll get away in the air," Esther said, the owl again growing and expanding to something the size of a horse. "I can get them a bit farther."

"Get them as far as you can." He lifted Nia and Asha onto the horse-sized owl. He kept half his gaze searching the mist around them and stretched his wings, kind of like rolling his shoulders. Time to see if they worked. "I'll try to keep up."

He turned to face the snarling soul devourer again, settling the gun in his hands. "If there's a way out, don't wait for me."

"Mal!" Nia cried as the owl leaped into the air and flapped its enormous wings. He caught a glimpse of her pale face and wide eyes before the owl's body blocked his view.

The soul devourer snarled and dove. Mal shot it out of the air, making the thing recoil from the bullets and land hard on its side.

But from the snarls rising behind him, its friends had just arrived.

Mal fitted the gun over his shoulder with the shoulder strap, flexed his wings again. Like another pair of limbs, he had control over those muscles and strength. His mouth settled into a dark smile. Hell, he wasn't just any old asshole with a gun. He was a Fomorian. They never went down without a fight and taking plenty of their enemies with them.

Two of the beasts leaped at him at the same time, and it seemed natural to jump into the air.

His wings flapped, like another muscle group he'd forgotten how to use, rusty from the disuse but still capable, still getting him higher. And higher. Shit. He kept going up, the beasts circling beneath him a little while. Then, as though they'd caught the scent, they and their wounded pack mate raced off in the direction Esther had headed.

Toward Nia and Asha.

He brought his arms and wings closer, and dove. He'd get there first. Fuck if he'd let Nia do this alone.

❧

Nia stared back at Mal as long as she could as darker shadowy copies of Fluffy emerged from the mist and encircled him, and then the mist swallowed any sight of him. They'd left him there. They'd left him there to die.

"We have to go back!" she screamed at Esther. It was her fault he was here. Her fault he'd dove in to protect her and Asha. While Nia had been powerless. She could create all the castles she wanted, but when it'd come down to it, and the soul devourer circled, her thoughts fell apart. She'd tried to create a wall around she and Asha but couldn't focus on any one idea, couldn't sink into the cold ether. All she could do was focus as Asha wheezed for air.

The owl shook her head. *"No. I...have to get...you two...to safety."* Her words were broken, almost as though she, too, gasped for breath, reduced to speaking telepathically even in the Gray.

Nia's chest hurt, and the sound of her heartbeat was like angry heavy metal music in her head.

Asha gasped, neck straining, her skin too pale and gray, her gasps shallow.

Heat burned Nia's eyes. What good were all the powers of Death if she couldn't do anything to protect and save her own daughter?

The owl began to flicker beneath them, like it usually did in the real world.

"Hold on!" Esther screeched. She stopped pumping her massive wings, and they glided, silent through the air a few more feet. Her form shimmered. The mist and the ground rose up to meet them. The owl stumbled and vanished.

Nia curled herself around Asha and held on tight, envisioning something soft as they fell.

She and Asha landed in the soft fluffiness of a pillow the size of a pickup.

There was a snarl out in the nearby gray mist, and an answering howl. Both much too close.

"We must get Asha out of the Gray," Esther said, fluttering next to Nia, back in moth form but, frighteningly, still flickering.

"How? I barely know how we got here, let alone how to get out!" she cried. Stupid, she'd been so stupid to come here without knowing how to get out. Could she just as easily fall through the veils? Worse, to leave Asha alone after what had happened this afternoon. When the child was weak, too likely to fall asleep and end up in the Gray unprotected.

"Think, betiya. How did you get here?"

Maybe it was because Esther reminded her of bibiji, but Nia flushed at the question. "Well, uh, Mal and I—"

"I don't mean *that*," Esther said, sounding almost as alarmed at the topic. "I mean, what is it about those times that allows you to get here? You've also come here when you contact water, and when you sleep."

When she slept, when she climaxed… What the hell was the same about either of those? How did it make her fall through the veils?

Asha moaned, tossing her head restlessly, her eyes closed, body limp. Nia was losing her. Asha's soul was fading.

There was another howl and snarl, the snap of the teeth nearby.

"Betiya, think!" Esther insisted again.

"I'm trying!" Similarity, what was the similarity... "I'm relaxed. That's it."

The low, prowling figure of one of Fluffy's twins emerged from the mist, rows of eyes all blinking, the teeth dripping saliva, the obsidian scales along muscled backs like snakeskin.

"I'm not feeling very relaxed right now!" Nia cried, just as another Fluffy triplet emerged on the other side of them. Oh, gods. They were surrounded. Those things were closing in.

The moth landed on Nia's shoulder. A sense of calm soaked through her, loosening the tight muscles in Nia's shoulders despite too many monsters, and way, *way* too many teeth.

One of them leaped. Nia hunched over Asha, curling her body over her daughter.

There was the sharp blast from a weapon, and the beast howled, falling away.

Wings flapped, making the mist whirl around them before Mal came down beside them, landing lightly on his feet. He fired at the second beast as it tried to leap. "What are you waiting for? Get us out of here!"

Esther pressed calm again over Nia, scented the air softly with jasmine tea.

Mal was there. He wouldn't let those things get to her or Asha. That thought was the only thing allowing Nia to close her eyes, kneel on the ground, and try to become calm, to enter a meditative state.

"Calm, I'm calm..." she murmured to herself.

The gun roared around another blast of shots.

No, she couldn't think of bullets. She had to think of calm. Of...

Wait...

She'd reached the crest of something. Just as she'd been able to see the ragged edges of Daphne's soul, she could see the edges of the Gray. It was like the Gray was made up of a whole bunch of them. Millions and millions of loose, tattered souls, millions of gossamer layers fluttering against each other. She could see them, could feel them parting as she reached her hand through, the brush of them like cool, damp silk against her fingers.

"Focus on where you want to go," Esther said, this time inside her head, the horse's voice soft and calm.

Nia thought of where she wanted to go. Somewhere safe. Somewhere her daughter wouldn't be chased and hunted. Somewhere she could trust the people around her, where there was some certainty of tomorrow. Somewhere Asha would be cared for. Somewhere they could try and make Asha well.

There. Just ahead of her, there was an opening, the layers like silk curtains rustling in a breeze.

"Mal, take my hand," Nia said, the sound of her voice making the image of what she saw flicker a second, but she held on tight, refused to let it go.

Warm fingers closed around hers and helped her to her feet, Asha over her shoulder. There was the sound of a gun firing, but it grew ever more distant as the gossamer layers folded over them, like settling beneath the water of a cool bath. They caught in her hair, pulled taut against her skin, and the air in her lungs tightened, as though she were holding her breath beneath water.

Then they stepped forward and emerged into a dim room. The only light came from the digital green numbers glowing from an appliance. The floor was hard and solid beneath their feet, and some glimmer of moonlight slid through the curtains over a small sitting area. The room was warm and welcoming compared to the damp of the Gray. Quiet snoring drew her attention to the dark shadowy form of a bed over to the left.

"Aunt Junie," Mal breathed quietly. "We're home."

CHAPTER 23

Mal did a quick pat down and back check to ensure, yep, he was in his regular body—no wings, no horns, no gun. He took a small step toward the bed, peering in the dim light. It was Aunt Junie all right, snoring softly. Her hair fell in loose silver waves around her head, prematurely gray, but there were more lines around her mouth and eyes. A certain soft vulnerability, her face empty of its usual vitality and life. She was still, the hollows in her cheeks too pronounced.

She'd done so much for him all through his life, and damn but he wanted a chance to make her proud. As much as he hated to think of it, she wasn't getting any younger. Someday, he'd lose her. What with the daughter he hadn't known about and potentially getting executed by the gods, making her proud in this lifetime seemed a lot less likely all the time.

"How did we get here?" he whispered to Nia.

Nia frowned at the sleeping older woman, Esther the moth on one of Nia's shoulders, Asha quiet and curled against Nia's other shoulder. Dark circles deepened Nia's eyes, and tension bracketed her lips. She adjusted Asha's weight, grimacing as she did so, her hands trembling. "I…I pictured somewhere safe. Somewhere we could take of Asha."

Asha. Big dark eyes, halo of dark curly hair, her skin a lighter bronze like his own. She wasn't as solid as a human would be, but he could see *her*, not just a shadow. Maybe part his Fomorian side, part seeing her fully in the Gray? From the way Nia held her, she had weight, too, enough that Nia looked ready to drop her.

Ma swallowed, then moved forward, hands out. "May I?"

Nia's eyes widened. "You can *see* her?"

"Yeah."

Nia's eyes were too dark to read in the dim light, her face all shadows. She hesitated a second, then nodded and allowed him to take the weight of Asha from her arms.

He gently lifted the weight of his daughter from Nia's arms. Asha was chilled, like her hands had been when he'd only been able to feel her. An electrical tingle skittered over his arms, raising his hairs with her slight weight, the reminder she didn't belong to this world. She had Nia's hair and eyes, nothing of him. She was too chill, her flesh pale, her breathing shallow and rapid. His throat tightened. She was in trouble.

What happened if a ghost died? Probably nothing good.

"Aunt Junie told me about the wendigo, a creature which feeds off souls. A pretty good description of the soul devourer. Maybe she can help," he whispered back. He moved forward to place a gentle hand on his aunt's shoulder, too boney, too fragile. When had Aunt Junie gotten old? Somehow, she'd always been that warm smile and loving arms, almost unchanged from what he remembered as a child. But he was a long way from childhood.

He shook her gently again. "Aunt Junie? It's Mal."

His aunt frowned in her sleep, turning away. Then her eyes opened. Her brow lowered again a moment before she leaned closer, peering at him in the dark.

"Malcolm?" she asked, as though confirming his identity. "Are you really here?"

"It's me, Aunt Junie. I'm sorry for waking you. I—we—need your help." He stepped back to give her some space.

She pushed back the blankets and stuck out first one small bare foot and then the other, the bare legs skinny where not concealed by her long flannel nightgown. After flicking on the bedside lamp and shoving her feet into a pair of slippers, she looked up at him with a smile and cupped his jaw, smiling like his showing up in her room in the middle of the night was perfectly normal. "What can I do for you then, Malcolm?"

His chest expanded, and warmth flooded him at the way she was, as ever, ready and willing to help however she could. That was Aunt Junie for you. Much more than an aunt, and always willing to see the best in him, even when no one else could.

Including himself.

He cleared his throat, thickened with gratitude and emotion, but before he could answer, Aunt Junie had turned to Nia.

"Hello, Nia. My, you've grown into such a lovely young woman. I can see why my Malcolm is so smitten." His aunt gave Nia a quick, warm hug before she pulled away, patted Nia's arm, and offered another welcoming smile.

Nia stood, frozen in place, like she wasn't sure what had just happened.

Now the heat was mostly rushing to his face. He could have been sixteen all over again.

Nia looked equally discomfited, pulling at the hem of her shirt and smoothing her hands down her slim fitting pants. "I, uh, hi! Sorry we kind of barged in on you."

"Oh, no trouble, no trouble," Aunt Junie said, turning back to Mal and raising her brow at him. "I'd hope you know I would always help you, however I can."

She reached forward and smoothed a dark curl back from Asha's forehead.

Mal just stared, exchanging a wide-eyed look with Nia. His aunt had said something about being able to see ghosts when he'd visited before, but she could *touch* Asha, too? Maybe it wasn't just his Fomorian side that gave him the ability to do the same.

"Poor little sweetie. She has her mother's hair, but I see her father here and there." Aunt Junie tsked and reached for Asha's slight form.

Mal held on a second longer than necessary because he still needed to keep Asha's little body close to his, to know she was here, and she was safe for now. Also, because what. The. Hell.

"How did— You don't even know who her father is," he sputtered, while his aunt cradled Asha and carried her over to the bed, pulling the covers up to the child's chin.

Some of the tension seemed to drain out of Asha, and maybe he imagined it, but it looked like she might have almost smiled and turned into his aunt's touch. Maybe she absorbed some of Aunt Junie's special kind of magic. Her love, too. She looked more like she was sleeping.

Tossing some of her long silver hair back over a shoulder, Aunt Junie perched on the edge of the bed and smoothed Asha's forehead, focusing on the child even as she answered.

"Oh, come, Malcolm. I'm not an idiot. You show up in the middle of the night with a child and you expect me to believe she isn't yours? I saw the way you looked at her." She cast a look back at he and Nia. "And the way you look at her mother."

He opened his mouth to say something but closed it; he was rendered speechless. He needed time to process. His parents sure the hell hadn't set a great example, he'd never planned to have kids. But now there was Asha. Plus, exactly how did he look at Asha? Maybe Aunt Junie really had put it together because even after all these years, he was still mooning over Nia Amort…and apparently being too obvious about it.

He raised his eyes and met Nia's dark gaze.

Amusement added a bright spark to her eyes, and there was the slightest smile on her face. She bit her lip a little, looking away, then meeting his gaze again.

What did she see when she looked at him? Did she see the kid he'd been, trying to play it cool, tossing paper airplanes in her direction and hoping she'd give him the time of day? Could she see what Aunt Junie saw, someone worthy, someone with a future worth looking forward to?

Someone she could trust with her heart and her daughter. She hadn't wanted to trust him with the truth. Would she ever have trusted him enough?

"Besides," Aunt Junie said, dragging him back into the present. "She has your elbows."

"Is there anything we can do to help her? I mean, do you know how?" Nia asked, her voice soft and raspy as she took a tentative step toward Aunt Junie. Her hand found Asha's arm under the blanket and gave it a gentle squeeze.

"Oh, my dear, I'm afraid that's well beyond my area of expertise. I can see she's failing. Can see the weakness in her. But beyond diagnoses I'm of little help. A wendigo did this, I expect?"

"A wendigo?" Nia asked, frowning.

"Aunt Junie gave me that name before. I think it's another name for the soul devourer, or Fluffy," Mal said.

"Then who can help?" Nia said softly.

"My friend Mr. Death might be able to. You've met him, haven't you? You're in the same business after all." Aunt Junie said this like Nia and Mr. Death were both dentists.

"Great! Can you give him a call?"

This was met with a frown. "Why, no. I thought…" Aunt Junie leaned closer to Nia. "You are the Death horsewoman, aren't you? I haven't gotten that confused? It happens sometimes, my getting confused. Or so I've been told."

"I, uh…" Nia's face flushed, and she pulled on a springy black curl. "I mean, technically…"

"Call him." Esther's voice, like a cold distant breeze but definitely audible, whispered through the room.

Mal's Fomorian side tensed, his hands fisted, and blue turned up in splotches along his forearms. Damn, but that was unsettling. He glanced at Nia, then Asha. Maybe a man could get used to anything, given the proper motivation.

℀

Nia's neck tightened, and the weight of the moth weighed on her shoulder like it was the owl perched there, along with the scent of jasmine tea. Esther pressed urgency to call him. To call Mr. Death. Evidently Esther was getting stronger if she could speak aloud in this world.

Mal's Aunt June looked around curiously, unfazed by the ghostly voice or freaked out like people usually were.

"Hello, is someone there?" The question seemed like she'd almost welcome the presence.

Yeah, well, maybe she'd only met the nice ghosts in the past. Even so, Nia had this crazy feeling Aunt June would probably welcome them with a warm hug and smile. Almost like she'd welcomed Nia. Even Mom had never been into hugs, what little Nia could remember of her before she'd left, then gone and met a semi head-on. Then when her abilities advanced and she read too much of a person's soul through touch, it'd been even more of a reason to avoid the things. Besides the people who had no business being all up in her face.

Except Aunt June's hug had been…nice. Surprising, yeah. But nice. Aunt June's essence matched her smile, her aura warm and golden, tinged with Caribbean blues and royal purples like a tropical beachside holiday. The hug had lifted some of the weight and fear off Nia's shoulders, however briefly. She'd never encountered anything or anyone like it. The love that woman had for Mal…most kids would be so lucky to see as much from a mother. Maybe that was what allowed her to ask the woman for help, as though a kind word and a warm hug really could make everything better.

"I said, call him," Esther repeated, her voice more wispy and ghostly than in the Gray, but no less audible.

"That's just Esther, my, er, horse," Nia said, hoping there was no need for a long explanation. She touched Asha's cheek, cool as ever to the touch, her breath still too fast. Not that she needed to breathe, but the soul was practiced in the symptoms of life the same way it held the shape of the body it had once possessed. "Esther, he doesn't like me, remember? Even if I did know how to call him, which I don't, he probably wouldn't come anyway."

"Oh, well that's nice. Does she like tea? I think I have a package of cookies here somewhere. I should make tea for when Mr. Death gets here," Aunt June said, rising and bustling over to her kitchenette with its single cupboard, sink, kettle, and microwave.

The moth fluttered off Nia's shoulder, and, barely flickering at all, though still semi-translucent, fluttered over the bed and landed lightly on Asha's hair. This time she spoke in Nia's head. *"She needs you. She needs all of you. You can't do this alone, betiya."*

Asha was more translucent, too.

Nia massaged her forehead where an Esther-shaped headache was forming. She wanted to shout that of course she could damned well do it on her own. It wasn't like either Mal or Aunt June could call Mr. Death. What did they know about saving Asha? He might not even know. He hadn't reattached Daphne's soul to her body, Nia had.

But then, she hadn't reached Asha in time in the Gray. Hadn't been able to focus enough to construct something or do anything other than cower while Mal and Esther did all the real work. Had spent her whole life avoiding water and her connection to ether…so she hadn't been able to use it when she'd needed to.

"You were frightened and protecting your child," Esther said, still in Nia's thoughts. *"Continue to protect her. Call him."*

"How?" Nia snapped, her voice cracking. How did she save Asha? How had she come this far only to keep messing up so badly, to be able to do so little to help her daughter?

"Use The Voice. Your Death voice ability," Esther said aloud this time, as though what she suggested were simple.

Using The Voice wasn't hard. Seeing people's reactions, the way they shied away from her even more after—like Daniel had, like even her friends had—that was the hard part. Her gaze found Mal's across the bed, every indication he'd heard Esther's suggestion.

He nodded, his blue gaze solemn.

She didn't want him to look at her like that after he heard The Voice. Even though that was stupid; it shouldn't matter. What they had between them, it wasn't real, it wouldn't last. Probably just the stress of the situation, their shared history…

The way he looked at her like she was the most beautiful woman he'd ever seen. The way he never once questioned her ability to became Death and was all-in to help her do it. The way he'd unquestioningly volunteered his life to act as her Defender and jumped off the side of a building and fought monsters to save Asha. Just the thought of it spilled warmth through her.

"Nia, please," Mal said, standing on one side of the bed, his hand resting near Asha's head on the pillow.

He'd leave her like everyone else did eventually. If she didn't get him killed before then. Hell, after what she'd kept from him, he was probably only around now because he had to be.

She closed her eyes and called to the darkness inside, the swell like cold water and the damp mist of the Gray. It was easier to connect to the ether all the time now, like allowing the cold water to envelope her until she could find the place where The Voice was, something she'd used to scare away weaker spirits and break up crowds occasionally, though frankly it'd never seemed especially useful otherwise.

"ER, MR. DEATH, I, UH, SUMMON YOU. PLEASE." The sound boomed through the room like thunder.

She'd barely finished speaking the words before the slim man appeared, in a striped white night shirt and cap. Plus his usual scowl.

"I might have been otherwise occupied," he said grumpily.

"Were you?" He had surprisingly knobby knees.

His glower deepened.

Nia whisked it aside with a quick movement of her hand. "You hate me, I'm not your boss, I don't deserve what I have, yada yada yada. Can we move on?" Her stomach quivered, and she frowned, tucking some hair behind both ears as she searched for the words. "I…I need your help. Can you help my daughter? Please?"

He gave her a long searching look before he nodded toward the bed. "She had a run-in with a soul devourer, I take it?"

"Yes. One has been stalking us for months now."

He gave Aunt June a nod in greeting but was all business as he approached the bed. He flicked a hand over his hair, and he was back in his usual dapper three-piece suit, complete with spectacles. He and Mal exchanged a look, as though Mal were giving him a non-verbal warning to be careful with Asha, before Mal stepped out of the way. "Probably not the same one. The crazed beasts don't make friends, even with each other. They don't usually stray too far out of their territory. She was marked, possibly you as well once the gods decided to get rid of you."

"I'm sorry, what?" Sorry, not sorry. She'd half-shouted that last part. "The gods did this?" They'd implied they knew about it in court. Mal had suggested they might have. To have marked Nia, that was fine. She was fair game. But Asha? Red fuzzed her vision for a moment or two. Her hands and jaw clenched until Esther fluttered over and settled on Nia's shoulder. Esther's calm and the scent of jasmine tea helped dull the red haze to merely murderous levels.

Mr. Death barely seemed to notice as he pressed a gentle hand to Asha's forehead and frowned. "Coming after you consistently, especially after a child, it's unusual behavior for them. They're creatures of hunger and rage, not reason and cunning. You, I mean, you're a couple of meals for them certainly," he said, tucking back the blanket to Asha's waist and picking up her hand, holding it to the light. "But a child this young? Hardly. They've fed from her before. And she's already fading from this world even without the attack. She's very weak."

Nia rushed forward. "We can do something, right? I can, I don't know, give her some of my energy or something?" She was grasping at straws, because while she'd seen spirits fade before, it was usually because of time, not an attack. If the soul devourers had been children, how could they attack one of their own?

"A soul graft is too risky." Mr. Death looked considering, then frowned. "But sharing some of the soul energy might work. For a time at any rate, but the damage is too extensive. I can see if I can find the marker the gods put on her, but even that I can't remove, only pass on. If she hadn't already been fading..." He shrugged. "I'm sorry, but you should probably prepare yourself."

Nia grabbed his arm and swung him around. There was that red hue again, creeping in at the edge of her vision. "No." Her voice was gravelly. "You take that marker, stick it on me, graft whatever the fuck you need to do, but she is not 'fading' and dying for good, we clear?"

Mal was right behind her, his warmth soaking into her, the promise he could tear this schmuck to pieces there, too.

Mr. Death didn't even glance at Mal. He looked down at her white fingers clutching his jacket sleeve, and a small tick started in his jaw before his gaze lifted to hers. "You may have acquired more abilities, but that does not make you Death," he said smoothly, a hint of hardness behind his words. "Even you can't just rebuild a soul. The universe requires balance and accounts whether you like it or not. She's turning back into the ether we're all made of, becoming part of the fabric that makes up the Gray.

Once the process starts, we can slow it down, but we can't stop it. *You* can't stop it."

"Then I bring her back to life. Give her soul a new body. That will help strengthen the soul again, won't it? Life?"

His brow flickered upward slightly, the only hint at what might have been surprise. "She doesn't have a body. It won't be that easy."

"I'll find, steal, or make a body. It would save her, right? A body?"

"It isn't—"

"TELL ME!" she roared, this time in the Death voice, the words reverberating around the walls, making the pictures rattle. To hell with all their rules. To hell with the gods. She would not lose Asha. She would not abandon her.

She would not lose Asha like she'd lost everyone else.

Mr. Death's lips compressed into a thin line before he straightened his spectacles. "Yes. The essence of life will make the soul stronger. Temporarily."

She dropped her grip on his arms, her fingers leaving creases in the expensive fabric. To hide her shaking hands.

"Good." She jerked her head toward Asha. "Get to it then. Take my soul energy, do whatever it is you need to do to slow down the deterioration. Then take the marker off her and put it on me."

"No, on me," Mal said, speaking up for the first time in a long time.

His words hardened a lump in her belly to stone. She turned to him. Gods, he was gorgeous, the way he looked, all broad and muscly. All mortal and human and killable. He hadn't tried to interrupt her rant, hadn't tried to take care of things for her. Hell, he hadn't told her to back down, either, which possibly would have been a good idea. Her heart hammered harder at the sight of him, and she could feel his, pounding in time with hers. Something, some feeling, swelled in her, so strong, so overwhelming, it threatened to engulf her. She tamped it down.

"No," she said softly, staring into those cobalt eyes.

His brow came down and his eyes narrowed. "I can defend—"

She stopped his words with a finger against those satiny lips. She leaned closer, sparks dancing between them, heating her core and zipping through her body. No, his aunt, his brother, they all loved him too much to lose him. He was too good of a man to lose his life because of her, with all the lies she'd told, the secrets she'd kept, the mistakes she'd made. She might lose him eventually, yeah. But it damned well wasn't going to be because he died.

"No," she said softly. "You said it yourself; I'm already easy to spot in the Gray anyway, right? What's one more target? I can take it."

His expression didn't soften. He lifted her hand from his lips, kissing it and then pressing it against his warm, hard chest, over the solid thud of his heart.

The healthy, living thud of his heart. Nope, no damned way was she going to let that stop.

"We spread out the risk between us. That's smarter."

"Well, tough shit. It's my way or the highway." She jerked a finger toward the door. "Highway's that way. What's your choice?"

Mr. Death cleared his throat. "If anyone is ready, I've located the mark and I'm ready to transfer it. Or would you rather waste all your time until the gods hunt you down themselves? They may have already noticed your absence, and they're not going to just let you go. Either of you."

"I'm ready," Nia said, giving Mal a hard look saying there would be serious consequences if he tried to interfere.

He scowled, a faint hint of blue flicking over his jawbones and along his forearms. But he raised his hands in defeat and stepped out of her way.

"Take a seat on the other side of the bed, please, opposite me," Mr. Death directed.

Nia did as he said, Asha unresponsive even with all the activity around her. Even with the sound of Nia's Death voice. Nia's heart squeezed, and she held out her hands. "'Kay. What's next?"

Mr. Death barely brushed over her hand, his fingers cool. "The mark is transferred. I'm not going to take any of your soul, just a bit of its energy. It will help refuel Asha's. But it won't last." His dark gaze, glinting behind the old-fashioned spectacles, was grim. "I've been around a long time, and I've never seen anyone bring a soul back from the dead. Not when they don't even have a body. Something can't be created out of nothing." He shook his head, lips tight. "There's so much you don't understand."

"Yeah, well, there's that saying about being better off not knowing, right? Ignorance is bliss, that's it. If I don't know how impossible it is, guess I can get the job done." If she could make a castle out of ether, maybe she could make a body for Asha.

He just shook his head, quite possibly rolling his eyes. "This will leave you rather fatigued. I'll take a bit from you, and then a bit from Aunt June's Fomorian."

"The Fomorian has a name. It's Mal," Mal said dryly, arms crossed over his chest.

The process, whatever it was Mr. Death did, was painless. She could see the energy, like a stream of silver and gold sparkles, float between her to Asha. The reaper repeated the process with Mal, and Asha's color and solidity continued to improve until, had someone not known differently, had her skin not remained so chilled, one might have even thought she was alive.

Nia chewed her lip. "Shouldn't she be waking up? Opening her eyes? She's stronger, right?"

"Stronger, yes, but still fatigued, still fading. She's sleeping." Mr. Death looked down at the child, his hand holding hers. "I can keep her here, out of the Gray in case the soul devourers are still waiting just on the other side. The longer she rests, the less it will deplete her energy."

The soul devourers, right on the other side and waiting. Set on Asha by the gods. If they could do that, who was to say they wouldn't do it again? A hint of red blurred her gaze again. She fought to tamp it down. For now. Those fuckers were toast.

"He's right, isn't he?" she said to Mal, his gaze coming up to meet hers. "We have to go back."

He gave her one short nod, his expression grim.

Go back to whatever the gods had planned for the actual trial. In the prelim they'd put her daughter in a cage like an animal. If that was their opening volley, tomorrow wasn't looking good.

Her stomach squeezed again, and her throat thickened.

"It's okay. Ask them," Esther said. The moth settled again on Nia's shoulder, with the grandma hug feeling. *"You're stronger with them. She will be safer here."*

When she'd been in the Gray, she'd tried to think of a safe place for Asha. After all the ways she'd sometimes wondered if coming back home had been a mistake, all the ways the locals had made it clear they weren't so sure having a Death heir among them was awesome-sauce, all of that, yet Beckwell was where she'd brought them all when she'd searched for haven. Here, in Beckwell, with Mal's loveable Aunt June and even Mr. Death—who was a lot less lovable—Asha was safe.

"I, uh." She had to clear her throat twice to get past the thickness, and she couldn't meet Mr. Death's gaze. Instead, she looked up and found herself the target of Aunt June's gentle, patient smile. Maybe that was what gave her the courage to ask for the favor, to depend on someone in a way she'd never really trusted anyone before. Until Mal. And now these two. "Can you take care of her?" Her voice was a soft rasp. She forced herself to turn to Mr. Death, who looked at her, expression unreadable. "Keep her safe?"

Aunt June squeezed her arm. "Of course, dear. She's family. Family takes care of family. No matter what."

Mr. Death didn't reply as quickly. Probably because the jerk wanted to see her squirm. He settled his dark spectacled gaze on her, studying her like a pinned bug. Asshole. Finally, though, he nodded.

Aww, damn. There went those warm squidgies, welling up inside her, settling over her, both weight and comfort. Two more people to add to her list of responsibilities. Two more people she needed to keep safe. But she couldn't face the gods while worrying about Asha, too. If things ended badly, at least she could go knowing Asha wasn't there to see it, and hopefully, somehow, might survive.

She and Mal both gave Asha a tender kiss on her forehead and whispered their love to her. Nia's eyes were stinging again, and she rubbed at them impatiently. What the hell. Seriously? She was not going to become a crier.

Esther settled on her shoulder. *"It's time to go, betiya. Time to face the gods and teach those monsters a lesson for what they've done to our Asha."*

This time, she wasn't alone as determination burned through her, burned through the moth. That same determination glowed in Mal's cobalt gaze. He nodded, his jaw hard. He held out a hand, and she reached for him.

"You said it," Nia murmured, before she let Esther calm her. Let Esther push away the flush of fury, the roiling unease that still wondered how the hell she was supposed to just assume Death powers and defeat the gods. Well, guess she'd figure that out later. Because she wasn't letting them take Asha, and she wasn't letting them take Mal. Nia parted the silken layers of the Gray, and they prepared for their return to Braelyn and the gods.

CHAPTER 24

Early dawn's pink light spilled in through the windows lining the hall, and Mal massaged the lump on his forehead where one of the angels had given him a good conk last night after he and Nia had returned to Braelyn. At least his horns had receded, and his skin was back to normal bronze, even though the Fomorian was still definitely ready for a fight, energy buzzing through his veins. He turned to one of the small army of angels marching him through more of Braelyn's endless marble hallways. Gave the guy a smirk and earned a dark look. Good. At least they knew he and Nia weren't going down without a fight in Act Two of the gods' revenge scheme. Unfortunately, giving the gods their comeuppance was beyond his pay grade. He'd have to let Nia do her thing.

Typical angels had polished their armor and their swords, and the seven who marched him along were all at least as big as he was. His lips twitched at the idea there were seven of them, like the seven dwarfs. The angel with the black eye swollen shut gave Mal a dirty look—Bruisy

Angel—who was accompanied by Pushy Angel, the guy with the staff who kept poking Mal in the back. Keeping pace were Broken Arm Angel, Bruised Jaw Angel, Bandaged Foot Angel, Broken Nose Angel, and Face Stitches Angel, all of whom Mal remembered in a vague sense after they'd all come after him. He sent them a hard grin at the thought he'd been the source of those bruises. Even angels couldn't take on a Fomorian and walk away unharmed.

Turned out a short visit with Aunt Junie had translated into missing a whole damned day in Braelyn. The gods and the angels weren't happy. Well, too damned bad. Neither was he. He was still determined to make sure they ended up more miserable than he was. Because he wasn't letting them take Nia down.

The gods were going to pay for the pain they'd caused Nia, and how they'd terrified and tortured Asha in that cage. Yes, he still wanted to be the hero, but if his experiences had taught him nothing, he wasn't the same kind of hero as Daniel. He was a Fomorian one. Which meant he probably did some dumb shit, pounded a few heads, but he was also too flipping stubborn to ever give up. Death and suffering be damned.

He scowled at yet another supposed idyllic view of that damned pink sky and their fake-looking buildings. Being back in Braelyn made his inner Fomorian grouchy. That, the whole Asha situation, her declining health, a night spent fighting soul devourers, and potential sleep deprivation might have contributed. Last night, after the punching match with the angels, he'd been tossed into one of those smooth blank prisons like the one they'd held Nia in when they first dragged her here. Hopefully his temper tantrum hadn't resulted in the same thing for Nia. At least he'd been able to have a few hours of sleep before reviewing the little book Anna had secreted him and preparing for the case. Facts and figures looked great on paper, but the gods were out to make a point: no one was more powerful than they were, and anyone who tried would be destroyed.

As they neared the massive courtroom doors, the buzz of voices reached his ears, far louder than it'd been for the prelim. When Bruisy Angel pushed open the doors, the noise got even louder.

It was a good thing Pushy Angel kept Mal headed in a relatively straight line, the others surrounding Mal like linebackers but blocking his line of sight.

Even with them on all sides, it was clear the enormous courtroom with its incredible sky ceiling was packed to the rafters with people. Some gods, but more of them looking relatively human. A lot of them very damned familiar. They were the outsiders, the gods and paranormals no one ever invited to the party. The Beckwellians. Here they all were. Ready for a very different kind of party.

Of course, as soon as he came in, maybe just with the Fomorian presence, the rowdiness level and potential for violence grew. Hecklers shouted louder. Protestors chanted with more vehemence.

Looked like he was going to get his chance to play the hero after all. To prove to Nia and all of them he wasn't just Daniel's evil twin. He was Malcolm Quilan, Defender. If this all ended up in making the ultimate sacrifice, maybe there was some redemption in there, maybe it evened out the tallies. Maybe it would make a difference for Nia and Asha, give them, his family, the added strength to fight.

The angels backed off, leaving him at the battered defense table. His heart stuttered. The empty table. Nia wasn't there.

☙

Nia kicked the angel in front of her in the ankle and elbowed the other one. She ignored the shaky uncertainty in her stomach, the sick feeling that hadn't allowed her to eat a bite again this morning. There were only four angels, and they were hardly trying, but damn it, she was pissed.

"Where is he?" she demanded, going in for another kick.

Stupid angel dodged that one about as easy as the last. One of them snickered.

Nia's lip curled back, and she prepared to use the Death voice on them. The stupid necklace trap they'd put on her burned like hell, leaving her doubled over and gasping.

Last night when she and Mal had stepped back through the veil from the Gray, the angels had been waiting for them. They'd thrown that damned gold necklace trap around her neck. It itched like hell and singed her skin if Esther approached. Then they'd locked her in her room, like she was a freaking kid. The last she'd seen of Mal was kicking and fighting the angels who were trying to take him before they'd dragged him out and the door had closed.

That was last night. She hadn't seen him since. Her chest ached. They couldn't have killed him, right? Because he was her Defender. He was supposed to suffer the same fate. She couldn't have lost him already. She couldn't have failed him like she'd failed Asha. That squidgy warm feeling inside, the one that could barely hold back a scream wondering where Mal was, if he was safe… That feeling was one she'd tried not to examine all that close, but she had a sinking feeling it was a four-letter word she'd never allowed herself to consider, let alone fall for.

That kind of four-letter word left you aching when you ended up alone.

It was the four-letter word that made her picture Mal's face, his smile, the twinkle in those cobalt eyes when he was up to mischief, which was pretty much most the time. It was the four-letter word that made her think she'd have been better off pushing him away when she still had a chance before it hurt so much she couldn't breathe when he left or when she lost him. It was the four-letter word making her insides swell with immense and mixed-up gratitude and guilt when he'd kissed Asha goodbye last night, the look on his face obvious he didn't know if they'd make it back.

Love. Bloody stinkin' love. The most dangerous four-letter word she'd ever encountered.

Her throat was thick, and she uttered only a few cuss words at the angels as they hauled her upright and then marched her out the door and toward the courtroom. Maybe she was on her own now. Maybe this was it. Maybe she'd really failed.

Esther in owl form flew at her side, swooping in at the angels, much to their irritation. Every time they swatted at her, she dematerialized so they couldn't hit her. It was almost enough to make Nia smile.

The owl spoke to Nia in her thoughts. *"Don't give up, betiya. There is always hope."*

Oh, yeah. That other deadly four-letter word.

⅓

The courtroom was in an uproar by the time Nia entered, led by her four angels, through the back from the door to the left of the bench. Her knees were weak, the sound made her head pound, and her stomach was rock hard. Holy crap. There were people packing the aisles, all four levels of the courtroom, since it looked like another mezzanine had been somehow added. She could barely crane her neck back far enough to see up there. They came in every hue and shape, with all sorts of added appendages and growths, like extra arms, tails, and horns.

Her hands trembled.

Most of them were wearing shirts black T-shirts reading "Justice for Death."

Huh…not sure that translated quite as well as they might have hoped, but the sentiment was there. Her ears rang with the immense noise of the crowd.

More angels packed the front of the room in front of the bench, probably to protect the gods. Another group of angels had been called in for crowd control, but they weren't having much luck of it as more people tried to push their way in. She was sandwiched between her four angels as they pushed and shoved their way toward her table.

She looked up.

Mal jumped to his feet out of the chair at the defense table.

She scrambled around the table and flung herself into his arms. Into the comforting warmth of his strong embrace, the spicy scent of him. His arms were hard bands around her, holding on to her as tightly as she did him.

"You're okay. They didn't hurt you. You're okay," she kept repeating, couldn't seem to make herself stop.

Finally, they pulled apart, or maybe he pulled back from her. She couldn't tell, didn't care, because at least he hadn't dropped his arms from around her. This way she could look up into his face, into those cobalt—

"What the hell?" Her fingers gingerly examined the purpling goose egg on his forehead. "What did they do? Who did this?"

Mal just shook his head then pulled her close and pressed his lips to hers.

The world, the noise, all vanished beneath the touch of his lips to hers. His heat melted through to thaw the ice built up inside, until she shivered in response. Desire flared through her, even as a smaller spot inside began to cry.

Damn that four-letter word and how vulnerable it made her.

His lips made her hope, made her dream, made her yearn for impossible things. This time he'd suffered a few bruises, but what about next time? The time after that? Even if they did survive this, even if he didn't leave her by choice, what if someone went after her through him?

She pulled back from the kiss, her face heating to the cheers around the room despite the repeated harp sound and a gavel. She smoothed the square outlines of his jaw, the soft prickle of whiskers beneath her fingertips, memorizing every plane. She leaned in close. "If things go badly, I'm going to push you through into the Gray. Mr. Death can find you there."

"Nia, I'm not running."

"Well, you should!"

"He doesn't have to. We have a solid case here," Anna said over the whistles and cheers. It sounded like someone had started a chant of "Justice for Death." The War horsewoman clambered clumsily over the stone barricade separating the lower gallery from the front portion of the courtroom.

Mal gave her a hand, half-lifting her the rest of the way so she didn't do a face-plant.

Anna grabbed Nia in a fierce hug. "We've gathered as many supporters as we can. I bullied Loki into getting a friend to transport me here pretty much the same afternoon I left. I couldn't risk the others coming, what with Piper's pregnancy and Ginny likely to be pregnant any moment." She glanced back at the galleries proudly. "There's widespread division all over the different communities. That's largely Loki's doing. Some of the gods are in on it, too, after Loki 'might' have suggested they had less power than they should because of those currently in charge."

"That mayhem could blow up in our faces," Mal said slowly. "We'll have to play it carefully."

Anna waved a hand. "Oh, that'll blow over. We've

divided support and antagonism mostly just to split the vote." She leaned closer and nodded toward the upper bench where the judges began to file in. "We've sown a little division in some of those hierarchies, too, put a bit of pressure on their verdict."

Mal cleared his throat. "Sown division…you mean tampered with the judges?"

Anna turned on him, her expression hard. She put her hands on her hips. "You think they're going to play fair? The crime Nia is accused of is bringing someone back to life. Let that sink in."

Mal raised his hands. "Fair point."

"What's our next move?" Nia's voice had risen, and her heart pounded, still in a kind-of-wanted-to-puke way, but with that faint hint of hope. Maybe there was a chance here. She stole a long glance at Mal.

"We'll get a chance to make an opening statement. Then, after the prosecution presents their case against you, we'll have a chance to present our case," Mal explained.

Anna nodded. "Yes, we've got very convincing evidence of the lack of threat you or any of the horsewomen pose, based on Piper and Ginny's actions, as well as historical evidence of past horsemen. The gods' entire case is based on their belief you subvert the natural laws and that you're dangerous to other gods and all the realms. We need to prove you're not. Next, we move on to Nia's actions themselves, the situation with the League and—"

Someone had finally found a suitably large, loud gavel, and they banged it on the upper bench. That, coupled with the angel muscle, got everyone to settle down.

Nia's heart pounded in her throat. It was a good thing she hadn't been able to eat this morning.

The harp played, and the judges took their seats.

They collectively glowered at Anna.

The angels started moving in.

"You better go," Mal said. He and Nia helped Anna back into the public side of the gallery.

It was the same snake-faced judge, Judge Thesku, in the center and apparently responsible for most of the talking. The guy made Nia's skin crawl.

"Now that the defendants have been recovered, we can continue with the trial," he said, giving Mal and Nia a cold glare.

Mal stood, prepared probably to give the opening statement Anna had talked about.

Judge Thesku's smile broadened, and he lifted a hand, freezing Mal. "Oh, I think the decision to flee criminal prosecution clearly makes your statement for you, Defender. Besides which, we're now behind schedule. We—" here he included the rest of the judges with a look down both sides of the bench, "—have concluded the trial process will be somewhat altered."

Mal's hands clenched at his sides.

Nia's stomach started doing somersaults again.

Judge Thesku indicated the prosecution. "You may begin presentation of your case."

This time it was the sphinx who came to his feet, his lion's tail extending from the back of his expensive double-breasted gray suit. "We would like to call our first witness. Will Defender Malcolm Quilan please step forward?"

CHAPTER 25

Adrenaline raced through Mal's body at the prosecutor's words, and he tamped it down before he turned full Fomorian. Tempting as it was, better to hold on to that card if they needed it. The distraction wouldn't help Nia. There had to still be a chance she could get out of this alive.

There were cries from the galleries, boos and hisses, cries of "cheat!" shouted at the judges' bench. The chant for "Justice for Death" was taken up again, louder than before.

It was all an indiscriminate thrum to Mal beyond the thud of his heart in his ears. He'd been called to the stand. A trap. His fingers were cold as he came to his feet, and there was a heavy feeling in his chest. Screw the gods. The more human and professional he looked, the worse it would make the gods look in front of all these witnesses.

"This is highly irregular," he said, facing Judge Thesku. He forced himself to think in official terms rather than a general WTF. "Objection to the opening statements being waived and procedure changes.”

“Overruled,” Judge Thesku said with a slight smile, his forked tongue flicking. “Having the defendants disappear mid-trial has allowed some…flexibility.”

Yeah, fuck you too, buddy. Mal nodded, because what the hell else was he supposed to do. He pushed back his chair, every movement precise, every moment stretched and taut.

Nia grabbed his hand and held on tight. Her eyes wide, face pale, her fingers trembled against his.

“Don’t go. Make up some reason you can’t go.” She turned to Anna. “The Defender can’t be called up, right? He’s supposed to be on my side. They’re breaking the rules. Tell Mal how to tell them they’re breaking the rules and he doesn’t have to go.”

Anna met his gaze above Nia’s head, her lips tight, the look in her eyes grim. “They’re the gods. They make the rules. Which seems to mean they can break them however they like.”

Nia turned back to him, her eyes shimmering. “Mal, please. You can’t.”

He lifted her hand to his lips and pressed a soft kiss there before he disentangled her from him. Too bad they hadn’t had time to figure things out, for her to finally trust him. For him to figure out the Asha situation.

“They’re just opening the trial. Screw them, remember?” He gave her a cheeky grin and a wink before he turned, his jaw and expression hardening as he strode toward the small witness box on the far side of the room, between the judges’ bench and the prosecution. Blood pounded through his veins. He could probably wring that snake-headed judge’s neck before they took him down, but there were too many angels and gods in the room to take them all out. The back of his neck itched, every inch of exposed skin vulnerable.

Anna would know what to do. She was the kind to

have a backup plan. Maybe this was what Nia needed. After all, there'd never been a chance they'd end up together, no happy ending in store for him. Not with all he'd done, not with all his sins. His own mother had never loved him. It was hard to see why anyone else could.

A sour taste filled his mouth as he took his seat and glared defiantly out at the judges and prosecution. Nia would make it out of here. Whatever happened, even if he didn't make it out of this, he knew she would. She was so much stronger and closer to becoming what she was meant to be than she knew. He could feel it, the heady perfume of power that wafted off her his Formorian side could pick up. He'd willingly sacrifice himself for her.

And for Asha. His insides pinched. Never had a chance to even get to know her. Never even figured out how what it meant that he was a father.

Yeah, well, maybe his sacrifice proved he wasn't an irredeemable asshole.

The sphinx in his expensive suit, hands behind his back, strolled across the courtroom toward Mal, taking his time as the angels and the judges struggled to get back control and silent the public.

"If you cannot maintain decorum, the public will be banned from this trial!" Judge Snakehead said.

"If you continue to bully innocent paranormals and think you're better than the rest of us, it won't matter whether we're banned. We won't stand for it. We stand for justice!" Someone from up in the one of the upper galleries shouted down. The crowd was so restless and angry, it was hard to see who had spoken specifically.

This got the crowd all stirred up again, and again the gavel was pounded and the angels moved in. Word was rebellion was spreading throughout the paranormal world. About time.

As order was resumed, the sphinx and Mal had time to take each other's measure. Sphinx were widely known for their intellect, although they were also very rare. Chances were this was the head of the gods' legal team.

Which did not mean good things for him.

The sphinx twitched an ear as he regarded Mal with his almost-human face. "Mr. Quilan. You are part Fomorian by birth, correct?"

"Yes."

"What is the nature of your relationship with Petunia Amort, Death clan?"

Even across the room, he tried to read Nia's expression. The nature of their relationship, huh? Tricky question. They had a history, where it seemed like his crush had been one-sided. They had a child together. Sometimes they drove each other nuts. He'd willingly lay down his life for her, and just recently, he'd wondered if maybe they could have had a chance. In another life, with different choices.

Maybe then she could have loved him like he loved her.

"We're old friends, and I'm her Defender." He sat back in the chair and rolled his shoulders to stretch out some of the tension.

The sphinx made a slight twisting of his lips, an attempt at a smile, his hands still behind his back. "That's all?"

"That's all."

"Well, then. As Defender, you accepted the possibility your life would be forfeit. We commend your willing sacrifice and generosity, however misplaced. You have performed admirably. And you will continue to fulfill your purpose." He brought his hand forward and opened his fingers.

Mal only had time to see the flash of light.

CHAPTER 26

Nia's breath clogged in her lungs. Time slowed and her throat ached with a suppressed scream. All she could see was Mal, looking at her the second before the light flashed and his body slumped in the chair. His head rolled back. His eyes still frozen open.

A million images of the way he smiled, the spark of humor in his eyes flitted through her mind. And the emptiness. The hollow, gnawing emptiness as her heart was wrenched out and flattened. It stole her voice, stole her ability to move.

Mal, slumped and growing pale.

In the dim background, a cry went up from the galleries. Esther screeched and swooped through the air toward him, as though to see for herself what Nia already knew.

He wasn't there. That tiny blue spark that was his soul was gone, stolen, thrown out into the ether. The temperature in the room dropped, a chill lifting the hair on her arms. Mal, beautiful, sweet, sexy Mal.

Dead.

She held her breath until her body forced her to wheeze inward. Dug into the rough wood table until blood pearled at the end of two fingers where she'd broken the nails.

The gallery went wild. There were shouts, even screams.

Anna pulled at Nia's arm. "They want you to bring him back to life. This will be their proof. That you're dangerous. That you're willing to contravene the natural order, contravene death."

Was she? Dangerous? Did she even have a choice in any of this?

Anna's voice, the shouts, it was all a dull roar against the thrum of her pulse in her ears, the rush of blood drowning it all out. All she could see was Mal's beautiful body, slumped over in the chair.

They'd *killed* him.

They'd killed him because he was her Defender, because he'd been stupid and generous enough to volunteer his life to defend hers. Look where that had gotten him. Dead. How could she go home now, with what they'd done to him? What would she tell Asha? What would she tell his brother, and Aunt June, and her friends?

Some of the audience began to charge the judges' bench. The angels marched forward, forming a protective ring around the gods. Almost blocking her view of Mal's body. The healthy bronze was rapidly fading from his skin. Any hint of life.

Her skin had turned icy, her insides almost as empty and hollowed out. Here she'd thought the worst thing that could happen was she'd open herself up, she might even start to care for him, and then he'd leave. He'd betray her. Like Mom and Bibiji had left. Like Dad had hurt her. Love meant pain.

How much more it hurt when he left her like this. When he died because she wasn't strong enough. Because they killed him.

Her eyes narrowed on the judges behind the bench, behind their army of angels, and blood began to pound through her veins. Because they'd killed him. He wouldn't have been here if they hadn't decided she and her friends needed to be punished for trying to become powerful, for somehow posing a threat to the gods when they couldn't have given a shit. She'd barely heard of Braelyn before this, let alone had any plans to take over, to cause problems.

That was then.

They'd tried to take Asha. They'd tried to take Mal. They were trying to break her. Why should the bullies always win while everyone else suffered?

Cold began to soak through her. First the damp cold of the ether, then the iciness of water, filling the hollowness inside. It spread up from the pit of her belly and the dark corners of her heart. It coalesced in her veins like a dark ominous fog, rising around her, sheltering her.

Nia climbed to her feet.

Today, things were going to be different.

Today, the bullies weren't going to win.

The courtroom was still in chaos. Some of the public were chanting about justice. Others were shouting at the gods. The angels and the judges were shouting for order. The gavel was like the thud of a heart.

The cold settled over her, clarified her vision, slowed her heart, and chilled her breath.

Esther flew through the room back from Mal on soundless wings. Her talons perched on Nia's shoulder, but neither they nor the weight were any bother.

Nia closed her eyes. She could see the edges of the veil and layers of ether forming Braelyn and keeping it apart from the other realms. She saw the brightly colored layers that were the living souls, the more muted colors of the dead.

Anna pulled on Nia's arm. "Don't. Please."

Nia turned, her eyes narrowing and then blinking around the fiery aura of the War horsewoman.

Anna's face crumpled, and tears streaked her face. "You…you can't do it."

"It isn't a choice." Nia gently pulled away, or maybe it was like she just dissolved the part of her Anna held, and re-solidified it later. The dark mist knew how. "I GUESS THEY'RE ABOUT TO GET WHAT THEY WISHED FOR," she said.

She had to get back to Asha. She wasn't going alone. To hell with letting them kill Mal and get away with it.

Esther rose into the air with a screech, flapping her wings but making no other sound as she swept around the room.

Nia walked through the crazed courtroom without hesitation, without stopping. She passed through any who got in her way, was too insubstantial to be held by any who tried to stop her. Until she reached Mal.

No. Beautiful Mal, this wasn't him, this was just his shell. She stepped through the witness box holding him until she stood in front of him and could gently lift his jaw and his lips to hers.

She pressed a kiss to his cool lips, but hers were colder. A breath sighed out between them, fogging the air. She closed her eyes and searched for him through every molecule of moisture, every river and sea, through all the veils and all the planes. Her search swept far and wide, both endless and over within moments.

She smiled as she found him and opened her eyes.

"RETURN, MAL. IT'S NOT TIME FOR YOU TO REST," she commanded with a whisper.

A streak of blue light flashed through the room and slammed into his body with such force, he jerked. He sucked in a breath and his eyes popped open. Pupils dilated and shrank in his deep blue eyes before they latched on to her.

She checked and secured the few ragged edges of the soul that hadn't attached themselves. She inspected his aura for health, ensured he hadn't brought anything back from wherever he'd been sent, but there were no ill effects.

He looked at her, blinked, his eyes narrowing in focus. He lifted a hand to touch her face, hesitated, then cupped her jaw, the warmth of him making her solid, making her real.

"Thanks," he said with a cheeky grin that held a small tremor.

The gavel pounded. It was hard to hear over the rest of the chaos of the room.

"Petunia Amort, Death clan, you have proved your dangerous nature. You have proved your willingness to subvert the natural order and balance of life and death with no care for the consequences," Judge Thesku roared, the look on his face triumphant.

Nia turned and stared at the judges, at the angels flanking them. All afraid of her and her friends. For what? She and the girls didn't want to take over the world. But maybe if fear and anger was the only way the gods knew how to hold onto power and they'd gotten away with it for so long, they'd never had reason to change.

They would now.

Mal stepped out of the witness box behind her, and though she didn't turn to see him, his warmth radiated toward her. His living, vibrant warmth. His aura brushed hers like sunshine.

She could see the veils now, see the pathway to the Gray and the ether. She stretched out her hand through the veils into the Gray, let the dampness of the ether soak into her skin, solidify into the weapon that had waited hundreds of years for her. Her fingers curled around the icy, worn handle, and like pulling it from water, she pulled it into the physical world, water droplets still clinging to the shaft. The wood grain beneath her fingers was worn smooth by generations, but the length was just right for her height, adjusting as it came into being, the sharp curved blade of the scythe gleaming. Death's scythe. Her scythe.

Nia's lips slowly curled up in a dark smile of her own. "Oh, yeah, asshole. You're toast now."

Judge Thesku's snakey smile wavered, ever so slightly.

"Neither my friends nor I ever wanted anything to do with your world or your power. But you think someone's always out to get you because that's how you live your lives." She cocked her head and raised a challenging brow. "Maybe it's time you learn why you shouldn't mess with Death or any of the four horsewomen."

The snake-faced judge leaned over the bench. "Just what are you going to do about it?"

Good question. The overwhelming knowledge of power wavered as Nia considered the army of angels throughout the room. She squeezed her hands together.

Esther screeched, swooped through the room, then toward the floor.

"Escape," she said in Nia's head. *"Hurry, betiya. No time to waste."*

Esther began to transform before she hit the ground. Growing, lengthening, and morphing until the two rubber tires hit the ground, the large chopper motorcycle all polished chrome and pale gray paint air-brushed with the image of a moth, an owl, and a skull. She pulled to a stop in front of Nia, the set of keys already in the ignition with a little skull key fob, the license plate reading "2DEAD." Like the scythe pulled from the Gray, small droplets of water clung to Esther, as though the ether had just been pulled through the doorway.

"Well, damn." Nia eyed the size of the thing. "Piper and Ginny both got cars. I get a bike?"

Esther gunned her engine. *"You get style."*

"Okay, climb on. Anna, you coming?" Nia called while she struggled to climb astride the bike.

Mal climbed on behind her.

Anna ran over, her lips a thin line, but perched on the back behind Mal, like she was riding sidesaddle.

"You can't possibly think you can just walk out of here," Judge Thesku sputtered. He whipped a hand toward the angels. "Arrest them. No. Kill them!"

The angels rushed toward them.

Nia used the tip of the scythe to slash a thin hole in the veil between this world and the Gray. Then with the Death voice, she whistled.

Spirits poured out of the Gray in a blur, faster than a rushing river. They filled the room and put themselves between Nia, her friends, and the angels. She'd have to put them back afterward, but whatever.

Esther gunned her engine again, a big rumbling sound that growled through the room, though barely louder than the cries of the spirits and the curses of the angels.

Nia tucked the end of the scythe into the little holder that supported the end and hooked on to the handle. Then she leaned forward, gripped the handlebars while Mal held on to her and Anna.

Esther squealed her tires on the marble floors as she skidded through the courtroom. The gallery emptied quickly as the public streamed out, too, getting away from the angry gods and even angrier spirits.

Esther aimed for the wall. Nia closed her eyes, guiding the bike through the layers of the veil, into the barren desolation of the Gray. Beyond that, home.

<h1 style="text-align:center">CHAPTER 27</h1>

Colder air rushed past them, a harsh winter wind biting through her thin shirt and slicking her hair against her head as Nia cut the small entrance from the Gray through the veils. They bounced through the damp layers onto slick, shining asphalt a few meters from the four-way stop in downtown Beckwell. Mal's warm arms around her were the only warmth in her body as they pulled into the gravel parking lot of the Senior Center and skidded to a stop beside the rear door. They'd left Asha in the care of Aunt June and Mr. Death, and they had to reach her immediately. Finish what she'd promised her daughter for too long now.

Nia scrambled off the bike, Mal and Anna doing the same. Anna was making horrible retching sounds, but there wasn't time to focus on her. She'd almost lost Mal today. She wouldn't lose anyone else, especially not Asha. She was running out of time.

Esther transformed out of bike form, the bike and the scythe vanishing. The owl screeched as she swooped in owl form ahead of Nia and they both stormed through the entrance of the Senior Center into the bright and deserted atrium. Must have been snack time, because even though it was late afternoon, there wasn't a senior citizen in range.

Nia's hands trembled, and she blinked back the image of Mal's cold and lifeless body. A shiver chased over her, and she clenched her fingers into fists. She couldn't survive that again. She'd brought Mal back to life alone. Surely, she could do the same for Asha. She'd make a body for Asha out of ether in the Gray.

No matter what people thought, death came alone. She refused to let any of her friends be hurt like Mal. Because what if she couldn't bring them back? No one else would be hurt because of her. She had to do this alone.

"Nia? Is that you? Hold up," the masculine voice called from behind her.

She glanced back, and for half a second, she thought it was Mal. No, the khaki dress pants and sedate polo were too boring for Mal. Daniel's smile was too soft, without Mal's sexy edge.

She slowed, just barely, but Daniel's long stride ate up the distance between them. She gestured toward the hall where, she hoped, his aunt was located. Appearing in the middle of the night in Aunt June's room before meant she'd have to read door labels to find the right one. One advantage of a small town. "I'm sorry. I've got to get to a meeting…" she said lamely. She couldn't look at him, and worse, she'd caught sight of Mal behind his brother, jogging to catch up.

"Nia, wait," Mal called.

She was too weak. She couldn't resist a momentary comparison of the two gorgeous men, at the contrast they made, Mal in dark denim, fitted charcoal shirt stretched over his pecs, and that leather jacket. Mal, who'd brought warmth and life back into her life when she'd almost forgotten what it could feel like. Her insides ached, and she turned away quickly, trying to cool her burning eyes. She caught only a glimpse of the brothers greeting to each other, the quick back pound.

It'd be okay. Mal would have Daniel. Mal could have anyone he wanted if they just looked at him for half a second longer and saw the incredible, heroic man she did. The man who'd literally fought monsters for her. The man who'd made a doll for Asha just to make her smile. The man who saw her completely, all the ugliness, and still looked at her like she was beautiful.

The man who'd died for her.

She pressed trembling lips together and squeezed her hands hard enough her nails dug into her palms. The coldness of Death's powers was draining out of her, leaving her reeling and trembling over all that had happened. Tears blurred her vision and she blinked them away, searching for Aunt June's name.

She left the Quilan men in her wake, rounding the bend in the hallway. Her stomach rolled, her throat ached, and she wanted to curl up in a ball somewhere and hide. Because, oh, hell, this was going to hurt. But she had to. She had to push away Mal for his own safety. For his very life. Because if it wasn't the gods coming after her, it'd be someone else. They'd die. They'd all die. He might be Fomorian, he might be strong, but he'd died all too easily today. Because of *her*.

She stopped dead, swiping at her eyes, trying to suck in calming breaths that weren't doing any good. Her shoulders heaved with the effort.

Fuckfuckfuckfuck. Which room was it? She couldn't even find Asha now?

Mal caught her shoulder gently, his hand slipping down her arm and his warm fingers tangling with hers. "This way. It's this one."

He didn't waste time or words, leading her quickly a few doors back. Mal rapped on the door, giving her fingers a squeeze.

She bit her lip against fresh tears. This wasn't time for crying. She didn't even like crying. She was doing the right thing. She had to be. It was safer for everyone if she did this on her own.

If she was on her own.

Daniel flanked her on the other side. "I just texted Piper. She's excited you're home. We've been feeding the kids, checking up on the place. I take it this means…you won?"

A tiny whimper escaped her lips.

Mal squeezed her hand harder. "No," he said, voice hard.

The door opened before Daniel could ask anything else, and there was Aunt June. Her face broke into a smile that traveled over both the twins, and she wrapped her arms around first Mal, then Daniel. "My boys!"

The back of Nia's throat burned, and she tried to duck around them and sneak into the room. Poor Aunt June, if she knew what had happened. Because of Nia.

Aunt June, not much taller than Nia, caught her in a quick hug and kept one arm around her as she led them all into the room, pausing near the entrance and pitching her voice low. "I'm glad you're all back so quickly. I've been telling Asha stories about her family. Well, her father's side," Aunt June said softly.

More inner somersaults. Nia gave Aunt June a wide-eyed, panicked look. She'd been dreading the "Asha, here's the father I kept from you" talk, but she didn't want anyone else to break the news first.

Aunt June must have picked up on it. She waved a hand. "I mean about my family." She leaned close and whispered. "I haven't said anything. Not my place." She raised her voice, and they moved toward the bed together.

"Asha, Mr. Death, look who it is," Aunt June said cheerfully.

The everything-will-be-okay smile came too easily to Nia's lips as she parted from Aunt June and perched on the edge of the bed. Asha's eyes were open, but she was still too translucent, her smile tired. Her hand, when Nia touched it, was not only cold, but just a shade thicker than fog.

"Hey, sweetie. I missed you. You about ready to head home now?" Was she already too late? What if her plan didn't work?

"Mommy, Aunt June and Mr. Death are funny," Asha said. "They told stories. We had cookies. And tea parties."

"A lot of tea parties, heavy on the cookies," Mr. Death said with an almost affectionate smile for the child. He had a hand on Asha's thin shoulder, and his look was telling as he met Nia's gaze.

Nia blinked to let the veil fall and she could see the energy transferring from Mr. Death to Asha. It seemed to wash through the child, very little of it sticking. Her aura was almost colorless and as wispy as the rest of her.

She fought for calm for a second or two. Her knees trembled.

Esther settled on her shoulder with a comforting hug feeling, but oh, hell, it still hurt. Her eyes burned.

She was losing Asha all over again. This time, there wouldn't be any bringing her back.

"Hey, peanut," Mal said, giving Nia's arm a squeeze as he took a seat on the bed next to her, his hand huge where it lightly lay on her hand. "Remember me? It's good to see you." He gave Asha a lopsided grin.

"Where are your wings?" she asked.

Mal frowned a second but figured it out a second before Nia did. "Oh, those. I only wear them on special occasions. You know, dinners out, trips to the Gray, that kind of thing." This he accompanied with a wink, and Asha grinned back, as though the two of them shared a private joke.

The light twinkled in their eyes the same way, and Asha's smile, the way one side was slightly higher than other, almost as though she knew something no one else did... Nia's breath caught. It was Mal's smile.

Mr. Death cleared his throat and extricated his hand. "You just hold Mr. Quilan's hand." He patted the connection, with a look at Mal that said not to let go. Then his gaze turned to Nia. "I think she's fine with the Fomorian for a second. Can I speak with you privately?" He stood, giving Asha a quick bow. "Thank you for the lovely tea and cookies, dear lady. I hope we may enjoy the same in the future."

Asha giggled at his silliness, and Mal whispered something to her that made her laugh.

Nia looked back at them as she followed Mr. Death out into the hall. She didn't need to talk to him. She already knew what he was going to say. Dreaded hearing him confirm it.

"Looks like you had an interesting night," he said, giving her a quick up and down. He quirked a brow.

"Spit it out. She's not getting better, is she?" Nia said quietly.

He sighed as he looked downward. "It's only been a few hours since you were here, but she's deteriorating more quickly than I'd anticipated. A bad combination of her previous fading and the soul devourer's attack. June and I have tried supplementing her strength, but whatever you plan on doing, I'd suggest you do it quickly."

Nia's throat burned, and all the air had been knocked from her lungs. She stared at the wall ahead of her as the mauve and beige panels faded in and out of focus.

Mr. Death's brow wrinkled. "For what it's worth, I'm sorry." He struck her a quick bow from the waist, then turned and left, walking through one of the walls, probably back to the Gray or maybe Death Corp, wherever reapers went.

Nia inhaled and exhaled as slowly as she could. There wasn't time for dramatics or feeling sorry for herself right now. That would be like defeat. That would mean she accepted the gods had won, and because of their machinations, she'd lose Asha. Nope. Not going to happen.

She straightened, grasped the doorknob, and let herself back into the room. "Okay, kiddo. Let's get going. I think we've kept Aunt June occupied for long enough." Probably should have called the woman Mrs. Benoit or whatever, but somehow, Aunt June just felt right.

She helped Asha out of the bed, and when the child stumbled, her knees going out from beneath her, Nia scooped her up and onto her shoulder.

Asha laid her head on Nia's shoulder without complaint, not even squirming to readjust herself like she usually would. It made Nia's knees weak, the pliability of the child.

"It'll feel good to be back in your own bed," she said, all false optimism and sincerity.

Mal rose, too. "I'll drive."

"Oh, Esther. Help me! I don't think I can do this," she communicated to her horse in panic. The moment had arrived. She had to do it. She had to push Mal away, and it would hurt, it would hurt so damned bad, but she had to, for his sake.

"Then don't do it, betiya," Esther scolded, her voice echoing through Nia's head. She settled into moth form on Nia's shoulder, a warm comforting squeeze, the soft scent of jasmine. *"You do need him. You need each other."*

"No. I can do this on my own. I have to."

"Betiya—"

"No! No one else dies because of me. Sticking around Death, he'll end up dead, too."

Esther fell silent.

Mal just watched her, his lips tight as he looked at Asha.

Nia took a quick step away from him, away from the temptation he was. "I— You should stay here. With your aunt."

Mal's gaze snapped back to her, his eyes narrowing. He took a step after her, blue-gray climbing up his neck and over his forearms. "No. I'm coming with you."

She scuttled back another step, like the coward she was. Her throat burned, and a tear slid down her face, dribbled down her chin. She shook her head, slowly. "You can't." Her voice was barely more than a whisper.

His jaw hardened. He closed the distance between them again, grasped her elbow gently when she tried to scramble away from him. "Nia, what's going on? Why are you doing this? You're going to need protection, backup." He leaned closer, pressing his forehead to hers. "I'll do anything you need."

She squeezed her eyes against the pain and struggled not to squeeze Asha too hard. She struggled for breath, for words, her throat too tight to speak for a few moments. Finally, she managed to force her eyes open, to pull back from Mal and meet his eyes. There was no stopping the tears now as they ran in hot rivulets down her face.

"Don't you get it? That's exactly the problem. You would give up anything to help me, to help Asha. And I..." Her voice cracked, again the image of how he'd looked, how lost she'd been when the gods had killed him. She shook her head, closing her eyes again for just a moment. "I can't lose you again."

She opened her eyes to stare back at him, the look in his cobalt gaze mutinous.

Blotches of blue-gray peppered his neck, giving

away the strong emotion he was obviously trying to hold back, and his jaw was tight.

"Who says it's your choice to make? You think you get to make all the choices about what I know and what I do?" He gave a hard look at Asha's back. His daughter's back. The daughter she'd kept secret from him.

Behind Mal, Daniel seemed to have purposely turned to stare out the window, while Aunt June, frowning, hands trembling, was cleaning up Asha's tea party on the bed. They'd be there for him. So long as Mal was alive, he could be around for them.

And when she'd brought Asha back, they'd all be there for her daughter. Because it wasn't safe for any of the living to be around her. The gods had made that clear.

She forced herself to meet Mal's gaze and pushed the words past her lips. "You're a good man, Mal. The best I've ever met, probably ever will. But the gods are going to come after me again, and what if I can't bring you back a second time?"

Mal caught the doorframe, gripping so hard his knuckles were white, and he dropped his gaze from hers, blue-gray splotches appearing on his whiskered jaw. "Then so be it."

"No. No, you don't get to decide that. I just…I can't!"

He lifted his gaze at her cry. "Then why do you get to decide it?" A hard edge tinged his words.

Even Asha managed to lift her head and frowned into Nia's eyes. "Don't be sad, Mama." She wiped at Nia's tears.

Somehow, she managed to force a watery smile.

"I'm not sad, sweetie." She met Mal's eyes over their daughter's head. "I have to do this alone. Then…then you'll get more time to get to know Asha, I promise. But please, Mal. I'm asking you as a friend. No, I'm begging you. Let me do this alone. I must do this alone. There is nothing to love about death."

Death had taken everything from her. Mom, Bibiji, Asha, even Mal, while she was left standing, alone in her pain. If she was alone, at least death couldn't take anyone else.

He leaned in close, his harsh whisper only for her ears. "This is bullshit. You call when you figure that out." Then he shrugged out of his leather jacket and stepped forward to wrap it around Asha's slight form. "Bye, Peanut. I'll see you later, 'kay?" he said, ruffling her dark curls and stepping back.

His gaze met Nia's again, pinning her in place. But he didn't move closer. He didn't reach for her.

She just shook her head. She had no words. She couldn't tell him how much he meant to her, that this was killing her, filling her belly with jagged shards of glass. Because he might come after her, and she couldn't let him. This time, she had to be the one to leave. For his sake, and even though he didn't know it yet, for Asha's, too.

She forced herself to turn. Then, carrying Asha and the weight of the universe on her shoulders, she raced for the door. Esther sent mute disapproval through their connection before she fluttered off, transforming as they stepped through the front doors and transformed back into the chopper bike. It was a good thing she could drive herself, since Nia couldn't see past all the tears.

CHAPTER 28

For fuck's sake. Mal glared at Nia as she half-ran down the hall as if the soul devourer was nipping at her fingers. He fisted his hands and gripped every ounce of willpower to let her and Asha go, even though every instinct he had told him not to let her walk out that door alone. Because she'd begged him. Nia Amort had begged him. His Formorian side said to hell with it; she was being an idiot and she needed him, she had no damned right to make this kind of decision for him, like she had keeping Asha from him.

For a second, the image of Mom came to mind. Her flouncing off inside after she'd thrown the bouquet he'd collected her on the ground, his little hands sticky and green, the flowers wilting and scattered around him. All those flowers, all his love, gathered up in a hopeful bouquet for her. Thrown back in his face.

He straightened. Yeah, not a little kid anymore.

"Oh, sweetie," Aunt Junie began, her voice soft.

He didn't avoid her hug but gave her a quick, hard

squeeze before backing out of it. The Fomorian wanted blood, alcohol, and violence. He wouldn't let Aunt Junie see that. "I've got some things I better deal with. But I'll pick up some fresh cookies and be back tomorrow, 'kay?" His smile felt hard and crumbly around the edges, just like the cookies he'd promised his aunt. He turned on his heel and headed for the door before she made him feel like a foolish little boy, looking for love in the wrong places.

Daniel's long stride caught up and kept pace in the halls and as they entered the wide, bright foyer of the Senior Center. No flying senior citizens today, either. A shame. Might have been a nice distraction.

"Want to talk?" Daniel said quietly.

"Nope," Mal bit out.

"What about a ride?"

"No. Back off." Mal stalked out of the Senior Center, the bracing sting of the cold sleet and the wind against his face welcome. Even if the leather jacket hadn't been warm enough for the weather, it'd been a hell of a lot better than his bare shirtsleeves were now. He paused a second, hands opening and fisting, his jaw clenched. The urge to chase Nia back to her place rode him hard.

Didn't have his bike, so couldn't get farther than his feet would carry him. Didn't want to go back inside. Aunt Junie and Daniel would just make the pain worse. Across the street warm light spilled out of the store, and just beyond, the welcoming porch and protective steel door of the bar, Loki's place. The red "open" sign flashed in the window like a siren's call.

He'd died today. Outrun the gods. Then been summarily dumped—if they'd ever been in a relationship in the first place. He deserved a beer. Hell, he deserved several beers, to get rip-roaring drunk and feel sorry for himself. Let the Fomorian loose.

He'd reached the four-way stop when a pickup truck barreled through without stopping.

He took off after it, boots slipping on black ice, but it hadn't passed the emergency station before Mal caught up with it, grabbed the door. The brakes squealed.

The driver inside, barely more than a teenager with scruffy beard and orange skin, someone Mal didn't recognize, looked wide-eyed at Mal, his hand fumbling as he rolled down the window. The driver gulped.

"It's a fucking stop sign. That means you stop," Mal snarled. "What if there'd been someone else going through? Kids playing? You want to be responsible for that?"

The orange-skinned kid's head bobbed obediently. "Yes, sir. I'm sorry, sir."

"This time's a warning. Next time you're looking at a ticket or worse. Got it?" Mal didn't have the authority to hand out tickets…but judging from the kid's wide eyes, kid didn't know that.

"Y-yes, sir."

Mal peeled his hands off the door, realized blue-gray had crept all the way up his arms, probably colored his entire face the way the adrenaline raced through him. "You get someone hurt, there's no going back from that, you understand? Now go on. But drive safe and obey the damn laws."

The kid did a good imitation of a bobblehead as he rolled up the window then slowly pulled away from Mal, barely doing more than thirty.

Mal's hands still shook as he watched the kid drive away, then moved to the side of the road as another car drove up to the four-way. This one stopped.

Stupid kid. Too damned young and invincible to think of what the consequences of breaking the law could lead to. The rules were there for a reason. What if there had been another person?

What if a kid had run out, a little kid, like Asha had been?

The thought set his jaw harder and dragged a growl out of his throat. Asha. Who Nia hadn't told him about. Little Asha, fighting for her fucking life while he stood around like a traffic cop. Where did Nia get off pushing him around like that? Didn't she get that it was his damned life and he could do what he wanted with it?

That he wanted to be there for her?

And shit. He wanted to be there for Asha, too.

His gaze was drawn to the blue metal building on the corner, maybe twenty feet away, opposite the bar and store. The windows were dark, but the large bulk of the white pickup hunched beside the emergency building. The ragged tarp someone had thrown over it flapped wildly in the wind, threatening to blow off into the road.

Well, shit. He could at least save the truck and any passing vehicles. He stalked toward the truck. The wind had shredded and pulled the tarp off the windshield and the front half of the truck, sending trapped autumn leaves racing for cover.

Sleet soaked his shirt to his back, trickling in icy rivulets down his neck. Mal jerked impatiently on the remains of the tarp, freeing the truck. The patrol vehicle Daniel had convinced Loki to buy, to give the town a local peace officer.

To give Mal a place where he belonged. To be what, a traffic cop?

The wind howled, fighting his grip. His lips drew back in a snarl, and he crushed the tarp into a ball between his hands, glared at the truck. The symbol of how he'd been supposed to come back to Beckwell, find the purpose he'd had with the RCMP that had died the night the little boy had.

Head down, melting snow dripping in his eyes, he stalked toward the building. The past few days, he'd been stupid enough to almost feel like he could become that man again, for Nia and Asha. Nia sure the hell didn't see it that way, though.

The blue metal building was little more than a glorified shed with "Beckwell Emergency" written on the sign over the white steel door. The two windows on either side showed no lights, and when he pulled on the door, it opened.

He shook his head at the trusting nature of some residents. Didn't they know rural crime was on a rise for this exact reason? As he stepped inside, the door closing behind him, it blocked out the wind, leaving only the sound of his harsh breath and water dripping onto the linoleum floor. His Fomorian vision kicked in, defining the room into shadowy forms rather than shapeless black. He hit the light, squinted as it stung his eyes, and tossed the tarp on a table beside the doors.

This was what was left for him, was it? A medium-sized room, four battered metal desks out front in a small office, around fifteen feet square. A couple of mismatched chairs…maybe that was the waiting area. A red backboard stood in one corner, and various medical supplies lined a metal shelf beside it, flanked by filing cabinet soldiers.

The deck of cards spread out over the two desks, two five-card hands laid facedown on their respective desks said just how busy it was around here for the volunteer paramedics.

Maybe this was the best he could hope for. Nia didn't want him. Asha didn't know he was her father. Geezus, how was she? He should be there. With them.

Restless, directionless anger stalked through him, propelled him farther into the room. Toward the door between the desks and filing cabinets that looked like it led back to more rooms in the back.

"Chief Quilan" was printed in neat white letters on the name plaque stuck to the door.

He swallowed, hard. Well, damn.

He hadn't been Corporal Quilan or any other kind of

police officer for some time now. Not since he'd turned in his badge and his gun two days after little Paul had been killed. Finished the hearing and investigation a week after Mom and Dad's funeral.

Still, his hand reached for the knob. He snorted when it turned easily in his hand. Yeah, well, they hadn't locked the front door, why lock this one?

This room was even darker than the outer one had been, and he flicked the switch. Stale fluorescent light revealed a basic office, maybe ten-feet square, with a bulletin board and window on one wall, white boards on another, some filing cabinets. A quality wood desk and nice office chair, two matching chairs in front of it. On the desk was a closed laptop, a stack of folded uniforms, and two pairs of shiny new black boots. Mal poked through the clothes. Two pairs dark green slacks, four undershirts, and four deep-green button-downs—two with short sleeves, two with long, all of them with dark green pocket flaps and a hint of gold braid.

He shivered, the cool room and his soaked clothes not helping the matter.

He considered the clothes again, then the room outside. Well, hell. He was cold, and the clothes were dry and warm. In case the paramedics did show up for work, he closed the office door and quickly changed. The slacks and the shirt were still stiff with starch, the creases sharp. They fit well.

The first time he'd put on a uniform, it'd been like dressing up in someone else's clothes, pretending to be someone else. Until the uniform and what it represented had started to represent him, too. Until it'd become important to live up to the uniform and what it meant.

He straightened. The heavy twill pulled at his shoulders, large enough to accommodate his bigger self. For the first time in four years, he fit into that uniform again.

Like maybe, just maybe, he belonged there, he deserved to be there.

Fuck, yeah, he deserved to be. Who else would be?

And who else would help Nia? And Asha. To hell with promising to back off. Nia was being an idiot, but he wouldn't let it cost her. Wouldn't let it cost Asha. He'd do the only damned thing he was good at—taking care of them.

He jerked open the door to the office.

Loki sat on the corner of one of the desks. This wasn't Lou, the plaid-loving big guy everyone generally liked and didn't worry about. This was Loki, in charcoal slacks and a dark green shirt, open a few buttons at the neck, muscular and of similar size to Mal, his hair dark and wavy.

Mal fisted his hands and bit back the temptation to make excuses, to explain his clothes had just been wet.

Loki looked Mal up and down, then nodded. "It looks good on you."

"You're spying on me now?"

The other man's lips curved upward slightly. "I prefer the term 'looking out for' rather than spying." He pushed off from the desk, sauntering closer. "I saw you from the bar when you stopped that truck. I wondered what you were doing."

"What were you doing out there? It's cold and snowing."

"Sleeting is the term, I believe. I was considering whether it would be wise to stop in on Anna, just to see how she was doing. She wouldn't listen to me when I advised her not to return to Braelyn for the trial. I'm just the villain. I can't imagine today was easy."

"They killed me. Nia rose as Death, we rode off on a chopper. Are you? A villain?" How much of this had Loki foreseen when he'd set Mal up as Nia's bodyguard? Maybe it was all that'd happened in such a short time, but it sure the hell felt a lot longer than a week since Nia had walked back into his life. A lifetime. The only life worth coming back to in more than four years.

Fine. Maybe he didn't know bupkis about bringing Asha back from the dead, but those soul devourers would be after them. Who'd have their backs?

Loki shrugged and tucked a hand into his pocket. "The state of my villainy or otherwise depends on who you ask." He looked up and met Mal's gaze directly. "Of course, the issue has always been whether you're the villain, isn't it?" He nodded at the uniform. "I hope this means you've figured out where you belong."

Mal shoved a hand back through his wet hair. "Look, it's been one hell of a day. I'm not up for riddles."

"Neither am I." Loki reached into his pocket and pulled out a jingling set of keys. He tossed them toward Mal.

Mal caught them one-handed.

Loki had already turned and was striding out of the building.

"What do I need these for? Is this a game?"

"They're the keys for the truck outside, dumbass. I expect a rural peace officer is useless if he has to run everyone down on foot. Even if he is a Fomorian. Best of luck, Malcolm."

The door closed behind the demigod.

Mal looked down at the keys in his hand. Was he the Beckwell peace officer?

Well, he had the uniform. He had the office. And wheels.

He turned back to the office. Spotted the dark green heavy winter coat hanging beside a closet. Went back for it and pulled it on, the down-filled warmth surrounding him.

He took a deep breath, the weight of the uniform on his shoulders. The rightness of it.

Maybe he was Beckwell's peace officer. Maybe he was finally ready for that.

Almost.

Nia and Asha needed him, whether they knew it or not. Hell, maybe even if Nia was ready for it or not. He could try to be patient, but he couldn't just sit around while they were in danger.

He stalked toward the door and headed outside to see if the truck started and just what kind of bribery could be bought at the corner store.

CHAPTER 29

When Nia, Esther, and Asha pulled into the driveway of her house, they were forced to dodge around the ghosts that almost formed a solid wall. Nia hugged Asha against her, the wind drying her tears as Esther wove through the ghosts. There were the usuals: the cowboy, the First Nations hunters and their elk, the mother and child among them. But there were a hell of lot more than that now. Some queued up at the front door, others wandered lost, dressed in clothes ranging from the medieval knight who didn't belong in Canada, to the hippies dancing in their bellbottoms. All of them turned to silently watch her cross the yard.

Only to find two vehicles pulled up at the front door. Ginny's horse, Roger, in his black ice-cream truck form, the license plate "2HUNGRY." Beside the black ice cream truck stood Piper's snot-green Porta Potty truck, Queenie, license plate "2SICK."

Her insides were raw and aching. She did not want freaking company, dead or otherwise.

She climbed off Esther, putting Asha on her shoulder, wrapped in the warmth of Mal's jacket. Nia's throat squeezed again at the image of him as he'd wrapped it around their daughter, the look in his eyes as she'd left him behind.

Esther flashed from chopper into owl form and swooped in front of Nia as she tried to climb the porch steps. *"Foolish! You need him, betiya. You both need him."*

Nia sidestepped the owl. "It's better this way. For everyone."

There was a flash of light, a shimmer in the air behind her, and the Porta Potty truck and the ice cream truck transformed into their respective animals. A skunk—Piper's horse, Queenie—and a black pig—Ginny's horse, Roger—climbed the steps behind Nia.

"Ooh, I smell a fight," Roger said inside her head, the first time she'd ever heard his voice, his hooves scrambling on the wood steps. *"What's wrong, my loves? Anyone call for a big black sausage?"* He winked at her in a way that said he wanted to get her to smile. Like a creepy guy.

Queenie the skunk tried to project warmth and kindness at Nia.

"Back off. All of you." Nia stomped past all three animals and reached for the front door. Esther in her head was more than enough without her friends' horses, too.

The knob was pulled out of her hand as Piper and Ginny answered, their faces wreathed in smiles.

"You're back!" they cried, practically in unison before they swarmed Nia and enveloped her in a smothering hug.

A hug that reminded her these were two more living people in danger because of her. Because she'd gone and pissed off the gods. She'd embarrassed them in their own home, proved she was as powerful as they feared, had run out on their so-called justice, and stirred unrest in the courtroom and the paranormal community. The gods would hunt her down and hurt anyone else who got too close. Even worse, the hug made her insides pinch again, and her eyes sting, all that warmth reminding her of Mal. Almost made her want to curl up with ice cream and these girls and tell them what had happened and let them make her feel better.

Until she'd wasted what little time Asha had.

Or the gods came, and her friends, just like Mal, ended up innocent bystanders and victims.

She wouldn't let death get them.

"Ugh, get off me," she grumbled, trying to summon her bitchiest voice. Not the one clogged by tears. She didn't have time for tears. She had to get to the Gray and get Asha into a body before anything else went to shit.

Her friends pulled back.

"We've fed the kids as best as we could," Ginny said. "I'm really getting the hang of the incinerator."

"I've been trying to take notes and stuff for Anna since she was gone, answer the phones, help coordinate things for Loki and Anna with everyone getting back to us and wanting to help," Piper said. "Louise Dole, the Fate who shot Daphne? She died yesterday. It's only Ms. Boniface left now. Plus, that crazy loon Daphne, who Loki has locked up."

Esther swooped over in owl form, the other animals nosing in between the women's legs. "Nia has pushed Malcolm away, and she needs your help. She needs all of you," Esther said aloud, her voice whispery, but from Piper and Ginny's widening eyes, they'd understood her just fine. Understood Esther just as Nia had understood their horses for the first time.

"Yeah, apparently it was this really crushing scene," Roger added telepathically.

Queenie tried to rub against Nia's leg.

Ginny and Piper turned to Nia, their expressions turning to confusion. "What happened between you and Mal?" Piper asked.

Ginny's eyes narrowed. "Do we need to 'talk' to him?" she said in an almost-Anna voice that was kind of terrifying.

But also, a good excuse to get rid of them. Nia edged around them, backing into the house. "Yeah, you know, that'd be great." Because she couldn't talk to them. She didn't have time. She glanced out at the spirits, who'd started moving toward the house. Shit. Chances were, it was going to get less safe and less comfortable around here quick.

She'd managed to shift her friends and their animals, so they'd switched places, and now Nia stood within the doorway alone with Asha. "Look, guys, maybe someday we can chat about this. Not today. Mal's at the Senior Center, though." She slammed the door in her friends' faces and flipped the locks.

There was a heartbeat before Piper pounded on the door. "Nia! What the hell, let us in."

Ginny joined her. "Nia, your owl says you need us. Let us help!"

Nia leaned against the door a second, hugging Asha against her chest. Her fingers trembled, and she closed her eyes, one stupid tear escaping all over again. Then time was up on her break, and she pushed off from the door.

"I'm sorry, guys. I can't let anything happen to you. I have to do this on my own. I can't let me being Death hurt you."

Her kids started to swarm her then. Asking about where she'd been, what was wrong with Asha, telling her stories about the interesting people who'd been in the house and a million other things. She tried to murmur the right things, making her way up the stairs, up to her room. Told them she loved them, would talk to them later.

If there was a later.

Reaching her bedroom, she closed the door on them, too. Closed them out, lying to her kids and telling them she just needed a moment alone.

She took Asha to the bed and laid her down, smoothing back her daughter's dark hair.

Asha's eyes opened, their shade grayer than brown. "Am I going to be okay, Mommy?"

Nia smoothed Asha's forehead and tried to smile, refused to let any more tears fall. "Of course, sweetie. You don't think I'd let anything happen to you, do you?"

"But—"

"Shh, it's going to be okay, baby. I promise."

Asha settled back against the pillows, her eyes like dark bruises.

Nia held her hand, then blinked aside the veil to see Asha, to try and see her soul, but it was pale and waning still. Struggling to swallow back her rising panic, Nia pressed a soft kiss to Asha's cold forehead. Okay, first she'd try like she'd done with Mal. She let the cold Death ability well up through her, fill her body, then she leaned over Asha, her voice like a cold mist.

"LIVE," she whispered in Death's voice.

"But, Mama…" Asha began.

"I'm trying to figure this out, Asha. Just give me a second. I've got this, I promise, I've got this."

Except, did she? This meant she had to risk taking Asha to the Gray, where Nia could build a body out of ether, since Nia was pretty sure you couldn't order a body online, even with Prime.

She lifted Asha into her arms, reached through the air, and tried to feel the edges of the veils, to create the doorway into the Gray.

Slicing her hand through the air with no effect. She couldn't feel the cold or damp of the veils.

She tried again.

Nada. Her heartbeat started to race.

The moth fluttered through the door, flickering as it did so before solidifying and then growing into owl form. Esther perched on the corner of the dresser and glared at her. The scent of singed jasmine tea floated through the room.

"What? You don't think I'm trying to help her? I'm Death. If anyone can bring her back, it's me. Besides, the closer they are to me, the more danger they're in. This is for their own good."

Esther still glared.

Nia tried slashing her hand through the realms again. Still nothing. "Remember my scythe? It'd be really handy about now, if you hadn't made it vanish when you transformed out of a bike." When that didn't work, she tried focusing, tried to see the edges of the veils. But her heart pounded too hard, and Asha's fingers were too cold in Nia's. Was Asha getting more translucent all the time? Nia couldn't see any damned veils, just her own hand waving around. No water, no cold, no ether, no Death abilities. Tears pinched her eyes, her breath came in fast huffs.

Esther hooted softly, then took flight, swooping down to land beside Nia on the bed. She walked over and stood on Nia's thigh.

The calm soaked over Nia. Slowed her heartbeat until she could see the micro thin silky veils of reality rustling against each other, overlaying each other and keeping this world apart from the others. Until she could feel the damp slide of ether in the veils, wafting through from the Gray, could sink into the ether and let it guide her. She slid her hand between the damp silken curtains, easily making a small portal she could step through, carrying Asha with her.

She knelt on the ground, Asha leaning against her.

From there, it was easy to picture a solid body for the

child. The same proportions, the same size, built from the ether of the Gray. The damp ether solidified first into an icy form, then a diaphanous body.

A howl came from nearby.

A growl from in the mist to Nia's left.

The diaphanous form rippled, losing stability.

She licked her lips. Okay. She could do this. She closed her eyes, let the ether flow over her like water, let it enclose her as she formed the body.

The growl grew closer.

Esther grew, holding her wings over them as she shrieked her warning. "Hurry, betiya. Hurry."

Nia opened her eyes, lifted Asha, and set her down in the body. Tried to connect the two. But…there was nothing to connect. She set Asha down and the ether body collapsed into mist.

The snarling grew louder. Something leaped.

Nia swept a high wall up, up, up around them, towering to an impossible height and surrounding them on all sides. She scraped more ether together. Again, formed another body. She must have done something wrong the first time. She could figure it out. She chafed her hands against her thighs, her fingers almost numb from the cold of forming the ether.

Howling and scratching from outside, then the sound of claws scaling her wall.

She swept a roof over them, blocking out the light until it was only her own glow providing light to see her trembling hands, Asha's pale form, and Esther's worried expression as she looked upward.

There. It looked like a little child. Nia bit her lip and again tried lifting and putting Asha over the body. Seeing the edges and trying to take it to the body, as she'd done with Daphne.

Only…it was like there was nothing to tack it to.

Again, the body collapsed into damp mist, returned

to ether.

More howling. Clawing on the outside of the tower. Pebbles and pieces of dislodged stone showered down on them as Nia again tried to build a body. How hard could this be?

Maybe, maybe she needed to combine what she'd done with Mal and the new body thing.

This time, as she lowered Asha into the body, she willed life into her daughter.

"LIVE," she commanded.

For a second, there were edges she could almost attach to the soul. A bit of something to connect.

Light broke through the top of the tower. Along with a hissing, howling, horrible screech.

The body collapsed into nothing.

"We have to run!" Esther cried. She landed on Nia's shoulder.

Nia scooped up Asha just as the soul devourer landed beside them and charged. Nia, Esther, and Asha slid through the veils.

The soul devourer lashed out.

Nia screamed. Pain tore through her flesh as its claw slid down her back. But a different pain, too.

The soul devourer's pain.

She could sense the echo of the child it had once been. A little boy, with dark brown hair and bronzy skin. Flashes of his memories, of visiting home tore through her. Listening to his parents talk about his death. Finding another child in his bed. A replacement. The raw fury and pain and confusion that scorched through him, every atom exploding out with furious speed until they burst and reformed. Into something darker, something stronger with claws and scales and the need to hunt, to feed.

Nia, Asha, and Esther collapsed into a tangled heap on the floor of Nia's bedroom.

Wet, liquid pain seeped down her back and stuck her

shirt to her back.

The soul devourer's memories—the child's memories—echoed through her head. The child's soul was inside that thing, trapped there, suffering. The soul devourers weren't just mindless beasts. They were still children. Trapped, tormented children.

Nia staggered to the bed, her vision blurring for a second or two. She slipped to the floor, her knees giving out beneath her. Tears stung her eyes. She couldn't seem to stop slipping. Couldn't stop the darkness from stealing over her.

Late afternoon, only maybe thirty minutes since he'd let Nia ditch him in the Senior Center, and Mal pulled the patrol truck up to the gas pump. It was so low in fuel it'd barely started. He joined another vehicle refueling, while two others were parked out from the store. The much longer row of vehicles filled in the spaces in front of Loki's bar, but this time, the warm glow of the open sign didn't even tempt Mal. No matter how long that had been his habit. The drinks were just an excuse to get in a fight. Or they had been. Until a few months ago when he'd started to feel the echo of Daniel's happiness with Piper and he'd started to think he wanted a taste, too. Hell, he hadn't wanted a drink since Nia. She was the only thing he was addicted to now. He'd convince Nia she needed him, one way or another. Once the truck had enough gas to reach her place.

He jumped out of the truck, the wind no longer as bitter with the protection of the parka, and strode into the store to pre-pay for his gas.

The bell tinkled as he stepped inside. A slim redhead perched on a stool behind the counter, serving the older man ahead of him. She looked vaguely familiar, and around here that probably meant they'd gone to school together. She glanced up from her book, then just as quickly did a double take, her gaze taking its time sliding over him. Maybe it was the uniform.

Not so long ago he might have accepted the invitation in her blatant appraisal. Instead, he nodded quickly and ducked down one of the aisles. Redheads just didn't appeal anymore. Not when there was black curly hair to tangle his fingers in, a petite, gorgeous body to lose himself in.

He cleared his throat, glanced at the aisle. Children's cereal. The kids were out of food at Nia's place, literally burning through boxes of cereal. Had any of Nia's friends bought more? Flowers might work for some women but were too cheesy for Nia.

He ducked out of line. Grabbed the first box of cereal he saw, something with a cartoon animal on it. Was this the kind Asha and her friends liked? He picked up two more varieties, too, just in case. His hand paused on picking up a fourth—the woman coming around the corner of the aisle had it in her cart, and she had a kid about Asha's age.

His insides clenched around the box. Asha looked young, but if she was his, that put her closer to nine or ten. Nine or ten years he'd missed out. Hell, hadn't even known he'd been missing out. He'd never considered kids. Especially not after Paul's death. But now… He couldn't get the slight weight of Asha's body out of his head any more than he could forget Nia. Couldn't forget the way she'd reached for his hand, squeezed his fingers, hers icy and tingling in his.

Nia needed him. Asha needed him, too. Even if she didn't know who he was. Hell, he wasn't sure he was ready for that anyway.

"Oh! Is that young Quilan? The younger one, not the doctor?" a purple-haired woman near the end of the aisle said to her possibly older friend. She might have even thought she said it quietly.

Her friend squinted at Mal. "Malcolm Quilan. Yes, that's him."

He tried to pretend he hadn't heard them and was reading the nutritional value of sugary cardboard. People fed this crap to their kids? Shouldn't there be vitamins and stuff, not just chemicals? He put it back, then started reading the other boxes he'd picked up. *Okay, ladies, put it together just which Quilan I am. The one who gets in trouble, the one who gets in drunken brawls. The usual.*

Crap, this one with the elephant on the front was terrible, too. He re-shelved it. He should forget the whole thing, just get gas, get to Nia's place.

"Oh, really?" The first old lady sounded kind of excited, like maybe she'd spotted a celebrity.

Yeah, well, everyone loved a bad boy. Even cougars.

"He is indeed. He's the one who defended our Nia against the gods. Didn't even flinch. Took on twenty angels, all by himself I hear." The second old woman repeated it with glee. With…pride.

For a second, Mal couldn't read the list of garbage filling the cereal he held in his hand. Our Nia? And twenty angels was exaggerating a bit. He put the cereal back on the shelf, knocking over all the rest behind it. They toppled, knocking his box toward the ground. He grabbed for it, shoving it back in place. Put back the other one he'd picked up, too, because those bright colors couldn't be natural, and instead grabbed good old Cheerios.

By the time he looked up, the old women in the aisle had been joined by four more people behind them. Down on the other end were five more. The lady with the little boy Asha's age. A few of the faces familiar, a few not. He was surrounded. They were all staring. At him.

His throat thickened. His hands went clammy. Usually this was the part when he was a kid where someone said to hold him, and someone else called the police. Except…he was the police.

Instead, he held up the box of Cheerios lamely. "So, uh, these are good for kids, right?"

"Oh, yes. Really good for developing fine motor skills," the mother said, moving closer and pulling the honey version off the shelf. "But these taste a bit better if you want to eat them, too." She beamed at him.

He smiled back, the action sickly. "Um, thanks." He managed to put the plain type back on the shelf without knocking everything down this time. Boy, that winter jacket sure was hot suddenly. He pulled at the collar. So long as he didn't make any sudden moves, maybe he could just get to the till and get out of here before whatever the hell was happening happened all over him.

The second older lady, the one who'd said all those nice things about him, turned her cart and blocked his escape. Her lips tight, her hands and motions a little shaky, she gave him a firm nod. "Good job, young man. You're the kind of man our town needs. Not afraid to stand up to the gods. Not afraid to fight for what's right."

He smoothed a hand over his face, mostly to make sure yep, he could feel his hand, which probably meant he wasn't dreaming, and nope, his mouth wasn't hanging open.

"Thanks," he said slowly. Waiting for her to add the part "just like your brother" or "about time you've lived up to your brother's reputation" or something like.

Only…she just smiled, a mostly toothless smile at him. She didn't say a damned thing about Daniel. She didn't compare him to his brother, like people had been doing since the second they'd been born.

Other people patted him on the back. Said how glad they were he'd made it out alive. How good it was to see a peace officer in town again. How they knew they could count on him to help defend their town, but how he wouldn't be alone against those "damned greedy gods."

The whole time, he edged slowly toward the till to

pay, trying to say the right things but not sure what those might be. The surreality of the situation was bonkers. Maybe he'd fallen and hit his head or something. Maybe too much stress in one day.

He made it to the till, people still saying nice things about him—that would take some getting used to.

The pretty redhead had lost her glasses, her book, and it looked like a couple of the top buttons off her uniform, since it was a lot more cleavage-y than he remembered. He made sure to keep his eyes on her face.

Then everyone started to fight over who got to pay for his cereal and gas.

Okay, this was insane. He cleared his throat loudly and raised his hands. "Hi. Can I have your attention?"

Everyone quieted and looked to him. Looked up at him. Not just because he was taller than most of them, but with something he'd never seen in Beckwell, not for him. They looked at him like he was important, like he was one of their own. Like he was one of the good guys.

Since he'd gotten back, that's kind of how he'd been feeling, too. Maybe it was the coming back from the dead thing, maybe it was standing up to the gods. He couldn't remember the last time he'd compared himself to his brother, not even this morning.

Maybe it was all of that and more. Maybe it was the way Nia looked at him, other than today. She might not have trusted him with the truth about Asha, but she'd never compared him to Daniel, had trusted him with her life in court.

"You were saying Malcolm, er, is that Officer Quilan?" the lady with the little boy said. Again, a bit friendlier. At least her T-shirt couldn't lose any buttons.

He cleared his throat. "I can pay for my own groceries, thanks. It wouldn't be appropriate letting any of you do so."

"Well, we need to thank you somehow," the eldest

little old lady said, frowning at him.

"That's my job. It's my town, too." And his Nia. He didn't say the last part since she wouldn't appreciate it. Hell, probably wasn't even PC with women's equality and stuff, but he'd be hers if she'd be his. He dug a twenty out of his wallet—his last twenty, as it happened. Needed to talk to Loki about the whole salary and getting paid thing. But the effect was worth it. More polite nods and smiles as he made his way out of the store.

After fueling up, he slid into the front seat of the truck, putting his groceries beside him. Then paused a second after he started the truck, the hot air blowing out of the vents, rock music blasting. He shut the music off. He needed to hear his thoughts.

That back there had been…nice. He'd waited a long time to feel accepted. To feel like he belonged in and to the town.

He put the truck in reverse. But those words didn't matter as much as they would coming from the lips of the woman he loved.

Yeah, loved.

She made him a better man. His love for her might even make him a hero. He skidded across the gravel as he backed out, turning around before he pulled up to the four-way, his blinker on, due west, due Nia. Maybe she didn't want his help saving Asha. Maybe she wasn't ready for whatever it was between them, whatever had always been between them. She'd begged him to keep his distance for his own protection. But what about her? Who had her back? He could be patient. But he couldn't leave her out there, frightened and alone as she fought to save their daughter. She didn't have to be alone ever again if she just said the word.

He needed to go help his family.

It was dark, the lamp on when Nia woke in her own bed. Her back burned like it was on fire, and there was a strong possibility she'd been run over by a bus. Every inch of her ached. Asha curled against her, her small form cold and translucent. Esther clung to the headboard above, peering down into Nia's face. Anna was over in the corner on the phone, glancing back toward Nia. Piper and Ginny both perched on either side of the bed, watching her intently. A skunk and a pig were curled up by her feet.

"She's waking up!" Ginny cried at a volume that should have been considered cruelty.

Anna rushed toward the bed. "She's awake." She hung up the phone. "How are you? Do you feel weak? Can you see us?"

"Don't move too quickly," Ginny advised.

"Daniel said she just needed rest, and I agree." Piper held out a hand over Nia's body. "I can feel her energy. She's weak, but she's getting stronger."

"Welcome back, betiya," Esther whispered in Nia's

mind.

"Hi, Mama," Asha said, cuddling against Nia.

The events of earlier in the day—her *failures* of earlier in the day—swept over Nia with the force of a tsunami. The bodies that had collapsed into nothing. The soul devourer that was really a trapped child. She gasped, tears filling her eyes. She tried to push her aching, bruised body upright, but moving was about as easy as shifting her house over a few feet to the right.

Mr. Death had told her it was impossible. Maybe he was right. She couldn't do it. She couldn't just build a body for Asha. She couldn't bring her back to life.

"Don't be silly. You just couldn't do it in a backward, ridiculous fashion," Esther said.

Ginny squeezed Nia's hand. "We're here to help now."

"That's because of the soul devourer," Esther said, this time her whispery voice audible to the others. "When it attacked her, it drained some of her spiritual energy, and she'd already given a lot to Asha earlier."

Nia flung back the blankets and gave Ginny a pathetic shove. Good thing her friend got up and moved, since Nia hadn't budged her. "Okay, you guys stay here, argue about how to help me. Meanwhile, I've got to get back to the Gray with Asha."

"Maybe these would help," Anna said, moving aside and pointing to a stack of old, worn, leather-bound books, five or six of them.

Cold dropped in Nia's core, and rushing air seemed to shuttle her back to the past. Back to the basement, forced to stand in the swimming pool while Dad did his experiments. On her. Or using her, depending on the day. All of it to become stronger. To not only prove his worth to the rest of the Death clan, but to defy death itself as a necromancer. While it left her broken, no barrier to keep her in this world, but torn between it and the Gray.

"Where did you get those?" she said, her voice a rough whisper.

"I—" Anna swallowed and licked her lips, glancing toward Asha momentarily. Even the War horsewoman, who was notoriously tone deaf when it came to picking up social cues, picked up that Nia wasn't happy. "I thought they might help." She straightened, as though finding confidence in her argument. "Some of them are extremely rare. I've looked through a few of them already, and I think—"

"No."

Anna frowned and took a step closer. "But they could help—"

"I said no. Are you deaf or something?" Nia snarled. "Put them back where you found them."

They must have been downstairs. Someone had boxed what was left of her childhood home, saved it, and kept it all the time she'd been away. A few days after she was back in town, they'd showed up on her porch, and she'd tossed them all in the basement. She'd always suspected Loki, but since he held her mortgage, it wasn't like she could go shout at him. Or at least, she'd been more hesitant to back then.

Anna on the other hand…

"You know how I feel about them. About the whole thing," she rasped.

"You mean about necromancy," Anna said quietly. "I know. I wouldn't have brought them up if we hadn't thought they might be of value."

"I'll find another way, I'll figure something out. Not with those." She managed to make it to her feet. Her knees collapsed beneath her about two seconds later. Only Ginny's quick reflexes prevented her from doing a faceplant.

Ginny guided Nia back to the bed.

Nia perched on the edge, her friends, Asha, and

Esther gathering around her.

Piper took her hand and closed her eyes. "This might help a little with the exhaustion," she said, and energy flowed out of her. Soothed the burning feeling on Nia's back, made it feel like at least if a bus had hit her, it'd been a small-ish one.

"Eat this," Ginny said, reaching into the basket by her feet and producing one of her muffins. "You probably haven't eaten anything all day, have you? Anna told us what happened in court."

Nia chewed on the muffin, mostly just hoping there was something to the building-up-her-strength thing, and…she was feeling a bit stronger. Her knees would hold her this time. Then she'd take Asha back to the Gray, and…and what? Try to make a body again and watch that fail? Let the soul devourers get them?

"I'm sorry, Mama. It wasn't Anna. It was me. I thought they might help," Asha said quietly. Her voice sounded different, less hesitant. More mature.

No. Couldn't be. It had to just be Nia's imagination.

Everyone in the room stilled.

Nia slowly turned to face her daughter. She twisted, bending one leg beneath her so she could cup Asha's face. She was paler than she had been. Hell, it was damned lucky she was even here, since Nia had been lying around at least an hour or so passed out.

"Sweetheart, there's nothing in those things to help us. I promise. I know last time didn't work, but—"

"No, Mama," Asha said, touching her fingers to Nia's lips and stilling her words. Her expression was solemn. Much more solemn than a three-year-old should be.

Nia's stomach quivered.

"You need to listen to me, please," Asha said, even her voice paler. But her words were clearer, not that of the younger child. There was no imagining that. "I know I don't have much time. I know you've done everything in your power to help me. The books are for you. To help you with your job. At Death Corp."

Nia tried to speak, to tell her none of it mattered without Asha there. Being Death only mattered if it meant she could bring Asha back. It was all a way to try and make up for what had happened, all those mistakes.

Asha just shook her head, tears forming in her eyes. "I thought… I wanted to say thank you. And that I know, everything you've done. Everything."

Nia took hold of her daughter's hand, pulling the fingers gently away from her lips. Her friends were there, and yes, she'd rather have said this in private, but maybe there really wasn't time. "But I haven't done everything. Maybe—"

Asha dropped her face, her dark curls hiding her face for a second. Then she looked up, her eyes impossibly dark. "I mean I know everything you've done to try and protect me. From the moment I was born, until right now. I remember, Mama. I remember everything."

Nia froze, her lips moving but incapable of speech for a few seconds. Chills chased up and down her arms, and her stomach churned. Her mind tripped over all she knew about Asha's short life. And tragic death. "E-everything?"

Her daughter's smile—too mature, too knowing for a three-year-old—was gentle, and she cupped Nia's face.

She sounded more like the ten-year-old she should have been.

"I heard your voice, the day I was born. Your whispered hopes for me, that I would find something better. You wished me only good things."

Her eyes blurring with tears, Nia couldn't seem to just blink these ones away. "You knew that?"

"They named me Manjula, but I always knew it wasn't my real name, even if for a while, I didn't know how I knew that. I knew I was Asha. Your Asha." She sighed and cocked her head, moisture and warmth mingling in her dark gaze. "I forgot again when I died, but you didn't. You took care of me then, too, Mama. You brought home this strange little spirit who didn't even know it was dead, and you made me food like a living child, and you bought me toys, and you read me stories, and you treated me like I was alive, because that's what I thought I was."

"How long have you known?" Nia rasped. How long had her daughter been pretending to still be sweet, innocent little Asha when all along she'd known the truth? The idea of it gutted Nia and made her chest impossibly tight.

"I started remembering a few weeks ago. When the soul devourer first attacked us in our sleep." Asha shrugged. "When we were with Aunt June, I heard you then, too. I heard…about Daddy."

Nia's stomach did a triple backflip and a few cartwheels. Oh, hell, maybe that conversation about "who's your daddy" would have been better, because this was infinitely worse.

"Asha, I'm so sorry. I should have told you. I should have—"

Asha looked up, blinked, then leaned closer, cupping Nia's jaw. "Oh, Mama, don't be sorry!" Her smile was tear-stained. "This is why I didn't want to tell you. I didn't want to hurt you."

Nia's smile was as hollowed out and empty as her insides. "Same reason I didn't want to tell you. To keep you from all of that. And all along you knew."

"I know that's all you meant. But, Mama?" Asha hesitated a moment, the look on her face uncertain. "I don't think it's supposed to work that way."

"You mean me trying to keep you safe? Nu-uh, it's definitely supposed to work that way."

"No. I mean…" Asha frowned, chewing her lip a bit. "Even you can't protect me from everything. Even if I was alive. Because if I was, I'd grow up, and I'd fall, and I'd get hurt." She shrugged. "Eventually, I'd grow old and die. Just like you. Just like pretty much everyone. The young eventually replace the old. That's what's supposed to happen."

Nia pictured the entire impossible reality in a split second. From Asha finishing elementary school, then graduating high school, then heading off with friends, and boyfriends, and then off to college. Until finally she didn't come back anymore. "Eventually, I'd lose you no matter what I did."

"I suppose so. I-I'm not sure that's what I mean. It doesn't matter anyway, does it?" That sweet child, too much knowledge in too young a face, held solemn peace. "I know I don't have long. I just wanted you to know that it isn't your fault. Any of it. The bad stuff at anyway. The good stuff I know was all you."

Asha was right about one thing. Nia had tried to keep Asha safe from birth, thinking she'd be safer away from Nia. That hadn't worked, had it? Instead, the guilt of abandoning her daughter had eaten at her, made worse when she'd discovered Asha's death. But even back in Beckwell, hiding Asha's existence, it hadn't been able to protect Asha from fading or the soul devourer.

Just like it hadn't worked to keep pushing her friends away, either. She looked at them now, standing at her side, listening silently, no judgment on their faces. Tears slid down Ginny's and Piper's faces, while Anna remained pale and tight-lipped.

When she'd needed them, they'd been there for her, taking care of her kids and her home even when she could barely ask. It didn't matter how much she tried to convince herself that pushing them away harder and faster meant she wouldn't get hurt, she still cared about them.

Like she cared about Mal.

She'd pushed him away for his own safety, no matter that this was his daughter, too. Without him, she'd been too weak, too alone in the Gray, prey for the soul devourers.

The image flickered of Mal with the battle-ax behind her eyes. Then Mal, placing himself firmly between her and Asha. The castle she'd built. The way she'd been able to call him back, and all she'd accomplished with him at her side.

Warmth sparked inside her, that first flickering light in the dark, one of those terrifying four-letter words, the tiniest hint of something precious: hope.

Maybe love did mean eventual pain. Maybe grief was just love. But the world was too damned cold and dark to live without it, the warmth it provided when it was there, and the desolate chill left in its wake. He might eventually leave her, through death or some other way. It was worth the risk. She needed him to help her save Asha.

She needed him, *wanted* him in her life. Period.

She wanted her happy ending, weddings and flowers and love and all the things she'd barely had the courage to imagine, but with Mal, with Mal she wanted it. And she wanted it to build the picture-perfect life for Asha.

She grabbed for her cell that'd been left on the bedside table, and no surprise, it was dead. But there was a wall phone in the kitchen.

She held Asha's face a second, then smoothed back her hair. "I should've known you'd be smarter than me."

Asha grinned. "Really?"

"Yes. Do you why I named you Asha?"

Asha shook her head.

"Because Asha means 'hope,' and when you were born, I wanted only the best for you, wished only the best for you. You are what makes me fight, makes me jump out of bed each day and try again. You are my hope, which means I'm never giving up on you, you understand?" She pressed another kiss on Asha's forehead, then stood.

"Yes, you stay right here. I'm going to be right back. I just need to run downstairs and make a call." She paused and looked at her friends. "Could you… Do you think…?" Even with them knowing the truth, the words to ask them for help were still thick and unwieldly in her mouth.

"We'd love to stay here with her," Ginny said and put her arms around air.

"I'll take care of them, too, Mama. But I don't think it's going to work," Asha said, looking worried.

Esther flew up into the air, transforming into a moth and landing on Nia's shoulder. *I do. I'm proud of you, betiya.*

"Just…don't go anywhere, okay? I'll be right back. For real." She came to her feet, and whether it was the muffins, or maybe Esther lent her some strength, but her legs were solid beneath her as she headed for her bedroom door. "I have to go put our family back together again. Then we'll try one more time. Together. I have to get Mal."

CHAPTER 31

Leaving Asha safe with her friends, Nia raced down the stairs to the second floor and toward the wall phone in the kitchen. Energy sizzled through her with the knowledge that if she put their family back together again, she, Mal, and Asha could do this. Finally, she could bring Asha back. There was that little niggle that wondered if Mal would forgive her. Could he? What if the gods came after them? Sure, she was Death, but could she really take on the gods, face them down for Mal and Asha?

She thundered down the main staircase. Only to skid to a stop at the base of the stairs. Her eyes widened. Her lips fell open.

Mal straightened beside the front door, where he'd removed his boots and hung his dripping coat on the coat tree. A green police uniform stretched over his muscles as he took a step toward her and held up his hand, a glint of silver there.

"I still had a key. And your plan to do this without me was stupid," he said quietly.

Heat and gratitude and butterflies all swarmed inside, and Nia took a hesitant step toward him. How could she explain what she'd realized in the few hours they'd been apart? She was still terrified for him, still dreaded losing him, the image of him slumped over in the courtroom forever etched in her mind. But, oh hell, it was like the sun had come out again in a world with endless night.

He took a small step toward her, his expression set, jaw hard. "Look, I know you said you didn't want my help. That you're worried something could happen to me. I get that, I do. And I'm not a big fan of death, but that's not all you are. You're also Nia, full of warmth and love and care." With each word, he moved slowly toward her, studying her expression. Blue-gray tinged his neck, his body larger, more muscular than usual. "But it's my life." His voice dropped. "She's my daughter, too. And—"

Nia closed the distance between them, threw herself against his chest, craning up on tiptoes, and pressed her lips against his. Pressed the horror of seeing him dead, the fear of it happening again, the clawing failure she'd suffered, the pain of the soul devourer and her own mistakes, all of it, into that kiss.

His arms closed around her, and his lips moved against hers.

Heat and life whirled through her. Headier than that was the faint flicker of hope deep inside, and the overwhelming warmth and need that expanded her chest and made her want to keep him locked up somewhere— probably the bedroom—but knew she couldn't do that. Because she needed and wanted him at her side.

He pulled back, his hands on either side of her jaw, smoothing back her hair, his thumb sliding over her lips.

"I take it you're not mad about the key?" he said, the one side of his lips quirking upward.

"I'm sorry. I still want to keep you safe, and it's still probably better if you stay as far away from me as you can, but, Mal…" Oh, hell, her eyes were tearing up again, and she tried to blink it away. "I'm selfish and I'm mean, and I want you next to me. In this life and the next, whatever is coming, I want you. Without you, I screw up everything, make it all so much worse, and I don't think anyone should let me be responsible for so many people and so many things, but I am, and guess I can't get out of it. And you better not die, you hear me? At least, not until we're really, old, and maybe by that time I'll have figured out immortality or something, and—"

He cut off her words with another kiss, this one harder. And hotter. He pulled away too soon again, which was getting annoying, but her friends and Asha were waiting upstairs.

"Okay," he said, the corners of his eyes crinkling.

"*Okay*? That's all you've got to say?"

Whatever he might have said was shattered by the sound of screams upstairs.

Time slowed.

Wood splintered behind them as the front door gave way.

Three shining, black-scaled soul devourers bounded through the opening. One launched itself at Mal's turned back.

Nia didn't think. She twisted, shoved Mal to safety, and turned in time for the soul devourer, terrible maw open with its rows of glistening, razor-sharp teeth coming toward her face. She fisted her hand and punched upward, beneath its jaw. The punch closed its mouth enough to grab it, grip it around the neck, and hold on with everything she had in her.

At the heart of the beast was the frantic, panicked fear of a child. A girl this time. Trapped inside this thing so long there was little of the girl itself to identify. But still a child. Still a soul there.

Well, they did say Death had an affinity for wild

beasts.

The two other soul devourers leaped over her and the one she had in a headlock, bounding up the stairs. Their claws scratched and skittered on the wood, their tails smashing into the railing and shattering spindles. One of them howled, the unmistakable unearthly roar of the soul devourer in her house. Headed upstairs, toward her friends and her daughter.

"Upstairs!" she shouted at Mal.

The weight of the soul devourer suddenly lifted, and it roared, twisting toward the new threat.

Nia scrambled back to her feet to find Mal's shiny new uniform straining and tearing to accommodate for his wider shoulders, his expansive wings. Oh, yeah, he was full blue-gray Fomorian now, grabbing the soul devourer by the tail and slamming it into the stairwell wall.

The monster shook its head, snarling back at them, before it too raced up the stairs.

Mal turned back.

"Go! Upstairs. My room."

His wings stretched, and he jumped, gliding up to the top of the stairs and disappearing into the darkness. Looked like his time in the Gray had finally taught him what those wings were for.

Nia grabbed the rail and pounded up the first two stairs before the first spirit grabbed on to her hand.

Lost souls poured through the front door, reaching for her, spilling over one another and through the walls as they reached for her. Outside, the weather had turned to rain. Rain, in the freakin' middle of winter.

Nia jerked and pulled away from the hands and fingers that clawed at her skin, at her hair. Their stories, their pain, leached through her.

"Let me go! I'll help you later. I have to get upstairs," she pleaded with them, dragging her weight and the weight of maybe fifty souls up two or three stairs with her.

She had to get upstairs. To Mal, Asha, and her friends.

There were so many spirits. More and more, far more than she'd ever seen in Beckwell, far more than those who had crowded her front yard when she'd returned home.

Another scream from upstairs, female. It sounded like one of her friends.

Esther swooped down the stairwell in owl form and landed on Nia's shoulder. Power spilled through their connection.

Nia turned on the spirits. "BACK OFF," she roared. She joined with the ether, melted her solidity, enough to slip away from those who hadn't released her at the sound of Death.

She raced for the stairs, scrambling up as fast as she could. These were spirits straight out of the Gray, hungry for life energy and dangerous. They formed a solid wall of cold behind her, their bottomless appetite meaning they would suck the life energy out of any living being they encountered. But it was Nia's brighter, stronger energy that called to them the most. Every footstep was just ahead of them as she pounded up one staircase. Then up the second.

Asha's scream echoed through the house, the hair on the back of Nia's neck standing up at attention.

The spirits still came after Nia, still reached for her.

She kicked them aside, almost fell up the stairs a couple of times, finally reached the bedroom door and fell inside.

Asha lay on the bed, pale and flickering. The sheets and blanket were shredded, half on the floor. The shattered remains of a chair were near the end of the bed. Anna was collapsed, blood streaming from the slash to her chest, gasping for air while Ginny and Piper knelt over her, the bright green and smoky black of their essences mingling. The skunk bounced, its tail held upright. The black pig lay bloody and motionless against the wall.

Mal stood between Asha and two of the soul devourers, wings spread, service revolver in hand.

"Nia, get back," he said calmly.

The shining black wetness of the soul devourers' scales was even more obscene in the bright lamplight. Their claws clicked on the wood floor as they came closer, hundreds of eyes blinking, and opening their shark-toothed maws and snarling, drawing back gums to reveal endless rows of teeth.

The beast swung toward her. Snarled, layers of black scales rippling over its back.

An answering snarl came from directly behind Nia. Oh, shit. There were three.

Esther screeched and dove. *"Run!"* she cried.

Nia dove toward Anna and her friends. She blinked, seeing the scene with her other vision. Anna's soul was partially detached and weak. Piper and Ginny were giving her energy, but it wouldn't be enough.

Souls crawled up the walls, seeped up through the floorboards like mist, and shoved through the bedroom door, reaching for her, oozing around her. They moaned as they touched her, absorbing parts of her energy.

There was a horrible snapping sound. The screech of the owl. Then a muffled thud.

Nia twisted in time to see the soul devourer toss what looked like a bloody lump of feathers to the side. Then the third beast advanced on her and her friends, while the other two closed in on Mal and Asha.

Asha flickered in and out of visibility. She tried to move closer to Mal. Fell back to the bed. Closed her eyes. Began to flicker wildly, like a lightbulb about to go out.

"Asha!" Nia cried, the sound of her heartbeat shutting out any other sound for a second. Spirits crawled over her, tried to climb inside her mouth.

Oh, fuck this. She snapped her eyes closed and reached inside, deep. Shoulders heaving, she pushed away the vision of everything she'd seen—Asha's faint flickering, Anna's injury, or Esther's bloodied lump of feathers. She reached for the cold mist that whirled deep inside her, for the icy water that connected her to the Gray, connected her to her ability. Out of the cold, Esther whirled upward until she settled with comforting weight on Nia's shoulder, the soft scent of jasmine tea. Esther created a safe zone around them, forcing the spirits back. Nia opened her eyes, the scene all in grays, light and darkness.

The two soul devourers crouched in front of Mal tensed, preparing to spring.

He steadied his weapon in his hand and lowered his head to face them, Asha a pale shadow behind his wings.

"HEEL," she commanded in the Death voice. She reached out a hand and gripped the one by the neck as it moved toward her friends. It froze, still as a statue.

The two near Mal stilled, sat back on their rumps, and shook their heads as though confused.

A flash of light momentarily blinded them all.

The soul devourers screeched.

Nia squinted against the light, though her other vision was less affected. She could see the form of a body appear in her bedroom doorway.

Judge Thesku, the snake-headed judge. He was flanked on either side by a pair of muscle-bound angels, their gold swords drawn. He took in the scene with a quick look, his tongue flickering before his scaled lips drew back in a smile and his gaze settled on her.

"Isn't this a delightful tableau? Do you like it? Our little surprise for you? The other gods and I have had enough of your machinations. You brought the spirits to Braelyn, now I've unleashed the Gray on this one. You're not the only one who can pass through the veils." His expression hardened. "You'll be last, don't worry. I might even let you survive long enough to see this entire town of miscreants razed to the ground first. Enough of this foolish rebellion and pretending you aren't all subject to the laws of the gods." He indicated the soul devourers with a sweep of a hand. "There are plenty more already making their rounds as we speak. More than you can imagine. All that we could find in the Gray."

The soul devourer within her grasp jerked away, like a spell had been broken, and she pulled her hand back just before it snapped. It advanced on Anna, her soul separating from her body, a pool of blood beneath her despite Piper and Ginny's best efforts.

The other two beasts crouched again, prepared to attack Mal and finish off Asha.

Asha, who barely flickered at all. She was almost out of time. There would be nothing left if she died this time.

Mal didn't take his eyes off the two soul devourers. His expression was hard, controlled, like he was calculating which one he'd take down first.

All these people she cared about. Had she ever even told them? Yet when she needed them, they were there for her, without question.

This time, it was her turn.

Nia had to turn away, had to face the god instead. For now. "Welcome to Beckwell, asshole. We don't much like the gods here, and you're about to find out what happens if you mess with our town. With my town." Oh, hell, this better work. "MR. DEATH, A HAND PLEASE."

Judge Thesku laughed. "You think a reaper scares me?" He raised a hand and the soul devourers froze like statues. "Oh, I don't want to miss this."

"I'm hardly here for your amusement," Mr. Death said, his voice at peak snootiness as he stepped through a wall and strode into her room.

Followed by a veritable army of other snappily dressed male and female spirits, all in dark gray pinstriped suits.

The god crossed his arms and snorted. "An army of reapers. How terrifying," he said dryly.

"Fired up the legal team and started the paperwork I hope?" Nia asked, seeing the thin, dark-haired Mr. Death only peripherally.

"We did indeed. It's about time the gods were reminded that Death does not work for them and is not subject to their laws or whims." Mr. Death held out a hand, and a scroll appeared in it. He shook it out, letting the paper roll out along the floor, long enough it only stopped when it bumped into the god's foot.

"This is a formal injunction against any further action taken against: Nia Amort, henceforth known as 'Death,' who is necessary for the duties of her office; any of the alleged horsewomen; Malcolm Quilan; Asha Amort; or, in fact, anyone who does, has, or ever will live in the protected sanctuary of Beckwell, Alberta." He held up another scroll, which he didn't unfurl. "This one's the call for your impeachment from the High Court signed by ten managed members of the United Supernatural Exalted Deities. Don't worry, every other judge that served on Death's travesty of a trial has matching ones."

Judge Thesku, the snake-headed god, looked at Mr. Death for a second, like he was insane. Then he started to laugh. "You've got to be joking." He lifted his hand to indicate the soul devourers to proceed.

"Oh, he doesn't have a sense of humor. Go on, tell him, Mr. Death." Nia took the opportunity to swiftly step toward Anna, Piper, and Ginny.

The ragged edges of Anna's soul fluttered in the wind, and Anna's soul stared at the other spirits around the walls, barely connected to her body at all.

For a second, Nia saw spots, like she yanked her head out of the icy water, out of her ability, and saw one of her oldest friends, lying in a pool of blood. Nia's chest squeezed and ached. Her hands shook.

Piper's usually pink aura was tinged with black and brown fear and uncertainty, her abilities flaring like a yellow-green rainbow as she fought to feed her energy into Anna's failing body.

Ginny sobbed, whispering something over and over to Anna, holding the War horsewoman's limp, bloodied hand, her usually green aura likewise tinged with black grief and depression.

This was why she hadn't wanted Mal involved, hadn't wanted any of her friends involved. Getting too close to Death was deadly. They didn't deserve this. This couldn't be happening—

Esther, flickering and pale, landed on Nia's shoulder. Pressed comfort and strength through the connection.

The moment allowed Nia to take a breath and plunge back into the icy waters of her ability, let them soak through her.

Nia knelt between her friends and stitched body and soul back together. Yes, she was Death. But she wouldn't let that be dangerous to her friends. One living War horsewoman, sometimes pain in the butt, always a friend. She reached for Ginny's and Piper's hands, and together they helped Anna draw back energy and strength that she'd lost.

Two of Mr. Death's gray-suit-clad spirits joined her, murmuring that they'd finish things off.

Only when Anna's eyelids flickered, her fiery red aura flaring back, did Nia let herself breathe, force herself to her feet and away from her friends.

She stood to find Mr. Death crossing his arms as he faced down Judge Thesku. "Do you want to be remembered as one of the ignorant asses who started one of the most widespread paranormal wars in history?"

The snake judge's eyes were narrowed to such narrow slits, it almost looked like they were closed.

"Nia!" Mal shouted, his voice hoarse.

Her heart jumped.

The soul devourers growled, but she raced to his side, striding through the glut of spirits all over the floor.

He cradled Asha in his arms. She was barely flickering. Barely visible.

"We've got this handled," Mr. Death said, clearing his throat. "Boss."

Nia nodded at him before she touched Mal's arm. Esther landed on her shoulder, and Nia slipped all four of them through the veils to the Gray.

CHAPTER 32

She couldn't lose her. It wouldn't happen. It couldn't happen. The moment they arrived in the Gray, Nia dropped to her knees and started making a new body for Asha, one more time, like she'd done before, but this time it would work. This time it had to work.

Asha didn't have the time if it didn't.

Mal cradled Asha in his arms, and when he looked up at Nia, moisture shone in his eyes. "We're losing her," he whispered, the words raw.

"No. No, we're not. Nu-uh," Nia snapped back. Okay, that looked about right. The body was the right size. To the touch, it could have been cold flesh beneath her fingertips. Just…blank. Icy because it was formed of pure ether. Like a piece of metal before it was stamped and turned into currency. Or in this case, brought to life as Asha.

"Bring her down near the ground," she told Mal. She squeezed her hands tight, trying to stop the shaking with no success. Just like she couldn't stop the chill stealing through her body, something so much deeper than the usual damp of the Gray.

Asha was barely visible. Her form was almost entirely faded. She turned toward Nia, tried to hold out her hand, but couldn't lift her arm.

"Mama," she whispered, her voice barely audible.

"I'm right here, baby. It's going to work. You're going to be okay."

Her fingertips brushed Mal's as together they slowly started to lower Asha over the body blank. She looked up at him, met his eyes.

His lips were bracketed, brow furrowed. He was following her lead.

Even if his expression said he didn't believe it would work.

"Betiya," Esther said gently, speaking easily in the Gray. "How will this work better than last time? What's different?" She fluttered over Asha.

"Because it has to!" Nia snapped. She focused on the glow of Asha's soul, of holding on to it, trying to feed energy into it.

The moth settled on her shoulder, soaking in calm and strength. "Yes, but—"

"I don't have time." She wiggled her shoulder, dislodging the moth. She had to focus. Mr. Death had called her boss. That meant she was officially Death, right? That meant she could do this. She could save Asha.

Asha's soul slid into the body blank. Her eyes fluttered.

"LIVE," Nia commanded in the Death voice, and then held her breath. There were the edges of the soul. If she could attach those, if she could...

Asha opened her eyes and took a breath.

The body blank collapsed to misty ether.

Mal caught Asha's head before she crashed into the hard ground.

Tears bit Nia's eyes. "No! I did it right. I…"

"You may be Death, betiya, but what do you know about being Life?" Esther said gently. "What do you know about bringing back the dead?"

Bringing back the dead. Necromancy. Dad. His experiments. Nia's breath sped.

Asha paled a little further. Her head lolled.

It was insane. Oh, god, it was disgusting and horrible and the last thing she wanted to do. She didn't want to touch those things, didn't want to remember, didn't want to feel all the souls and horror attached to them. Just the idea made her nauseous.

If it meant saving Asha, she'd do it.

"Dad's books? They're on the dresser, right?" she asked her horse.

Esther barely said yes before Nia closed her eyes, reached through the veils. Yes, there they were. She didn't need all of them. Most of them were relatively worthless, didn't seem to even understand the basics of how the Gray and the veils worked. She dug through them, each one like touching hot coals, hungry with the force of imprisoned souls, horror they'd enacted, horrors they'd witnessed. She wasn't usually affected by objects like she was people, but these books had taken on a life force of their own. A very dark one.

Not that one. She knew which one she'd need if any of them would be of any help.

She needed the one Dad had used when he'd broken her. The one with the water.

She shoved her hand through the stack of books, knocking many of them to the ground. They didn't matter. It was like she could sense it now. Eyes still closed, she shoved through the pile. It was close…

Her fingertips grazed over an ornate embossed leather cover, the book small. She gasped as the icy energy shot through her fingertips, cold enough to burn.

Didn't matter. She grabbed it hard, her fingers burning, aching. The book hissed and cried out in her head. It and the souls trapped inside, the experiences it had witnessed, screamed. She yanked them through the Gray.

Panting, she fell momentarily back, the book falling from her hands, droplets of water covering it from being pulled into this world so abruptly.

"Nia, I don't think she's breathing," Mal said, his voice cracking.

In Asha's case, even as a ghost, not breathing meant barely surviving.

Nia gripped the book, cold burning her fingers, and flipped it open. Then started shaking her head. No, no, this couldn't be. It was nonsense. Just scribbles and illegible symbols. Nothing made sense.

Esther landed on her shoulder. "It's a tool of Death. Use it."

"I'm trying!" Another glance toward Asha.

Mal rocked Asha slowly, singing a soft song, a tear sliding down his face. Asha flickered into visibility, then out. In…but so translucent…

Tears scalded Nia's cheeks. She couldn't have lost her. Please, please, no.

"Use it. Command it," Esther cried. "Quickly, before it's too late." She fluttered over to Asha and settled on the child's hair.

Asha gained a bit more in color, while Esther began to flicker.

"Hurry," she urged in Nia's head.

Command it. Nia blinked. The Death voice. "SHOW ME HOW TO SAVE MY DAUGHTER," she commanded the book.

It dropped to the ground and pages flipped wildly. Letters rearranged themselves into legible writing. It was like a recipe, kind of. Build the body. Check. Layer the soul. Check. Add the life force. Wait, what?

"How do I get a life force?" Nia asked the book.

It flipped back one page. Providing the clear directions to obtain a life force. Easy as pie.

You just needed to steal it out of another living body.

Nia's breath sagged out. Mr. Death had tried to tell her, hadn't he? Everything needed balance. A life…for a life.

"Did you figure out how to help her?" Mal asked, keeping his voice soft.

"Yes. But…but I need a life force. I need someone else's life."

"Then take mine," Mal said.

She turned and met his gaze. His clear, certain gaze. No hesitation. No question.

She could have her daughter, but she'd lose him. His laughter, the life he brought to her. The suffocating loss she'd experienced back in the courtroom, when they'd stolen his soul, shortened her breath.

"I don't even know what happens if I did that. If your soul is gone, if… Maybe we should take my life force. I can be the sacrifice."

Mal just shook his head. "I can't bring her back. Only you can."

She pictured how he'd looked in the courtroom, his skin starting to gray, the warmth gone out of him. The entire world had seemed to grow colder and grayer then. She'd grown so cold and gray herself before he came back into her life. Before he brought her back to life.

"I can't do that," she whispered, throat raw.

Mal cradled Asha in his arms and shifted until his big warm body brushed hers, his thigh pressed against hers. "Yes, you can. I'm going to help you. Because we're not losing our daughter this time. I've made a lot of mistakes, but this isn't one of them. It's worth it."

Nia's eyes filled with tears, her chest compressed. "But I don't want to lose you, either." Her voice cracked.

"I don't want to choose Asha over you."

He took her hands and placed one on Asha and one on his chest. Warmth soaked through her fingers, his heart a steady thud beneath her fingertips. "You don't have to choose. I will. I love you, Nia." He looked down at Asha, his smile bittersweet. "I love both of you, and if there's anything good I've ever done in my life, even by accident, she's it."

"You have to choose, betiya," Esther said, her voice faint in Nia's head. *"I'm trying to hold her…but she doesn't have much time left."*

Nia tried to start the process but froze. She couldn't do this. She'd said she'd do anything to save her daughter, but she couldn't kill another person.

She couldn't kill Mal. "Mal, I…"

"Wait! Wait! You two haven't done something stupid, have you?" Aunt June cried, rushing through the mist toward them.

Both Mal and Nia looked up at her, then at each other, as though confirming yes, they both saw her.

Mr. Death emerged behind her, walking more sedately, the arm of his pinstripe suit torn off, blood smeared down his leg. He grimaced. "There'll be just a little tidying up to do when you get back. But I knew you'd want to deal with this first."

Mal just shook his head. "Aunt Junie? What…what are you doing here?"

Nia's throat thickened as she saw the faint shimmer around Aunt June's form.

Humans couldn't come to the Gray.

Not living humans.

₧

Mal still couldn't make sense of the reality that his aunt was here, that this was somehow real. He was losing Asha, but if he could go in her place, he was more than good with the trade.

But…Aunt Junie was here. She shouldn't be here. His brain kept getting stuck on that, like it couldn't add it all up. His palms dampened, and his stomach twisted.

Aunt Junie came and knelt beside them, her smile soft as she brushed the hair back from Asha's forehead. Soft golden light flowed through her touch, illuminating Asha's face.

"She's even more beautiful here," she said softly, then looked up at him. "So are you. I always have been partial to blue. Can you fly, or are they more decorative?"

"They're real," he said. Maybe Nia had started the ceremony, and this was a farewell to life or something. "Aunt Junie, are you really here?"

This time she turned the smile up to him. "Yes, Malcolm." She frowned and leaned in close to search his face. "You're not forgetting things and getting confused, are you? Your brother calls in medical experts if you do that."

"He doesn't mean anything by it. He's just—"

She waved him away. "I know he doesn't mean anything by it. It's his way of taking care. But here I am chattering on." She turned to Nia. "Carry on, then. Complete the ritual."

"T-the ritual?" Mal said, the hair lifting at the back of his neck. A ghost of a thought skittered over his skin with icy feet. He shifted his wings. "Nia, what is she talking about?"

Nia, her eyes over bright and shining, turned to Mr. Death.

"There isn't any other way?" she whispered, her shoulders slumped.

Mr. Death stepped closer. "I'm sorry, no. Life can't be created from nothing, not even for you. But the life does not have to be stolen."

Mal came to his feet, Asha still in his arms as he put things together. His stomach hardened, his throat burned.

"No." He turned to Nia. His voice hardened. "Not her. Me. That's the deal. Me. My life force. You're going to use me to save Asha. That's it, that's final, that's how it's going to work."

Nia lowered her eyes and began to create the body blank, a new one.

"Oh, Malcolm," Aunt Junie said, standing and stepping toward him.

He took a step back, as though if he didn't hear it, if he didn't let her say it, it wouldn't happen, wasn't true. The possibility of what this meant settled on his shoulders with the weight of a truck.

Aunt Junie followed him, wouldn't let her push him away or outrun her. Just like she never had as a child, either. She'd always found him. The back of his throat ached, and a tremble slid through him. She'd always coaxed him back to the house with cookies and treats, the promise of her warm hug. The sweet scent of her, closed in her arms, was the safest he'd ever been when he was a child. Her scent was like fresh-baked cookies and soft perfume, surrounding him in her hug, in her safety and her love.

She cupped his jaw with her hand, her fingers soft.

He closed his eyes, unable to see her, the raw ache inside slicing through him. "I can't let you do this. I won't choose your life for another." Not even for Asha. Without Aunt Junie, he might not have survived childhood.

"Look at me," she said. Then a moment later, she gave him a light swat on his face. "Malcolm Quilan, you open your eyes and look at me young man, do you hear?"

He opened his eyes. He had to look down at her, even taller than he was in the human realm.

She smiled, as if to reward him for listening. Her eyes were deep brown and clear, with tiny flecks of gold. She patted his cheek. "Of course, you can't make that choice. Which is why I have."

"What? No! I—"

She shook her head, gripping his shoulder. "The deal is already done," she said, her voice soft yet firm. "I made the choice for you. For us." Her gaze landed on Asha, and a radiant smile spread over her face. "Not much longer now, don't worry."

He looked down at Asha. At the improved color in her face. At her increased solidity.

Back at Aunt Junie. The slight shimmer to her form. The growing translucency. Her cheekbones stood on in higher definition. His throat ached with rawness.

"No. You can't have. Please. Tell me you haven't."

She took his arm and tugged him back toward Nia. Then lifted Asha from his arms that had gone boneless. He could only watch as she lowered Asha into the body blank Nia had built.

Then his aunt stood and turned to him. "Most people don't get to choose how they go. Death steals up on them one day like a dirty thief, and all their plans, everyone else's plans, it's all torn away. But I get that choice. What greater gift than knowing it guarantees the future of our family?" She squeezed his elbow with a soft smile. "I'm ready, Malcolm. This is my choice."

"But Aunt Junie—"

"My choice," she said, more firmly. Then her voice softened. "Oh, my darling. Don't you think I know how lucky I am? I may not have borne you, but you are *my* son. You and Daniel both. I have been blessed to have two such wonderful men in my life, both of whom I am so very, very proud of."

His eyes burned, his insides clenched. He'd always thought they'd have more time, he'd be able to show her how much she meant to him, give her all she deserved for everything she'd brought into his life. "I've made so many mistakes…"

"We all make mistakes. It's how we rise from them

that matters." She gestured at Nia and Asha. "I think you've done very well."

She gave him a hug then, her body thin and growing increasingly insubstantial. Still, there was the sweet smell of her, that Aunt Junie smell of perfume and clean soap. Her body was frail in his arms, too small somehow, her arms stretched around him more bone than flesh. He tried to memorize that hug, that moment. When he couldn't give her another, at least he'd remember this one.

His hands shook as he lifted them and settled them on her shoulders.

"I know," he said. "I know you're ready to go." His voice cracked at the idea that after this, he wouldn't be able to speak to her, would never again hear her laughter, watch her face crinkle up with a smile. A few tears slid down his face. He brushed them away and tried to smile. "I—we—are so incredibly grateful for what you've done. For who you are and all you've done for us." His voice broke then, became raspy and thin with the knowledge he needed to tell her the things he needed to say now, because there'd never be another chance.

The world slowed around them, the sore tightness in his throat almost choking off all words. She'd be gone. No more smiles, no more visits to her house, no more tea and cookies. He clenched his teeth, burning pain seeping through him like lava. He wanted to be strong for her, but inside, oh gods, inside he was still that little boy who needed her, who loved her, who just wanted one more hug. And who knew that after this, there'd never be another.

"I'm not ready to let you go. I don't think I'll ever be ready," he managed to get out past the thickness in this throat.

She stepped back into his arms. "Oh, my darling. We're never ready. Not when it's someone we love." Wrapping her thin arms around him, she squeezed. Her warmth, her scent around him.

His lungs burned, and he squeezed his eyes tight a second and held on, gripped her narrow shoulders and burned the sight of her smile into his thoughts. Every memory of all she was, all she meant washed over him, clenched at his chest and weighed them down. All the things they wouldn't have. How empty the world would be without her.

It was Aunt Junie who pulled back. She patted his cheeks and smiled at him, a sheen of tears in her eyes. "Now, you be good to each other. Love each other." She sniffled and then laughed at herself, never letting her smile falter. "And remember, I'm not really gone. I'm just around another corner. I'll be waiting for you with some hot tea and cookies when I next see you. Hopefully not for many, many years. I love you, Malcom."

She stepped back, growing ever more translucent. A glow surrounded her form. She turned, lights blooming growing behind her. In that light, silhouettes stepped forward. Including two young men, barely into their twenties from the looks of them. They were similar in coloring and stature to Mal and Daniel, that other set of twins. Her brothers.

Aunt Junie's face broke into a huge smile, and she walked into the warm light. Toward her brothers and her family. She turned back for a moment, lifted her hand in a wave.

The light flared.

Light dimmed again, taking with it Aunt Junie.

His stomach plummeted, vision blurring as his knees gave out beneath him. He thudded down into the parched soil, his hands empty, insides hollowed out, body turning as cold as the surrounding Gray mist. He dropped his head, a low keening moan breaking from his throat. The sound echoed through the Gray, through all the empty rooms inside him where once Aunt Junie had protected him, kept him safe, loved him. Heated tears burned down his face, and he didn't stop them.

Aunt Junie was gone, part of his brain tried to say, whereas the other part said it wasn't possible. Someone so vibrant, so full of life and love couldn't just be gone.

Don't leave me behind, Aunt Junie. How am I supposed to do this all without you?

Small fingers closed in his. Small, *warm* fingers.

His face wet with tears, he looked down at the curly-haired little girl kneeling beside him. Tears streaked her face, too. She reached a hand up and wiped away his.

"Don't cry, Daddy. It's okay. Can we go home now?"

CHAPTER 33

Nia froze in her progress toward Mal and sucked in a breath as she heard Asha call him Daddy. Would he blame Nia for Aunt June's decision? He'd just lost his aunt to save Asha. Nia rubbed the spot over the ache in her chest.

Esther fluttered over, landing on Nia's shoulder with a warm hug feeling and speaking softly. "Give him time. Grief takes time."

Her chest ached with fullness and warmth for Aunt June and what she'd given them, even while her belly knotted. Grief might take its own time, but what about forgiveness?

Mr. Death cleared his throat.

She held up a hand, not taking her gaze off Mal and Asha, still staring at the spot where Aunt June had vanished into the bright golden light. "Just give me a second Mr. Death—"

"Leonard."

This made her turn to look at him. Really look at him.

His suit was torn, his spectacles slightly askew, and

the blood smeared across his suit and soaking a pantleg suggested reapers weren't entirely immune to harm.

"Leonard who? Is this some weird knock-knock joke?" she said.

He rubbed his lips and smoothed his moustache, pretending to study the fog in the distance. Was that the faintest hint of a blush? "Leonard Amort. It's my name."

"*Amort*? As in, we're related?" Okay, this kind of explained his extra-pissy behavior if he was Death clan, but he'd become a reaper, not Death.

Color stained Mr. D— Er, Leonard's cheekbones. "A great-uncle, I think. I thought knowing might be handy. If you need to get ahold of me, or when we're around the office."

Around the… Oh yeah. Death Corp. Breath filled her lungs, along with the hugeness of what that meant. Holy crap. *Death Corp.* It was hard not to wheeze a second or two. Her office now. Her… Well, "job" or "career" didn't really seem to cover it.

She shook her head. "But I called you before."

He, too, glanced toward the spot where the bright light had been, a small frown creasing his brow. "Mr. Death was what Ms. Benoit called me, so I answered to it." He paused a second. "She knew, you know. That you'd need more to save Asha. She made me tell her that night we took care of Asha, and she made me swear I'd tell her if there was anything she could do." His voice roughened. "One heck of a lady, that."

"Yeah," Nia said, the only thing she could think of saying. There went her stupid eyes, burning again. Seriously, crying was *not* going to become her thing. Heck of a lady wasn't the half of it. Aunt June had given her life to save Asha. It was her who'd made all the difference and really performed the miracle.

She looked toward Mal again, aching for him. She didn't have the words to tell him what his aunt's sacrifice meant. She hadn't even had the courage to tell him she'd known the second she saw Aunt June's spirit here in the Gray what it could mean.

And was selfishly grateful. Frick.

"I don't believe Aunt June would want you to feel badly about her sacrifice," Esther whispered in Nia's head, maybe so she wasn't overheard by the reaper. *"She said it was her choice."*

"I'm grateful, I am. But Mal must be so torn up. Aunt June gave us…everything."

"Because for her, love meant giving nothing less."

Still putting off talking to Mal and calling it giving him time, Nia turned back to the reaper. "Thank you. For helping us."

He shrugged, tucking his hands behind his back. "You'd probably have been a terrible grouch if I didn't. Self-preservation, really."

"Ah. Of course."

"Speaking of preservation? Your town is still overrun with soul devourers and some very angry ghosts. We should probably go deal with that."

The soul devourers. All those traumatized children transformed into deadly hunters because of their pain. Seemed unfair. Until Aunt June, she'd honestly never been sure if there was a real "light," or if it was a good thing.

But if Aunt June had gone there, it had to be. Both real, and good.

Nia's throat ached. "I can help them, can't I? Now that I'm Death."

"The dead? Indeed. It's something of the job description and the rules."

She considered her daughter, with her healthy, vital glow. A living three-year-old child, though only time would tell how much she remembered of the other world…and her life before. "Yeah, I'm thinking of changing some of those rules," she said darkly. "I meant I could help the soul devourers."

"Those destructive creatures? How could you help them?"

She turned to Leonard. "There is so much you don't know." She patted his arm. "It's okay. I'll let you revise the Death manual after I change things. But for now—" she glanced in Mal's direction again, "—you go ahead. We're right behind you."

Leonard's lips formed a tight moue, but he nodded, turned on his heel, and melted into the mist.

Nia forced herself to approach Mal, his wings and shoulders rigid, still facing the spot where Aunt June had vanished into the light. She stuffed her hands in her pockets, shoulders hunched. "Mal?"

"Yeah," he said, face set, staring off in the distance at something only he could see.

She couldn't ask him if he was okay. It hurt like hell to lose someone. She'd been five when Mom and Bibiji walked out, abandoned her with Dad. Mom had promised she'd come back…but death in the form of a speeding truck found her first. They'd never come back, no matter how many nights she'd cried for them, after Dad's experiments, the spirits who tried to break her, tear her apart. Mom and Bibiji had just been…gone.

But even after all these years it still hurt so damned much, she'd tried to shut herself off from people for so long to avoid just the pain. She looked down at Asha, beautiful, perfect Asha, glowing with health and vitality…who probably should have been attracting other spirits.

In fact, the whole being vulnerable and not watching their backs all the while they'd been here should have attracted spirits and lots of the dark hungry things in the Gray.

Which looked damned empty about now…

Oh, hell. Her heart picked up speed. Maybe it wasn't just the soul devourers the gods had let run amok in Beckwell. Maybe it was all the dark inhabitants of the Gray.

"Mal." She winced and squeezed her hands into fists, glad his back was to her. "I am so, so sorry to do this, but we have to get back to Beckwell. I think things are going really badly back there about now."

He slowly climbed to his feet, Asha at his side. His expression was bleak and set in a way that made her insides churn.

"Then let's go."

∾

Icy slush poured from the sky as they emerged from the veils into the human world, soaking them almost immediately. Mal was so numb, the cold almost didn't register. He tried to shelter Asha with his wings, but Nia had already stepped away, so he couldn't do the same for her. Could barely tear his mind away from that last glimpse at Aunt Junie, turning and disappearing into the light. He was supposed to fight now, but even the Fomorian ached, reacted sluggishly.

Nia froze for a second in the rain, like a wet cat, her eyes wide. Esther in owl form landed on Nia's shoulder, and her muscles seemed to relax. Her shoulders eased down. Spirits raced toward her, but none of them dared get close.

There was a dull heaviness in his chest and limbs, and his body chilled. Only Asha's little hand in his and Nia's soft hand resting on his forearm kept him moving forward. The second Asha's little fingers had touched his, the first time he'd walked into Nia's house, he'd been lost. Whether he'd known it or not, she'd given him the chance to prove he wasn't the evil twin, never had been.

He let the Fomorian stir, let it spiral energy through him as it breathed in the chaos in front of them and the thrill of the fight.

To say they emerged into chaos was putting it mildly. It took him a moment to recognize where they were when they arrived. Not back in Nia's house, but outside it, in what had been the yard. Which was now a battlefield. Like *Ghostbusters*, except a lot less funny. And unfortunately, not in someone else's fictional New York, far away from here.

Spirits covered almost every square inch, so thick, it was like the mist of the Gray had found its way here. Amid them were a few people he recognized. There were even more of the suited people from Death Corp, who seemed to be trying to stuff the spirits into large canvas sacks with medium success. Interesting approach.

Nia's three friends were on the house's porch. Piper spread green smoke and raised what appeared to be a hurricane around her, which blew some of the spirits off their feet, but not enough. Ginny then blasted them toward the suited Death Corp people, upending the earth beneath the spirits' feet. Anna sprayed ghosts with a hose, which did seem to hold them off. They stepped into the deep puddle she'd created, before sinking and vanishing from sight.

Nia scowled. "Well, sh—"

"Sugar," Mal supplied, a meaningful look down at Asha. The enormity of what Aunt Junie had done for them was still too huge to contemplate. The hole she left with her absence likewise too immense. Like ignoring the elephant, somehow it was easier to overlook it for a little while and focus on what he could understand and handle. Such as the fact that his town was under attack, and he needed to help them, to keep both his daughter and Nia alive.

That unearthly howl he was really starting to hate echoed through the yard and seemed to freak out everyone, dead or alive. Especially when it was answered by another.

Nia reached out, her hand momentarily vanishing before she pulled out the scythe, the blade gleaming in the dull afternoon light.

"Okay. Time to clean house. Mal, you take care of Asha and the kids. I'll get the girls, we'll round up the spirits, scoot them back to the Gray, then it's on to soul devourers and the gods."

"Wait, what about the soul devourers?" He strode after her, keeping close as she and Esther cut a path through the spirits as she made for her friends. "You have a bigger weapon hiding somewhere I hope?"

"Won't need one," she said, then waved her arms. "Esther, go round up the girls."

The owl swooped through the yard with a screech, attracting the attention of Nia's three friends, who abandoned what they were doing and headed for Nia, Anna in the lead.

"Boy, are we glad to see you," Ginny said. She waved at the ghosts. "How is it we can see them?"

"Because there's a lot of them, and because most people who've been close enough to death have more ability to see spirits." Nia put a hand on Anna's arm. "You okay?"

There was a strained tightness around Anna's lips, a narrowing around the eyes he recognized from friends on the force who'd seen and experienced too much. Hell, he'd seen it reflected at him in the mirror.

The War horsewoman shoved back her shoulders, a desolation in her eyes. Her brow came down, her voice brusque. "Glad to see you. We need to get rid of these ghosts and monsters, ASAP."

Nia studied her friend a bit longer, too, but nodded, rubbing her hands together as she turned and looked out at the yard.

"You know that rhyme about the Pied Piper? That's

what we're going with. You drive them toward me, I send them back to the Gray. If they look lost, kind of wandering around? Don't worry about those. I'll deal with them later. We're after the ones with sharp teeth, on a murderous rampage. Pretty easy to spot since they'll probably try to kill you."

"Gee, Nia, you throw the best parties," Piper said dryly, but there was an entirely inappropriate smile tugging at his sister-in-law's lips.

Nia turned away from him and her friends. Her form shimmered, seemed to grow larger. A dark cloak of smoke and cloud descended around her. The gray owl settled on her shoulder, and with the opposite arm, she tapped the end of the scythe on the slushy ground. A deep, sonorous bell tone echoed through the air. Then Nia, in the deep voice that sent a chill sliding up his spine, smiled and began to speak.

"ATTENTION DEAD JERKS." She spread her arms. "THIS WAY HOME."

Mal quickly lifted Asha onto his shoulders. "Hold on tight, Peanut. Whatever happens, don't let go." An ache tore through him, but he tried to swallow it down. To hell with losing anyone else today.

Then, along with the other three horsewomen, he stepped up beside Nia as the spirits roared toward her.

☋

Overall, possibly not her best plan. Nia braced herself as the spirits turned and looked at her like she was a twenty-four-hour buffet. Would have been nice if they'd formed a line. Instead, they came at her all at once, a giant, moving, twisting tsunami of mist and clawing hands.

For a second, she was three years old, down in the basement, and subject to Dad's experiments. For a second, she wanted nothing more but to duck her head and cry.

But Mal stood to her right, his wings spread, making

sure nothing could come at her from behind. Asha was on his shoulders, a fierce expression on the child's face as she opened her mouth and screeched at the spirits to go away. Anna, Piper, and Ginny had spread out to the left and right, corralling the mass toward her, just like she'd asked. Anna with her hose, Piper with a green roiling mass of disease, and Ginny with sections of earth forming walls and tunneling the spirits toward her.

Esther perched on Nia's shoulder, the grip of her talons like a firm hand on Nia's shoulder. *"Let them come, betiya. Let them pass through you."*

Her knees shook. The first hand clawed at her, but at Esther's urging, Nia unfisted her hands, closed her eyes against the mass moving toward her. She was back in that wading pool, but this time she fell backward into the cold water, splashed down until it covered her face, covered her body from head to toe. The icy cold cradled her and filled her, allowed her to reach for the ether and blend her spirit with it, to fade her physical form.

To become the bridge to the Gray.

The spirits crashed through her and beyond, into the Gray. If some of them wanted to stop when they saw what had happened to their friends, they didn't have a chance. The moving wave of rage was moving too fast, and she was like a ghost vacuum. They fell through her. All she felt was the silken brush of the veils against her skin, as if she were standing in a strong wind.

Anna and the other women called to each other. Mal threw a couple of spirits at her, through the doorway. It seemed to last forever, maybe just a few moments, or somewhere in between.

Nia opened her eyes and sagged. The yard was down to pre-insanity spirit levels, meaning there were still a lot more than usual, but no more than there'd been earlier this afternoon.

"THE REST OF YOU SHALL WAIT UNTIL

TOMORROW." Yeah, probably should have made it sound more official, but whatever. Her shoulders sagged. Scratch one item off the cleaning list.

The growl came from behind her. From out around the corner of the house.

"Nia," Mal said warningly. "You still have that marker from the gods. Those things are going to come right for you."

She rolled her shoulders, straightened, and turned. On to item number two.

"I'm counting on it." Yes, she could have just cleaned house by throwing everything back into the Gray and dealing with it later. But these children had waited too long already. She adjusted her grip on the scythe and balanced on the balls of her feet. "Mal, cover Asha's eyes, will you?"

"Mama, kick his ass!" Asha shrieked.

Both she and Mal turned to look at their daughter, then Nia back at Mal. "That's totally on you. I don't know where she'd have picked up language like that otherwise. Go on, cover her eyes."

The soul devourer emerged onto the damp lawn, scales clicking, all those eyes narrowing on Nia.

She turned to face the beast, biting her lip and crouching down. "On second thought, cover your eyes, too. You're not going to like this."

"Sh—sugar, Nia—"

Nia blocked out Mal and focused on the soul devourer. It launched itself at her.

And she launched herself right back.

Esther swooped in, transforming and growing, grasping Nia's shoulders and helping Nia land on the soul devourer's smooth back. There was nothing to grip, so she jerked the scythe handle beneath its neck, gripping either side, keeping those teeth away from her.

The soul devourer *really* hated her riding on its back.

Nia's fingers were slippery against the smooth shaft of the scythe, but she gripped it on either side—the blade would never cut her. If she didn't want to let go, she wouldn't lose her grip, either. She wasn't a big fan of riding the bucking, squirming beast, trying to avoid its teeth and find the edges of the soul.

She'd started thinking back in the Gray that she had to come back here and help clean things up. Just sweeping everything back into the Gray wasn't right. Not when she knew what lay beneath all the gnashing teeth and slippery black scales. She might not be able to bring in new rules where children didn't die, but she sure the hell wouldn't let any suffer on her watch.

Of course, try explaining that to a monster while riding on its back. This one was a boy. And it didn't much want to listen. It mostly wanted to destroy her.

It had wanted to destroy she and Asha for months as it hunted them through the Gray.

"You better have a plan!" Mal shouted at her, somewhere to the right. Guess he hadn't closed his eyes. Yep, he sounded pissed.

Not much time to worry about that as she and the soul devourer bowled through the herd of elk and First Nations hunters like they were playing ten pin and winning. The heat of the soul devourer's damp breath and the brief hint of teeth was way too close to her right wrist.

"You do have a plan?" Esther screeched from above, swooping overhead and keeping pace.

"I need to remove the soul." Remove the soul and free the child. No more soul devourer, no more suffering child. That was supposed to be one of Death's powers, right? Reaping souls. Trouble was, she'd gotten pretty good at sewing souls back to their bodies. Not much practice with pulling them out.

Esther swooped down, shrinking and transforming to a moth as she did so, then clutching Nia's shoulder.

"Plan first, action after," she scolded, but calm soaked through Nia anyway.

Nia's eyes drifted shut for a second to open her other eyes, her Death eyes. To see the edges of the veils fluttering, the semi-translucent physical form of the soul devourer. Below that, the gleaming blue shards of a human soul, scattered throughout the monstrous form. That sight obliterated any lingering animosity that this creature had hunted she and her daughter. The boy hadn't meant to hurt her. He'd just wanted to survive, just like all of them.

"Come here, kiddo," Nia said gently, sliding one hand free of the scythe to reach through the body and hold out a hand to that little soul. It took a little while, holding out healing and love to him, sorting through the shattered fragments and fury until from all that damage emerged a small boy. He blinked up at her, eyes wide, before slowly, he reached out a tremulous hand.

Nia grabbed him and pulled.

They both somersaulted forward onto the slushy lawn as the soul devourer crumpled beneath them. Nia hugged the child against her to protect him from the worst of it. When they looked up, Mal stood a few feet from the fallen body of the soul devourer. A little boy with curly dark hair sat beside her, looking confused. The body of the soul devourer was solid for a moment, looking like a monstrous fallen dragon, before it turned transparent and crashed in on itself, nothing but water and ether.

Nia came to her feet, scythe in one hand, and pulled the little boy up beside her. That was one.

The little boy gawked at the remaining spirits and her friends, shrinking against her legs.

She crouched next to the child, smoothed back his hair from his face. "Hi, sweetheart. It's good to see you. I know you're probably scared and confused right now, but it's going to be okay, I promise. I just need to gather more of your friends, and then I'm going to take you all somewhere good, where you're loved." She stood, and pointed at Mal. "This is Mal. He's a supercool, powerful warrior, and he's going to keep you safe until I get back."

Mal took the little boy's hand, frowning down at the child's curly head, then at Nia. "Please tell me you aren't going to do that again."

Another snarl approached from behind. That marker was making this almost easy. Nope, wait, not one of them. Two. Okay, not that easy. "Just keep him calm and safe. And of course, I'm not going to do that again."

She signaled to Esther, who transformed into a chopper, gliding up just as Nia jumped astride, and they both roared toward the soul devourer. "I'm going to change my technique!"

CHAPTER 34

Dealing with the soul devourers got easier after the second one. A lot less riding around on top of it. Less imitation of wrestling a bear. Nia improved her technique until she just needed to touch the soul devourer lightly to reach the soul. Pulling out the children was a bit tricky, since many of their shattered souls had to be pieced together in her mind with the memories she picked up before she could pull them out.

When she took the hand of and guided lucky number thirteen, another little girl not much older than Asha, back toward Mal and the other waiting children, Nia's knees trembled beneath her.

"She's the last of you, or the last of you willing to come out and play today." She still tried to give the kids a kind smile. "Come on. Let's get you home."

They trailed her into the middle of the yard, her tiny charges who made her heart squeeze. Mal, Asha, and her friends followed slightly farther behind.

"Okay, this is the part where you have to help. I need

you to place a hand on the scythe handle. Don't worry, it won't hurt you."

When thirteen small hands joined hers on the handle, she could follow the thin gold thread that led through the spirits, down through the scythe, and parted the veils, this time to a place she couldn't travel. Not yet anyway.

Warm light spilled through a doorway, so bright she had to shield her eyes. Beyond, shadowy figures moved and shifted. The first to break through was a young woman, little older than Nia, who fell to her knees, her body shimmering, tears on her face as she held out her hand to one of the little girls.

"Mama!" the child cried and raced toward the figure.

One by one, each of the children passed through. Until the thirteenth. The little boy she'd pulled from the first soul devourer. He turned back from the beckoning hands at the doorway and touched Nia's arm, removing a small glowing orb, which he tossed over his shoulder.

"I'm sorry for hurting you and your daughter. I was…" He frowned, searching for the words.

Nia knelt beside him. "You were lost. But you're not anymore. It's okay."

He nodded. "They will come after you. The gods. Their anger was even more frightening than my own. Please be careful. And…thank you." Then he too turned and passed into the light.

Her three friends came forward to join her.

"Is that it then?" Piper asked.

"Not quite." She changed to the Death voice. "LEONARD, YOU DIDN'T LET HIM GET AWAY, DID YOU?"

"Of course not. I'll leave such inefficiency to you," Leonard said, but softened his words with a wink as he stepped through the veils. In his right hand he gripped the nape of Judge Thesku, who squirmed and struggled ineffectually despite his larger size. Leonard dropped the god, letting him fall onto his knees in the slush. "I lost the angels in the Gray.

"You, all of you, will pay for this," Judge Thesku aka god of douchebags hissed, his forked tongue flicking as he clambered to his feet. He tried to run.

Ginny stepped forward and earth clamped around the god's feet.

"Yeah, see, here's the thing. You already tried to make us pay even before we did anything wrong." Nia cocked her head. "Ladies, I could use an assist here."

The gods must have feared The Four for a reason. And Nia was about to prove them right. Together, The Four were more powerful than gods.

The four friends joined hands. Nia breathed in, the powerful essences of her friends flowing through her like a shudder. Fiery War. Lush, green Famine. The yellow-green fog of Pestilence.

"You treat mortality and life so casually, when it is something you understand so little of." Nia blinked slowly, allowing the veil to fall over her eyes, to see the god's soul bare before her. The stains on it, the shiver of fear, the gold glow of immortality. Her friends' power flowed through her, making her even stronger than she was on her own. It allowed her to focus on the gold glow of the god's immortality.

"Piper, you first. Weaken him."

The pestilence horsewoman closed her eyes, her green power whirling around her like a sickly mist, setting boils on the god's scaled skin, slightly dimming the gold glow.

"Ginny, next up is you," Nia said, monitoring the golden light. "Anna, feel free to jump in whenever you like."

Ginny's black power oozed out like thick oil, coiling and climbing up the god's feet, dulling the gold of the mortality even further.

That had hardly finished climbing the struggling god's body before War's flames licked over his feet. He screamed.

Which let Nia reach forward and tweak his life thread. Turn it from gold to blue.

From immortality to mortality.

Judge Thesku's back bowed. The glow dimmed from around him, and he stared down at his hand. "No. No, you can't do this!"

"I think you have your tenses confused. I think the word is 'done.' We're done." She turned back to Leonard. "You can take it from here?"

Leonard inclined his head.

"Who's Leonard?" Anna said, leaning closer.

"He's Mr. Death, Aunt June's friend. You were almost dead last time we saw him," Piper supplied, waving at him.

He gave her a small smile, but his attention was largely on the god and Nia. His brows lifted. "I thought you'd have killed him. You can do that, you know."

"There will be consequences!" the god yowled.

Nia and Leonard ignored him. "I'm not into the whole death-touch thing. I mean, look how something similar turned out for Midas." She fake-shuddered then jerked a thumb toward the mortal god. "Do you think you can deal with him? Take him wherever he should be. You have all that legal stuff, right?"

"I do indeed have the 'legal stuff,'" Leonard said dryly. "I'll take care of transportation." He glanced at her friends. "Though I hope you are aware this is unlikely to be the end of the gods' pursuit of you."

"Let them come. We'll de-god all of them," Ginny said.

Nia made a face, turned to her friend. "That sounds kind of wrong."

"Definitely wrong," Piper agreed.

Ginny's face colored. "*Sugar cookies*. It didn't sound nearly that bad in my head…"

Leonard rolled his eyes, reached up, and put a hand on the collar of the snake-headed mortal god before they both vanished.

Yep, needed to learn that trick, too.

Nia caught a glimpse of Mal and Asha, taking a seat on the front porch as the rain turned to fluffy snowflakes. Mal was human colored again, and Asha hung around his neck, giving him a kiss. Esther swooped toward them, perching between them on the porch step. A strange, unfamiliar warmth spread through her just looking at them, seeing them there, in front of their house.

Her family.

Someday, they might not always be there. But as Aunt June had shown them, just because you couldn't see them didn't mean they still weren't there for her. Love meant sometimes it might hurt, it might not be easy, but it was so much harder without risking that connection. Love meant giving everything you had.

Nia turned back to her friends. "Thanks, guys. You're the best. I love you to bits."

Her friends' eyes widened.

She tried to ignore the heat in her face but glanced down at the ground a second before she could face them. "I know I can be kind of a jerk—"

"Kind of?" Piper inserted.

Nia stuck her tongue out at her. "Okay, a big jerk sometimes. But I really do care about you. All of you. And, I, um, I'm proud to be one of The Four. Just to be your friend. I've always felt that way. Just—" she snorted, "—well, I figured it would probably be this uncomfortable to actually ever say."

It was Anna who leaned forward and gave Nia the first hug before the others all joined in with a group hug.

Finally, they pulled back—all this hugging was

going to take some getting used to. Was it always going to be that way from now on? Maybe she better be a little less nice.

"We're good?" she asked her friends.

Anna looked at the other two, who nodded, then back at Nia. "We're good." She sent a significant look back toward Mal and Asha on the porch. "Now, you better go talk to them. We'll wait a day or two for all the juicy details."

Nia just grinned and turned away.

"I bet he totally changed color the first time." Piper's voice carried as Nia moved toward the porch.

Ginny snorted. "Of course, he did. Do you think them having sex makes more ghosts? Like ghost babies?"

Nia blocked out the rest of what they said, instead stepping up onto the porch.

"Mama!" Asha shrieked, jumped up, and raced toward Nia.

Nia scooped her up into her arms and breathed in the scent of her hair, the feel of her *warm* little body pressed against her. Tears pricked Nia's eyes. Okay, this was the last time for the month at least she'd let the whole crying thing happen. Thanks to Mal, Aunt June, Leonard, and Esther, she'd done it. She'd saved Asha. Something she never could have done alone.

Mal slowly came to his feet, his cobalt gaze meeting hers as he stepped closer. Muscles rippled and moved in his chest and his arms. It turned out there really was something to that whole man-in-uniform thing, despite the fact his uniform was looking a little worse for the wear. He wiped his hands down his slacks and nodded to her friends. A muscle worked in his jaw. "You're right. I didn't like you jumping on that thing at all." He blew out a breath. "But you did good. Those kids deserved to be free."

Nia took a step closer. Her throat and her heart were

so full, she didn't know how to say what she needed to say, to tell him how she how grateful she was to him, how sorry she was for what happened to Aunt June, to tell him everything she hoped, feared, and finally understood. She grabbed a handful of his wet shirt and pulled him closer until Asha was sandwiched between them in a hug. Damn, he was one gorgeous man. And so, so much more. Her eyes swam, warmth flooding through her. "Mal, I… I…"

"Might be willing to let me crash at your place for a while?" he said with a cheeky smile. But there was something behind it. Like he, too, maybe had more he wanted to say but didn't know how. Not quite yet.

Her eyebrow quirked. *Oh, hell, I love you.* "That's presumptive, don't you think?" It seemed like somehow, he sort of understood. How much she loved this banter between them, the life and laughter he brought to her life.

The love.

The possibility of a happy ending, the perfect fairytale life. For once, within her reach. She wanted that. For Asha. And for herself.

He loosened his arm from the hug to tuck a curl behind Nia's ear. He stroked his finger along her cheekbone, sparks dancing through her at the touch. "I can be pretty convincing."

Desire shuddered through her, and she closed her eyes a moment before she opened them to look at him again. "You can be kind of an as— jerk," she said, substituting the swear at the last moment. Her beloved jerk, forever and always if she had it her way.

"Right back at you." He leaned forward and pressed a kiss to Asha's head, then to Nia's. "Now come on, let's go inside. It's freezing out here." He lifted Asha up out of Nia's arms and swung her around until she made a delighted squeal and grabbed for Mal's shoulders. He gathered her close and held out his hand.

There was no hesitation as she stepped forward and

linked her fingers with his.

CHAPTER 35

Mal stomped snow off his boots and set the shovel beside the door after he finished shoveling the porch. He picked up the thin, nearly five-foot by one-foot box he'd leaned near the door and stepped inside the warmth of the house. There was the scent of warm melting cheese and baking pizza. A bit of char, but it was Nia cooking—there was a small chance it was intentional.

"Daddy!" Asha squealed, rounding the corner and barreling toward him, barely reaching his knees.

Warm lightness spread through him as he scooped her up in his arms, giving her a light toss in the air until she squealed and clutched at his hair. Chuckling, he set her back down on the ground before untying his boots, slipping them off, and putting them next to the small pair of black biker boots and the even smaller pink sparkly princess boots. He undid the heavy parka printed with the Beckwell coat of arms across the back, and Chief Quilan over the right upper pocket. Then he grabbed the long package and padded through the foyer.

Nearly a month and a half had passed since Judge Thesku's attack and Beckwell had been overrun by inhabitants of the Gray. It had taken almost that long to straighten things out afterward, since they'd had to triage the damage. First, the souls had to be reattached to any of the unlucky residents who'd met the soul devourers and some of the other nasty things he didn't even know the names for. Then there'd been sorting out the ghosts: who belonged in the Gray, who belonged in Beckwell. Mr. Death—or Leonard, as he was properly called—and Nia complained it was a lot of paperwork. Nia frequently said she'd bill Braelyn for all the overtime. She might get it, too, considering all the turmoil in the paranormal world. There were rumblings that the gods going after Nia and her friends was a step too far, exposed their paranoid delusions and the laws they'd break to cling to their power. There were even whispers that maybe it was time for new management. Fine with him, so long as the trouble didn't spill into his town.

He padded down the hall, past the stairwell into the kitchen, and found Nia at the table. Heavy, ancient-looking leather books surrounded the beautiful, dark-haired woman while she was busy writing in a different ancient, important-looking book. Esther wore glasses in owl-form, reviewing a book of her own. While Nia did go into Death Corp periodically, with Asha being so young, she did most of her work from home, with Leonard as her assistant and top manager. Plus, she'd increased the hours she said she used to hold in the library to deal with the dead that came looking for her. She helped them find peace, to move on, and did all the paperwork herself. Occasionally she and Mal went into the Gray to search for soul devourers who still needed saving, lost children who deserved peace.

She looked up with a smile that lit up her face, her hair pulled back in a ponytail, her shirt bright pink and probably one of the Asha's choices. Asha was very into pink and had somehow convinced Nia to add some color to her wardrobe.

He had, too, though his choices weren't exactly PG.

Nia met him around the side of the table, grasping his shoulders and lifting on tiptoe as her lips met his. Passion and heat blossomed between them, and he started thinking about that skimpy pink thong and lacy bra. Maybe she'd put them back on…if they'd survived his removing them last night.

"Well, hello to you." Her voice was raspy as they allowed air to pass between them.

"Hello to you," he said, his voice rough.

"Daddy, what's this?" Asha said, tugging at the package.

He tightened his hold so she didn't accidentally pull it down on herself, and found himself studying her smile. She remembered some of what she happened, and she would never be an average child—her parents were a Fomorian and Death, so that was probably unlikely anyway. But otherwise she was a sweet, happy, precocious three-year-old, doted on by her uncles and many aunts—the other horsewomen.

Sometimes he thought he saw a hint of Aunt Junie's smile when Asha looked at him, or the way she'd scold him without heat. While he'd explained to Daniel and their friends what had happened, to everyone else, Aunt Junie had suffered a stroke and passed away quietly in her sleep. Too young, too soon. She was probably right about that, too. There never would have been an age when he'd have been ready to say goodbye. At least she'd gotten to know Asha a little, and Asha her. And some of Asha's favorite bedtime stories were about Aunt Junie.

He cleared his throat and tried to push aside the emotion for now. "It's an early birthday present for your mom," he said.

No one would know it from the amount of snow outside, but it was mid-March, and close to Nia's birthday on the twenty-first. Fitting somehow, that she'd been born on the spring equinox, the date when day and night were almost identical, the divide between winter and spring.

"Not for me?" Asha looked crestfallen. For the first time this April, she'd truly age another year.

"You had an early birthday present two days ago. And the day before that, remember?" Turned out not spoiling your kid was a lot harder than he'd thought. He held the box out for Nia.

She raised a dark brow and nodded toward Asha. "It's okay she sees this?"

Oh, yeah. There'd been that early birthday present for Nia two days ago, too. That lingerie had been black. They'd celebrated the completion of her new and improved bathroom, which, while he'd worked on it had also been undertaken by other tradesmen, and all paid for by Loki. The shower was big enough for two…and some fun.

"This one's okay. Set it on the table. You don't want it to fall."

Still giving him a look, she did as he asked, laying it on an angle across the table and pulling the tab that tore the box open from one end to the other. When she pulled apart the cardboard and pushed aside the plastic and bubble wrap, she gave him another look, this one just as confused.

She pointed at the large, double-bladed and very shiny battle-ax. "Um, you thought I needed this?"

"Nia, you shouldn't criticize a gift from Malcolm," Esther scolded aloud in that whispery voice of hers, flying over to pull back the cardboard and see for herself. "Even if it is…unusual."

"Well, it's kind of for me. Kind of symbolic." This had seemed easier when he'd rehearsed it in his head. His neck warmed, and his tongue was thick. "It's a promise. To fight at your side. To protect Asha, our home, and our town, wherever and however you need it. Besides, you said it matched my wings."

Nia threw her head back and laughed, the sound rolling over him and worth the ridiculous amount of shipping he'd had to pay to get this thing here. Then she gave him another kiss, which quickly flared to heat and fire between them. The buzzer on the oven went, and while she pulled back, she still gave him another hug.

He held her in his arms another few seconds. "I love you, through this world, this life, and back again. You know that, right?"

She smoothed a hand down his jaw and along the side of his neck, sending up a riot of sparks and thoughts about how they could celebrate tonight, in their room, alone. "Yeah. I know that."

"Enough you're even okay with Daniel, Piper and the gang coming over tomorrow for dinner?"

She rolled her eyes and danced out of his arms. "Well, they are Asha's family. Creating a supportive environment is one of those things good parents do." She headed toward the kitchen.

He smiled, ignoring the small pang because she hadn't said the words yet. They were there, in her touch, in her smile. He knew she loved him, and the words shouldn't matter…but turned out they kind of did. He'd thought of getting a ring, proposing. He and Nia talked about the kind of life they wanted to build for Asha and the children. But so far, she'd stayed pretty noncommittal. He wanted to take things at her speed, didn't want to rush her, but damn, it wasn't easy.

"Supper!" Asha bellowed, then raced out of the room still shouting it. "Supper! It's supper." She hollered back to the kitchen. "In here?"

Nia and Mal exchanged a look.

"We said we wanted to start good habits," she said sternly. The repeat of almost every night.

Yeah, not spoiling either the kid or Nia was harder than he'd thought. He moved closer to Nia, wrapping his arms around her and rocking her lightly against him. "I know…but it is movie night. This could be a special occasion. Besides, anything happens to the couch, we're getting a new one anyway."

Nia smiled, and he knew he'd won.

He gave her a quick kiss on the lips, then turned and raced down the hall after Asha.

She squealed and raced off with a giggle.

"Let's get ready. It's dinner and a movie tonight!" he announced to Asha and the rest of the kids.

The process of getting the pizzas out and everyone settled on the sofa wasn't exactly a finely oiled machine, but it was getting more familiar all the time. Mal and Nia sat first on the sofa while the other kids and a few assorted cats and dogs settled around them. Since he'd died, he could see and interact with ghosts almost as well as Nia and Asha. Which meant at least he and Nia could have "the talk" with the kids together, one child at a time, introducing the idea of death and offering the possibility of going into the light. With the soul devourers, since they knew they were dead, they could help open the doorway to the light, the one place Nia couldn't reach through the veils. But with the others, with no one to open the door, the timing was up to them. For now, figuring out how to get them to cross over without causing them any additional pain was still a work in progress.

Esther perched on the back, settling her wings. *"As are we all."*

He sent the owl a small smile—he could hear her now, too—before he dished out the hot, tangible pizza for he, Nia, and Asha. Plus the small piece for Esther, who picked at it daintily.

Nia handled the spirit pizza for the other kids. It hadn't been easy rounding all of them up after, many of whom had been terrified and confused by what had happened. A few of the older children had moved on to the light; they'd introduced the concept to some of the younger ones, but with some new additions, there were still five plus Asha. They were taking it slow, not wanting to risk the traumatizing effect of the kids turning into soul devourers.

After a brief argument over which movie they should select, Mal made an executive decision and then laid his head back against the couch. Another movie with talking animals wasn't his first choice, but it was better than the cartoon they'd wanted. Still, a small smile curved his lips and satisfied warmth spread through him as he looked over his family lounged around him. Asha and Nia were curled against him, everyone else piled everywhere, a couple on the floor. This was his family. And they were perfect.

Damn, he was one lucky man.

"Hey," Nia whispered, leaning toward him, her dark eyes glittering. "Thank you. For the gift."

"You're welcome."

She plunked a small box down on his chest, looking away for a second, but her gaze quickly moved back to his. "This one's for you. I've been waiting for the right time."

The little black box flipped open. Inside was a silver ring with a winged skull on the front. Frowning and not sure what to think, he looked up.

To find Nia and all the kids staring at him. Nia shooed them off and dropped down on one knee in front of him and the sofa.

Well, holy hell. His heart fluttered—he'd swear it in court—and he could barely breathe. Letting Nia take the lead wasn't always easy, but it did have its rewards.

"Malcolm Quilan," Nia said, trying to be cocky, but something vulnerable and open glowed in her expression. "You can be a jerk. And difficult. And you usually don't listen to what I tell you to do."

He raised an eyebrow but couldn't help the way his lips lifted.

"Which is only part of why I love you completely and madly, and I want you in my life not just today, but forever." She paused, her eyes shining, her voice growing raspier. "I want the whole damn happy ending, the fairy tale life for us and the kids, all on our terms. So, what do you say? Will you marry me?"

He scooped her up and dragged her against him, pressing his lips to hers as the kids started to cheer. "I thought you'd never ask."

COMING SOON...

Must Love War, Early 2019
Anna and Loki's story, and the final book in the Sisters
of the Apocalypse Series!

In the meantime, read the rest of the series:

Must Love Plague
Must Love Famine

And for more adventures in Beckwell, look for the
Shades of Beckwell – a brand new series featuring
some of the characters you've met already, along with
many new ones.

ABOUT THE AUTHOR

Shelly Chalmers' first favorite book was Cinderella, so once she could form letters, naturally she turned to romance where everyone "loved" each other—though mostly because she didn't yet know how to spell "like."

A 2014 Golden Heart® finalist, she has a bachelor's degree in English and French, and has never lost her love of romances and their happily-ever-afters. Her stories run the gamut from Regency shifters to space opera. All include a touch of magic, a sense of humor, and a dab of geek. She makes her home in Western Canada, where when not reading, writing, crafting, or hunting unusual treasures and teapots, she wrangles a husband, two daughters, and two nutball cats.

She loves hearing from readers and chatting! You can find her at:

Website: shellychalmers.com
Email: shellychalmers@scchalmers.com
Twitter: @scchalmers
Facebook:
https://www.facebook.com/ShellyC.Chalmers

Check out her Facebook readers group: The Brazen Librarians. Chat about books, have some fun, and get the inside scoop on works in progress.

Plus, if you'd like to be the first to know about Shelly's new releases, giveaways, and other goings-on, sign up for her newsletter, and get Five Magical Things in your inbox once a month. shellychalmers.com

www.ingramcontent.com/pod-product-compliance
Lightning Source LLC
Chambersburg PA
CBHW051527100726
47898CB00005B/1603